A GIFT FOR THE DISTRICT NURSES

It's 1943, and the district nurses have two fresh recruits! As the country ramps up for D-Day, the new nurses are getting to know their patients on their patch in London's East End. Lily is quite sure of herself, and doesn't believe she has anything new to learn — but when she meets a man who promises her everything, she'll find out the hard way that anyone can be made a fool of. Ruby thinks that nursing might not be for her — is she as hopeless as she thinks, or will tough times bring out the best in her? As the war takes on a new urgency, everything is at stake. Can the nurses do what is right for the country, and for themselves?

ANNIE GROVES

A GIFT FOR THE DISTRICT NURSES

Complete and Unabridged

MAGNA
Leicester

First published in Great Britain in 2020 by
HarperCollins*Publishers*
London

First Ulverscroft Edition
published 2021
by arrangement with
HarperCollins*Publishers*
London

A catalogue record for this book is available
from the British Library.

ISBN 978–0–7505–4918–9

Published by
Ulverscroft Limited
Anstey, Leicestershire

Printed and bound in Great Britain by
TJ Books Ltd., Padstow, Cornwall

This book is printed on acid-free paper

This book is dedicated to all
district nurses, past and present

1

'Would you like my seat, miss?' The young man in army uniform stood up from his place in the corner of the already crowded railway carriage. 'Nice girl like you doesn't want to be standing all the way.'

Lily Chandler smiled in gratitude. She liked a show of manners. 'Thank you,' she said, bestowing a smile on him — a sergeant, she could see now she was a little closer to his khaki jacket. 'That's very kind.' He was quite right, she thought. She certainly didn't want to stand all the way from Liverpool's Lime Street Station the entire length of the journey down to London. She intended to look her best the moment she stepped down onto the platform in the capital. New year, new life, she told herself.

Not that she needed to strengthen her resolution, she thought as she settled into the seat the sergeant had vacated. She smoothed the lapels of her maroon wool coat; a rare bargain, as many of her home city's clothes shops had been destroyed in air raids earlier in the war. It suited her, she knew. It brought out the roses in her cheeks and contrasted with her hair. She counted herself fortunate to have been born a natural blonde. Not for her the desperate searching for bleach, or the hopeless task of hunting down lemons for their juice. She'd been dealt all the aces when it came to hair and complexion.

She almost broke into a private smile but then

1

remembered that nobody liked a smug expression. It didn't do to appear too pleased with yourself. It put people off. She'd have to be careful. Moving to a new place, with new colleagues, she'd have to try extra hard to be pleasant and make new friends. Everyone needed friends. She'd be starting from scratch somewhere nobody knew her. She'd have to be careful to get everything right.

There was a jolt as the train set off, and she quickly looked up at the rack overhead, where her suitcase was crammed in between army kitbags and leather grips. It seemed safe enough — it couldn't possibly tumble down as all the luggage was so tightly packed. She might as well make use of the time to catch up on her beauty sleep. There was no way of knowing how long the journey would take. Besides, if she closed her eyes then there was less chance of being drawn into conversation. She didn't fancy having to make small talk with strangers, for hours and hours. Or certainly not with a bunch of wet-behind-the-ears servicemen, little more than boys. That wasn't to her taste at all.

Her parents had been sad to see her go but they could understand that she was doing it for the best. 'Take care, love,' her mother had said, anxiously gazing into her daughter's determined face. 'Stay away from Hitler's bombs, won't you? Promise me you won't go doing anything daft.'

'I promise.' Lily had tried to reassure her mother, because it was simpler to do that than argue. Anyway, as if she would do anything daft. It wasn't her habit.

Besides, they'd already come through the Liverpool Blitz. It wasn't as if she was deliberately leaving safety to head into danger — they'd had plenty of that at home. The docks had been the main targets, and the city centre, but stray bombs had fallen all over the place, including in a neighbouring street. It had meant night after night of taking shelter in the church hall. Surely it couldn't get much worse than what she'd already been through.

She had been glad to get Christmas over and done with, to be truthful. She'd got the impression that her mother had pulled out all the stops in a last-ditch effort to persuade her to stay. Lily was all too aware that there was little money to spare and yet her mother had produced a roast of sorts, with plenty of vegetables to disguise the lack of turkey, and even a small plum pudding. Her father had done the honours and carved the scrawny chicken, and then afterwards had poured brandy over the pudding and set it alight, as he'd done for as long as Lily could remember. She had dutifully oohed and aahed, as she didn't want to upset them, but all the while she had been itching to leave.

Lily hadn't stinted on presents for them, turning her bargain-hunting skills to full advantage. She had managed to find a warm woollen waistcoat for her father, who was prone to chest infections. For her mother she had followed a rumour of jewellery for sale, and tracked down somebody who had worked in the city centre until the shop was destroyed by a direct hit. Now he was selling privately, if you knew where to go. Lily had ventured out to a semi-detached house, in a somewhat better road than her own, and was relieved to see a selection of items she could just about afford. Her mother had gasped with delight when she had unwrapped a small velvet box — the paper carefully saved from last year — which contained a turquoise necklace. Lily had been glad. She did love her parents; but she didn't want to end up living their lives. Guilty or not, she knew she had to leave for a better future. She deserved it, she told herself.

She gave a little shiver now, despite the crowded clamminess of the carriage. It was excitement, she told herself, not fear. There was nothing to be afraid of. She'd made her decision, applied for her transfer and that was that. She was needed where she was going; they'd be glad to have her. She would not look back. She was taking her future in her own hands and there was no room for doubt. That was all in the past.

Firmly, she shut her mind to the memories of the quiet celebrations with her family. Her parents weren't musical but a friendly neighbour a few doors down had a piano, and invited them in to sing carols on Boxing Day. Lily had always felt a little embarrassed at this tradition, as nobody could sing very well and the neighbour's dog usually snored loudly all the way through. It also smelled of wet dog and over-cooked vegetables rather noticeably. Yet her parents always reminded her that the offer was made out of kindness and you never knew when you would need a neighbour's helping hand. Lily had squirmed; that was exactly the sort of thing she was moving away from.

It had been funny to bump into somebody she knew at the station just before her train had pulled in. He'd been coming back to visit his parents, carrying a bag obviously full of presents, having had to miss the festive season itself. 'Where are you working now?' she had asked, curious to hear about someone else who had made the break from family and all things familiar.

'Oh, down south,' he'd said, tapping his nose.

4

'Loose lips sink ships, eh?' She had nodded, realising he couldn't really tell her precisely as he must be in the forces, despite his civilian clothes today. Then she'd told him what she was doing and he'd looked at her with keen interest. Not *that* kind of interest, she had soon recognised, as they continued to talk until her train was ready. Still, he was good company for the few minutes that they had, and she'd always liked him when they'd trained together. He wasn't what many people would call handsome, but his intelligent looks grew on you. Such a shame he didn't seem to be based in London. But she knew full well that plenty of doctors were attached to the airfields and naval ports along the south coast.

Absently she touched her fine wool collar once again. Soon it would be time to swap her elegant coat for something more practical. Carefully folded into her suitcase was a serviceable and warm navy cloak. That would be a vital part of her uniform where she was going. From tomorrow she would be a district nurse once again, but instead of working in the streets of Liverpool that she'd known for all her life, she'd be based in the East End. She didn't have to check the formal piece of paper for the details because the address was instantly memorable: Victory Walk, Dalston.

* * *

Ruby Butler folded her arms and glared at her big sister. For two pins she'd have stamped her foot, but that was exactly the sort of behaviour that Beryl would pick up on, and use it as an excuse to call her childish. Not that she ever needed an excuse.

'All I'm saying,' Beryl complained for the fiftieth time, 'is that I don't see why you have to go traipsing right across London to work when you could do the exact same job right here. Aren't we good enough for you?'

Ruby tsked in annoyance but refused to rise to the bait.

'After all,' Beryl went on, her voice high-pitched and relentless, 'it isn't as if you'll spend the rest of your life working. You won't want to do that for ever. It's not what you're made for. You'll want to get married, same as the rest of us. You'll meet someone like I did when I saw my Terry and that'll be that.'

My Terry, my Terry. If Ruby had a penny for every time her sister dropped her husband's name into the conversation, and always with that smug little expression on her smug little face, then she wouldn't have needed to go out to work at all.

'There aren't many eligible men left around here, if you hadn't noticed,' she pointed out. That was putting it mildly. Everyone remotely fit had been sent off to fight, leaving those too young, old or sick. There were a few young men in reserved professions, but they tended to work all hours of the day and night and be too worn out to socialise. Well, Ruby knew exactly what that felt like.

'No need to be snarky,' Beryl retorted, most unfairly. 'You wait till this war is over, and the place will be flooded by homecoming heroes, that's what they're saying. You'll be swept off your feet. It won't be long now. My Terry says that everything is going to plan with the army in Italy . . .'

'Can't wait,' mumbled Ruby, fed up with her sister's conviction that she knew best. That was how it

6

had always been: Ruby was the baby of the family, with Beryl and her twin Colin ten years older, and they had never even considered that Ruby might have a mind of her own. Then when Beryl had met her Terry — who to Ruby's mind was no great catch, being pasty-faced and short-sighted — it had become three against one. Four, if you counted their mother.

'Come, Beryl, Ruby will have her reasons,' their mother said now, belatedly riding to her youngest's rescue, although with a tone of voice that made it clear she didn't hold with those reasons, whatever they might be. 'We'll miss you, that's all. It's so far away. And going right to where all those bombs fell! It doesn't seem right.'

Ruby pressed her fingernails hard into her forearms to keep from screaming. It was hot in the kitchen from where the range was heated up to cook their barley stew for tea, and the window was fogged with condensation from the kettle. Would she miss this? Her mother's cooking, maybe. Not everything else that came with it.

'We didn't exactly avoid the bombs here,' she commented. It was true. Hammersmith had suffered during the Blitz and the very next street to theirs had caught a high-explosive bomb, something none of them would ever forget. She didn't want to go through that again, but she couldn't stay here any longer.

She'd thought when she began her nurse's training at the local hospital that, when she qualified, her family would finally respect her. Years of studying and practising had to count for something, surely — but as soon as she stepped through the front door to their house, it was as if she'd never left. Then she had gone on to do an extra period of specialist district-nurse training, a demanding role in which she'd dealt with life-or-death situations. It still made her nervous to think of the responsibility she'd been given. Yet her family continued to treat her like a baby.

It wasn't that they didn't love her. Quite the opposite, in fact. But that love came with a suffocating layer of protection that would have kept her safe indoors, wrapped in cotton wool, until the right man came along; someone who would also protect her to an overwhelmingly high degree. At least the war had meant she had to go out to work — it was the law.

Ruby had been terrified the first morning she'd gone to the hospital to start training. What if her mother and the twins were right — that she was too childish to do anything useful? Colin had just joined the navy and had received a hero's send-off. In contrast, Beryl's words to her that morning had been, 'Well, don't come running to me if you can't cope.'

Ruby sighed at the memory. She'd had the chance to stay in West London as a district nurse, based at the local home, which was a short bus ride from her mother's house. But to her mind that was not far enough. She had to put more distance between them, or she'd never gain the confidence she felt she so badly lacked. At the moment she felt like a fraud, going out into her patients' homes, afraid that one of them would cotton on to her ignorance and point out that she wasn't really a proper nurse. Every time she built up a reserve of resolution, a comment from her mother or, more likely, Beryl would raze it to the ground.

True to form, Beryl tutted as she went over to the range to stir the simmering stew. 'Well, don't come crying to us when you get homesick,' she said loftily.

'And you will, Ruby, you're a real home bird and no mistake. I just hope they look after you when they realise.'

Ruby felt a stab of guilt. There were things about her home that she knew she would miss. The Christmas period had been full of moments that took her back to her childhood: fetching the ancient wooden box full of decorations, carefully taking them from their nests of newspaper, checking none had broken. Finding her favourite, the glass angel with the wonky wings. Making paper chains and pinning them across the parlour ceiling, her mother anxiously holding the chair she'd had to stand on to reach. Carols playing on the wireless and her mother singing along under her breath, not realising Ruby could hear. Even Beryl had been almost bearable, until Twelfth Night arrived and it was time to take all the decorations down again and stow them safely away.

Now her mother wiped anxious hands down her striped pinafore. 'But you know you can always come back, Ruby,' she said seriously. 'You'll always be my precious little girl, you know that.'

That was the whole trouble in a nutshell. Ruby took a deep breath. 'I know,' she said, smiling wanly at the careworn woman in front of her, old beyond her years. 'It's only a couple of bus rides away. I'm not going to Scotland or something. Or Italy,' she added pointedly. 'We could meet in the middle.'

Her mother instantly recoiled. 'Oh, you know I don't hold with going to the West End. You never know what sort of people will be there.'

'Never mind, then.' Ruby wondered if nervousness could be catching. Or passed down from mother to daughter. She had to fight it or she wouldn't be able to do her job, and she desperately wanted to be a success. She'd got this far, after all.

Slowly, she walked from the kitchen, through the slightly shabby but immaculately clean hall, and headed upstairs. She had packing to do. Tomorrow, she would take those couple of buses, or as many as she needed to take if they were rerouted yet again, and make her way to the East End. She touched the pocket of her skirt for good luck, as it contained her letter from the nurses' home on Victory Walk, Dalston.

2

'If I say so myself, I'm quite pleased. That was a good idea of mine.' Fiona Dewar, superintendent of the North Hackney Queen's Nurses' Association, stood back from the narrow wooden doorway with pride. 'It may not be ideal but it'll serve its purpose for now.'

Gwen, her dour-faced deputy, looked dubious. 'It's highly irregular.'

Fiona shot her a swift glance. 'That's as maybe. Needs must. This new girl is joining us and she has to sleep somewhere. If there's no vacant bedroom then this is the next best thing.'

What had once been a large store cupboard and an underused alcove just off the main downstairs hallway had been knocked together to form a makeshift bedroom, large enough to fit a single bed but not much else. At least it had a window, although the view was of the bike rack in the back yard of the nurses' home.

'It will at least afford her a wee bit of privacy,' Fiona pointed out. 'I hope she'll not be too cold. Still, it's only temporary.' She checked the newly installed electric light switch. 'See, all mod cons. We'll have to make the best of it.'

Gwen remained unconvinced. 'If you say so. I hope it won't affect her work. She might be disturbed by the other nurses going in and out of the district room.'

Fiona raised her eyebrows. 'Well, we'll just have to inform them that they are to re-equip their bags more quietly for now. They're intelligent young women. I'm sure they can manage.' She switched the light off

11

again and nodded with satisfaction. 'Come, we'll go up to my office and make a note that all is ready for our new recruits. Whatever happens we cannot shirk the paperwork.'

'Heaven forbid,' said Gwen as she followed her diminutive colleague up the wide stairs to the first floor. Though in truth she was more of a stickler for the rules than any of them. Bombs might fall and fires might blaze, but Gwen would see to it that the proper regulations were adhered to.

Fiona led the way into the office, its shelves crammed with medical textbooks and files, bright in the sharp winter light. She swung herself into her wooden chair and Gwen took her usual place opposite the old wooden desk, polished to within an inch of its life, as Fiona picked up her fountain pen and made a note on the form placed in readiness in front of her.

'At least we have one regular room for our other recruit,' the superintendent said, blotting the dark blue ink.

Gwen nodded. 'Who would have thought that Primrose would leave us to get married. After all her years of training. She seemed so steady. I'd have assumed she'd have carried on with us, no matter what.'

Fiona leant back and laughed. 'Who would have thought you'd say such a thing, Gwen? Before the war you'd never have countenanced the idea of a nurse staying on after her wedding.' Her eyes gleamed in merriment.

Gwen sighed, caught on the horns of the dilemma. Strictly speaking, all nurses were meant to cease work after getting married, but that rule had been enforced less and less as the war had gone on. Hospitals and district nursing organisations simply could not afford to lose young women with medical expertise, and besides, many of the new husbands were away, serving in the armed forces. Added to that, in many areas of the country — the East End being one of them — a young married couple would struggle to find a home of their own, as so much of the housing stock had suffered bomb damage. The result was, more and more nurses married their sweethearts and then returned to work, living in their respective nurses' homes.

Gwen disapproved in principle but was forced to concede in practice. The real problem came when the inevitable consequence followed.

'That's as maybe,' she admitted, accustomed to her friend's teasing. 'The fact remains that we must keep a careful eye on Nurse Gillespie — I mean Nurse Banham, as she is now. When is her baby due?'

Fiona thought for a moment. 'Not until June, I believe. She'll be fine for a while yet. She's made of strong stuff, is Edith.'

Gwen nodded in acknowledgement. She could not argue with that; Edith would never have come through the past few years had she not been. Edith's fiancé had gone missing at Dunkirk and everyone thought he had died, along with so many others. Then they had learned that he had been so badly injured he'd been unable to tell his rescuers who he was or where he was from. He had been discovered in hospital in Portsmouth, close to death and almost unrecognisable. It had taken many operations and changes of treatment before he miraculously recovered enough to marry Edith.

'She's hiding her morning sickness as best she can, but I'm not fooled,' Gwen said now. 'If she becomes too weak to perform her duties, we must step in. She

13

won't like it but it's our job to protect both her and her baby. Also, we must protect our patients.'

'Gwen.' Fiona looked up sharply. 'You're not suggesting that our patients will object to their nurse being pregnant? I know it's unusual but they'll have to accept it.'

'No, no,' Gwen said hurriedly. 'Besides, Edith is almost as tiny as you are. There's no sign of her bump showing yet. What I meant was, the daily rounds of working on the district require physical exertion. Just riding those bikes takes considerable effort. I regret not obtaining new ones while they were still available. There's no chance now.' She shook her head and then returned to her main point. 'The fact is, Edith might reach a stage where she's simply not able to manage the physical side of the job. She'll be the last to admit it — you know as well as I do how hard she drives herself. So that is when you or I must be prepared to step in.'

It was Fiona's turn to sigh. 'I hate to deprive a nurse who takes such joy in her work of her chance to practise.' She twirled her pen around on the completed form. 'But you're right, of course. She may continue as long as she's able. But for her own sake, at the first sign of trouble, we must step in.'

★ ★ ★

Lily had debated whether to keep her elegant maroon coat on, or if it would be best to change into her uniform cloak. She knew she would make a more attractive impression in the wool coat, as its fabric swung from her waist as she walked. She'd opted to wear it as she descended from the train when it finally pulled in to

14

its destination, and noticed the appreciative glances as she made her way along the crowded platform to the concourse. Then she had second thoughts. What sort of impression did she want to make on her new colleagues and superiors?

Swiftly ducking into the waiting room, she opened her case and drew out the navy cloak, changing into it and carefully folding her precious coat on top of her packed clothes. It pained her to crease it, but perhaps she could steam it over the bath in her new accommodation. What sort of bathrooms would the place have? She hadn't been told. Would they be expected to keep to the government limit of a measly few inches of bathwater? She hoped not but suspected that they would.

It took two buses to cross London, which made her slightly nervous; she had been lucky to visit the capital just before she started her training but she didn't know it well at all. It was already close to dark when she stepped off the second bus, the conductor kindly telling her where the right stop was. 'Now you just cross this main road and head down there,' he said, pointing to a street of tall terraced houses, dimly visible against the last of the daylight. 'Don't hang about, mind. You don't want to be caught out on unfamiliar streets in the blackout.' He helpfully lifted her case to the platform at the back.

'Thank you, I won't,' Lily assured him with a smile, knowing all too well from experience in Liverpool how easy it was to have an accident in the absence of street lighting.

There was just enough receding twilight to guide her along the road, and then to illuminate a street sign, clearly made crooked by bomb damage: Victory

Walk. Lily breathed a sigh of relief. Despite all her brave talk, she had been dreading finding her way here. The end of a very long journey was in sight. All she had to do now was find the right building, before it was completely dark. Where had she put her torch? Nowhere easily to hand, she realised.

Her task was made easier when she noticed in the gloom a figure at the far end of the road, wearing an identical cloak to her own. Another nurse. That must be the place, and not a moment too soon, because there really was very little light left. She hurried to the end of the pavement, and the other nurse swung around in alarm at the sound of footsteps.

'It's all right,' Lily called out hurriedly, swinging her suitcase in one hand, her nurse's Gladstone bag in the other. She was keen to set them down after the long day of hauling them around. 'I'm looking for the nurses' home. Is this the right place?'

She could scarcely see the other woman's face, but the voice that replied was tinged with relief. 'Yes. Yes, I think so. I haven't been here before. I'm new.'

Lily recognised the accent as being from London, so perhaps this other nurse came from a different district. 'So am I,' she said. 'I'm joining the Queen's Nurses here.'

'Oh. Yes, me too.' The young woman seemed anxious, so Lily took control.

'We'd better go in, then. I'm Lily, by the way.' She strode up the short path to the front door of what looked to be a double-fronted house, taller than its neighbour, at the end of the terrace.

'Ruby,' said the other nurse, following on her heels, and dragging her case along behind her.

Before they could even knock, the door swung open.

16

'Come inside, come inside!' The light from the hall silhouetted a small figure, whose instruction came in an accent that was distinctly Scottish. 'Hurry now, or the ARP warden will have conniptions. We've been waiting for you and we're very glad you're here.' She ushered them into the hall and swiftly shut the door, shiny in its glossy navy paint, behind them. 'There now! You've arrived safely, and we've made sure it's good and warm for you. Leave your bags right here and come along to our canteen-cum-common room — it's just down these steps at the back. Now along the way, take note that this is our refuge room. We don't have a bomb shelter as such but we've all survived the Blitz just fine in here. I don't want to alarm you unduly, but you should know that this is where you'll need to go if the siren sounds.'

Lily did as she was bid, unable to get a word in edgeways with the small woman in full swing. She did her best to take in her surroundings: high ceilings in the corridor, several doors, a telephone; every wooden surface highly polished and a distinct tang of beeswax in the air. Clearly standards were not allowed to slip around here, war or no war.

'Take a seat, take a seat.' The woman indicated a well-worn sofa, with patchwork cushions against its padded arms. She drew a chair across for herself, waving at a small, dark-haired young woman across the room as she did so. 'Edith, we have our new recruits at last! Could I trouble you to put the kettle on? They'll be in need of something to warm them after their travels, I should think.' She turned back to Lily and Ruby. 'I'm Fiona, Fiona Dewar.'

Lily tried to hide her shock as she realised this was the superintendent who had written to her confirming

17

her position. She had never come across any nurse in authority who didn't stand on ceremony and insist on her full title. 'Pleased to meet you,' she managed. 'I'm Lily Chandler.'

Fiona beamed, and turned to the other newcomer, clearly expecting a similar response.

Ruby swallowed with obvious nerves before stuttering, 'I'm Ruby Butler.' She blushed.

'Excellent! Good to see you've made it safe and sound. Now don't go getting the idea that you'll be waited on hand and foot, but I can see your kind colleague Nurse Banham has made you a hot drink. Here she comes. Three cups — you'll be joining us then, Edith?'

Edith set down the tray with its jug of steaming, sweet-smelling cocoa and three cups, clinking on their saucers. 'No, no. This is for you.'

Lily wondered at Fiona's raised eyebrow as she inclined her head towards the obliging nurse, but Edith just said, 'Really, it's all right, I had some not long ago.'

'Very well. I'll not keep you long.' Edith faded into the background and Fiona pressed on, while pouring the welcome drinks for them all. 'You'll want to get settled. So now, the only small thing to mention is that we have just the one proper bedroom at the moment, and the other one is temporary. It's absolutely fine, there's a real bed and all you'll need, but it's on the small side and doesn't have a desk or wardrobe — though there are hooks to hang up your things.' She paused, taking a sip of her drink.

Lily wondered what she was meant to do. Of course it would make a good impression if she offered to take the smaller room. Then again, she had no inclination to do so. She wanted to unpack her lovely clothes, collected with such dedication, and to be sure there was a mirror and a space for her hairbrushes and precious but limited cosmetics. She didn't like the sound of a cramped room at all.

She was saved the decision by Ruby speaking up. 'I don't mind,' she said. 'I haven't brought much with me. I'm just glad to be here. Besides,' she met Lily's eyes for the first time, 'you're taller than me. I dare say I'll fit into a smaller space more easily.'

Fiona regarded her seriously. 'That's very generous of you, Ruby. Like I say, it will only be temporary. So I'll show you to your quarters as soon as you've drunk up, and then we can discuss your work tomorrow morning, after you've had a proper meal and a full night's sleep.' Draining her own cup, she rose, and Lily felt obliged to do the same, although she would sooner have lingered on the comfy sofa in the warm, homely room.

★　★　★

Well, well, thought Edith, after Fiona had led the new nurses away again. She had watched the superintendent's technique with interest. Fiona had left her question hanging, no doubt deliberately, and Edith had seen from her vantage point the look that had passed across the blonde nurse's face at the notion of taking a less than ideal bedroom. Lily, was it? She was someone who thought a lot of herself, if Edith was any judge of character, and she'd had a fair amount of practice. She wondered if she should approach Ruby and explain why the room was temporary.

They were all waiting for her to move out. She

could tell when she turned down the cup of cocoa that Fiona was checking that she didn't still feel sick. True, her morning sickness often extended into the afternoon and sometimes into the evening as well, but Edith had no intention of stopping work before she absolutely had to. It was a shame that this meant Ruby, who from that one brief encounter seemed very pleasant if a bit anxious, would have to rough it for a while. But that was just how things were. Nothing was going to prevent Edith working until the very last moment, if she had any say in the matter.

3

If Ruby could have wheeled her bike along the pavement while squeezing her eyes shut, she would have done. She wanted to block out what she'd just seen. It had been too depressing for words and she wished she hadn't had to be there.

It wasn't as if she had come from a wealthy area or hadn't been into patients' homes before. Of course she had; that was what the specialist district nurse training had been about. The area where she had worked had plenty of families who were far from well off, and she had steeled herself to expect more of the same now she had come east. All the same, the house she had just visited was on a whole new level of poverty.

Ruby had been called there to see the mother, who had had an accident falling off a kitchen stool some weeks ago and was taking a long time to get better. She needed her dressings changed, and that had sounded simple enough. But when she got to the address, Ruby had been overwhelmed by the number of people crammed into the small red-brick terraced house, which showed signs of bomb damage. The house next to it was uninhabitable, and so one wall was left exposed, meaning the place was even colder and damper than it might have been before. No wonder the poor woman was recovering so slowly. She should have been taking it easy but instead was trying to look after a host of small children — Ruby had lost count — and an infirm elderly woman who sat in one corner of the cramped living room and complained loudly, even as Ruby was trying to talk to her patient.

Ruby had done her best but had gasped with relief once she had shut the front door behind her again — carefully, in case it came away from its half-rotten frame. She had gulped in the cold fresh air of the street, fighting down the urge to gag at the smell of the little house. It had been like a nightmare.

Now she slowly wheeled her bike along, knowing she had to get to her next appointment but desperate for some time to recover first. You wanted this, she told herself. You knew what it was going to be like. That was half the trouble; she had jumped into this and thought she was prepared, but the reality of it was only now hitting her.

She screwed her eyes shut again, just briefly. She'd done it now; she had to cope. She couldn't go running home with her tail between her legs. Her mother and particularly her sister would never let her forget it. She shook her head. She couldn't let their voices fill her mind. She'd lose every ounce of confidence if she did. Then they would have won.

Right, my girl, she muttered. Show some backbone. The other nurses deal with such things day in, day out. There's no earthly reason why you can't, either. You'll have to, simple as that. You can't back out now, not just because somewhere smelled terrible and was dark and noisy and damp.

Besides, Ruby realised, she was needed. She must remember that. What would the poor mother have done if nobody came to change her dressings? Her legs might never heal properly and then all those children would have been even worse off. It was, what? Ten minutes of the day. Ten minutes that would have made all the difference to her patient, and therefore to all the family.

Ruby felt her mood brighten and she began to take in her surroundings. This must be the market that some of the other nurses had told her about. There were stalls with bright awnings, and even with the restrictions of rationing there seemed to be plenty of things for sale. Colourful goods were cleverly arranged to make them seem plentiful. Voices drifted across the road, stallholders shouting their wares, the buzz of conversations, arguments, gossip. She decided that she would explore it properly on her first day off.

Her new colleagues had been kind, filling her in on the local area, and she had been surprised to find that they came from far and wide themselves. Fiona was Scottish, of course; then there were two nurses from Ireland, who had come to London because they knew there was a shortage of trained medical staff. The nurse with the thick chestnut hair sounded rather posh; Edith — on the other hand — spoke very like Ruby did, though she said she came from south London, not west. She hadn't met all of the others yet, and it was a job to remember their names. She wondered if Lily had the same trouble, although she'd bet that the other new nurse wouldn't admit to it even if she did.

Ruby paused and smiled to herself. Lily hadn't fooled her for a moment. There was no way on this earth that her fellow newcomer would have volunteered to take the temporary bedroom. She'd been all gratitude and are-you-sure, I'll-swap-if-you-like, but Ruby couldn't imagine her anywhere that didn't have a big mirror and a decent light above it. That and somewhere to hang up her many clothes. How her glamorous colleague had managed to come by so many while everyone Ruby knew was struggling with clothing coupons and make do and mend, she couldn't comprehend.

Not that she begrudged her. Ruby was quite content with her makeshift room; she didn't need anywhere bigger. She had very few dresses to hang up, aside from her uniforms. She had enjoyed the freedom of living in at the nurses' home while training, but once she'd been back under the family roof, she'd had a glorified box room no bigger than where she was now. Her sister had commandeered the bigger room as her husband Terry might come home on leave. Her brother Colin had a room fit for a fighting hero. Ruby knew her place.

She checked the address for her next patient and squinted at the map. She'd soon get the hang of the unfamiliar streets, she told herself. The others had done so before her; she didn't like to confess that she'd hardly ever left Hammersmith and the areas immediately around it. She would learn, she'd have to. Rather reluctantly she turned her back on the lively market and traced the route she had just memorised. She would cope, and things would get better. She didn't need to believe what her family had told her, the doubts they had sown. She would not let their voices win.

★ ★ ★

'So how have you been?' Alice set down her canvas weekend bag on her bed and looked at her fellow nurse and best friend, Edith Banham. 'You're still very pale. Are you sure you're eating properly?'

Edith stretched out along the narrow bed as best

24

she could, around the bulging bag. 'Don't fuss, Al. I've had it up to here with Fiona checking me over every two minutes. Blimey, you've only been gone a few days. I hope you haven't spent all your time worrying about me.'

Alice nodded. 'As I thought, then. You haven't been eating. Seriously, Edith, you can't live on dry toast.'

Edith shuffled around on the candlewick bedspread. 'I happen to like dry toast.'

'Just as well.' Alice wasn't giving up.

'It's filling and there's plenty of it, even if it's from that horrible national wheatmeal loaf. How does that rhyme go? "It builds up my health, and its taste is good, I find that I like eating just what I should." Must be true, the government says so.'

'Oh well, in that case . . . ' Alice relented a little, as she took her clothes from the bag and shook them out.

'So how were your parents? Oooh, is that new?' Edith's eyes were drawn to the fine wool boat-neck jumper that her friend was holding up.

Alice smiled. 'My mother made it. Must have taken her ages, it's got all these complicated bits at the cuffs. See, these pearl buttons.'

Edith felt the delicate cuffs and sighed. 'It's just your colour, Al. Turquoise blue.'

Alice had dark blonde hair that she nearly always wore up, as it was more practical for work, but this evening it hung down to her shoulders. 'She's had the wool for ages, waiting for the right moment to make me something.'

'That's lovely.' Edith didn't say anything more but she didn't have to. Alice could tell she was thinking of her own mother, who scarcely bothered to send a

25

Christmas card, and never remembered her daughter's birthday. There had been no special festive gift in the post, not this year or any year that she could recall. Then again, Edith was from a big family and Alice was an only child.

'I don't know why we didn't think of doing this before,' she said, folding the new jumper and carefully placing it in her dressing-table drawer. 'It always seems such a long journey back to Liverpool, but meeting halfway wasn't nearly as bad. My father's always wanted to see Stratford.'

Edith nodded. 'Bet he wouldn't have been quite so keen when the Luftwaffe were bombing Coventry. A bit close for comfort, isn't it?'

'True. But they haven't done that for ages.' Alice brought out a brightly coloured tin from the bottom of the bag. 'As you're eating only dry toast, I don't suppose you'd be interested in my mother's spicy biscuits.'

Edith immediately sat up. 'I could make an exception for those. Besides, ginger is good for nausea, as you must know, Nurse Lake. Go on, hand them over.'

Alice grinned as she passed the tin to Edith and then sat down beside her, moving the empty bag to the rag rug on the floor.

'What have I missed? I know it's only been a few days but it feels like ages.'

Edith finished her mouthful before replying. 'As it happens you have missed something. The two new nurses have arrived. One's had to go into the broom cupboard downstairs as I've not thrown in the towel yet.' Her eyes flashed defiantly.

'Well, they've done it up, haven't they, so it isn't a cupboard any more,' said Alice, not getting drawn in

26

to Edith's mood. 'They'd started before I left. It won't be too bad.'

'She seems nice,' Edith reported. 'Well, maybe a bit green, but we must all have been like that when we started out on the district for the first time.'

'I was very nervous,' Alice recalled, casting her mind back to the day when she and Edith had come to Victory Walk together, just weeks before the war began. That made them virtually veterans.

'Her name's Ruby,' Edith went on, 'and the other one is Lily. She's from Liverpool too. I wonder if you know each other?'

Alice laughed. 'I wouldn't have thought so. Liverpool's a pretty big place, you know.'

Edith shrugged. 'Yes, but it's possible, isn't it? She sounds a bit like you, though her accent's stronger — even more than yours was when you first left home.'

Alice smiled at the memory. 'Maybe . . . but there are loads of hospitals in and around there. The doctors and nurses I knew back then could be anywhere by now, posted to all four corners of the globe.'

Edith nodded, knowing full well that this was the case for everyone — families, friends, colleagues now split up, sent to wherever they were of most use. Her own brothers were now serving in the forces — not that she was in touch with them much. 'Shall we go down for the evening meal, then? Hasn't travelling given you an appetite?'

Alice sat back, eyebrows raised. 'What, do you actually feel like eating?'

Edith nodded with determination. 'Must have been the magic properties of your mother's biscuits. Suddenly I feel as if I could eat a horse.'

'Careful what you wish for,' Alice said cheerfully, getting to her feet. 'Maybe better sticking to the lentil rissoles.'

'Don't really care,' said Edith, standing up and brushing crumbs from her faded green skirt. 'Lentils, horse, I'll eat the lot.'

Alice followed her down the corridor and stairs, beaming at the idea that her friend finally wanted to eat something, knowing that she had been so sick.

★ ★ ★

Lily tucked into her breakfast with relish. It had been hours and hours since she'd eaten properly. The day before she had had an early evening meal and then found she had forgotten to buy any snacks to leave in her service-room locker, for those occasions when she needed something extra between the canteen meal-times.

She wouldn't make that mistake again. Somehow on her morning rounds she would find a moment to visit a shop or a stall and see what was available. Three meals a day were provided for the nurses, but it was hard work riding on those old boneshaker bikes around the still-unfamiliar streets of Dalston, and she needed more fuel.

It was a wonderful novelty to have porridge ready and waiting rather than having to cook it herself. Even if there wasn't much sugar to put in it, let alone cream or fruit, simply sitting down to something warm and filling to begin the day was very welcome. She wondered if she would get used to it, take it for granted. But it was still her first week and the joy had yet to wear off.

There weren't many others up at this early hour. Lily had been awoken by the rumbling of her stomach. Good job she had the lovely bedroom to herself and there was nobody else to hear. While it was not exactly luxurious, the room was better than any she'd had before. It was on a corner of the building, with one window facing over the front gate and the opposite terrace of Victory Walk, the other at right angles giving a view over neighbouring rooftops. She could see the havoc the Blitz had wrought on the area, but also catch the last rays of the setting sun, if she was back on time. That would only get better once spring came.

The porridge had been served to her by a young woman, perhaps in her early twenties, with scraped-back straight brown hair and shadows of tiredness under her eyes, but with a bright manner that suggested she was used to being up and about at this unearthly hour. Lily had been unsure of how to behave with her. At her previous nurses' home, she had cultivated a gracious manner with the various helpers, showing that she was friendly but that her position of a trained professional must be respected. She didn't want to appear too patronising; you never knew when you might need a favour. Yet she had to admit she saw herself as above those who cooked and cleaned, keeping the medical establishments ticking over.

She had been prepared to extend the same attitude to this young woman, but then one of the others had mentioned in passing that Gladys was also a nurse with the Civil Nursing Reserve. That made Lily feel slightly confused. Should she treat the young woman with an air of friendliness tinged with rightfully earned superiority, or acknowledge her as an equal? Yet the

Reserve weren't as well-trained as regular nurses, were they? Some had served for many hours in hospitals, though, as well as at first-aid outposts; there they would have had to cope with whatever horrors the bombings threw at them until the ARP could organise ambulances to bear the casualties away. It was a dilemma.

Somebody had dropped into conversation that Gladys worked all day at the nurses' home, including the early start, then helped to look after her many younger siblings at home before spending most evenings at a first-aid post at a local church hall. That would explain the dark rings under her eyes. Perhaps condescension was the wrong approach. Lily had smiled gratefully when collecting her porridge, deciding she would bide her time with this one.

It also helped explain why everyone was expected to fetch their food from the kitchen hatch and then collect their used plates, bowls and cutlery and take them to a counter at the end of the room, ready to be washed. Gladys and the cook couldn't spare the time to wait upon the nurses. Lily decided she didn't mind, even though — on the few occasions she had been in a restaurant — she had loved being waited on. A sigh escaped her. Not much chance of that at the moment.

As she set her empty bowl down on the battered countertop, two figures came through the canteen door, talking earnestly. They sat at a table in the far corner, too intent on their conversation to pay her any attention. One, the smaller woman with dark hair, was Edith, who had been kind that first night and brought over the cocoa. Lily hadn't seen much of her since.

The other young woman was a good half a head taller, with dark blonde hair — or would it be better classified as light brown, Lily wondered, proud as ever of her own true blonde locks? Then she looked again more closely. The dawn was still to break fully and the light was not the best, but still that taller nurse seemed familiar somehow. Lily wrinkled her nose in concentration.

She'd seen her before, no doubt about it. Lily hadn't been in London for long enough to have met anyone apart from here at the home, or the patients. That couldn't be it. Back in Liverpool, then? Someone passing through one of the hospitals?

Or . . . or . . . the pieces were beginning to fall into place. Not passing through. Someone who had trained at the same place that Lily had, although maybe a year or two ahead of her. But they had overlapped, and she was certain that they knew people in common.

What on earth was her name? Lily drummed her fingers against the counter. Somebody had actually mentioned the name to her recently. Of course. That tall nurse on the far side of the room was Alice Lake.

4

Edith knocked on the front door and then opened it, without waiting for an answer. The knock was just for politeness' sake; she didn't really have to let anyone know she was here. This house was practically her home, and as soon as she had to give up work this was where she would be living. Three generations of the Banham family were to be found under this roof, and they had never been anything but welcoming — to her and to any of her friends.

'Come on in,' she said to Ruby, who was shyly hanging back.

'Are you sure they won't mind?' Ruby asked for the umpteenth time that morning. She drew her cloak around her against the bitterly cold wind as she hesitated on the doorstep of the terraced house.

'Not a bit, they'll be glad to meet you. Now get yourself inside before all the heat goes out of the door.' Edith knew that her mother-in-law, Flo, would have the range stoked up in the kitchen at the back and she could feel its warmth radiating down the corridor, but it wouldn't do to let the temperature drop. Fuel was not easy to come by.

Ruby gingerly stepped inside. She had been delighted when Edith, who had rather taken her under her wing, had invited her to the Banham family home, but now she was having second thoughts. She was not used to people opening their doors to strangers. Her mother never had anyone round and her sister would have been highly suspicious of the invitation. Ruby could hear her now: why would any-one want to meet you, Ruby? What makes you think they'd be interested?

Before she could change her mind, a small child ran into the corridor from a door at the far end, swiftly followed by a woman of around Edith's age.

'Edie, Edie!' shouted the child, holding out two arms to be picked up. As the figure approached, the light from the front fanlight showed it to be a little boy. Edith immediately bent down and lifted him up, even as the other woman protested.

'Edie, you're meant to be taking it easy! Alan, what have I told you!' she scolded, but Ruby could tell she wasn't really cross. Her tone was full of exasperated affection.

'I know, I know, but he's not doing any harm. Are you, Alan? Down you go.' Edith set the toddler back on the ground. 'You don't need to wrap me in cotton wool, I'm not half as sick as at the beginning.' She led the way into the room at the back, and Ruby followed, drawn by the promise of warmth and the enticing smell of something cooking.

'Mattie, this is Ruby.' Edith made the full introductions as they stepped into the muted winter sunlight of the big room.

Ruby stopped biting her lip and smiled at Edith's sister-in-law, who gave her a lively smile back. Ruby couldn't help but notice her hair was a complete mess, escaping from pins on both sides, a chunk of it ineffectively tied back at an odd angle. For some reason it helped to settle her nerves. 'Pleased to meet you,' she said. 'Thank you for having me.'

'Not at all. Any friend of Edie is a friend of ours,' Mattie insisted, nudging Alan out of the way as she turned around. 'Ma, is the kettle on? Our visitors are here.'

Ruby looked towards the door at the far side of the room, which appeared to lead to a back kitchen, as a bustling figure came through — a middle-aged woman, with greying hair and faded apron, but who moved as swiftly as her daughter. 'Oh, you're here, Edie!' she called in evident delight. 'And your new friend too. Come in, come in . . . Hasn't Mattie taken your coats? Whatever were you thinking of, Mattie? Now do sit down and tell me how you're settling in.'

Edith grinned wryly as Ruby took a small step back, caught in the full beam of her mother-in-law's energetic welcome. She slipped off her own worn winter coat and cheerfully took Ruby's cloak, as Mattie was busy keeping Alan out from under their feet by steering him towards his toys under the window.

There was a rocking chair near the range, and Flo indicated that Ruby should take it. Then she swung the large tin kettle onto the hot plate. Ruby's professional brain registered that the older woman winced slightly as she lifted its heavy weight, and noticed that her wrist and fingers were swollen. The cold weather must have brought on a bout of arthritis, but Flo was obviously determined to ignore it.

'So, now, how are you finding the nurses' home?' she asked her guest.

Ruby cleared her throat. 'I like it,' she said honestly. 'Everyone's been very kind.'

Flo nodded, as if this was only proper and what she would have expected.

'I'm still getting used to where everything is,' she admitted. 'Inside the house and out of it, I mean. I haven't been to the East End before. It's taking a

34

while to get my bearings.'

Flo's face creased in sympathy. 'It will do, I expect. You'll have to learn all the alleyways and shortcuts, won't you, nipping from patient to patient like you do. Then you got to keep away from all the potholes and what-nots. Our streets ain't like they were before, that's for certain.' She paused as the kettle began to whistle.

'I'll do it, Ma.' Mattie stepped in, bringing a large china teapot across the room. 'You'll both have a cuppa, won't you.' It wasn't really a question. Tea might be rationed but that didn't mean a guest would ever go thirsty, or not in this house.

Edith nodded for both of them. 'I remember getting completely lost when I first came.' She laughed at the thought. 'Seems like ages ago now, things have changed so much. You get the hang of it before long.'

'Hope so,' Ruby replied.

'And have you been to the market yet?' Flo wanted to know, settling herself on the old sofa with its much-mended cushions. 'That's the place to pick up what's really going on, never mind what you hear on the wireless.'

'Not yet.' Ruby could sense disapproval at this. 'I've seen it though. I thought I'd go back when I have a day off. It looks bigger than the one near my house — my old house, I mean.'

'I'll take you,' Edith offered. 'It's always best to get to know the stallholders, then you get a better bargain. We know some of them pretty well.'

'Especially Brendan,' Mattie said. 'He's also an ARP warden, works in the same section as my dad. You get Edie to introduce you and he'll always see you right.'

'Helps to know the ARP wardens too,' Edith added cheerfully. 'The other one in their section is Billy, and he went to school with Mattie.'

'And now he's married my best friend Kath from school, so we see a lot of him,' Mattie chipped in as she poured the tea into cups arranged on the big dining table. 'Sometimes I mind their little girl — she's about a year younger than Alan. Or sometimes my friend minds him, cos I work in a factory most of the time. I got today off cos I worked a double shift yesterday.' She came across with a cup and saucer for each of her guests.

Edith took hers gratefully. 'So you've gone full time now, then?'

Mattie nodded, taking a cup for herself and one for her mother. 'They need as many workers as they can get. It's much easier for me, now that Gillian's started school — that's my eldest.'

'How's she getting on?' Edith wanted to know.

Mattie raised her eyebrows. 'Only been there a week or so and she's practically running the place already. You know what she's like. It's strange to think of her in the same classroom as we used to be in.'

Flo sipped her tea and gave a nostalgic smile. 'It's no time at all since she was a baby.' She glanced across the room to where a large wooden cot was pushed against the far wall. 'Remember how she used to sleep there while you helped me with the housework, Mattie? And then Kath would bring Brian round and they'd share it.'

Ruby glanced over to the cot.

'Yes, we never got around to moving it,' said Flo happily. 'First Gillian and Brian, and not that long afterwards, Alan here, and little Barbara as often as not. Used to nap in it when they were tiny and then it's as good as a playpen once they get crawling. Not long before your baby has its turn, Edie.'

Edith laughed in acknowledgement and Ruby widened her eyes.

'It's due in June, but don't worry, I'll have to give up work before then,' Edith said, mistaking Ruby's expression. 'So you won't have to sleep in the broom cupboard for ever.'

'Oh, it's not that.' Ruby hurriedly put her right, but couldn't say what it was that had bothered her. It would sound silly in this generously sized room with its generous family, but something about the cot had shocked her.

Her mother had always been extremely proud of the fact that — even though she and Ruby's father had been short of money and space — the twins had never needed to share anything. It had been some kind of point of honour: whatever misfortunes might befall the family, Colin and Beryl would not be lumped together, but would have their own clothes and little beds. Not for them the big, unwieldy prams with a baby at either end. People who did that to their children were to be disapproved of, condemned even. As if it showed they didn't love them enough.

Yet here were a mother and grandmother who obviously doted on the children, and those of their friends too, who had no problem with them sharing a cot. Ruby knew on one level there was no sense in her reaction; as a nurse she knew there would be little risk to the children, providing normal rules of hygiene were observed, and this house was as clean as any could be with a toddler around. It was yet another part of the way she had been brought up, she realised,

37

having extra things to worry about that simply didn't bother most people. It was a burden she feared she could not shake.

'Have you heard from Harry?' Mattie asked Edith.

Edith turned to Ruby. 'That's my husband,' she explained. 'He's just got a posting as a PT instructor with the army, and he's had to move up north — we won't see him for months now.' Automatically one hand went to her stomach where there was just the beginning of a new bump. 'He's not a great one for letter writing, so all I know is that he's arrived.'

Mattie grimaced. 'He's better at it than Lennie is — sorry, he's my husband. He's been a prisoner of war since Dunkirk. Never was much good at writing home and now he doesn't have much chance to.' She smiled as if she had grown used to the situation, and that would have fooled anyone but Edith and her mother. They were well aware that she was covering her daily heartbreak with a show of bravery.

'Oh, that must be hard,' Ruby said, realising that this young woman had some very genuine causes for concern. 'My brother's in the navy. You can't help worrying.'

Mattie nodded. 'That's true enough. As for my big brother, Joe's in the navy as well and we never know where he is or what he's doing. That's unless Alice has said anything?' She looked hopefully at Edith.

Edith shook her head. 'I don't think she's heard from him since New Year. She always tells me if there's any news from him.' Once again she felt obliged to explain to Ruby. 'Joe's good friends with Alice, and everyone always teases them that there's more to it, but really it's because they're the only ones among us who read all the papers and follow current affairs.

She's always been like that and the war has made her even worse — you'll soon find out, if you ever try to get her head out of a book.'

'They're the brainy ones all right,' Mattie agreed. 'Most of us haven't got a clue what they're on about half the time. Still, that's not much use to either of them now. Didn't she think he was in Italy, or on the way there?'

'It was a guess,' said Edith sadly. 'I'll tell you if I hear, of course I will.'

Ruby let the conversation flow on around her, enjoying being part of the warmth of the group but not joining in. The heat from the range was enough to make her pleasantly drowsy. Somehow it felt more like a home than her own. She shifted a little in the chair, knowing her thoughts were disloyal, and her gaze fell upon an open newspaper, tucked behind a cushion. It had been folded to show a photo, a little blurred, of prisoners of war opening Christmas presents. She wondered if Mattie had searched the men's faces for her own husband's, hoping for confirmation that he was still alive and safe, or at least at the time the picture had been taken, a few weeks ago now. It must be horribly difficult.

Edith noticed her movement and turned to her. 'We ought to be going,' she said, her voice full of reluctance. 'Sorry to drag you away, Ruby, but I promised to help restock the district room this afternoon. It's my turn. We had better make a move.' She rose, pausing to ruffle Alan on the head as he raced by with his toy plane. 'We'll see you again soon. Thanks for the tea.'

'Don't stay away so long this time,' Flo scolded, as Mattie went to fetch the coats. She gently took Ruby's arm for a second. 'That means you too, Ruby. We said it before; any friend of Edith's is a friend of ours.

Even if you aren't as far away from your family as some of your colleagues, if you ever want a bit of home comfort then we're always here. You make sure you remember that.'

Ruby swallowed hard. 'I will,' she said.

Walking back to the high road that ran between the Banham household on Jeeves Street and the side road that led to Victory Walk, Edith noticed that the new nurse was very quiet. 'You all right, Ruby?'

'Of course.'

'Because you don't need to worry; like I said, I will have to give up work in the not-too-distant future and then you'll have my room on the top floor, up next to Alice and along from Mary. I just hope you aren't too uncomfortable in the meantime.'

They stopped and waited at the kerb for the Liverpool Street bus to go by, and Ruby gave a small smile. 'Really,' she told Edith, 'I don't mind. I like it.'

Edith frowned. 'But you must be able to hear everyone coming and going. Isn't that annoying? I'd be annoyed.' She stuck her hands into the patch pockets of her coat, feeling around for her gloves.

Ruby shrugged, a little embarrassed. 'I'm a heavy sleeper so I don't get woken up easily. Then sometimes it's useful.' She almost stopped but then ploughed on, despite having to admit her ignorance. 'I didn't know what to do about my Gladstone bag. I knew I was meant to refill it but I'd forgotten how — we never did it on our own when we were training and I felt a fool for not knowing.' The bus left the stop near them and they crossed the wide road. 'Then I heard voices and so stuck my head out. Two of the others — the one with the posh voice and the very tall one with black hair . . . '

'Mary and Belinda, I bet.'

'Yes, that's it. Well, they were about to restock their bags and so I asked if the room opposite was where everything was kept. They said yes and showed me what to do. So you see, it's the ideal place.'

Edith looked up at the new nurse, with her pale face and sharp features, noticing for the first time the reserves of humour in her grey eyes. 'I'm pleased to hear it!' she said with some relief. 'I hated to think I was stopping you settling in.'

Ruby shook her head. 'No, it's quite the opposite,' she said with feeling. As they walked on past the tall terraced houses she reflected that she had truly struck it lucky — getting to know Edith had not only helped her at the nurses' home, but now she had also seen a taste of family life that, if she was honest, made her ever so slightly jealous. What she wouldn't give to have a warm welcome like that to go back to.

5

Lily was grateful to be back indoors and out of the freezing January wind. She set down her Gladstone bag and rubbed her hands, trying to bring circulation back into her fingers. She'd only just managed to work the brakes on her rickety old bike, she was so chilly. Those bikes were terrible to ride, far worse than the one she'd had during her training in Liverpool. It was a wonder that none of the nurses had come a cropper.

She decided to head straight for the service room and get herself a hot drink. Restocking the bag could wait. She'd only fumble everything while her fingers were cold and stiff, she thought, hurrying down the short flight of steps at the end of the corridor and into the common room.

Others had clearly had the same idea, and several nurses were huddled around the fire burning in the grate on the far side of the big room. Lily hastily made a cup of tea and then went to join them. 'Room for another,' said one of the Irish nurses as she let Lily squeeze in. 'I'm late already, so I'll see you all later,' she called over her shoulder as she headed off.

Lily edged into the vacant carver chair that either Bridget or Ellen — she couldn't remember which was which — had left behind. She sighed in relief as the warmth from the fire hit her, making her tingle all over. 'That's better,' she breathed.

'I'll say.' The tall, dark-haired nurse raised her eyebrows in sympathy. 'Bit of a shocker out there today, isn't it?'

Lily nodded, her teeth chattering a little against the rim of her cup as she raised it to her mouth. She knew it was important to appear to be friendly but she didn't want to seem weak. 'It certainly is, but I'm used to it. It gets pretty cold where I'm from.'

Belinda smiled. 'Liverpool, wasn't it? Alice says it rains a lot there.'

Lily took another sip. 'It does, there's no denying it. Is Nurse Lake back from her rounds yet? I've hardly seen her since I moved in, but it would be nice to talk to her, given that we come from the same place.'

The nurse on her other side frowned. 'No, she's teaching one of the WVS groups today,' she said in a refined accent. 'She'll be gone all day, I expect. I'm sure she'd be glad to, though, another time.'

Lily could finally feel her hands properly. 'Well, we're bound to see each other soon, then.' She tried hard to remember this nurse's name. Mary, that was it. And the tall one was Belinda.

'How were your rounds today?' Belinda was asking now.

Lily set down her cup on the nearest table. 'Oh, nothing I couldn't handle,' she said lightly. 'One of the women was making a right fuss over nothing. You'd think nobody had ever had flu before. She kept asking me for a new vaccine, said she'd read about it in the paper, and that she wanted it for her family. I had to tell her she couldn't have any such thing and that her little boy would get better as long as she kept him in bed.'

Mary looked puzzled. 'I haven't heard about a vaccine.'

Belinda grinned. 'Yes, but you hardly ever read the papers, Mary. Don't worry, it won't affect us. It's a

43

new thing the Americans are giving to their servicemen. It wasn't exactly in the headlines.'

'I'm sure if it was important then Charles would
have told me,' Mary replied staunchly, unconcerned
that Belinda was teasing her.

'In that case I'm surprised this woman knew about
it,' Lily said, keen to keep Mary on side. 'It didn't look
like the sort of house where people read very much.'

Belinda widened her eyes at this but didn't comment directly. Instead she said, 'Was this a place just
off Cricketfield Road by any chance?'

Lily paused to think. She was still trying to remember the names of the streets. 'Yes. Yes it was.'

Belinda nodded. 'Thought so. It's the Peterson
family, isn't it? I've treated them before now.'

Lily shrugged. 'Yes, I think that was her name. Mrs
Peterson. And her little boy is Bobby.'

'Oh, I know who you mean now,' Mary said. 'No
wonder she was upset. She can't help it. She's terrified of the flu; happens every winter, of course, but
this year there's been a bit of an epidemic and that's
made it worse. Poor soul, I hadn't realised that her little boy had gone down with it or I might have popped
in.'

Lily was confused. People got flu all the time;
what could possibly be so different about this family?
They'd all been in a right state and she'd had to struggle hard not to show her impatience with them.

'Mrs Peterson's parents caught the Spanish flu
when it was going round at the end of the Great War,'
Belinda explained. 'They both died. It was especially
sad because her father hadn't long got back from
fighting. He'd survived the trenches only to be killed
by the flu. She was brought up by her aunt and she

44

must have put the fear of God into her about it. She's always extra-careful about hygiene but it looks as if her son's gone and caught it anyway.'

Lily bit back her annoyance. She couldn't possibly have known but now she'd come across as uncaring. It made her dislike the family even more. 'Well, he's in no danger,' she pointed out. 'He seemed a healthy little thing otherwise. He'll be over it in no time.'

Mary nodded. 'He probably will. I might go round anyhow, just to reassure her.'

Lily wanted to snap in exasperation; hadn't she reassured the woman, despite her being so aggravating? But it would do no good to object.

'At least people are better fed now,' Belinda pointed out. 'I know we all complain about the rationing but it does mean that families like that have better nutrition than they would have done otherwise. He most likely got it from school. You can't stop kiddies passing it on when they're all over each other in the playground.'

Mary brightened up. 'We could use that as an excuse to visit the local schools and give them extra hygiene lessons. We haven't done that for ages. Remind them that washing their hands properly isn't just something their mothers tell them for the sake of it.'

'Good idea. We could speak to Janet.' Belinda's expression grew animated. 'That's a teacher we're friendly with. She's very keen on that sort of thing, that's how we know her in the first place — she got Alice in to teach the little ones how to brush their teeth, ages ago.'

'Oh.' Lily wasn't sure how to react. It looked as if her casual comment had spawned a whole lot of extra work for her colleagues. That hadn't been her intention at all. She'd better leave before they roped her in any further. 'Nice talking to you,' she said hurriedly, 'but I'd better go and see to my bag as I'm running low on lots of things. See you later.' She headed for the door as quickly as she could without seeming rude.

'Golly,' said Mary when she'd gone. 'Was it something we said?'

* * *

There was no better way to end a shift, even one that involved teaching rather than nursing, than to come back and find a letter, thought Alice, picking up the envelope from the special shelf near the front door. Telegrams usually meant bad news; postcards cheered you up but never actually said much and besides, everyone could read what was written on the back. Letters were special.

Particularly ones with this handwriting on the front. Alice tucked it into her pocket as she went upstairs to her attic bedroom, singing to herself in anticipation. She had heard nothing from Joe for six weeks, unless you counted the quick note at New Year. That wasn't a proper letter. True, it had been a relief to get it, confirming he was still alive at any rate, but it wasn't like pages of news, his opinions and thoughts on what he'd read recently. Joe had the knack of making his writing sound just like how he spoke, so that she could imagine him sitting opposite her, telling her what he'd been doing, what he'd heard on the wireless, funny observations of his life as an engineer in the Navy.

She didn't rush to open the envelope, but changed out of her uniform, wrapped herself in her new turquoise jumper and made herself comfortable, before reaching for her little paperknife and carefully slitting

46

the flap, edging out the flimsy sheets from inside.

Alice had grown into the habit of skimming the whole letter from start to finish, almost as a way of ensuring it contained no bad news. She knew it was silly and superstitious but she did it anyway. Obviously if Joe had been able to write the letter, seal it and post it, he must be all right — or at least up until the time of sending it. Yet the habit had stuck. She would then go back and reread the whole thing through, slowly, savouring every sentence.

Running her eyes over the words now, she reflected that he'd already had one near miss that she knew of; she couldn't be sure if there had been others that he'd not mentioned for fear of worrying her. Or perhaps it was more that he didn't want to worry his family. When he had one of his leaves, which was all too rare, she and he would talk about anything and everything, no subject off limits, no matter how uncomfortable. Yet Joe would know that whatever he wrote to her would end up being shared with his family. He couldn't expect Alice to keep news to herself when she was so close to Edith and to all the Banhams.

She released a breath she hadn't realised she had been holding as she reached his signature on the last page. No accidents, no brushes with death this time. Every time he wrote with no tales of close escapes, she felt it was one step closer to his surviving the war. She knew there was no logic to it, but felt it keenly all the same.

Leaning back on her pillows she began to reread the pages, laughing at his description of his messmates, but realising he had given absolutely no indication of where he was. While a direct statement would have fallen foul of the censor, Joe usually got around it by

47

naming a book or author that was associated with the location. But there was nothing here. The only books he spoke of were ones he'd recently read. For a while they had tried to read the same ones so that they could swap notes afterwards, but after he had left his base in Plymouth it had become too difficult; he had to make do with whatever was available, exchanging books with his crewmates. Alice sighed again, in sympathy. It was easy for her to wander up the road to the lending library. She counted herself lucky.

Where was he, and when was he coming home, she wondered. It felt like half a lifetime since she'd seen him. She found it difficult to admit, even to herself, just how much she missed him. They never spoke of their feelings for each other, insisting that it was purely friendship. With the war separating them by force, this was simply practical.

However, Alice knew that they had a special connection, something only they could share. Joe was the one person who totally understood her, to whom she could say anything. It wasn't solely that they were both avid readers or followers of current affairs, though that was what those on the outside usually commented on. It went far deeper than that and she struggled to put a name to it. There was a sensation of being connected in a way that defied description. Even though she was close to her parents, and extremely close to Edith, somehow her friendship with Joe was on another level.

It was not a fanciful romance, though. Alice had been badly hurt before and was determined never to risk her heart again. When first training as a nurse in the big hospital back in Liverpool, she had fallen hard for a young doctor, Mark. They had planned a future together and she had never doubted him — until he left her, not for another woman but for something altogether more potent: a cause. He had gone to fight in the Spanish Civil War and she had been abandoned. Even to this day she scarcely ever spoke of it. Her parents knew and so did Edith, but she had seen no reason to tell anybody else.

This determination had come unravelled when one of the other doctors from the old days, Mark's best friend Dermot McGillicuddy, had briefly turned up in Dalston, working as a locum. Alice had learnt that Mark had survived Spain and knew that he was now a doctor at a base on the south coast, as was Dermot. That was all she wished to know. He was nothing to her any more and she had no desire to reopen such a painful wound.

A knock on the door brought her out of her daydreams, and Edith poked her head inside the cosy room. 'Time for tea!' she called brightly, and then stopped at the sight of the letter. She too instantly recognised the handwriting. 'Oh, Al, how is he?' she cried eagerly. 'Has he got leave? Does he say?'

Alice shook her head and fought hard to hide her disappointment. Edith had enough on her plate, she didn't need to see how much her friend had been hoping for just that very news.

'Not yet,' she said with a brightness that sounded horribly false to her ears. 'But soon. He's bound to come back soon.'

6

Lily was still in a bad mood the next morning. It being a Saturday, she had no rounds, and she decided to do something to cheer herself up. If she had been home in Liverpool she would have gone into the city centre, even though so much of it had been destroyed by bombs. She sighed, remembering how she had loved to go to John Lewis in the sales. Not much chance of that now.

She considered making a trip to the West End, to see if there was anything on offer in the big shops on Oxford Street, but knew from what she'd overheard in the canteen that the buses were often disrupted and the whole expedition could take the best part of a day. Really, it was too bad. She didn't want to spend her day off cooped up in the nurses' home. She was sure that Mary and Belinda would have thought badly of her after yesterday's conversation. She had to hope they'd forget about it if she stayed out of their way for a while.

Her gaze fell on her collection of cosmetics, carefully set out on the dressing table next to the window. Light was peeping from behind the curtains and she could make out the outlines of her lipstick, mascara and powder compacts, all several years old and reaching the end of their serviceable lives. She'd been eking them out even before she applied for the transfer to London, keeping them for special occasions. She hadn't yet stooped to using boot polish instead of mascara, but that day was not too far off. She shuddered as she swung her legs out of bed, edging her feet around the rag rug until they made contact with her slippers.

Then she remembered what one of her patients had said yesterday morning, before the visit to the little boy with flu had driven it from her mind. The young woman had cut her arm on broken glass from a bomb-damaged window, and needed her stitches taken out. She'd had slippers very similar to Lily's own — that was what had reminded her. They had been trimmed with pale apricot ribbons, with a little bow at the back, and Lily had admired them. This had been a useful distraction as the young woman was still talking about them as Lily removed the stitches.

Then she had mentioned that a chemist's shop not too far away was rumoured to be getting some cosmetic supplies. 'I'm not sure if I'll be able to go, I'll have to see how I feel tomorrow, but you should try it,' she'd said, gingerly rubbing her injured arm. 'It's easy to find.'

Lily knew that if there was anything to be had then it would be expensive, but she reckoned it would be a worthwhile purchase. An investment. You couldn't put a price on looking good. It made her feel better if she dressed up smartly, and it wasn't big-headed to notice that plenty of bystanders enjoyed the way she looked as well. You could say that she was doing them a service, giving them a moment of pleasure in their dull day.

Carefully she chose an outfit — not too gaudy but stylish, a cream blouse with a pin-tucked bodice, teamed with a warm russet skirt with a little flare to it. She knew it swung around her knees as she walked. Perfect.

51

After a hurried breakfast sitting by herself in the corner of the canteen, pretending to read a magazine so that nobody would try to talk to her, she made good her escape, along Victory Walk and down the side street to the main road through Dalston. Remembering her patient's instructions, she headed south, through the busy crowds of weekend shoppers. She passed the end of the market, tempting but unlikely to sell what she'd set her heart upon. She could always drop by on the way back.

She was entering new territory now, beyond the roads she was slowly becoming familiar with. These houses would be covered by a different team of district nurses, living in another nurses' home. Lily smiled, drawing the collar of her maroon coat more tightly around her neck. There would be nobody she knew to see her, so it wouldn't matter if she failed to buy what she was after.

She peered at the signs above the shops, looking for the right number. What a long road it was. Perhaps her patient had got it wrong? She hoped it wouldn't be a wild goose chase after all.

Then it became clear which was the right shop, as she noticed women gathering around a doorway. Lily realised it was a rather unruly queue. She didn't know if that was a good or bad thing; would it mean there was a better chance that the rumour was right, or would whatever stock there might have been already be sold out?

Well, there was no point in turning back now. Lily took her place behind a middle-aged woman who, Lily thought unkindly, could certainly do with a bit of makeup to improve her appearance. She looked down at her pretty brown boots so that her less than

52

generous thoughts did not show on her face.

Two younger women joined the queue behind her, jostling each other, their hair caught up in bright scarves. From their conversation Lily guessed they had come direct from a shift at a nearby factory. She idly listened in as one complained that they were having to work even longer hours than usual.

'Makes you think something's up,' she finished.

'Stop it, you mustn't say that,' her friend replied, elbowing the first girl in the ribs. 'Loose lips sink ships, ain't that what they tell you on the wireless? You're just lazy.'

'Lazy! I just worked twelve hours straight through and I'm going back this evening for fire-watching,' the first girl groaned, shuffling forward a little.

Lily was inside the door now, gazing around the small shop. Whoever owned it had done their best to make it appear that there was a lot for sale, but the gaps on the shelves were painfully evident. Everything was spaced out as far as could be, and the products, such as they were, stood only one item deep along the shelves. Bright posters advertised Tangee and Helena Rubinstein cosmetics, but Lily couldn't see any of those once-familiar boxes.

All the same, the pictures strengthened her resolve to buy something, anything, to give herself some of that glamour. Finally reaching the front of the queue, she drew a breath. Painting on her brightest smile, she did her best to make eye contact with the elderly man behind the counter. 'Do you have any lipstick?' she asked, trying not to sound too desperate.

His eyes were semi-hidden behind thick glasses. 'Sorry,' he said. 'Just sold the last one.'

Lily could have screamed. Had that old woman in

front of her pipped her at the post? She drew another breath, slower this time. 'How about mascara? Or face powder?'

The old man shook his head, his face almost expressionless. Lily decided that he'd probably already made a packet this morning, and all these remaining disappointed customers were a waste of his time. 'Maybe not the ones in their original packaging . . .' she added, dropping her voice.

His chin came up a little — he was scarcely taller than she was. 'I'll tell you what we do have,' he said confidingly. 'As you probably know, materials to make powder compacts are hard to get hold of. Government says all the metal and suchlike have to go for munitions. Can't even get the wherewithal for a powder puff.' Lily nodded encouragingly, wishing he'd come to the point. 'But we get little blocks of powder, no puff, and you can slip them into whatever compact you've already got,' he went on. 'How would that suit you?'

Normally Lily would have demurred, played the game, hoping not to seem too eager and keen to negotiate. But this morning she sensed that any delay would see her leaving the grim little shop with precisely nothing. 'Hmm, not quite what I was after, but yes, that would do,' she said, and watched as the shopkeeper's hand darted beneath the counter and reappeared with a cardboard box, small and plain but for some dull lines of print. She almost gasped at the eye-watering price he named, but then reminded herself she had known this little expedition wouldn't be cheap. Pursing her lips she handed over the money, turned on her heel and hurried back outside.

'Oh, I'm terribly sorry.' A man standing just by the

door knocked against her shoulder, making her stumble. 'I didn't realise you were coming through. Are you all right? Not hurt?'

Lily instinctively checked her coat pocket for the box of face powder — that was the most important thing. 'No, no, I'm not hurt at all,' she assured him. As her eyes adjusted to the daylight back on the street, she noticed with some satisfaction that this man was the virtual opposite of the miserable mean old shopkeeper. He was tall, for a start, with a head of dark brown hair, slicked back but not showily so. He was perhaps thirty, maybe a little older. His eyes crinkled with good humour and she could see that he liked what he saw when he looked at her. Best of all, he was definitely handsome. He put her in mind of Clark Gable.

She smiled at him, certain that her cheeks would be flushed gently pink as she emerged into the cold winter air once more.

'There's quite a crowd here,' he observed. 'I'd hoped to buy some lipstick for my sister as a belated Christmas present, but it would seem I'm out of luck.'

'Me too,' said Lily, thinking that bumping into this handsome man was no bad luck at all. 'I'll just have to manage without, I suppose.' She gave him another bright smile.

'That would be a shame.' He raised an eyebrow. 'This country needs our ladies to look their best. It's good for morale.'

Lily pretended to look down in modesty. 'So they say.' She glanced up again.

'If you don't mind me saying, I'd lay good money on you looking like a film star when you wear lipstick,' he grinned.

55

Lily knew he was stringing her along but couldn't resist it. It had been ages since she'd been flirted with by anyone remotely interesting. 'I hardly ever get the chance,' she said primly.

'What, you don't wear it for work? You're not a model, then?'

She laughed at that. 'Of course not. I'm a nurse, as it happens.'

He nodded approvingly. 'In that case, your patients are very lucky.'

'I'm sure it's very kind of you to say so.' She brought her hand to her collar and adjusted it.

'Which way are you going?' he asked.

She angled her head up the main road. 'I have to get back to the nurses' home. It's not far.'

He nodded. 'Well, I'm sad to say I go the opposite way. My sister will be waiting.' He paused. 'You'll think me very forward, but it so happens that every now and again I can obtain the occasional lipstick, through work contacts. All above board, just in the course of business,' he added quickly, as Lily stepped back. 'It would make me very happy if you would accept some as a gift, the next time the chance comes my way, to make up for me almost knocking you over just now.'

'Oh, I couldn't possibly . . . ' Lily's mind was racing, trying to work out if it was worth the gamble. 'But what about your sister? Won't she want it?'

'I dare say I can get some for you both.' He gave her a charming open smile. 'If you'd care to write down your name and how I may contact you . . . ' Again he raised an eyebrow.

What did she have to lose? It wasn't as if she was agreeing to anything serious. Lily bit her lip and let him wait just a little longer than necessary. Then she nodded. 'All right. Thank you.'

★ ★ ★

Alice tried to concentrate on the note she was writing, the sheet of paper catching a ray of sunshine sloping in at a low angle through the big common-room windows. Her mind was still racing though, thoughts of Joe and the mystery of his current whereabouts crowding out everything else. She'd slept badly, her convoluted dreams revolving around Joe's ship being bombed, water rushing into the bulkheads, his crew-mates struggling to escape. Then she'd woken up to find it was raining hard and the noise was the raindrops pounding at her attic window. She had tried to go back to sleep but it hadn't worked, and she had fallen into an uneasy doze.

Finally, she had given up and risen early, despite it being a Saturday. Rubbing her red and itching eyes she had dragged herself downstairs and attempted to compose a note to her teacher friend, Janet. Mary had told her about the idea of giving new lessons in hygiene, and Alice had agreed that would be a good plan. She had offered to be the one to contact the school because, after all, she knew Janet better than the others.

Yet the words refused to form and, after several goes, she had abandoned the effort. Instead she'd passed the morning chatting to whoever was around — Gladys to begin with, then Belinda on her way out to meet up with her ambulance-driver friend Geraldine, then the Irish nurses who lived in the annexe next door came over for some company. Gwen came in with the daily papers, and that had been another excuse to while away the time. Alice had battled with the crossword with mixed success, but failed to find anyone to help her out. Nobody else had much time for cryptic clues. Which brought her full circle, to missing Joe. He was always game to have a go at a tricky crossword.

Alice didn't like to give in to defeat but her tired brain was unequal to the task of finishing the puzzle. Sighing, she set the newspaper aside and returned to her note. Just holding her pen felt like an effort. She put it down again.

The door from the hallway opened and in came one of the new nurses, the one with bright blonde hair. Her cheeks were flushed with cold from being outside and she was smiling as she walked across the room. Alice realised she was heading her way, and half welcomed another source of distraction.

'Hello.' The new nurse stopped beside the little writing table. 'Nurse Lake, isn't it? Do you mind if I join you?' She gave a big smile and Alice couldn't help but respond.

'Of course not — and do call me Alice.' It was always good to hear a voice with that familiar accent. Alice might have lived in London for five years, but she would always think of Liverpool as home. The new nurse's words took her back to that city, where there were reminders of the sea everywhere — the gulls, the ships, the salt tang when the wind was a westerly. 'And you're Lily, is that right?'

Lily nodded and drew up a chair, positioning it so that the sun fell across it. She sat down and smiled again. 'Yes, I'm Lily. I'm glad to have a chance to say hello. I've been meaning to since I got here and found you came from the same place as I do.'

Alice nodded, noting that the young woman seemed very confident and was in an evident good mood, rather in contrast to her own. She stirred herself to be polite and interested. 'Yes, isn't that a coincidence?'

Lily cocked her head to one side in acknowledgement. 'It is, but actually I think it's even more of a coincidence than that.' She paused. 'I'm sure I remember you from training. Weren't we at the same hospital?'

Alice frowned and struggled to recall. Her brain was too sluggish and she could not bring the young nurse to mind. Surely she would have remembered someone with hair like that, and yet no image presented itself. 'I'm not sure,' she said honestly.

Lily persisted. 'I'm sure we were. I think you were a year or two ahead of me. We weren't in the same lectures or anything like that.'

Alice thought that sounded possible. She could recall nurses who had been in their final stages of training when she was just beginning, wondering if she would ever be as good at her job as they had appeared to be. She had been envious of their competence and the easy way they handled themselves. How strange if Lily had thought the same about her.

'I finished my basic training in 1938 and then moved down here to specialise as a district nurse,' Alice explained now. 'Would that fit?'

The younger woman's eyes lit up. 'That's it. I was two years behind you, then. That makes sense. Do you know, I used to look up to you — you always seemed to know exactly what you were doing, when I was struggling to get used to everything.'

Alice grinned. 'I'm sure I wasn't as good as all that. It didn't feel like that at the time — there was always

59

more to learn, a new ward to get the hang of.' She cast her mind back to the intensity of hospital training. 'And some of the matrons were terrifying. We were afraid of lots of them. If we made the smallest mistake we'd get a proper dressing down in front of everybody.'

Lily laughed in delight. 'They were real dragons, weren't they? Made you feel about five years old if you stepped the smallest bit out of line. Not like Fiona here — I couldn't believe she was the supervisor at first.'

Alice laughed as well. 'I know what you mean, but don't be fooled. She's sharper than all those dragons put together. She might be informal but that doesn't mean she tolerates mistakes. You'd see another side to her then.'

'Oooh, I wouldn't like that.' Lily pretended to shudder. 'No, I'm sure you're right. It helps though, doesn't it, to be treated like a grown-up?'

Alice shifted in her seat, telling herself that she should make more of an effort to be friendly and welcoming. It was just tiredness making her tetchy, she decided. 'She trusts us, that's the difference. Besides, all of us have passed our exams, taken an extra period of specialist training and then practised on the district. We ought to have some idea of what we're doing, even though it doesn't always feel like that.'

'Gosh.' Lily looked surprised that such an experienced nurse as Alice should admit to feeling uncertain. 'Well, it's true I sometimes wonder if I've done the right thing. I've read all the books and try to keep up by reading the magazine, but you can't always see what's coming from around the corner, can you?'

Alice nodded vigorously. 'Exactly. You can't be fully

prepared for absolutely everything. The trick is to admit it and not to be afraid to ask for help. We've all got areas we feel more comfortable in — I like training children and volunteer nurses, Mary's the best when it comes to elderly patients, for example.'

Lily's eyes opened wide. 'Can I really come to you if I need it? That would be so reassuring.'

Alice nodded again, although a little voice in her head wondered what she had let herself in for. 'Of course. Not just me but any of the others would be happy to help.'

Lily smiled broadly. 'I can't thank you enough.' Then she frowned a little, as another thought struck her. 'Do you remember those two student doctors in your year? I can see them now — that very good-looking one with dark hair and his friend, the quieter one.'

Alice forced her face to give nothing away. This was a subject she didn't share with her closest friends unless she absolutely had to, much less with a young woman she'd only just met. 'Yes. Everyone always noticed Dermot McGillicuddy.'

'That's right,' Lily exclaimed. 'I knew he had a funny name. He was so handsome!' she laughed. 'We used to try to change our rotas so that we could be on the same ward.'

Alice smiled back. Perhaps all would be well if they could keep the conversation on the topic of Dermot.

'Can you believe it,' Lily sailed on, blithely unaware that she had steered into dangerous waters, 'when I was waiting for the train at Lime Street, on my way down here, I bumped into that friend of his — the clever one, Mark I think he was called. He'd come back to see his parents and we got talking. I told him where I was going and he said he knew someone here — well it was you, of course.' She smiled again, oblivi.ous to Alice's reaction. 'He seemed very keen to know how you were, but I couldn't tell him anything as I'd not met you.' She smiled happily and looked at Alice. 'He kept saying what a lovely person you were and how very sorry he was not to be in touch with you still. I suppose you lost contact what with the war and all . . . In fact, perhaps I should have got his address for you,' she chattered on, 'but the train came in and I had to run. Small world, though!'

Alice gripped her chair so hard she thought she would break it. Taking a deep breath she managed to answer. 'Yes, as you say, it's a small world.' She could think of nothing else. Her world had just been ripped wide open.

Lily got to her feet, perhaps sensing she had said too much. 'Well, it's been lovely talking to you but I really must get on. I can see you're writing a letter and I've interrupted you. TTFN!' She waved breezily and headed out of the door the way she had come.

Slowly Alice turned to face the big windows, away from anyone who might be able to see her. The angle of the sun had changed and the back yard was now in shadow, forming a background to her own reflection. There was no escape from the sight of her tear-filled eyes and utterly devastated face.

7

Ruby was lost. She'd been so sure that she could find this morning's patients that she hadn't brought her map. The trouble was, many of the terraces looked the same, give or take the patterns of bomb damage. Red bricks or dull stone, doors opening directly onto the pavement or with a small area that could never be called a garden, barely big enough for her to leave her bike. The upshot was, she could be almost there or miles away — she had no idea.

She didn't like to ask. It made her feel a failure and that she was letting down her profession. Nurses shouldn't get lost.

Now she turned her head this way and that, searching for anything even slightly familiar. It was to no avail. She could feel her temperature rising as she pedalled faster, her heartbeat increasing, sweat beginning to bead on her forehead despite the chilly air. She knew she shouldn't panic but it was hard not to. She would be letting down the patients waiting for her.

Then again, what if this wasn't panic and the symptoms were the first signs of flu? More and more people were going down with it; it would be hardly surprising if she caught it too. There was a limit to how much stringent hygiene could stave it off. That little girl on Friday had sneezed all over Ruby before she could turn away. It wasn't deliberate, but perhaps that was when infection happened? The mother had been desperately apologetic, but maybe the damage had been done?

The sensible part of Ruby's brain told her to calm

down, but now the familiar pattern of low confidence was spiralling faster and faster. She was no good at this, she'd never been any good. It was pure fluke that she'd passed her exams in the first place. Perhaps it was better that she missed her appointments as that way she couldn't harm her patients. She could hear her sister's voice saying over and over, 'I told you so.'

Then a dog dashed out from behind a baker's cart, and she was forced to swerve and brake hard. It was touch and go whether she'd stay on the bike, and once she'd regained control she was shaking with effort, but at least it had broken her train of thought.

'Miss, I'm ever so sorry.' A middle-aged woman came around the side of the cart, wiping her hands on her dusty coat. 'Buster, come here, bad dog. You almost got this lady hurt. Oh, you're a nurse. Are you all right?'

Ruby was trembling but nodded. 'Y-yes, I think so. No harm done. It was just a bit of a shock, that's all.'

She held on to the heavy old bike for support, her knees weak.

'He's never done that before. He usually stays inside when I collect me orders.' The woman shook her head. 'Can I do anything, nurse? I hope I've not made you late or nothing.'

Ruby saw her chance. This woman must be a local. 'As a matter of fact, maybe you can help me. I'm looking for Butterfield Green. Could you point me in the right direction?'

'Oh, nurse, you must be all confused what with Buster running out like that. No wonder you don't know. You're only a couple of streets away. See where the road bends up there? Turn left at the house with the dark blue door and then next left after that. It'll be

64

right in front of you, you can't miss it.' She grabbed the little dog by his collar and pulled him close to her feet. The dog, having had his brief adventure, made no protest.

Ruby smiled in gratitude. 'Of course. It's all coming back to me now,' she said, stretching the truth. 'I'd best be off, but thank you.'

'Oh no, thank you, nurse. For not making a fuss,' the woman insisted, evidently relieved that she wasn't going to get into trouble for her pet causing an accident. 'I'm happy to be of assistance, I am.'

Ruby swung her leg over the saddle and began to pedal once more, calmer now that she knew where she was going. That had been a lucky escape. The naughty little dog had done her a favour. She banished all thoughts of her doubting sister to the back of her mind. Now she had a job to do and she had to believe that she could do it. Breathing deeply she willed her heartbeat to go back to normal. Already she was feeling better. She didn't have flu. Just as well, she thought — with all the patients they had to attend to, none of them had time to be sick themselves.

★ ★ ★

Of all the weekends for Edith to spend at the Banhams' . . . Alice had been pacing around the nurses' home, her mind in turmoil since Lily had thrown out her casual thunderbolt of a remark, knowing the only person she could confide in was her best friend. Edith, however, had spent both Saturday and Sunday night at her in-laws' house, having planned to go through their pile of baby clothes and pick out what might be suitable for her own baby when it was born.

65

Alice could hardly object to that but she could not control her tumbling thoughts. Why did Mark still have the power to disturb her in this way? Why couldn't he have stayed away and out of her thoughts, when it had taken so much time and painful effort to banish him in the first place? Only Edith could advise her, but Edith was not around to ask. Nor did she see her on Monday morning and, as bad luck would have it, Alice was busy on the Monday lunchtime dropping off leaflets for the new band of Civil Nursing Reserve recruits.

So it was not until she had finished her rounds on Monday afternoon that she had a chance to see what Edith made of this unlooked-for turn of events.

When Alice knocked on her door Edith was taking a surreptitious nap, tired from a hectic day on the district but unwilling to admit it.

'Oh, it's you. Thank goodness for that.' Edith swung her legs off the bed to make room, rubbing the sleep from her eyes.

'Are you all right? Shall I come back later?' Alice felt bad for disturbing her friend, still quietly battling lingering morning sickness but not making a fuss about it. 'I didn't mean to wake you.'

'You didn't. It doesn't matter.' Edith sat upright, wedging a pillow behind her to soothe her aching back. 'What's happened? Don't say it's nothing, I can see by your face that something's up. Tell me all about it.'

Gratefully, Alice poured out the conversation she had had with Lily on Saturday. She strove to get every detail right, not to distort it with all the anxieties that had swirled around her head ever since. 'Am I making a fuss out of nothing?' she demanded.

66

'No. Well, maybe. It's bound to upset you.' Edith rubbed her eyes again. 'Give me a mo, we need to think this through.'

Alice sat back against the wall, with its pale pattern of leaves and birds on the slightly faded wallpaper. She forced herself to breathe deeply and study the edge of the rag rug that lay not quite straight on the floor alongside the bed. 'What do you reckon?' she asked at last.

Edith sighed. 'It's a bit of a shock, isn't it? After all this time.'

Alice stared at the crooked rug. 'It's been years since I've seen him. Not since he went to Spain. That was before I even knew you. I couldn't stay in Liverpool any longer, knowing he might come back, or I could bump into his parents. That's why I ended up doing my district nurse specialist training in Richmond.'

'I know.' Edith's voice was full of sympathy.

'Of course I knew he was back, ever since Dermot got that locum posting here. That was bad enough, but I got used to it. In some ways it was a relief, knowing that he hadn't been killed in Spain, that he was a forces doctor now. Not that it would have been much safer, around the airfields and ports during the Battle of Britain and the bombings on the south coast . . . but we were all in that together, weren't we? We just got on with it. All that time, he was nothing to do with me, and I could concentrate on working here. It was what I wanted.'

Edith glanced sideways. 'Was it, Al?' she asked gently.

Alice nodded without hesitation. 'It was, it really was. I thought I knew what I was doing when I met Mark but it turns out I got it totally wrong. That

67

was a hard thing to admit. I'd fooled myself and got caught up in this dream of us being together for ever. Well, it wasn't to be.' Suddenly the anger she had been suppressing all weekend burst out. 'It doesn't change the fact that he decided to go off to Spain without so much as asking me what I felt about it. He makes all the arrangements and then he tells me as an after-thought. One minute we're talking about where we'll go on honeymoon, the next he's off to fight. Everything that went before counted for nothing.' She gasped, her whole body trembling.

'It's all right, it's all right.' Edith patted her arm, but Alice was not to be calmed.

'I thought I would die, it hurt so much. I couldn't believe he would betray me like that, not after all he'd promised, that what we had could count for so little. Well, I didn't die. I put it behind me and got on with things. I know you all think I'm boring when I don't go out dancing but I don't care. I like staying in. I'd rather read a good book than come anywhere near that sort of pain again.' Exhausted, she flopped back onto the candlewick bedspread.

'Well, if he couldn't see how stupid he was being then he didn't deserve you,' Edith said loyally.

'He didn't. He doesn't,' Alice replied fervently. 'He can wonder and worry all he likes. He had his chance, he blew it. He can't have another go. What, so he can let me down all over again? I don't think so.' Her mouth set in a straight, determined line.

'Of course.' Edith paused. 'Although to be fair, I suppose we don't know that's what he intended. He was just making conversation by the sounds of it.'

Alice exhaled noisily. 'All right, yes. Perhaps he was just being polite, but even so. Claiming he would still like to be in contact — whose fault was it that we lost touch in the first place? Well, see if I care.'

Edith bit her lip, and held back from pointing out the obvious: that if Alice no longer cared, she would not be in such a state.

'He needn't think I'm going to go running after him. Not on your life. He's nothing to me, nothing at all.'

'You're right,' Edith said staunchly. She'd never seen her friend so emotional in all the years she'd known her. Cautiously she pursed her lips. 'I suppose you could always write to Dermot and drop it in casually, to see if he can shed any light . . . you write to each other quite often, don't you?'

Alice shrugged, and her usually neat bun of dark blonde hair fell loose. 'We do. Not sure how I could just drop it in, though. It'd stand out a mile. Besides,' she tucked her heavy hair behind one ear, 'I don't want to drag him into it. He's a good friend to both of us. It was bad enough when it all happened and he tried so hard not to take sides. It's not fair on him. No,' she continued with growing resolution, 'I'm going to forget all about the whole incident. Thank you, Edie, for hearing me out. I'm sorry I woke you up — no, I know I did.'

Edith smiled wryly. 'Well, maybe I was just starting to doze. Anyway, don't be daft — what are friends for? What would I have done without you these last few years?' She turned to look Alice full in the face. 'You can tell me anything, you know that.'

69

8

Lily had tried hard to put the handsome stranger out of her head since the chance encounter outside the shop, but he kept appearing in her mind's eye at the most inopportune moments. She would be taking a patient's temperature and there he would be, smiling in that devil-may-care way and commiserating about the lack of lipstick for sale. Or she would take a patient's hand to check the pulse at the wrist and the most inappropriate thought would pop up: what would it be like to hold his hand?

It wouldn't be wet and clammy like her patient's, she'd put good money on it. He'd have a strong, reassuring grip, not too aggressive but definite and forceful. He would smell very slightly of cigar smoke, or a refined aftershave with a hint of cedar wood. Although his hair had been slicked back, she felt sure he wouldn't reek of oil, as had some of the young men who'd tried to win her favour in Liverpool. They'd piled it on too thick and their heads shone in the lights of the dance halls like so many slippery eels.

No, this man would take a more subtle approach. He'd know just how far to go and then stop.

She checked herself as she came downstairs from her corner bedroom, knowing that she was losing concentration. That wouldn't do. She had to refill her Gladstone bag and any mistakes could cost her dearly.

Mary was rounding the newel post in the main hallway. 'Lily! Just who I wanted to see. Do you think you'd be interested in helping out with those hygiene classes

70

we spoke about? Our teacher friend Janet thinks it's a tremendous idea. I said we'd had some inspiration from our most recent colleague.' She beamed expectantly.

Lily's heart sank. No way did she want to be stuck in a freezing classroom full of noisy brats, all coughing and sniffing. What had she got herself into? 'Ah, I'm not sure . . . ' she began, not wanting to commit herself to anything so unpleasant but not wanting to lose face in front of Mary either. She had not failed to notice that Mary was the nurse with the nicest clothes, the poshest voice and, if what she'd heard was true, the highest-ranking boyfriend. Just the sort of sophisticated friend she would like to have.

She was let off the hook by Belinda swooping by with a bundle of post. 'Letter for you, Lily! Who's the secret admirer?' Her dark eyes flashed with humour but she didn't stay around for a reply, linking her arm through Mary's and pulling her down the corridor.

Just as well, for Lily didn't recognise the handwriting on the envelope, but she would have sworn it was masculine. There was something about the assertive slope of the letters. She ran her finger over the address, noticing how the paper was of good quality and the pen nib had made decisive indentations. Not the mark of anyone she'd known in Liverpool.

Checking that there was nobody else around, she stepped into the district room and put down her bag on the floor. Restocking it could wait. Intrigued and excited, she gently teased open the envelope and took out the single sheet of paper — again a good-quality vellum in an elegant off-white. The ink was a deep blue, almost purple. Lily approved.

Avidly she scanned the message and as she read it

a slow smile crept onto her face. Well, she'd certainly made an impression that Saturday morning. It was, as she had hoped, from the mysterious man outside the shop, and he offered to make good on his promise.

If she'd care to meet him, he would be pleased to put right the disappointment of her shopping trip. He had managed to obtain some lipstick — and his sister had already tried it and reckoned it was of good quality. If Lily was still keen, would she like to see him to receive her gift? Only after her work had finished, of course — he respected her profession as a nurse. He suggested a café not far from Victoria Park. If that suited her, would she please confirm which day would be best?

Lily hugged the sheet of paper to her, feeling a delicious thrill. She didn't know the café but recognised that it was fairly near to the nurses' home, without it being so close by that she would run the risk of bumping into someone she knew. While there was nothing underhand about the fact she was meeting this man, she definitely didn't want to share him with any of the other nurses. She checked his signature: Donald. Donald Parker. That had a nice ring to it — respectable, but not too stuffy.

She glanced at the return address. It was an office, in Bethnal Green. She wasn't sure where that was, but she knew it was in East London. Didn't the bus to Liverpool Street go past Bethnal Green Road? It couldn't be that far away. Good.

Footsteps coming down the corridor made her hastily tuck the letter into her pocket, and not a moment too soon. It was Mary again, with a small box in her hands. 'Just putting away these spares of calamine lotion,' she said cheerfully. 'Have you thought any

72

further about those lessons, Lily? It would be a great help to have you on board, you know. We're thinking of Thursday for the first one.'

Lily's mind raced. Donald hadn't suggested a particular day, leaving it up to her, but what if Thursday was best for him? She didn't want to miss this chance.

'I'm so sorry,' she said, making sure her tone was as genuine as she could get it. 'I've got a previous engagement. Otherwise I would have loved to.'

Mary took it well. 'Never mind. Perhaps another day. I'll let you know how it goes, of course.'

Lily smiled, more warmly this time. Mary sounded as if she cared for her opinion. 'Yes please,' she said, but already she was thinking ahead, to what she might wear for the rendezvous at the café. Donald wanted to meet her, and suddenly the future looked very bright indeed.

★ ★ ★

Days off were meant to make you feel better, not worse, Ruby thought glumly. She'd been given a free afternoon because one of her cases earlier in the week had overrun well into the evening, as she'd had to wait with a patient until an ambulance arrived. As often happened, the ambulance had been diverted, as a water main had burst — not because of any new bombing, for which they were all thankful, but most likely from damage sustained earlier in the war.

That had counted for nothing with the patient's indignant family, who had protested that they were being treated badly because they weren't able to pay the insurance. Ruby had done her best to persuade them that it wasn't the case and it was nobody's fault, but it had been a tough few hours. Even when the ambulance finally arrived, she had stayed on to soothe the frayed tempers. For a while she had feared the husband might turn nasty. When she finally got back to Victory Walk, she was at her wits' end.

To her surprise, the usually stern assistant superintendent had come to her rescue. Gwen had spotted the signs of an inexperienced nurse feeling overwhelmed and had taken her to one side. They had sat together in a corner of the common room, which by then was emptying out as most of the nurses were retiring to their individual rooms. Gwen had made sure the exhausted young woman had something hot to eat and then she herself made a pot of tea for two.

'These things happen,' she reassured her. 'It sounds as if it was a very difficult situation. It's one of the things they don't tell you much about when you're working in a hospital.'

Ruby had almost cried at the unexpected sympathy. 'No, they tell you what illnesses you are likely to come across and how to treat the sick person, but not that you could get threatened by their family.'

Gwen had nodded seriously. 'They didn't try to hurt you, did they?'

'Not really.' Ruby wiped her hand across her face. 'I thought the husband might though. He was older than her, and even though he had a limp he never sat down, he just couldn't keep still. He was between me and the front door. I kept thinking, if I've got to run for help I don't know how I'll get out.'

'That must have been very frightening,' Gwen replied, her brow creasing. 'A limp, you say? I expect he's one of those men who wanted to go and fight but got turned down. That can make them frustrated and

74

so they get particularly angry. You just happened to be there. It wasn't your fault. You were doing your job.'

Ruby sniffed and fought back the tears that she had driven away during the crisis but which threatened to erupt now. 'I tried, I really did. And it was such a dark little road, all the houses close together. Moses Street.'

Gwen sighed. 'I know the one. Yes, we get called there fairly often and some of the families can be tricky. Let me just check one thing. You said it was for an especially bad case of flu?'

Ruby nodded. 'That's what the doctor said, although I'm not sure when he saw her. I think it was right — her temperature was all over the place.'

Gwen tapped her forefinger against the table top. 'This might sound like a daft question, but did you ask the patient when she had last been to the toilet? Was she drinking normally, maybe cool water to help with the fever?'

'I'm not sure . . . ' Ruby was puzzled. 'I gave her a cup of water more than once, but I didn't ask — and she was too weak to move anyway, while I was there.'

Gwen hesitated, as if wondering whether she should say anything more. 'Don't take this the wrong way, Ruby, but I'm going to give you some advice for the future — just an extra thing to bear in mind, and not all hospitals cover it.' She drew herself up a little more on her wooden chair. 'It's not your place to make diagnoses like this, it's for the doctor, but sometimes there isn't one around. I'm only saying this because I know what has happened in that street before.'

Ruby wondered what was coming, and felt a sense of dread.

'It's easy to mistake some symptoms of flu for something else. Particularly now, when there have been so many cases. One of the conditions that often gets missed is blood poisoning. Septicaemia.'

Ruby felt on safer territory. 'I've heard of that.'

'Of course you have.' Gwen took a sip of her tea and decided to continue. 'I'm talking about one distinct cause of it, among women of child-bearing age. Do you know what I'm referring to?'

Ruby shook her head. 'I don't think so.'

Gwen set her cup down again. 'Well, it's not an easy thing to discuss but, as nurses, we must acknowledge that it happens. You'll know as well as I do that some pregnant women do not wish to have their baby. That can be for many reasons — overcrowding and poverty among them. Two reasons that go hand in hand and which are prevalent in Moses Street, wouldn't you say?'

Ruby blinked, still not completely sure what Gwen meant.

'What happens is, they try to get rid of the baby. If they're poor they won't have access to any means of doing so safely, and so they try to bring it about by themselves. There are lots of ways and none of them are pleasant. Many are downright dangerous — and one of the consequences can be septicaemia.' Ruby's hand went to her throat. 'I . . . I didn't think . . .'

'No, no.' Gwen tutted. 'As I said, it's not your job to diagnose. I'm simply saying, it is something you may well come across. What made me extra suspicious was the husband's reaction. He will know that such a procedure is illegal. He'll be defensive and therefore angry. Some men try to hide what's happened, others go on the offensive. Of course now we are at war often there isn't a man around at all — another reason why women resort to such measures.'

76

'So was that what was wrong with the woman? Not flu?' Gwen shrugged. 'I can't say. Even if I'd seen her, I might not have been able to tell. Plenty of women wouldn't admit it, even more so to anyone in a position of authority. They're caught between the devil and the deep blue sea. I'm telling you this so that you bear it in mind in future. You don't go wading in reading them the riot act; you act as fast as you safely can because, as you know, if left untreated then septicaemia can prove fatal.'

Ruby gasped.

'And it sounds as if that's what you did, no matter what underlying reason lay behind her symptoms,' Gwen assured her. 'Even if you'd known for sure that the poor woman had tried to give herself an abortion, you wouldn't have acted any differently. You've given her the best possible chance of recovery. Just keep this in mind — not urinating for a long time, maybe a day in the case of an adult, can be a sign of blood poisoning. So it doesn't hurt to ask that question.'

'I shan't forget,' Ruby said.

'No, I dare say you won't,' Gwen replied wryly. 'Tell you what. You have acted above and beyond tonight, and that family has every reason to feel grateful. Why don't you have a half-day off in recompense? Perhaps you'd like to see your own family? This won't happen every time, I am compelled to warn you.'

Ruby's eyes widened. 'Really? That's kind of you!'

Gwen made as if to rise. 'Really. Make the most of it — when we are busier you won't have the chance. What do you say?'

Ruby smiled, for the first time since she had knocked on the grim front door in Moses Street. 'Yes. Oh, yes please.'

77

When Ruby approached the Lyons' Corner House on the Strand she was buoyant, hopeful that this meeting would mark a change. Even though she had been so afraid at the incident in Moses Street, the conversation with Gwen had done her a world of good. Despite not knowing the full story of the poor family, she had done the right thing. Whatever had led to the woman's symptoms, she had ensured she was safely taken to hospital, which would be the best place for her.

Surely her mother and sister would notice the difference in her. She consciously put her shoulders back and drew herself up to her full five feet four. Her hair was neatly pulled away from her face in a band and she wore her one good winter jacket, as a change from her nurse's cloak. Edith had noticed her on the way out from the home on Victory Walk, and had stopped to lend her a scarf. 'This colour suits you and goes with the jacket,' she'd observed, tucking the pale blue length of wool around the other nurse's neck. 'We don't want you to get cold up there in the West End.'

So Ruby had another reason to feel proud: not only did her deputy supervisor trust her enough to share the warning about botched abortions, but one of the most experienced nurses had shown her friendship. This move to Hackney was the best thing she'd ever done.

The good mood lasted about two minutes. That was how long it took Beryl to get into full flow, casting aspersions left and right, while their mother sat and nodded. Ruby took the lead, boldly ordering teacakes for all of them from the smartly uniformed waitress, and that set Beryl off. Had she forgotten how tasty their mother's cakes were, and did she think they had money to waste eating out?

'I thought that's why we came here,' Ruby objected.

'We could have just had a cuppa and saved our pennies. You know Ma doesn't like the West End at the best of times,' Beryl snapped. 'I won't make a show of myself changing our order but, honestly, you should have asked first, Ruby. Looks as if you're getting above yourself already.'

Ruby had had to grip hard on her teaspoon to stop herself from screaming.

'We've managed all right without you since you left, thank you for asking,' her sister rattled on relentlessly. 'Never mind that Ma's sciatica has been playing up, isn't that right, Ma? And we couldn't get hold of no wintergreen. Of course we used to rely on you for that, Ruby, but you never thought of us when you made your decision to go, did you?'

The unfairness of that took Ruby's breath away.

'Sorry to hear that,' she managed to mutter. She didn't wish her mother any pain, of course she didn't, but to blame her for it was a step too far.

Her mother nodded tremulously. 'I'm all right really, dear. Don't you worry about me.' She gave a small sniff. 'Don't make the girl feel bad, Beryl.'

Beryl huffed. 'I'm just letting her know the state of affairs. Don't imagine you can swan off across town and forget all about us, Ruby.'

'I wouldn't do that,' Ruby protested, thinking that chance would be a fine thing. The next time she got a day off she would take herself to the cinema and not waste it being told off for something she could not control.

'Your trouble is, you don't know what's what.' Beryl

79

was well under way now on her favourite complaint.

Ruby sat back as the teacakes arrived and let her get on with it. There was no point in trying to stop her. Finally she would come to a halt, if only so she could eat her teacake. Beryl might protest that they were an extravagance, but she would soon demolish hers with great speed. Sure enough, having complained for five solid minutes, she set to swallowing her cake in record time. Their mother was still finishing her final crumbs.

'I'll pay, it's my treat,' Ruby said into the brief gap of silence.

'Oh, thank you, dear,' said her mother, surprised and pleased.

Beryl scowled. 'I'm amazed they're paying you enough. Don't go thinking we'll be so grateful that you can ask for favours in future.'

'That isn't why I offered,' Ruby retorted, stung. 'I thought you might like it, that's all.' The final crumbs of her cake tasted like dust in her mouth. Her little treat had been spoiled. What had she expected, really? In all honesty, she should have known better.

'Well, we'd best be getting back,' Beryl asserted.

'Get you back to where you belong, eh, Ma? Away from all this noise and kerfuffle.' She glared at Ruby. 'Next time, see if you can't get yourself over to Hammersmith.'

Ruby nodded dumbly. She certainly wouldn't be inviting them to Dalston. She wanted to keep that all to herself — somewhere that people valued her and didn't think she was a waste of space.

As she sat on the bus, slowly making its way back to the east of the city and trying to avoid the potholes, she felt that her wonderful sensation of happy confidence had vanished, gone up in smoke like the toasted edges of the teacake. Was it true that she didn't know what was what? How could Beryl blame her for her lack of worldly experience, when she and their mother had gone to great lengths to prevent her getting any?

Recognising the big crossroads, she stood up and prepared to get off, edging down the aisle of the bus between boxes and shopping bags. She gritted her teeth. She couldn't pretend to be worldly wise, but at least she was now mixing with people who were, and who might teach her how to get on in life. She fingered the warm scarf. At least some of her new colleagues believed in her. That was a start.

9

It had taken Lily ages to decide what to wear, and now she feared she was late. She didn't want to appear red in the face or untidy and so she couldn't actually run. So she walked as fast as she feasibly could, balancing expertly on her court shoes, not so high as to seem showy but definitely enough to enhance the elegant shape of her calves. She'd once again picked out her rust-coloured skirt; she didn't want to give the impression of having an enormous wardrobe, as that might make her seem frivolous. She was aiming for sophisticated and professional.

There was little option but to wear the maroon coat again, this time with its belt even more tightly cinched. The choice of blouse had been the hardest. Lily had no way of knowing what sort of colour the lipstick might be and hadn't wanted to risk a shade that might clash. She'd worn cream last time. Her navy blouse, which was deliciously silky, didn't go with the skirt. At last she had decided upon a neat knitted sweater with a round neck, edged with a ribbon of jade green against the more muted green of the main garment. That should cover all eventualities.

Where was that café? Lily hesitated on the unfamiliar street; it was even more confusing because it was almost dark. She had her shaded torch to hand, but knew it would make her stand out as a stranger so early in the dusk, and she didn't want to come across as being cautious or anxious. That would contradict all her plans.

That must be it, on the corner of the next road. Its window was warm and inviting under its awning, the glass steamed from condensation. As she drew closer, an indistinct figure reached up and drew the blackout blinds, and so by the time she was near enough to see inside, the view was blocked.

She had wanted to arrive after Donald, but now she would just have to chance it that he'd got there before her. Given how close to being late she was, it was a fair bet he would have. There was nothing for it but to push open the door.

She tried not to gasp as the warm air hit her as soon as she went in — there was a fire blazing merrily in the grate opposite. It would make her face flush but that was quite attractive as long as she didn't have to sit right next to the flames. Glancing around swiftly, she saw him, just at the moment he saw her.

Donald got to his feet, folding away the newspaper he'd clearly been reading as he did so. His face broke into a wide smile. 'Hello,' he said as she came towards him, and his voice was even deeper than she remembered. Sure enough, when she reached the table with its cheerful chequered cloth, she could detect the faint aroma of cedar wood.

He came around the table and pulled out a chair for her. 'It's good to see you,' he said, and sounded as if he really meant it. 'I wasn't sure when I wrote to you if you would come or not.'

Lily laughed lightly. 'Well, as you can see, I did.'

Donald sat back down. 'I wondered if you would think it very forward.'

Lily pressed her hand to her collar. 'Oh no, not at all.' She carefully unbelted and unbuttoned her coat and wriggled out of it.

83

'Here, let me.' He reached for it and took it to the row of hooks mounted on the wall nearby. 'If I may say so, that colour suits you beautifully.' His eyes lingered on her green top.

Lily glowed with pleasure that her deliberations had had the desired effect. 'Why, thank you. It's just something I picked up in the sales.' After hours of hunting, she neglected to add.

'You obviously have a good eye,' he said with a smile.

Lily could recognise flattery when she heard it but still wasn't immune from its charms. 'I do my best,' she said modestly, lowering her gaze a little. His hands rested on the tablecloth. They were still a little brown from the summer sun, and his nails were neatly trimmed and clean. She liked that — it showed he cared about the details. Such things were important.

A waitress came over, in a serviceable but well-washed cotton apron. Lily could tell the middle-aged woman was tired but she covered it with a welcoming smile. 'What would you like?' she asked. 'I must warn you we've run out of eggs. They've been even harder than usual to get hold of this week.'

Lily shook her head, knowing she would have her evening meal provided back at the nurses' home. 'Oh, don't worry, I'll just have a hot drink. But you go ahead,' she added, not sure what Donald's domestic circumstances might be.

He shook his head. 'A hot drink is just what I need as well. May I interest you in a cup of coffee, Miss Chandler?' He turned to the waitress. 'Do you have coffee, please?'

The harassed waitress frowned. 'We've got Camp

coffee. Most folk just want tea.' She looked dubious.

'Oh, Camp coffee will be perfect!' Lily assured her. She was glad they weren't simply having tea. She could get that at any time. It was harder to track down supplies of Camp and none of the nurses seemed to have it; if they wanted a change from tea they would have hot chocolate, which did not strike her as the right sort of drink to have at a meeting like this. Or some of them liked Ovaltine, which would be even worse. It brought to mind listening to the wireless with her parents when she was younger, humming along to the Ovaltineys' jingle.

'Then we'll have two Camp coffees,' Donald said firmly, and the waitress put away her notepad and went back through a beaded curtain, making it rattle.

'I like a woman who doesn't always choose tea,' he said confidingly.

Lily gave a little chuckle. 'I'm offered tea at nearly every home I visit, and it's often hard to say no. There are days when I think I can't bear to see another cup. Not that I'm ungrateful,' she added hurriedly. 'It's just there's only so much of it you can drink.'

'I totally agree,' he said solemnly. 'A place for everything, isn't that right?'

He really was quite handsome, she thought as they waited for the coffee. He was telling her about how he came to know this café, it being somewhere his sister would go with her friends, and she nodded in all the right places, but really she was watching how he moved his hands and how his lively expressions changed, along with the timbre of his voice. It was one she could listen to for a long time without becoming bored, she decided.

The waitress reappeared with a tray and set down

85

two cups of coffee, a small amount of milk in a glass jug and an even smaller amount of sugar, before retreating once more behind the curtain. Other customers' conversation provided a background hum. Donald pushed the sugar towards Lily.

'I'll just have a little,' she said, anxious not to take it all and appear greedy.

'Finish it off,' he suggested. 'I don't take it, myself. Sweet enough already.' He flashed her a dazzling smile, as if he knew how silly that sounded.

'Well, maybe just this once.' Lily added some more to her cup, relishing the prospect of a properly sweet drink for once. Ever since sugar had been rationed it had been hard to come by, and she loved the taste of it. She had hoped it might be more widely available in London than it had been back home, but if anything it was worse.

'Heavenly,' she pronounced, setting down the cup on its pale yellow saucer.

He smiled again, more gently this time, and she could feel his gaze was on her lips. She resisted the urge to lick them.

'Let me show you what I found the other day.' Donald reached into his pocket. She observed that it was a very well-cut jacket, its tailoring sharp and no trace of fraying anywhere about the cuffs or collar. Definitely classy.

He set down a paper bag and pushed it across the table to her. 'Sorry about the wrapping.'

Lily was far more interested in the contents than the wrapping, and for two pins would have thrown the bag to the floor in her eagerness to see what was inside. She made herself be patient, to assure him that it didn't matter, before drawing out two narrow

86

cardboard tubes. 'Oh!' she couldn't help but exclaim. 'They're by Tangee. My favourite.'

'Don't you want to see the colours?' he teased.

'Shall I?' She knew she was flirting now but he seemed such good fun.

'Of course. I want to know if I've made the right choice,' he said solemnly.

'Oh, well. In that case.' Carefully she drew out the first lipstick and unscrewed its cover. 'It's a real, proper lipstick. Not even a refill. How ever did you manage to come by this?'

'Through a business contact,' he said breezily. 'Think nothing of it. He owed me a favour. I've mentioned now and again that my sister was running out of cosmetics and how downhearted that made her, and so he's come good.' He raised an eyebrow. 'So, do you approve?'

'I most certainly do.' Lily turned the lipstick around, noting its dark red colour. 'This one will go exactly with my coat. It's absolutely perfect.'

Donald sat back in his chair, nodding judiciously. 'That's precisely what I thought. I remembered what you were wearing and reckoned this was the closest match.'

Lily was extremely impressed but worked hard not to show it. 'Did you, now?' She raised an eyebrow at him and gave a small smile.

'I most certainly did. Try the other one.' He was watching her intently, as if sharing her delight.

Breathing deliberately steadily so that her hands didn't shake and give away her excitement, she gently drew out the second lipstick. A more subtle shade but rich all the same; it would complement the green of her top, or the navy blouse she had had to leave in the wardrobe. 'This is beautiful,' she said honestly. 'It's exactly what I would have picked for myself.'

'I'd hoped that would be the case,' he said, his voice warm. 'I don't suppose you can wear it when you're working . . .'

'Good heavens, no.' Lily's face took on an expression of mock horror. 'We can't do that. The rules are very strict, you see.'

He beamed back at her. 'But when you're not at work, well, it's almost a public service, isn't it? All beautiful women are obliged to keep up morale. I've seen the posters. It's almost like an order, in fact.'

Lily nodded, again registering the outrageous flattery but overlooking it as she was enjoying herself so much. 'That's true. It's our duty to keep everyone's spirits up.' She reached for her handbag. 'How much do I owe you?'

Instantly he shook his head. 'Put that away. It's a gift, like I said. It's payment enough to see that it's made you happy.'

Lily demurred. 'I hardly know you. I can't let you do that.'

'I insist.' He gave a slow smile. 'However, if you're worried that you don't know me, I might have the answer to that.'

'Really?' She kept her voice light but her heart was hammering fast.

'Oh yes. It's the obvious solution.' He paused and his eyes were bright. 'We simply get to know one another better. Wouldn't that make sense? Then you wouldn't have to worry about accepting presents from a stranger.'

Lily made a show of protesting, but knew if she was honest with herself, this was exactly the outcome she had hoped for as soon as she'd opened the letter. This was not a one-off encounter; it was the start of something else entirely.

'Besides,' he pressed, 'that would give me the chance to see you wearing these.' He reached forward and tapped a forefinger against the little tubes, almost but not quite brushing her hand as he did so. 'Wouldn't that work out well for both of us?'

Lily inclined her head. 'I'd be raising morale, you mean?'

His eyes crinkled in appreciation. 'You most certainly would, Miss Chandler.'

Lily levelly met his gaze. 'Call me Lily,' she said.

10

'It's ever so busy.' Ruby hesitated at the corner of the main road. 'Is it always like this?'

Edith nodded. 'On a Saturday it usually is. Everyone's got the same idea — go down the market and see if there's a bargain to be had.' She grinned up at her new colleague. 'You had markets over in Hammersmith, didn't you? You must have gone to some before.'

Ruby rubbed her gloved hands together for warmth. 'There's a big one up Shepherd's Bush way. Sometimes I'd walk there with my sister.' She gave a slight shudder. Beryl would instruct her to stay close, not to get lost, to keep right behind her and on no account dawdle and get caught daydreaming in front of the stalls. The whole expedition would have to be run with military precision: decide what was needed, get in and get out in as short a time as possible. They had never been relaxing days out.

'Well, then.' Edith linked her arm through Ruby's and encouraged her to join the fray. Ridley Road on a Saturday morning was as good an entertainment as you could hope for, in her opinion. 'Let's see what we can find. Alice asked me to keep an eye out for some wool, though I told her she'd be lucky. Are you after anything in particular?'

'Not really.' Ruby was trying hard not to be overwhelmed by the press of people, all jostling to get to the stalls, the noise of the stallholders shouting about their wares, the buzz of conversations and the mixture

90

of different food smells that wafted through the air. She stepped back hurriedly as a large woman pushed past, her wicker shopping bag jabbing her in the rib-cage. 'I thought I'd look around a bit, to get the hang of the place.'

'Good idea.' Edith pulled her over to the central aisle and along to a stall heaped with scraps of mate-rial. 'This used to sell lots of clothes but of course there aren't many to be had now. Still, if I found something in wool then we could unravel it and Alice could use that. She's going to knit a scarf if she can.'

Ruby looked dubiously at the pile. 'I can't see any-thing. And I thought she had a scarf? Several, in fact.' She had been quietly admiring Alice's way of dress-ing, which was far less showy than the likes of Lily, but subtly elegant all the same.

'Oh, it's not for her. It's for one of the school kids she knows. The family never have two pennies to rub together and the granny wouldn't bother checking if the kids had warm things for winter. In fact, I remem-ber now the idea is to teach the oldest child to knit so she won't have to rely on her gran, who's more likely to be off down the pub.' Edith shrugged, and rummaged through the heap. 'Any old jumpers in here?' she asked hopefully as the stallholder turned from serving a customer.

The man frowned. 'There might be, right under-neath that lot. It's mostly lighter stuff — you could make yourself a decent blouse from this,' he sug-gested, holding up a piece of cotton in cheerful yellow and white stripes.

Edith's expression was doubtful. 'I'm not sure it would be large enough, even for me.'

Ruby agreed. 'Maybe for a child,' she said. 'I don't

91

think you would fit in it, Edith, even if it was sleeve-less.'

'Anyway, I'll be too big for that soon,' Edith reminded her. 'By the time the weather's warm enough for sleeveless cotton tops, I'll be out here.' She held her hands out in front of her.

The stallholder broke into a smile. 'Ah, it's like that, is it?' He was maybe in his fifties, his face lined from a lifetime of worry, but it transformed into friendliness when he smiled. 'Here, you're Stan Banham's daugh-ter-in-law, aren't you?'

'That's right.'

'Well, in that case — hang on a mo, I just thought of something.' He bent down and undid the string on a cardboard box next to where he was standing. 'We got some stuff delivered last night, I ain't had time to go through it yet. Let me see, now.' He crouched down, huffing as he did so, and disappeared from view.

'Does everyone know each other here?' Ruby asked, bemused. She stamped her feet in her sturdy black shoes to keep them from growing numb with cold.

'Just about everyone knows the Banhams,' Edith told her. 'What with Stan being in the ARP, and Flo in the WVS, and then Harry was pretty famous locally for his boxing — you can't get away with any-thing once you're one of the Banham family. Not that I would want to get away with anything,' she added hurriedly.

Ruby relaxed and laughed. 'I didn't think you would. No, it's just not like where I'm from.' Or, more likely, not like how it is in my family, she thought honestly. There were probably plenty of people who were sim-ilar to the Banhams in west London — well known, well liked. Just not her family.

The stallholder reappeared, holding up a bright red jumper. 'What about this? I got to be frank, it's seen better days, what with these holes at the elbow and all that. Still, you could darn it. I dare say you two young ladies are dab hands at darning.'

'We are.' Edith's eyes sparkled. 'We have to be these days. It won't matter about the holes, though. I need the wool for my friend. She's going to teach a little girl how to knit and that looks just right. She'll love that colour, I just know it.'

'Yes, it's gorgeous. Lovely and bright,' Ruby agreed.

'Lifts the spirits, don't it?' the stallholder said, comfortable now it looked as if he had a sale on his hands and that he could do a good turn for one of the Banhams.

Ruby watched in amusement as Edith haggled for the best price, clearly an old hand at this game. She herself never had the nerve to bargain, always afraid that she would be taken advantage of, but Edith came away with both the jumper and a big grin on her face, while the stallholder didn't seem unhappy either.

They wandered down the main aisle, pausing now and again to admire a stall or to listen in to a particularly promising conversation. Towards the far end, Edith waved at another man in late middle age who was selling shoes. 'That's where I got my little blue pumps that I wore for my wedding,' she said. 'You've seen them, haven't you? I had them on last weekend when I went out to meet Mattie and Kath. They're a bit cold for this weather though.'

'Oh, yes. I remember them all right.' Ruby had been very taken with her friend's smart shoes, which were clearly kept for best. The man was waving back and she could see he was missing some teeth from

93

one side of his mouth. 'Do you want to go over and say hello?'

Edith paused. 'Probably not. See, he's busy, and neither of us will be buying anything from him today. Let's go and find Brendan.' She wheeled Ruby around and headed down a side aisle, back towards the main road.

'Who's Brendan again?' Ruby couldn't remember if she was meant to know. She had met and heard of so many new people in the past month that she was finding it hard to keep up.

'There he is! The man in the brown overall, putting carrots in that woman's bag.' Edith pointed. 'He's had a stall here for as long as I've been in Dalston, and for years before that. He's the kindest stallholder here. He always gave Kath a bit extra when she didn't have much money, and all the kids love him. Oh, and he's in the ARP with Harry's dad and Kath's husband, Billy. I don't know how he does it, patrolling all night and then working here in the daytime. He's one of those people who never seem to get tired.'

All the same, Ruby thought as they drew closer, the fellow had bags under his eyes and, if she'd been asked to assess him from a professional point of view, she would have said his skin was too pale. She suspected he was simply exhausted.

You wouldn't have known it from his demeanour though. 'Now you put that in a nice carrot cake, that'll put a smile on yer old man's face,' he was saying cheerfully to his customer, who laughed like a woman half her age at the good-humoured exchange. Then his face lit up as he caught sight of Edith. 'Edie! Edie Banham, as I live and breathe. How are you? Mattie said you'd been a bit under the weather — all cleared up now, I hope?'

94

Edith nodded. 'Much better now, thanks. Mattie's been a great help. Well, she's been through it twice, she knows what it's like.' She turned. 'This is our friend Ruby, who's come to work with us at Victory Walk.'

'Pleased to meet you,' Brendan said at once, holding out his broad hand to shake. 'If you ever need anything, Ruby, you just come to me and I'll see if I can get it for you. At least in the way of fruit and veg. Within the current restrictions of course.' He pulled a face.

'Of course.' Ruby let her hand drop again and smiled at the kind offer.

'How's it going, Brendan?' Edith asked. 'I heard you had a spot of bother last weekend.'

The man sighed at the memory. 'Yes, Green Lanes took a bit of a pasting. Incendiary bombs, we think they was. Kept me busy and no mistake. Billy as well. I know it isn't exactly our patch but they was a few wardens short so we all had to muck in.'

'Just when we thought all that was over with,' Edith said sadly.

'Let's not count our chickens,' Brendan warned. 'Didn't you hear there was more trouble up Clapton last night? Another incendiary, off the Lea Bridge Road. That's why I'm not quite my lively self this morning. I didn't get much kip, if I'm honest. And there was some anti-aircraft shell nearer you nurses, on Dalston Lane, not far from here. We was all working flat out.'

'Ah, I wondered about that.' Edith shook her head. 'You wouldn't have seen it from the ground floor, Ruby, but I knew something had happened last night. I thought we might all have to turf out of our beds and go to the refuge room, but we got away with it.

95

Sorry you got caught up in it all, Brendan.'

The man shrugged. 'It's me job, isn't it. I knew what it would be like when Billy recruited me. I got to do something. I'm not eligible for the services on account of having TB when I was a nipper, so this is my way of doing my bit.'

Edith's eyebrows rose. 'I never knew you had that, Brendan. You make sure you take care of yourself. It can leave you more susceptible to things that other people can just shake off, you know.'

Brendan wiped his hands on his overall. 'Yes, I know, that's what the doctors told me at the time. Still, can't ask the Jerries to leave off their fighting cos I got a bit of leftover lung trouble, now can I? I don't see them backing off on account of that.'

'Probably not.' Edith cast her eyes over the available goods on the stall. 'Even so, Brendan, you make sure you watch out.'

'Don't go saying nothing to Stan or Billy now, will you? I mean, they knew about it when I joined the ARP, I had to tell them, but they'll have forgotten all about it by now. I don't want them going all soft on me. Anyway,' he changed his tone before Edith could remonstrate further, 'I expect you two would like a little something special to keep in your service room for a nice snack, wouldn't you?'

Ruby nodded, but wondered what that could possibly be, since his stock seemed mostly to consist of dried goods or root vegetables. She didn't much fancy munching on a parsnip when hunger pangs struck in the evening.

'Seeing as it's you, Edie, I have the very thing. It's not strictly rationed as it's from me auntie down in Wiltshire. She's got a lovely garden with apple trees, and she dries the fruit when it all ripens at once, like yer apples tend to do.'

He expertly folded a sheet of newspaper to make a packet, and scooped in slices of dried fruit. 'There you are. They'll be lovely and sweet. Or you could plump them up in a bit of water or something stronger if you take my meaning, give you a lovely dessert, that will.'

Ruby stared in delight. 'That sounds delicious!' she said. 'You're very kind, Mr . . . '

'Brendan. Don't even think about the Mr bit,' he said happily. 'You put that in your basket now, Edie. No,' he objected as Edith reached for her purse, 'put that away. This is a little welcoming gift for your new colleague. I won't take payment. Auntie sends me this for next to nothing, so I'm quite at liberty to give it to whoever I please.'

'Well, I'll make sure I share it with the rest of them and they all know who it's come from,' Edith declared, putting the precious packet safely in her basket with the red jumper. 'You're one in a million, Brendan.'

Brendan beamed at them and then was forced to turn his attention to a new customer, as the two nurses made their way back to the main road and out of the bustling market.

Blimey, thought Ruby on the way home to Victory Walk. It certainly paid to go shopping with Edith. Knowing one of the Banhams opened all the doors.

★ ★ ★

Lily had been surprised when there was no immediate note from Donald to suggest another meeting. She was confident that she'd made the right impression and that he'd soon want to see her again, after their successful rendezvous in the café. Yet the days went by and there was nothing.

She didn't want to appear too keen and send a note herself, even though she had kept his address. Or at least the address of his office. Men didn't like women to be too pushy. She would have to be more subtle, but she couldn't start that part of her campaign until he asked her out again.

Sometimes she couldn't resist breaking the rules and taking a tiny smear of lipstick to spread across her mouth. Nothing obvious, just enough for a faint tint and to remind herself of his kindness. It gave her a little lift before the start of her rounds, an illicit thrill, even though it was harmless. It was a way of taking a little bit of him with her as she set off to see her patients.

With no pressing engagements, she'd run out of excuses to avoid the dreaded hygiene lessons, and Mary had dragooned her into taking part. At least she hadn't had to miss an evening; Mary had arranged a lunchtime class at a school in Clapton, a short bike ride away. Lily's heart had sunk, as she knew it would involve missing the hot lunchtime meal at Victory Walk, but Mary was adamant. 'We'll have Spam sandwiches afterwards,' she promised.

Lily found it hard to regard that as a treat as they were bound to be made with the disgusting National loaf, and therefore the equivalent of swallowing a brick, but she'd had no real option.

So she had gone along, telling herself to look willing, as she was desperate to impress Mary. Smiling for all she was worth, she had faced a class of small children, not all of whom seemed to know what they were doing there. She had pressed home the need to wash their hands at every opportunity, preferably with hot water and soap. From the looks of them, not all were well acquainted with the idea of soap, but she'd carried on anyway.

Mary had come prepared. She'd remembered Alice's experiences of years ago, trying to teach children to clean their teeth when they had no toothbrushes or toothpaste. Even though soap was rationed, she had got hold of a big bar of carbolic and cut it into individual pieces, so that each child could take one home. 'That's to get you into the habit,' she'd said, solemnly handing them out. 'Coughs and sneezes spread diseases, remember that. Try to sneeze and cough into your hankies and then wash your hands.'

Lily had nodded encouragingly, and repeated the message as she'd helped hand out soap, but really she couldn't get out of there soon enough. It was surely a haven for germs, and some children hadn't learnt to wipe their noses, let alone wash afterwards. She could sense a fit of sneezing coming on at the very idea. She felt out of place, uneasy with the sea of young faces.

Mary talked to them easily — it seemed to come naturally. Perhaps she was one of those women who simply liked children. Lily was not. Of course she'd been around young children, as there had been plenty on her street back home in Liverpool, but she had no younger siblings and harboured no great urge to have any babies of her own. No, the sooner she got out of there the better. Mary had said nothing in front of the children but had been a little brusque afterwards, hinting that Lily might try to be more understanding, and take the time to get to know some of the little ones. Lily had nodded but had no intention of going that far.

99

It had been a relief to get back on her rounds where, even though she was visiting obviously sick people, it somehow wasn't so bad. She knew this was illogical but there it was. She'd rather treat an ill adult rather than be cloistered with a roomful of apparently healthy children.

Lily got her just reward when she arrived back at Victory Walk that evening. At last — another envelope, with that dramatic handwriting, in the pile of post. She grabbed it eagerly and hid it in her pocket before anyone could see it and tease her again. She felt very protective of this burgeoning friendship and certainly didn't want the other nurses to know about it.

It wasn't exactly that she feared rivalry; she knew she stood out thanks to her looks, particularly her hair and creamy complexion. Not all of the others would be interested anyway. Yet some were pretty enough, she supposed, and could perhaps run her a close second on a good day. Where she really lacked experience was in her knowledge of how to carry herself in new situations, now she was in London. In short, she didn't feel sophisticated enough.

In her cosy bedroom, with its corner views, she raced to open the letter. Another invitation — but this time to dinner. Not to a pleasant little café, in what some would call an out-of-the-way corner of the capital, but to a proper restaurant in the centre of town. Somewhere where her new glamorous lipstick would be appreciated, he wrote, and she could picture his smile as he put pen to paper.

That would certainly call for sophistication. Lily gave a small smile of her own. What a good job she'd helped Mary out after all. She would use that to grow their friendship. Maybe sophistication could be learnt.

* * *

'How did it go?' Edith demanded as Alice plonked herself down on one of the comfy chairs in the common room. 'Was the gran there?'

Alice pulled a face. 'Give me a moment to take the weight off my feet and then I'll fetch us both a cup of tea. No, thank goodness. I shouldn't be mean but, oh boy, does she make everything more difficult.'

Edith grinned. 'Yes, but at least she likes you.'

'I wouldn't go that far. Perhaps she dislikes me less than she used to, that's about the extent of it.' Alice exhaled ruefully. 'Anyhow, it was just Pauline and her brother. He wasn't interested, of course, but at least I could keep a bit of an eye on him.'

'And Pauline? How was she?' Although they weren't meant to have favourites, both Alice and Edith had a soft spot for young Pauline, a schoolgirl they'd known since the teeth-brushing classes. Pauline battled valiantly to look after her younger brother and present a fairly respectable face to the world, largely in the absence of any useful adult help.

'In good spirits. She'd had a letter from Dottie, that classmate of hers who was evacuated. They were best friends all those years ago. To begin with they weren't old enough to read or write proper letters, and of course Gran was no help. These days, as long as she can scrape together the cost of a stamp, Pauline can write to her friend. Now she'll be able to tell her she's learning to knit.'

'So you made a start, then?' Edith was pleased the red jumper had been useful. She'd unravelled it the night she'd bought it.

'We did. It's strange trying to explain something

101

when you've done it without thinking for so long. It was harder than I thought.' Alice rubbed her hands. 'I was all fingers and thumbs. But she took to it like a duck to water. I've left it with her to practise — doesn't matter if she gets it wrong, we can always start again. Here, let me get you that tea. No, sit down, if you don't let people wait on you hand and foot when you're having a baby, then when will you?'

Edith shrugged and made no further protest. 'I hope you told Pauline to hide it all from her gran or the old dear will try to flog the needles for the price of her gin.'

11

Lily pressed her dark red lips together. She was trying to avoid the temptation of licking them, to taste that rare and luxurious flavour of a new tube of Tangee. She'd spent a considerable amount of time applying it, after she'd carefully used her recent purchase of the face powder. She was sure she looked as good as she possibly could.

Earlier, she'd persuaded Mary to share some hot chocolate, and she'd done her best to steer the conversation round to how to behave in a West End restaurant. Mary was more keen to discuss the hygiene classes, hinting that Lily had room for improvement in her dealings with the children, but Lily resisted the subject. She knew she was in danger of blurting out how much she disliked them, and recognised this would not go down well with the more senior nurse.

Instead, she praised Mary's jewellery, which was obviously expensive although not remotely showy.

'Oh, this old thing.' Mary's hand went to her necklace, as if she'd forgotten she'd put it on. 'It was one of Mummy's. She let me borrow it and then didn't mind if I kept it. She says I'll get more wear out of it than she will, as she's stuck in the country. Though she seems to like it there.'

Lily didn't have an opinion about living in the country as she'd never done so and couldn't think of anybody who had. Instead she saw the opening she had wanted. 'Where do you go, then?' she asked casually. 'I bet they must be nice places if you wear that necklace.'

Mary wrinkled her nose. 'Oh, here and there. Usually I let Charles choose. That's when he has time at all.'

Lily could sense this was a delicate area. 'Where does he take you, then? It must be very exciting.' From Mary's expression she realised this was too much, and she reined in her enthusiasm. 'I don't know many places in London, you see.'

Mary smiled easily. 'I forget that you're new to the place. I'm sorry, forgive me. I just assume everyone goes to the same old spots, and that's not fair.'

Lily thought she would burst with envy. 'I went out quite a bit in Liverpool but I've still not got to know anywhere down here.' It was true about Liverpool, but stretching things to imply that many of them had been top quality.

Mary obligingly listed some of Charles's top favourites, which included hotel names even Lily was familiar with: the Savoy, Claridge's, the Dorchester. Somehow she doubted that Donald would ever take her there.

Still, she encouraged Mary to go into detail, what she'd worn, how a typical evening would be spent, what sort of food they'd eat. 'Of course we used to enjoy a night out at the Café de Paris but then it got bombed, so that was that,' Mary finished. 'He's usually too tied up with work these days. He keeps saying that when it's all over then we can go where we please.' She sighed deeply. 'I can't wait.'

Lily nodded in sympathy. 'I bet.' How perfect it would be, to be taken to beautiful hotels on the arm of a captain. She could imagine Mary in a silky dress, her wonderful abundant hair piled high, her beautiful family jewellery twinkling in the opulent lighting. Whereas for her, that might be aiming a little high just yet. She had snapped out of her daydream.

Now she walked slowly along St Martin's Lane, not entirely certain that she was headed in the right direction. If she'd known the streets were so long she would have worn her lower heels again. She'd chosen her most glamorous shoes in honour of the invitation but they weren't really designed for walking far. But they did make her legs look fabulous.

Donald had suggested meeting at Leicester Square underground station, but she'd arrived by bus and had to make her way there. She'd studied the map but it was all so much more confusing in reality: the sheer number of people, the height of the buildings, the clamour of vehicles. She caught a few glances aimed at her and sped up. It didn't do to show you didn't know where you were — it made you vulnerable. That was not the impression she was seeking to make.

You can do this, she told herself. You're every bit as good as any of these women, however toffee-nosed they are. You are more beautiful, and all those men are wondering if they are in with a chance. You're meeting a handsome man.

What if he didn't come? If he'd had second thoughts? She gave a little gasp at the horrible prospect. Anything could have happened between the letters and this evening. No, she mustn't think this way.

Just as she was wondering if she should turn around, she caught sight of the Tube station entrance, the instantly recognisable symbol of the Underground displayed above it. Drawing closer, she could pick out people hanging around, waiting, in groups and couples and individuals. So many people, so much noise.

How did you ever become used to this place?

Then, she saw him.

For a moment she stood still, to take in just how handsome he was. Compared to the other men milling around, he was far better-looking. And he was here, waiting for her! Lily's heart skipped a beat.

He caught sight of her and she forced herself not to give in and run to him. Instead she walked as enticingly as she could on her high heels, allowing a smile to grow as she got closer. 'Hello, Donald,' she breathed, controlling her building excitement.

'Miss Chandler. Lily. You came.' His eyes crinkled as he too smiled.

'I did.' She felt as if time was standing still around them. All the other people in the teeming crowds faded away and there was just the two of them, and his gaze on her. She could tell that he liked what he saw.

He offered her his arm. 'You look just as I imagined you would in that lipstick,' he said. 'It suits you to a T.'

She tipped her head in acknowledgement, secretly thrilling at tucking her hand through his arm. His coat was a good-quality heavy tweed, reassuringly expensive. 'That's because it was well chosen.'

'I'm glad it's to your taste,' he said, leading her along through the crowds and towards a smart-looking side street. She glowed with pleasure that he was so unhesitating, knowing exactly where to go. She tried to memorise the route and to work out where they were in relation to the Underground station and her bus stop. She desperately wanted to know her way around the bustling centre of her newly adopted city.

'Here we are.' He brought them to a halt outside a small restaurant with a simple but elegant window and door. 'I hope you like Italian food — I took the liberty of booking us a table.'

'I'm sure I shall,' Lily replied as he held open the door for her. She had no idea what Italian cooking was like, although she knew there had been plenty of Italians in Liverpool, at least until the war had broken out. She'd had their ice creams as a child, but that was as far as her knowledge of Italian food went.

The waiter who came to greet them reminded her of the young man who used to sell the ice creams, with his dark eyes and even darker hair, and she allowed herself to be led to a table for two inside the warm room. 'So nice to see you again, Signor Parker,' he was saying to Donald as he pulled back her chair. She was so keen to sit in an elegant fashion that she missed the look that flashed between the two men.

She was also keen to hide the fact that she hadn't got a clue what the items on the menu might be. However, if he noticed, Donald hid it well, and instead offered to order for both of them. 'Would you like some wine?' he suggested.

'Oh, I'm not sure . . . '

Lily knew some men didn't approve of women who drank, but Donald didn't seem to be one of them. She'd hardly ever had wine — only on those few occasions back home that she now tried not to remember. In truth she would have preferred a shandy, but sensed that would not be the right answer. 'I'll have a little, as long as you're having some.'

Donald nodded sagely. 'Red or white?'

'Whatever you are having,' Lily said at once.

Donald turned in his seat and murmured something to the waiter, who was hovering nearby. He had few other customers, as only a couple of tables were

107

occupied. Maybe people ate later here, Lily thought, gazing around. The lights were dim but she could see the place was lined with dark wood panels, the tablecloths were a deep red and all the cutlery and glassware shone like as many little mirrors. It was a far cry from the canteen back at the nurses' home.

The food appeared and Donald apologised, informing her that they did their best but it wasn't a patch on what it had been like before rationing. Lily thought she was in heaven, with unfamiliar tomato sauces and the sharp taste of the wine, which was getting better with every cautious sip. If this was inferior to the meals they used to serve, she couldn't imagine what they must have been like. She blotted her lips very carefully on the heavy napkin, trying to preserve the lipstick. She would have to refresh it in the powder room once they'd finished.

In the meantime, Donald had kept her amused with anecdotes about his colleagues, even though he did not specify exactly what line of business they were in. 'I do my share of fire-watching of course,' he assured her. 'You know my office is in Bethnal Green, and we caught it bad during the Blitz. So I spend a couple of nights a week, when I'm not away, standing up on the rooftops, watching for any enemy aircraft, or things like that.'

Lily widened her eyes. 'Isn't that terribly dangerous? I don't like to think of you up there where you could get hurt.'

He laughed indulgently. 'That's sweet of you to say so. Of course it's not dangerous, not really.' He said it in such a way as to imply it certainly was.

Lily didn't argue, but knew of old that it was no picnic. Her own mother would go fire-watching for their street, and used to come home with hair-raising tales, so knowing he did this difficult work put Donald even further up in her estimation. When he suggested a final course of a dark liqueur served with tiny Italian biscuits, she was delighted. Every taste was a new adventure. All the while, the dim lighting accentuated the clean lines of his face, his strong chin, his angled cheekbones. She wished they could stay here for ever.

More and more customers began to arrive, and Lily realised they could not stay in this haven for much longer. 'It's not that I want to leave but I hate to share you,' Donald breathed as they rose, and the waiter went to fetch their coats. 'Allow me,' and he held her maroon coat for her to put on. As he did so she sensed his strong, warm hands on her shoulders, and briefly, deliciously, on her waist. She pursed her now-retouched lips prettily as the waiter held open the door. 'Maybe we will see you again soon,' he said charmingly.

'I do hope so,' she said, stepping out into the cold air.

Once again Donald took her arm. 'I wish I could escort you all the way home but I'm afraid I have to go back to the office,' he said regretfully.

Lily was surprised; it was Saturday night. 'Really? Oh, that's a shame.' She didn't want to come across as too demanding though. 'Never mind, I know the way back by bus. That's how I came in, after all.'

'Then I'll walk you to your bus stop. I promise I'll do better next time.' He followed her lead back to St Martin's Lane and down the road from which she had started.

Lily smiled to herself. So there was to be a next time. She hadn't put him off with her lack of knowledge of Italian food. 'I might hold you to that,' she replied archly.

'You can certainly do that,' he breathed, his voice full of suggestion, and she caught her breath. His implication was clear and yet there was nothing to be done about it in this busy street. Perhaps he was teasing her. Well, time would tell.

'Here we are.' She came to a halt by the queue of people all waiting to travel east. 'Is this your stop too?'

For a second he looked confused. 'Ah, no. Mine's been diverted. I have to go down to Piccadilly,' he explained, indicating in the opposite direction with his head, though Lily wasn't sure where Piccadilly was.

'I see.' She was determined to play it cool now that he'd promised they would see each other again. 'Well, thank you for a lovely evening. I enjoyed every moment,' she said honestly, catching sight of the bus at the far end of the street.

'The pleasure was all mine.' Suddenly he was deadly serious. Swiftly he dropped his head and brought his lips to hers, just for a fleeting moment, then he was all propriety as the bus drew up and the queue began to move. 'I'll send you a note when I'm back from my next work trip.' And he was gone.

Lily climbed aboard, her heart pounding. He'd started to kiss her and then drawn back. If the bus hadn't come just then, what might he have done? Or if the restaurant hadn't filled up so quickly? A little gasp escaped her, even as her head swam slightly from the unfamiliar alcohol. Whatever his intentions, he had most definitely left her craving more. She couldn't wait until their next meeting.

'What's up, Al?' Edith had popped into her friend's room to borrow a needle and thread, and found her sitting on the narrow bed, a sheet of notepaper in her hand. 'You look as if something's worrying you.'

Alice glanced up and smiled distractedly. 'I'm not sure if I should be worried or not.' She waved the piece of paper. 'It's from home, from my mother. Her handwriting isn't quite right, it's a bit shaky. She mentions that she's had a bad cold so maybe that's all there is to it.'

Edith flopped down beside her, wondering how many times they had sat like this over the past few years, in one another's rooms, side by side, facing news of one sort or the other. 'Maybe that's what it is. You know how shaky you get after being ill.'

'Hmmmm.' Alice wasn't convinced. 'You're right, of course, but this is my mother we're talking about. She never, ever admits to weakness. It's just not in her to do so. So simply dropping it in, in passing, is a huge signal. Something's not right, but I don't know what.'

Edith looked quizzical. 'Are you sure, Al? She's not just saying she's had a cold, like half of the rest of the country?'

'No. Well, perhaps. Maybe.' Alice sighed. 'I don't want to get worried about it unnecessarily, but . . . I don't know. At times like this, Liverpool feels very far away.' She tried to remember the last time she'd gone back. She'd seen her parents fairly recently of course, but then they'd met halfway. It was months — no, more than a year — since she'd been home to the city of her birth.

Edith patted her hand. 'If it was anything really serious, wouldn't she have said something? She wouldn't have deliberately left you hanging in mid-air. She's not mean.' Not like my own mother, she thought.

'Yes, you're right.' Alice rubbed her temples. 'I won't worry if there's nothing to worry about. And even if there were, I couldn't do much. Maybe I should try to go back there though. Perhaps Easter — mind you, it's late this year, so possibly sooner.'

Edith nodded. 'That sounds like a good idea. You never take all your days off. You won't get them back, you know.' She paused. 'When I saw that look on your face I thought something else had happened.'

'Like what?'

Edith hesitated. 'I dunno . . . maybe to do with Mark. That you were thinking about him or something.'

Alice turned her face up to stare at the ceiling. 'It's not like that. I'm trying hard not to think about it.'

Edith recognised that it wasn't quite as simple as Alice would have liked to make out, but she let it go nevertheless. 'As long as you're all right,' she said. 'You're not secretly tormenting yourself about him, all over again.'

'Pffff.' Alice laughed off the idea. 'No, I'm not. I spent long enough reliving all that — I've had enough of it to last me a lifetime.'

'Good,' said Edith fervently.

12

Lily realised she had hardly spoken to her fellow new recruit, Ruby, since they had both joined the nurses' home. However, this was not how she had imagined becoming close to her. The two of them were squashed together in one corner of the refuge room, imprisoned there by an air raid. The attacks from January and the beginning of February had continued, and now the action sounded very close indeed, with anti-aircraft defences crackling from nearby roofs and lights flashing through the small gaps in the blackout blinds.

All the nurses who were in residence this Friday evening were huddled in the one room on the ground floor, just along from the common room, well sheltered as its only windows faced a nearby wall, and with sturdy internal walls on its other three sides. Short of being in a protected underground bunker, this was as good as they could get. Yet Ruby was trembling and Lily could easily have given in to her fears and done the same.

'It's all right,' she said as heartily as she could. 'We'll be safe in here.'

Ruby shuddered against her. 'I hope so. I hate it when it's like this. Have you been caught in a raid before? You had them in Liverpool, didn't you?'

Lily groaned. 'Oh boy, did we have raids. Our docks got a proper pasting — that was when the Jerries were trying to stop any supplies getting in from America. Then they went after the city centre. Our poor churches — and the shops! That was awful, you couldn't even go out to buy something to cheer yourself up. Lots of the big ones got damaged and shut down.'

Ruby sounded as if she was stifling a sob. 'And did you have a shelter?'

Lily gave a shudder herself as the memories came flooding back. 'Not exactly,' she said. 'Our garden wasn't big enough for one of those Anderson dugouts. We started by going under the stairs, but everything shook so much we knew we weren't safe. So we had to take our chances and dash along to the church hall, down the road. Everyone from streets around used to go there. Filthy, it was, and the smell! You've never come across anything like it. Think of the worst home visit you've ever been on and then imagine it ten times worse. I'd as soon have been under the stairs back home but my mother wouldn't let me.'

Ruby cleared her throat. 'I know what you mean. I went down our church hall a few times with my sister and mum but it was horrible. I bet they're in there now.' She coughed. 'I was lucky — there was a big basement in my hospital. We used to have to get the patients down there, which was a right palaver, but once we were all crammed in, we knew we'd be all right.'

'Just as well we're in here, isn't it?' Lily knew that plenty of Londoners went to the Underground stations and slept on the platforms, but had absolutely no desire to try that. All those strange bodies pressed in together — not on your nelly, she thought. Besides, there weren't any Tube stations close enough to get to around here. She shifted a little on the cushion on the floor, against a wall. 'This isn't too bad.'

'No, you're right,' Ruby declared, sounding a little

less scared. 'We'll be fine, won't we?'

'Course you will,' said a voice in an Irish accent, and Lily realised the nurse on the other side of Ruby must be either Ellen or Bridget. She could never remember which was which, even though they looked entirely different. There was scarcely enough light to make out her outline, let alone any distinguishing features, so she didn't have a clue which one it might be.

'Have you been through many raids down here?' Lily asked.

'I certainly have.' The Irish nurse sounded almost cheerful. 'All hell might be breaking loose outside, but we were all unscathed in here. It's the best place to be. My colleague Bridget — you know, the one with all the freckles — she got caught out in the middle of one, coming back from her rounds. She ended up in the doctor's surgery where she had to help him out doing an emergency diabetes clinic in the near-dark. Much better to be here.'

So it was Ellen.

'I wouldn't like that — how would you know where you were sticking the needle?' Lily wondered.

Ruby giggled. 'Could be nasty.'

Lily agreed, and asked herself why she hadn't made more of an effort to get to know the other newcomer. She'd thought her a bit shy and retiring, not much fun. But in all the horror of the raid, Ruby sounded as if she was battling her fear and letting her good humour shine through. She might be fun after all. Lily resolved to make amends once this never-ending night was over. Lily had to admit that another reason she'd made little effort was that Ruby didn't look as if she might be useful to Lily in any way. Not like Mary, or Alice.

115

Lily was slightly disappointed that there had been no further chance to talk to the other nurse from Liverpool, even after she'd broken the ice. It was almost as if Alice was avoiding her, although she couldn't think why. She'd been as friendly as she knew how. She must be imagining it.

The crashes and banging from outside were growing louder, and she bit her lip to stop herself from crying out.

'That sounds as if it's coming from Clapton,' said a voice, and Lily recognised that it was Alice, from over in the corner. She could just about discern a figure sitting back-to-front on a chair, resting her hands and head on the ladder back. 'I hope the lending library is all right.'

'And the cinema. Don't forget the cinema,' said another voice — Mary's, the tone unmistakable. 'We all deserve a trip there once this beastly raid is over. Any idea what's on?'

'I think Old Mother Riley's back again,' Ellen said.

'Oh no! I'm not going to that. I didn't like it the first time round,' Mary protested. 'I prefer a bit of romance myself.'

'Well you would, with a boyfriend like that . . . ' someone else, possibly Belinda, began, when there was another bang, louder this time.

'There goes your library, Alice,' Belinda added darkly.

Lily was surprised, but then realised a degree of gallows humour was what got people through the worst times. She was more surprised that she wasn't sleepy; it was the middle of the night and yet she was fully alert. She'd gone past the fear stage now, and her thoughts were racing. She'd hoped to be able to meet up with Donald again this weekend, but if they were in for more of this, she wasn't sure if she'd be able to.

'Where's Edith?' someone else asked. 'Will she be all right? She's not here, is she?'

Alice spoke up. 'No, she's over with the Banhams. She left just before it got dark so there's no need to worry. She'll be in their shelter, along with Mattie and Flo and the children.'

'Will there be room?' asked Lily, amazed. The only ones she'd seen were very poky.

Alice laughed, but not unkindly. 'It's amazing what you can fit in there when you have to. Mattie managed to give birth in there, with Edith and me helping, and Kath coming in and out. They'll all be fine.'

Lily exhaled loudly as a realisation struck her. She'd been thinking only about herself, about her chances of meeting Donald, and further to that making a success of herself in the big city. All the individual nurses were possible means to that end. She'd overlooked what was right in front of her nose all the while: that they all looked out for one another. They would do the same for her. And they would also expect the same of her.

She shuddered involuntarily. Was she up to it? It was a new feeling for her. Putting others before herself didn't come easily. As the chatter slowly died out, and the noise of the raid receded, she slipped back into delicious dreams of Donald, imagining him rescuing her from a dangerous street, being crushed up against him in a private hiding place. If only he would wait for her and not think she didn't care if they couldn't manage to meet this weekend. Her last thoughts as she fell asleep were of his strong arms around her, the perils of the raid forgotten.

117

'Oh, dear.' Fiona was almost speechless at the scene before her. She looked up at Gwen, who was equally dumbstruck.

The weekend of raids had been exhausting but somehow they had come through it relatively untouched. Several of the emergency patients had had their evening visits cut short as the nurses dashed back to be safe before the action got fully underway, and they'd been called out to attend various people who'd been struck by falling roof tiles or bricks — nothing too bad, compared to the horrors of the Blitz. Throughout all of that, the building at Victory Walk had stood firm.

However, last night's midweek raid had hit home. The main damage had been to the neighbouring street, but the big windows in the common room faced that way. The large panes of glass overlooking the yard had shattered, the shards on the rug now sparkling like diamonds in the snow. A knife-like wind blew through the ruined windows, dispelling the usual cosy atmosphere.

Fiona exhaled deeply. 'Well, there's nothing for it. Plenty of folk have had far worse. We'd better get this cleared up before everyone starts to come down for breakfast.' She ran her hand through her short auburn hair which now showed streaks of grey.

Gwen frowned. 'Don't even think about touching any of that with your bare hands. We'll get gloves before we even begin to set about finding a dustpan and brush. Where do they keep the ones they use for the victory garden? I'm sure they're around here . . . '

'I'll get them.' The slender figure of Gladys emerged from the service room. She always arrived early, in time to help make the nurses' breakfasts, and shook

118

her head as she came closer to the superintendent and her deputy. 'So it's as bad as we thought, then. Was anyone hurt?'

'Mercifully, no.' It was Gwen's turn to sigh.

'Somehow the damage was all to this side of the lower floor. We were lucky, when you come to think of it.'

Fiona nodded vigorously. 'That's the spirit. What's a bit of glass? We'll patch it up and make the best of it. We won't be in the dark as the side windows weren't broken.'

'What about the bikes?' Gwen wondered, peering out through the jagged panes to the bike rack in the yard beyond.

Fiona came to join her. 'Looks as if the big wall sheltered them,' she said with relief.

'So we shan't have to replace any,' Gwen said.

'Just as well,' Fiona observed, wheeling round and pushing up her sleeves. 'Because there aren't any to be had.'

★ ★ ★

Twenty minutes later and the room was looking more like its old self, but many degrees colder. Gladys and Fiona had carefully picked up the broken glass and Gwen had swept and brushed, shaking the cushions to dislodge the smallest slivers, rendering the place ready for the influx of hungry nurses.

'I'd better get back to the kitchen,' Gladys said. 'Cook was going to make a start on the porridge but I should fetch the toast racks and boil the kettle. Here, let me take that bundle of newspaper. I'll put it some-where safe out of the way and get rid of it later when the rush has died down.' She took the parcel from Fiona, gingerly as they'd wrapped up some of the big shards in it. 'Good job we'd saved all that paper.'

'It was intended for the fire,' Gwen replied sadly. 'We'll have to be more economical with our kindling for a while, I'm afraid.'

'Well, at least there's one benefit from all this.' Fiona was recovering her usual positive mood.

'What's that?' Gwen asked doubtfully.

Fiona grinned. 'Well, you're always complaining about the nurses who break curfew and creep back in through the unlocked window. They won't be able to do that when it's boarded up, will they?'

Gwen shook her head, knowing that she was being teased. It was true that she disapproved of any breach of discipline, and she was aware that many of the nurses over the years had used this very window to flout the curfew. Fiona had been more pragmatic; transport was often disrupted and she would cut them some slack as long as their work didn't suffer. She was particularly lenient towards Belinda, who would meet up with her brother and parents on the other side of north London as often as he had leave from the RAF. They all knew what the fate of a Jewish airman would be, should he fall into enemy hands.

Before she could object, Gladys came back in to the common room, followed by a man in ARP uniform. 'Look who I found,' she said, wiping crumbs from her hands on her damp apron. 'Brendan was coming to check on us. I said we'd bring him some tea.'

The broad-shouldered warden smiled through his evident exhaustion. 'Morning, ladies. That's a very kind offer. I won't say no — I tell you straight, that was one devil of a night.'

'I'm sure, I'm sure.' Fiona hastened to pull up a chair for him. 'I'd take your coat but you might wish to keep it on. As you can see, we're not very weather-proof at the moment.'

The big man sank gratefully onto the seat and passed his hand across his brow. For a moment he seemed too tired to take in the change in the usually warm and welcoming room. Then his eyes widened as he realised what had happened. 'Oh, ladies. That's a dreadful shame. Your lovely windows. I'm sorry to see that, I am.'

Fiona bustled back with a tray of tea and toast. 'Plenty of fresh air,' she beamed. 'That's what we always recommend for our patients, and now we shall all have to practise what we preach.'

Brendan snorted. 'That's the spirit.' He took a long gulp of the hot liquid. 'Ah, that's better. I been on my feet all night so that is the best cup of tea ever. You wouldn't believe the mess Jerry's made of the next road over. We've been at it from dusk till dawn, non-stop. Makes me realise I'm not as young as I used to be.' He set down the china cup and his big hand shook.

'We none of us are,' Fiona agreed. 'Here, let me butter this toast. And a dollop of marmalade? Gladys always has some kept at the back of the cupboard for a special occasion.'

Brendan's smile brightened at this news. 'Now don't tell me that, or I'll be breaking in to find it. I love a good marmalade, I do. My missus used to make it when we had Seville oranges in season, but now she don't have enough sugar. Or oranges, come to that.'

'So this is special.' He took a bite of the toast, his eyes dancing. 'Speaking of which, you won't want those windows left like that or you'll have every Tom, Dick and Harry wandering in and taking what they please — marmalade or whatever. Your medical supplies for instance — they'd make a pretty penny on the black market.'

Gwen nodded. 'You're right, of course. We can't let that happen. We'll make arrangements to have them properly boarded up while we start enquiries about replacing the glass — no doubt there will be a bit of a queue.'

Brendan shook his head. 'No need for that. I'll do it. Just let me enjoy me toast then I'll pop down the market and get me tools. They'll have spare boards down there — they always got something like that knocking around.'

Fiona protested. 'But you haven't slept. And what about your stall?'

Brendan took a final gulp of the tea. 'Don't you worry about that. I got me nephew helping out. He's a bit of a wild 'un and I offered to take him on to sort him out. Me sister was proper worried about him cos he got in with the wrong crowd. Too old for school but too young to join up — so I said, let him come along with me, I'll show him what's what. Do him good to have a bit of responsibility this morning. Maurice can open up while I fix this and then get some kip. It'll be doing me and me sister a favour, in fact.'

Gwen raised her eyebrows. 'Well, if you're sure . . . ' It was too good an offer to turn down. Just finding big enough boards would have been a major enterprise.

Brendan stood up. 'Course I'm sure. We got to look after you nurses, haven't we? Cos you look after us when we need you. That's the way it goes.'

122

13

'There you are! I wasn't sure if you'd come. I wondered if you'd had second thoughts.' Donald smiled his easy grin and Lily rushed towards him, dodging the crowds heading for the nearby cinema. A big poster featuring the unmistakable face of George Formby beamed down at them but she had eyes only for the man in the elegantly tailored suit in front of her.

Lily smiled back, her lips carefully coated in the precious rich red lipstick. 'Second thoughts? Now why ever would I have those?'

He shrugged, and she noticed the way the gorgeous material of his jacket moved. 'You might have decided I'm too old and staid to be seen out with a beautiful young woman like yourself.'

Lily laughed. He was a dreadful flatterer but she couldn't help herself. 'Not a bit of it.'

Donald offered her his arm and she linked her own into it. He squeezed her upper arm against him a little as they began to walk away from Leicester Square. 'Well, you couldn't make our previous appointment.'

Lily tossed her head. 'You have Mr Hitler to thank for that,' she said pertly. 'He seemed to take a personal interest in the East End that evening. He ruined every.one's plans for the weekend, and not to mention our poor canteen just after. We've got to sit in the near-dark to eat our meals now as more than half of the glass has had to be replaced by horrible old boards. Well, you'd know — I bet Bethnal Green took a pasting too.'

Donald cleared his throat. 'I'm sorry to hear that. You nurses deserve better — you're all heroines to be working through the conditions that you do.'

Lily turned her face up to him, enjoying the fact that he was a good half-head taller than her. She liked a decent height in a man. 'It's what we signed up for,' she said simply. 'We knew what we were doing. So, was your office all right? There weren't any explosions nearby?'

For a moment she thought he looked confused, but she must have imagined it as he shook his head. 'No, no, we were lucky. Well, inasmuch as anybody caught up in all of this can be called lucky.'

'I'll say,' Lily agreed heartily.

He swung them into a side street where the crowds were thinner.

'Tell you what,' he said, his voice a little husky, 'I consider myself lucky. Want to know why?'

She turned to face him, smiling again. 'Go on then, tell me.'

He loosened his hold on her arm and then gripped both of her hands in his own. 'Because I chanced to meet you. That was pure luck, that you should be at that little shop at the same time as I was. Blind fate, nothing else. Another couple of minutes and we would have missed each other entirely and been none the wiser. So yes, I reckon I'm lucky.' His face was so close to hers that she could feel his breath.

For a moment she was almost at a loss for words, his intensity so sudden that she was not sure how to react. Her heart thudded in her chest and she felt short of breath. Then she recovered her poise. She didn't want to appear too unsophisticated. 'It was fate, wasn't it.' She fought to keep her voice light and steady. 'Who knows what might have happened if things had turned out otherwise? You could have bumped into the woman in the queue behind me. She might be here with you now, wearing this lipstick.'

Donald relaxed the tightness of his grip. 'Impossible!' He was back to his joking, debonair self. 'The very idea! You are a very special young lady. I knew that from the moment I saw you.'

Lily was doing her best to ignore his deliberate charm but was swept up despite herself. He really did say the most wonderful things, and a girl couldn't be blamed for wanting to believe them. 'You're too kind,' she purred.

Donald took her arm once more and began to lead her along the pavement, rain-splattered after a teatime shower. 'And what a beautiful young lady deserves is a delicious cocktail,' he proclaimed. 'How would that suit you? You do like cocktails, don't you?'

'Of course,' said Lily at once, without knowing if it was true or not. Cocktails had not been part of her life thus far. For a fleeting moment she imagined she was Mary, accustomed to such things from the moment she was old enough to drink them. What would she have? Lily racked her brains for the name of any. How would Mary talk if she was in one of those posh hotels with her army captain?

'Martinis are my favourite,' she said boldly. She had no idea if she would like one, but she remembered Mary mentioning that she'd gone to meet her godmother one Sunday afternoon and that was what they had had. If it was good enough for Mary then she would damn well make sure she enjoyed it.

'Martinis, eh?' Donald raised his eyebrows but in delight, not mockery, Lily was fairly sure. 'What fine taste you have, Lily. Not that I would have expected anything else.'

Lily inwardly thanked Mary and her godmother as Donald ushered her through a door — the kind of door you would normally pass by and hardly notice. A uniformed doorman greeted them, drawing aside a thick velvet curtain as he ushered them in. All at once Lily was assailed by a wave of noise — chatter, a dance band, the clinking of glass and metal.

'I say,' she breathed, taken by surprise. That nondescript little door had concealed a busy club and, from her vantage point at the entrance, they looked to be exactly the sort of sophisticated crowd she had always dreamt of mixing with.

'Caught you out there, didn't I?' Donald was pleased by her reaction. 'You'd never guess this was here, would you? Slap bang in the centre of the city. Welcome, Lily, to the Magpie Club. Strictly members only — and a very select number of special guests.' He held out his hand to her. 'Come this way. I usually sit over here, and — don't worry — they'll come to take your coat.'

Lily was glad she'd paid even more attention than usual to her outfit for this evening. She'd suspected they would go somewhere smart, and she felt she didn't have to be quite so buttoned up this time. Nothing risqué, obviously; she didn't want to give the wrong message. But something a little more fun than her respectable blouse from their last date, to show that she could let her hair down to a certain degree.

She had one black dress, quite plain in itself but with the right sparkly belt and a string of mock pearls and pearl clip earrings, she thought she could pass as relaxed and stylish. Gazing around, she would be

126

prepared to bet that many of the other strings of pearls being sported by the female guests were the real thing. Well, one day, maybe that would be her. One step at a time, she told herself, as Donald helped her out of her maroon coat and handed it over to be taken to the cloakroom.

Before she could change her mind about sampling a martini for the first time, Donald was off to the bar, returning with two gleaming glasses. His was a tumbler with an inch or so of a darkish amber liquid — whisky, she supposed. Her glass was one that she'd seen only in the films, a shallow cup filled with oily-looking clear liquid.

'Sorry, no olives available tonight.' He sat back down. 'You don't mind, do you?'

Olives? Whatever did he mean? 'No, not at all,' she assured him honestly.

'Quite right. I knew you weren't the sort to make a fuss about a little detail like that.' He picked up his glass. 'Well, cheers.'

She did the same. 'Cheers.' They touched glasses and she raised hers to her lips, wondering what she was in for. A man in a beautifully cut suit caught Donald's eye and they waved briefly at one another, so Lily took the opportunity to take a sip. She wanted to test her reaction to the new drink while his attention was elsewhere. It was freezing cold and astonishingly strong. She wasn't sure if she liked it or not — but she would teach herself to love it. If it was good enough for Mary and her godmother, then she'd damn well make sure she loved it too.

Donald's gaze returned to her.

'Delicious,' she announced determinedly.

'There's nothing like it, is there,' he said and his

eyes crinkled in the way she was coming to love as he smiled again. 'I can tell you are someone who appreciates the finer things in life.'

Lily carefully put the glass down. This was not a drink to finish in a hurry. Her head swam a little as she gave a small laugh. 'I like to think so,' she said. Maybe it was true — or coming true. She desperately wanted to be someone who could recognise the finer things and enjoy them. The nurses' home and the sense of solidarity she had felt with her colleagues on the night of the raid felt like a world away.

The murmur of the crowd was loud and so their conversation petered out, but Donald didn't seem to mind and neither did Lily. It gave her a chance to look around, to commit to memory the smaller details. That was how these women wore their scarves — like Mary sometimes did, of course, dashingly tied at an angle, for show and not for warmth. This was how to hold the unusual glass. That was how to adjust a cigarette holder. She wondered what her mother would make of this place — no, best not to think about her. She would not approve.

Lily liked it that she and Donald could be so at ease with one another so quickly and there was no pressure to make small talk. She didn't want to be one of those girls who babbled on incessantly, trying the patience of everyone around them. That would be common. She didn't want to seem like that. She'd save her thoughts and maybe share them with Ruby tomorrow.

'Penny for 'em,' Donald said, his mouth close to her ear. She shivered with pleasure. His aftershave was subtle but unmissable.

'Oh, I was just wondering where that lovely scarf

might have come from,' she improvised hastily.

'Which one — that green one over there?' He squinted in the direction she had indicated. 'That will have come from Liberty. It's a most distinctive print.'

Lily struggled not to reveal how impressed she was.

Fancy him knowing such a thing. That was true sophistication.

'I know that woman slightly. Shall I find out if she bought it recently?' He made as if to get up.

'Oh, no. Don't trouble yourself,' Lily said quickly. She would die with embarrassment if he went over to ask her. 'It's just that it's such a gorgeous colour.'

Donald cocked his head and looked at her in that magnetically intense way once more. 'It would suit you,' he said.

'Do you think so?' Her voice wanted to tremble.

'Oh yes. And you must remember, I've got a good eye for colour. Especially when it comes to which ones suit you.' That smile again — those wonderful laughter lines around his eyes.

'You have,' she managed to say lightly, taking a bigger sip from her glass. How funny — it was empty already.

'Another?' he asked, beginning to rise from his seat.

'Oh, I shouldn't, really I shouldn't . . . '

'Oh go on, you'll be keeping me company.' He finished what was left of his whisky. 'I've had a tremen. dously busy week and could do with another one of these. Look upon it as doing an old man a favour.' His face showed he didn't mean the old bit.

'In that case . . . ' Lily didn't feel she could say no; and besides, she needed to practise drinking cocktails if she was ever to genuinely enjoy them. Her vision was slightly blurry but she forced herself not to reveal any effects from the first one. Mary wouldn't, she was sure. She had to be just like Mary. She sat up straighter, absorbing the lively music issuing from the small group of musicians in one corner. The lead player's trumpet gleamed in the spotlights trained upon him.

'Here you are.' Donald was back, flashing her his smile, and yet she thought it wasn't quite as easy as before. Perhaps somebody at the bar had said something to irritate him. People could be so thoughtless.

'Thank you very much.' She lowered her eyelids and peeped up at him and sure enough his smile widened as he settled himself back down at the little table, with its highly polished wooden surface. No scratches or ring marks from old drinks around here. This was a classy place and no mistake. Lily took a sip from the new glass.

Donald began to hum along to a tune and then to tell her about what music he liked, which he then neatly turned into which film themes he thought were best.

'I loved the one in *Gone with the Wind*,' Lily said, sipping again.

'I bet that's because you liked Rhett Butler,' Donald suggested.

'Perhaps,' she admitted, batting her eyelashes some more. She wondered if he was leading up to asking her to go to the cinema with him. She would bet they wouldn't have to queue up at the crowded box office like they did when she went out with the nurses to the Hackney pictures. 'He was so much more handsome than poor Ashley, you have to admit.'

'Scarlett certainly thought so.' He raised his own glass. 'Maybe it's because you prefer dark-haired types to fair?'

'Maybe.' She gave what she knew was her prettiest little smile.

He held her gaze and his eyes grew dark with appreciation, joining in the game. She inhaled and kept her gaze steady, relishing every second, knowing how interested he was. Then the moment was spoilt as a man came across and touched Donald on the shoulder. It was quietly done but she was in no doubt that this was not something that could be ignored. Donald's initial look of annoyance was swiftly masked. 'Excuse me for a minute,' he said, and rose to follow the other man, who was shorter than him and whose clothing was by no means as elegant.

Lily was highly displeased that their little moment had been ruined, but told herself to buck up and not mind. Donald was after all a busy man, and apparently widely connected. These sorts of things were bound to happen. She swirled the oily cocktail around in its shallow glass, watching how the liquid moved and clung to the side before rolling back down again. The music pulsed through her and she tapped her foot in time with the rhythm.

'I'm so sorry.' Donald was back at their table. 'Would you believe it, an urgent work matter has just arisen. There's really no alternative — I have to go right away and deal with it.' His face showed his disappointment.

That odd little man was something to do with Donald's work? Lily's brain fought to understand.

She had imagined he dealt with people exactly like himself: worldly types in expensive suits, who all wore aftershave that smelt of wild forests. She shook her head.

'I know, I know,' Donald said, misunderstanding

and thinking she was cross. 'I would give my eye teeth for it to be otherwise. I'd hoped we might go on somewhere, but I'm afraid I really can't. Not this time.'

Lily knew she must be magnanimous. 'It's all right,' she said, a little unsteadily. 'These things happen. I know your work is very important.'

He exhaled sharply. 'Yes, but it shouldn't spoil our enjoyment like this. I'm mortified, I truly am. You must allow me to make it up to you. Will you do that? You aren't so angry that you'd deny me that chance?' His expression was pleading and deadly serious.

Lily's heart melted. He really, honestly wanted to see her again and was desperate for her to accept. Perhaps this hitch would work in her favour. Perhaps he would take her somewhere even more special the next time.

'Of course,' she said, tilting her head up to his. Before the coats could be brought back to them, he swooped swiftly down and kissed her, right there in the crowded club. His hand came to the side of her face and she could have leant into it for ever, it was so warm and wonderfully smooth. Not the hand of someone who worked down at the docks all day, and there again was that intoxicating aftershave. Then he released her as the coats arrived and he was all propriety, helping her back into hers.

'Just you wait,' he murmured. 'The next time we'll do something to make up for this. I promise you.' He had his hand in the small of her back as he guided her back through the modest entrance and out onto the street. 'I mean it, Lily. I promise you.'

She met his gaze in the dull light of the winter night. 'I accept,' she breathed.

132

14

Edith gritted her teeth as her front wheel hit yet another pothole. The roads were getting worse than ever. Heaven knew they'd been bad enough before, but since the last round of air raids some of them seemed to be more hole than road. At least the raids had died off — there hadn't been any more bombs in the area after the one that had destroyed the canteen's big windows.

She pulled on the heavy handlebars and tried to negotiate a path along the narrow street, but almost immediately the tyre caught on a dislodged brick and she almost fell off. She jerked sideways to maintain her balance and just about managed to right herself, but it had been touch and go for a moment.

'This is stupid,' she muttered, pulling up at the kerb and dismounting. She'd prefer to push the old bone-shaker rather than take a tumble. It wouldn't be good for a nurse to be seen sprawled on the ground.

It was more than that, though. Edith had been try-ing to put off the inevitable but the day was coming ever closer; she was going to have to admit to her-self that she could no longer manage the practicalities of her job. She'd coped with the morning sickness, which had been all-day sickness for a while. She'd got through the tiredness. However, there was no getting around the size of her bump. It was almost at the point where her centre of gravity was altered and she simply could not ride the bike the way she was used to doing.

It would have been hard enough on undamaged

roads with nice level surfaces. In the current conditions it veered towards the impossible on some
streets — and this was one of them. There was no
avoiding it; she had a regular patient here and that
was all there was to it. If she was to continue working,
she would have to pass along this street. If she could
no longer ride the bike then she would have to stop
working.

She came to a halt. That was the crux of the
dilemma. No bike, no work. She couldn't expect to
walk everywhere, carrying her bag. It would take far
longer and the bag was heavy. It was ride the bike or
nothing.

Edith bit her lip. She didn't want to give up work.
She loved her job and was tremendously proud of her
profession. She knew she was good at what she did.
Yet if she could no longer do the work safely, it was not
just herself she put in danger — it was her baby too.
Nothing must damage the health of her baby. What
sort of nurse would she be if she couldn't assess risk?

This baby growing inside her was a miracle. Any
new life was precious, but this one more than most,
as it so nearly had not come into being. When Harry
had gone missing after Dunkirk, they had all thought
he was dead. Then when he was found alive, there
had still been a high chance that he would not make
it. Even when it became clear that he would eventually be out of danger, there had been no guarantee
he would ever be well enough to lead a normal life.
That he was back in the army, working as a physical
training instructor on a base in the north, was almost
a miracle in itself. It was a testament to modern medicine and to his sheer stubbornness. Harry just did
not know the meaning of the words 'give up'.

Edith began to push the bike along again. She loved his stubbornness — it was a part of who he was. She must take care not to be stubborn herself, though. If the moment was near when she had to stop working then she must recognise that and do something about it. She had to concentrate on the most important thing: keeping her baby safe.

With a shake of her head, she put on her brave face and gave a smile. A patient was waiting, and they wouldn't want to see a miserable nurse. It was an elderly woman with a case of pneumonia. Her husband, equally elderly, was trying to look after her, but he had little idea of what to do around the house. Edith began to list what she would do to help: he must learn how to store food, especially milk, to avoid it going off or becoming contaminated. Small tips like this could make all the difference. It was her duty to care not only for her patient but also the other members of the household, and this old man was in dire need of her practical advice.

Edith vowed she would do her very best for these last few visits; and then she would go to speak to Fiona.

* * *

Gladys cursed under her breath as she caught her foot on the edge of the big rug at the back of the common room. No matter how she tried she could never remember exactly where it was, and now that part of the room was so much darker, it was even worse. She couldn't justify turning on the light or wasting a candle, but when it came to clearing up this end of the place she struggled to see what she was doing.

'Are you all right?'

Gladys looked up. The cups and saucers she had been carrying must have knocked against each other and made a noise when she'd tripped. 'No damage done!' she made herself call out, although she couldn't yet see who it was that had asked.

Ruby stepped in front of the side windows, which had not been damaged by the recent explosion. Early spring sunlight streamed through and glinted on her sharp features.

'Oh, Ruby, it's you.' Gladys came over and set down her tray of crockery on the counter by the service room entrance. 'I'm glad, I didn't want anyone telling me off for being so clumsy. There would've been such a to-do if I'd broken all this lot. I don't know how we'd have replaced them.'

Ruby chuckled. 'I bet someone down the market would have known a way. Those stallholders have all sorts of tricks.'

Gladys grinned back. 'I wish they could find a way of replacing these boards with new glass. Makes me proper down in the dumps, being in half-darkness like this.'

Ruby shrugged. 'I bet Fiona's on to it somehow.' She had great faith in the superintendent's abilities to magic something out of nothing.

'New glass this size might be beyond even Fiona,' Gladys sighed. 'Then again, if anyone can find some, she can.' She took her rag cloth from her pocket and automatically began to dust the nearest picture frame; she didn't like to be idle for one moment. 'So how are you settling in, Ruby? It's been, what, almost two months now.'

'That's right,' said Ruby, impressed that Gladys had noticed. 'It's funny — it's flown by, and yet sometimes I think I've been here for ages.'

'That must be a good sign, that you're at home here,' Gladys suggested. 'Even if you've got the smallest room.'

'Oh, I don't mind that,' Ruby said at once. 'I'm not in there much, after all. And a bed's a bed; as long as it's comfy then I can sleep anywhere. My room at home was tiny.'

Gladys nodded in recognition. Her own home was cramped and crowded with all her siblings. 'I know what you mean. But do you miss your home? Your family?'

Ruby pursed her lips. 'Here, let me help you with that,' she offered, taking a pile of saucers from the tray so that it would be less heavy and carrying them through to the kitchen. Gladys followed her.

'Just set them down by the draining board — thank you, that made it easier.' She looked at the nurse, still waiting for an answer, and realising that it wasn't simple.

Ruby turned away slightly, her face thoughtful. 'I do miss them at times, of course I do,' she said slowly, 'but it's much better to be here and get a chance to spread my wings a bit. That's the trouble when you're the youngest — everyone thinks they know what's best for you, no matter what you want for yourself.'

'I wouldn't know,' Gladys replied honestly. 'I'm the eldest and I've spent my whole life looking after the others. It's only now that some of them can muck in that I don't have to spend every waking minute wondering what they're up to. The sister next to me in age has gone away with the Land Army, but the one after that, Shirley, is a big help now. She's a better cook than I ever was for a start.'

137

'I'm sure that's not true.' Ruby knew that Gladys was responsible for some of the ingenious meals that fed them all.

'Anyway, it means I can do more nights on the first-aid post,' Gladys said happily. 'I know some of you nurses think that's a bit of a busman's holiday, but I love it. There's one thing to be said for bringing up your brothers and sisters — you can't be squeamish. They were always falling over, getting cuts and bruises, doing damage to themselves or each other. So I don't mind a drop of blood or whatever. Some of our recruits go all funny, but I've never minded.'

Ruby laughed. 'Well, I never had to clean up anyone when I was young but I don't mind either. To tell you the truth, when I began training I didn't know what I was in for, but it turned out I was all right. Not like some of them — one girl fainted clean away the first time she saw an open wound on a ward rather than in a textbook.'

Gladys tutted. 'No, she wouldn't have lasted long at the first-aid post, then. We get all sorts, and of course we're the first people on hand. We take them in, clean them up, patch them up as good as we can. It's the best thing I've ever done.' She beamed in contentment. 'Does that sound odd?'

Ruby shook her head. 'Not a bit. I feel exactly the same. I was nervous when I was first on the district on my own, but I'm getting used to it. Sometimes I'm not sure I'm doing things right but then it helps to come back here and talk about it with those who've been doing it for longer. I couldn't have done that at home. My mum would worry that I'd make a mistake and my sister would use it as an excuse to try to make me give up.'

Gladys finished unloading the tray of crockery. 'You mustn't — give up nursing, I mean. You can't let them persuade you. Do you see them often? They're in London too, aren't they?'

Ruby followed Gladys back into the bright area of the canteen. 'Not as often as they'd like,' she admitted.

'I thought I'd be going back every day off or meeting them halfway, and that now I'm away from them they'd begin to see that I knew what I was doing. But it didn't turn out like that.' She shrugged. 'So I go down the market with Edith instead, or she's introduced me to some of her friends.'

Gladys nodded in approval. 'That sounds like a good idea. You don't get much time off — you don't want to be dragging yourself across town only to feel miserable.' She gave a swift smile. 'So you've got to know Mattie and that gang who all went to school together? They're nice, they are.' She began to dust the frames again.

'Yes, there were several of them last time — we went to a café down near Victoria Park. There was Mattie, cos her mum had the children, and Kath, and a shorter girl called Peggy and a tall one with red hair called Clarrie — they work in the gas mask factory.'

Gladys nodded even more vigorously. 'I know them. You won't be miserable if they're around. It's good to have friends who aren't nurses sometimes.' She gave that little smile again.

Ruby picked up on it. 'And who are your friends who aren't nurses, Gladys? Do you even have time for friends, what with working here, seeing to your brothers and sisters and then evenings at the first-aid post?' She grinned back. 'What aren't you telling me?

Is there someone special?'

Gladys blushed a bit but didn't shy away from the question. 'It's not secret.' She hesitated but then ploughed ahead. 'Yes, I've got a young man. He's one of their friends and he's ever so nice. He works down the docks with Kath's husband — you know, Billy the ARP warden. His name is Ron and he asked me out at the carol concert just before Christmas.' Now she'd started, Gladys couldn't stop. She hardly ever talked about Ron and that was partly because so many of the nurses had known him before she did. Ruby was new to the area and so Gladys could describe just how wonderful he was.

'He's been ever so brave — you know what it was like when the docks kept being bombed. He can't leave, he's got to take care of his mum and his auntie. His big brother got shot down in the Battle of Britain and ended up losing his sight. So Ron's got to take care of everyone — he's a bit like me, that's how we get along so well.'

Gladys was almost breathless by the time she'd finished speaking.

Ruby was impressed. 'You're very lucky,' she said seriously. 'I never had no luck with boys. My big brother's so much older than me that none of his friends were interested, just thought I was a pesky little sister. Most of them weren't no good anyway. Then in the hospital all the doctors had their choice of the nurses and I never got a chance. I'm too plain.'

'Don't you go doing yourself down,' Gladys scolded. 'There's nothing wrong with the way you look. I'm no oil painting meself, but that's just how it is. You got lovely dark eyes, for example. Look at my lanky locks, you should count your blessings. You just need to have a bit of confidence. Now you're here and away from your family you can grow up some more, decide how you want your life to go. Sorry if that sounds too grand and serious.'

Ruby swallowed hard. She barely knew Gladys, and yet the young woman had summed up how she felt. Perhaps not all big sisters were interfering busybodies. 'Yes, you're right,' she said quietly.

Gladys halted her dusting and a broad smile creased her face. 'I just had an idea. Ron's best friend could come out with us. You might like him. He works down the docks too, so he's been through it like the rest of us. He could do with some cheering up; it turned out his last girlfriend was married all along and then she gave him the push. He don't deserve such harsh treatment.'

Ruby looked dubious. She wasn't sure she fancied mopping up a stranger's heartbreak. 'Maybe . . .'

Gladys clapped her hand to her mouth. 'Look at me, I always say too much and the wrong thing. Never you mind. We'll see. If a group of us goes out to the pictures, perhaps you can come too and then we'll see how things turn out.'

Ruby could see that Gladys wasn't going to abandon this idea now that she had aired it, but still wasn't certain. On the other hand, she'd moved away to have a few adventures. 'Perhaps,' she said.

15

Gwen pushed open the door to the superintendent's office, only to find Fiona was on the newly installed telephone. For ages they had managed with just the one in the ground-floor hallway, but since the last round of bombing — what people were beginning to call the Baby Blitz — it had been decided that they merited a second. Fiona was delighted as she had been lobbying for one for a long time.

'Then yes, we'll make sure one of our nurses is available,' she was saying now. 'Let me double-check the address. Number sixty-two, you said? Very well. You may depend upon it.' She set the handset back in its cradle. 'Ah, Gwen. Yes, of course, you're here to look at the rotas.'

For one brief moment, Fiona seemed to sag as she sat down behind the big wooden desk. Gwen was taken aback; she so rarely saw her senior display anything other than tremendous energy. Still, even Fiona must feel tired sometimes.

'All right?' she asked quietly.

Fiona gave herself a shake and straightened her shoulders, resuming her usual purposeful posture. 'Yes, quite all right. Thank you.' Her eyes met her friend's with a wry expression. 'That is to say, one too many late nights reviewing papers from too many committees. Then staying up even later to catch up on the news in The Times. Did you know the Vatican has been bombed? While at home there's so much going on and, whatever happens, we're all going to have to be prepared. Yet again.'

'A big push?' Gwen ventured.

'They're saying nothing officially, of course. But I'd say something major is brewing. Just you wait; we'll start to hear about some of the forces getting extra leave. It'll be embarkation leave in all but name.'

'Do you know when?' Gwen pressed.

'They aren't saying. We'll have to watch and wait, as usual.' Fiona sighed. 'Anyway, that telephone call. It was a last-minute request for one of our nurses to attend an operation in the patient's home. I really wonder if the poor child should be in hospital for the procedure, but of course there are so few beds — what with all the injuries from the last set of raids combined with the last hurrah of the flu season.' She gave a deep sigh.

Gwen could see Fiona was in need of encouragement. 'They are all trained to maintain hospital conditions of hygiene within a domestic situation,' she pointed out. 'I take it the doctor will provide an anaesthetist? What manner of operation are we talking about?'

'A tonsillectomy, for tomorrow. On a boy of nine.' Fiona skim-read her notes from the conversation. 'They wanted to do it tonight but it's too late, so it will be first thing in the morning. Yes, an anaesthetist will attend. It's as good as we are likely to get, to be honest. We'll have to find the most suitable nurse.'

Gwen sat down, frowning in thought. 'Surely it should be the one who has best knowledge of the family already? She will have established a bond of trust.'

Fiona folded her hands together on top of her notes. 'Ah, well, usually that would be the case. Alice Lake knows the mother well and has had dealings with all of the children on . . . ' she looked down at the top page ' . . . three previous occasions. However, Alice is on leave for a few days from tomorrow to visit her parents. So we shall just have to find somebody else.'

'Yes, I gathered her mother might be unwell.' Gwen pursed her lips. 'I do hope she won't be away for too long. We all benefit from her steadiness and sensible approach.'

'Now don't you go saying that some of the younger ones aren't capable,' Fiona said, cutting off Gwen's favourite subject of complaint before she could get started. 'Let's look at who else we have.'

'Very well.' Gwen looked up at the ceiling as she listed the names. 'I'd prefer Ellen and Bridget to be discounted; they both have the extra midwifery training and ideally need to stay away from such procedures to prevent cross-infection. Mary is booked to give a talk to a WVS group and I'd rather she didn't miss it. Belinda has finally managed to persuade that poor lady with the suspected cancer to attend a special clinic with her — let's not jeopardise that. There's Edith — '

'Who, as if you haven't spotted it already, is rapidly approaching the point where she'll no longer be able to work,' Fiona interrupted. 'I don't want to be brutal, but if she doesn't say something very soon then I shall.'

'Well, that's our most experienced nurses all accounted for.' Gwen looked cross. 'If only Primrose hadn't left to get married. What a waste of her training! And she was so proficient.'

Fiona raised her eyebrows. 'Nothing to be done about it, Gwen. I was as surprised as you but it was her choice. So that leaves us with the less experienced

144

members of the team.'

Gwen shuffled in her hard chair. 'I suppose so.'

Fiona tapped her fingertips on the notepaper. 'I've had an idea,' she said, and some of her familiar energy seemed to come back. 'Yes! We'll kill two birds with one stone. It cannot have escaped your notice that one of our latest recruits, young Ruby, is a little lacking in confidence. Yet I hear excellent reports of her work. This could be just the thing for her. Bring her out of herself by setting her a challenge. Dr Patcham will be there, she won't be able to do any damage if she does funk it; if she gets it right then she'll have every reason to feel pleased with herself, and we will be in the happy position of knowing we have yet another nurse who can cope with the surgical side of the job. Excellent! Will you ask her or shall I?'

'Goodness me,' Gwen said with a smile at her friend's recovery. 'It's not so much asking as telling, isn't it?'

Fiona beamed. 'No, no. I always like to give them the choice. I'll simply word it in such a way that she can't really say no.'

★ ★ ★

What had she agreed to? Ruby had scarcely slept a wink since the astonishing news yesterday evening that she, of all people, had been selected to assist at an operation this morning. She'd been in theatres in the big West London training hospital, of course, but the very idea that she would be responsible for preparing a room in somebody's house to the same standard of cleanliness was almost unbearably daunting.

Still, there was no getting out of it now. Here she

145

was, in the patient's home, speedily making it ready while attempting to appear calm. She'd managed to encourage the mother to take her other children across the road to stay with their auntie until it was time for them to go to school; the little sister's curiosity was more hindrance than help, and the mother was on the verge of tears.

At least this house had a copper in the back kitchen for heating hot water. Ruby's first task was to boil some towels to sterilise them, and then put them in the oven to dry while she readied the parlour, where the surgery was to take place. She lit the fire in the grate, so that the patient would be warm enough. She scrubbed the floor. The father had removed the armchairs last night before the family went to bed, and had brought in the dining table. It was the biggest available flat surface, and it was where the little boy would undergo the operation. Ruby dragged it across to the window, where it would get the most light. Ideally there should be another small table at the head of the big one, but there was nothing suitable available and so they would have to make do.

Ruby fetched a hard kitchen chair and covered it in clean paper, then set out the various implements that the doctor might need. She had sterilised two basins by swabbing them with meths and setting them on fire at the edge of the hearth. Good job the little sister wasn't around to poke her nose into that.

She counted off items on her list. Cover the floor under the dining table with newspaper, to catch the splashes. Buckets under the table for used swabs and instruments. Then the tricky business of folding the big sheet of mackintosh cloth — kept in the district room cupboard for moments like this — into a

146

funnel shape. That would go from the table into another bucket, so no discharge would come into contact with household or surgical items.

She looked up and caught sight of the little sister in the window of the house opposite. Sighing, Ruby realised that gave the child a ringside seat. She couldn't draw the curtains — they had been removed already. However, the nursing handbook had the answer: whiten the window with starch water to prevent anyone peering in. It was an extra duty but might save anxious moments later on. She hurried to do it while there was still time.

Dr Patcham arrived and pronounced himself satisfied. 'You may bring in the patient, nurse,' he said, not noticeably worried about the somewhat cramped setting. Ruby supposed he had done this many times before. 'And, by the way, ignore any comments from my colleague.' He nodded towards the hallway, where the anaesthetist could be heard taking off his coat. 'Bark's worse than his bite. Knows his job but has all the subtlety of a mallet when it comes to conversation.'

Ruby gasped at this remark; in her experience, all doctors stuck together. But there was no time to dwell on it; she had a small child to reassure and prepare for what could well be a terrifying and painful ordeal. Placing her operating overalls in readiness for when the operation proper began, along with the cap for her hair, she took a deep breath and began to climb the stairs.

There was a moment when Ruby had been nearly overcome with panic, thinking she couldn't cope. It wasn't the patient — bless him, little Roy had been immensely brave. In fact, just before he'd been lifted onto the makeshift operating table, he had confided to her that he didn't care what they did as long as his throat didn't hurt any more. He'd allowed himself to be knocked out, Ruby holding his hand and encouraging him to count backwards, even though the anaesthetist glared at her all the while.

It wasn't the blood either. Ruby hadn't been lying when she'd told Gladys that she didn't mind it. For some reason the sight of it had little effect on her, and she also didn't mind the smell, which caught out some nurses who were unprepared for its rich metallic tang. She was pleased that she had remembered all the right implements and ordered them in such a way that Dr Patcham wasn't left waiting for anything.

No, it was that miserable anaesthetist. Ruby supposed it wasn't a very nice job, putting people to sleep and watching while they were operated on, making adjustments and keeping a careful eye on the patient. You didn't get to know them before and after like a nurse or family doctor did. There would be none of that sense of reward when somebody thanked you, or you bumped into them out shopping and fully recovered. It was moments like those when you remembered why you became a nurse.

This man had a gaunt, lined face, such that Ruby found it hard to guess his age. Dr Patcham had more lines, but his were so very clearly from laughing or creasing his forehead with wry humour. She knew he was well into his sixties, if not more. This other man could have been anywhere from forty to sixty, and seemed to have spent most of his time sucking on lemons. Disapproval radiated off him like the heat from the fire.

Dr Patcham ignored it and carried on, carefully

148

removing the infected tonsils, occasionally asking for an implement or towel, checking his work at every stage, moving so that the daylight was at its best as the weak sun changed its position in the sky. Finally he pronounced himself satisfied, and took the last clean towel. He stood back to admire his own stitches. 'Bet you can't darn as neatly as this, nurse,' he said cheerfully, his eyes twinkling.

Ruby realised she had been holding her breath as he'd finished sewing up the last part of the wound. 'No, I don't think I can,' she said honestly. She could sense her knees going weak with relief but her job wasn't over yet. She would have to clear away all the used instruments and make sure the dirty swabs and rags were burnt, and stay with the patient while he came round. There was always the risk of bleeding after an operation, and patients often vomited after being anaesthetised, so she would have her work cut out.

The other man glared at them for daring to contaminate the scene with a small joke. It was evident that he could not wait to leave, and strode out of the parlour just as soon as he could. Dr Patcham was in no such rush and he put a hand out to Ruby's arm as she made to collect the enamel basins.

'You mustn't think too badly of him,' he sighed. 'At least he was reasonably polite today.'

Ruby raised her eyebrows. That was polite?

'He lost a child, you see. Not so very different in age to this one.' Dr Patcham turned to Roy, now beginning to stir a little, making a soft snuffle. 'Let's check the bed is ready if he comes round sooner rather than later — of course it is, you're very efficient, nurse . . . Well, yes,' he went on, 'it was near the beginning of the war — the war proper, not the phoney war — but when the bombs began to drop in earnest. He and his wife did the right thing, took the offer of evacuation — and then a German aircraft got lost and dumped its bombs on the return flight, right over a little village in Suffolk.' He sighed. 'Just one small tragedy in among all the others. My colleague has never been the same. He's only thirty-seven, would you believe it? Anyway, do forgive me rattling on. I know his demeanour can be off-putting.'

Ruby added some more instruments to the basins ready for cleaning. 'No, not at all,' she said, somewhat embarrassed.

Dr Patcham gave a wide smile. 'That's the spirit. You didn't let him distract you and that's important. You may be very pleased with your conduct this morning, nurse.'

Ruby stopped her tidying. 'Really? I only did what I've been trained to.'

The old doctor nodded. 'Yes, and you remembered it all and carried out everything calmly and in an orderly and organised manner. I understand you're quite new to working on the district, but believe me when I say you could not have done a better job. I shall inform your superintendent.'

'I . . . I . . . well, thank you.' Ruby could feel her face reddening, and not from the heat of the fire.

'You'll be here again tomorrow, I take it? Yes, good. I shall pop in later myself.' With that Dr Patcham bade her goodbye.

Blimey, Ruby thought, once Roy was tucked up into a makeshift bed on three chairs pushed together in the corner of the room, wrapped in blankets. As she bundled up the bloodied newspapers ready for

150

burning, and then scrubbed the starch from the window to restore it to its previous state, she sensed something shift inside her. She had handled a difficult situation and won praise from the doctor. No matter how shaky she'd felt, she'd appeared calm and kept her young patient cheerful and safe. Perhaps she wasn't going to fail. Never mind what those everpresent voices of her sister and mother said in her mind. She had succeeded. She was good at her job.

★ ★ ★

By the time Ruby returned to Victory Walk, news of the successful operation had beaten her to it. Fiona bustled down the stairs to greet her. 'Congratulations, Ruby. You did sterling work.' She paused on the bottom step but was still noticeably shorter than the young nurse. 'And the wee boy, how was he when you left him?'

Ruby set down her Gladstone bag. 'He was doing very nicely. His mother was quite tearful and so his auntie stepped in, heating up some beef tea for when he was ready to take it, getting the other children out of the way. He felt sick but wasn't, in the end.'

'Good, good.' Fiona nodded. 'I'm delighted you did so well — not that we expected anything other, mind you. It was lucky the auntie was there to help out — the benefit of a close family.'

Ruby smiled but couldn't help thinking of her own sister and how unlikely it would be that she would step in under similar circumstances.

'Ah, here's Edith,' Fiona went on. The other nurse appeared on the stairs from the first floor, descending in that new way she had of moving now that her bump was much more obvious. 'Edith's got some news that will affect you, isn't that the case, Nurse Banham?'

Edith grinned as she moved past Fiona and into the hallway. 'Well done, Ruby. Sounds as if you did everything you could possibly do this morning. Now here's your deserved reward.' She held out a little key.

Ruby looked at it in bafflement.

'It's to the cupboard in my room,' Edith explained.

Ruby was none the wiser. 'Why would I want a key to your cupboard?' she asked, frowning.

'It won't be my cupboard any more, it'll be yours,' Edith said.

Ruby shook her head. 'But there's no space in my little room — '

Fiona stepped in. 'What Edith means to say,' she said, rolling her eyes, 'is that it's not going to be your room any more. The time has come for Nurse Banham to hang up her cloak, at least for the foreseeable future. So she'll be moving out — which means you take her room on the top floor.'

Ruby had known that this was the plan but had secretly doubted the day would ever come. 'Are you sure? I don't mind — '

'No, no, it's best for all concerned,' said Fiona firmly. 'Edith's baby has to take priority now. Luckily you, Ruby, have just proved that you are able to step into her shoes with the most demanding cases. You will definitely need a proper room. You can't write up complicated notes and reports in that cramped broom cupboard, which was only ever temporary.'

Edith nodded. 'I'll pack my things tomorrow, and take them over to Jeeves Street. They've been expecting me for ages. Brendan said he'd pile them all on his delivery cart so I don't have to carry as much as a box.'

'Won't you mind?' Ruby asked carefully.

Edith shrugged. 'I'll miss the nursing, of course I will. Seeing all the patients, working out what's best for them, never knowing what you're going to find behind each front door. But then,' she spread her hands wide, 'I've been waiting to have a baby ever since I got married. Besides, only I can be a mother to this baby. But now we know that you can take my place here. The nurse who can cope with everything.'

153

16

'Try not to worry.'

Alice gazed into her father's face, registering yet again how much more lined it had become since their trip to Stratford. That felt like a lifetime ago. 'I'll do my best,' she choked.

Richard Lake smiled at his only child. 'She'll be better now that we're clear it isn't cancer. It's only that she couldn't shake off the flu. Well, you know all this.'

Alice nodded. She'd arrived back in Liverpool to find her mother much thinner and coughing constantly, her usually strong voice reduced to a feeble croak. No wonder her writing had been shaky. Her hands trembled and she had not left the house for the entire course of the visit. Yet both her parents insisted that she was on the mend. Alice was ashamed to admit that she was glad she hadn't seen her mother at her worst in that case. Heaven knew what that must have been like.

She thought she had adjusted to the idea that their roles were now reversed, and she was in a position of looking after them rather than the other way around. This brought it home in a completely new way though. Her mother wasn't just a little older, she was ill. Alice had wanted to see the doctor at the hospital who'd examined her for possible cancer, but Esther Lake had been dead set against it. 'You won't be able to do anything,' she'd insisted. 'He won't tell you anything that he hasn't said to me already. It's the aftermath of a bad case of flu, that's all.'

Alice could only hope that she was right. She tried to be rational. She herself had nursed umpteen cases this winter, and not everyone recovered quickly. Older people were likely to take longer. But this was different — it was her mother. She felt that she should be able to put things right, to make her better, or else what was the point of all her training? And yet she knew it didn't work like that.

Now she stood at the end of the platform at Lime Street Station, ready to catch the train down to London once more. She had said farewell to her mother back at their home with its faded, familiar furniture and the old rose wallpaper in the hallway. Esther Lake had apologised for not coming to the station but Alice had been horrified at the very idea. Even though it was March it was a cold morning, and she could never have forgiven herself if her mother took a chill. The older woman had conceded that her daughter was probably right.

'You'd best get back now,' Alice said to her father. 'We'll be boarding any minute.' Even though she wanted to cling on to these last moments with him, she knew it was more important that he looked after his wife.

He smiled at her. 'Don't want me to get caught in the last-minute stampede, you mean?' She laughed, trying to keep the mood light. 'All right, you don't want me waving you off. Some say it's bad luck, don't they? Still, you take this.' He reached into his coat's inner pocket and drew out a five-pound note. 'No, don't say anything. I know you earn your wage, but have this just in case you can manage a little treat.'

Alice felt her eyes welling up. 'That's more than a

little treat.'

'You deserve it.' Her father put his hands on her shoulders. 'Now off you go. I'll be off too.'

Alice would have hugged him but her father wasn't one for shows of public affection. So she kissed him quickly on his cold cheek and watched him as he moved across the concourse to the exit, more slowly than she remembered him doing. However, he still had his upright posture and calm bearing. She must not worry. It wouldn't help.

Then came the announcement that her train would be delayed.

Alice shut her eyes in frustration. It was hardly unexpected, and her journey up had been more than three hours late, but she had been hanging on to the idea that soon she would be on a warm train heading back. She shook herself and picked up her grip. She'd only brought a few things with her so at least she didn't have to worry about heavy luggage. She would see if there was a cup of tea to be had anywhere.

The crowds on the concourse had swelled with the arrival of a train from Crewe. Men and women in the uniforms of all the services, khaki, navy and grey-blue, flowed across the open space towards the exit. Alice decided to wait for them to disperse, dodging out of the way of a young army corporal whose duffle bag was so overstuffed he was struggling to carry it. She edged towards a side wall where she could wait without the risk of being pushed over.

Some of the recently arrived passengers were civilians — or perhaps, like her, they were in mufti for travelling. She rubbed her hands together in the gloves her mother had insisted on giving her — gorgeous ones from her own wardrobe, in fine dark green leather. They would be all but unobtainable in the shops now. It was such a thoughtful gift, typical of the woman, always alert to what others needed, even if she was too sick to care for herself.

Now the press of people was starting to thin out, and Alice turned once more to pick up her grip. As she did so she caught a flash of movement in the corner of her eye. Some deep memory in her brain must have registered that this was a figure well known to her, in among so many others. She nearly did not glance across to check but when she followed her instinct she wished she had not. There was no mistaking who it was. Older now, of course, but still distinctly him. Mark. The doctor who had broken her heart.

★ ★ ★

Moments seemed to pass, and Alice was glad that she was standing against the wall or she might have fallen. Her legs had turned to jelly. Why did he have to be here, of all places — and yet she knew that his parents still lived in Liverpool, and so he was just as likely to be up here visiting as she was. If she stayed right where she was, he would not notice her. He would be making his way towards the exit like everybody else.

As luck would have it, he stepped aside to make way for a young woman with a toddler tugging on each arm, and looked up, his gaze aimed straight at her. He came to an abrupt halt and the Wren behind almost collided with him. Swiftly he turned to apologise and then returned his gaze to Alice. Pointless to pretend she hadn't seen him. There was no escape. He was coming over, his weekend bag swinging at his side. He wore a heavy overcoat in grey wool and a warm-looking deep blue scarf wound around his neck, but his head was bare. She couldn't help noticing his hair, although still the same mid-brown, was receding slightly on each side. A few more years and he would have a widow's peak. Unconsciously she straightened up, ready to face whatever came next.

'Hello, Alice.' He came to a stop just in front of her. He set down his bag and paused. 'Fancy seeing you here. Have you been to see your family?'

She couldn't believe the nerve of the man — talking as if they were casual acquaintances. She fought to keep the welter of emotions from her voice.

'Yes, my mother wasn't well. She's on the mend now.'

'I'm glad to hear it.'

This was ridiculous. She couldn't think of anything polite to say that wouldn't give away what she was feeling — anger, confusion, bitter resentment.

He seemed to realise that such a bland conversation would not do. 'Look, do you have a minute? I mean, I can see you're waiting for a train, but maybe we could have a quick cup of tea? It's been a long time . . . '

'Six years,' she said at once. 'Are you sure you don't have to be somewhere urgently?' She knew she sounded sharp, but honestly. The cheek of it.

'No, I've . . . ' Uncertainty was creeping in. 'I'm on the way to my parents', but I'll find a taxi — they won't mind when I get there. There's a tea shop around the corner; let me take your bag.'

For a brief moment, despite herself, she was tempted. Then common sense returned.

'I'd better not. My train's delayed but they haven't said for how long.'

'Typical.' He tried to get her to join in his flash of

humour, but she wasn't inclined to play along. Why should she make it easy for him after all he had done to her? He had let her down in the worst possible way, making her believe they had a future together.

'Ah, right. Yes, I do see.' He looked down at his feet and then met her gaze. His eyes were the same: bright and intelligent and wry. How she had loved those eyes.

'How have you been?' he asked. 'I come back quite often but I've never seen you here until now.'

She shook her head. 'I can't get away from my work unless it's urgent. I've hardly been home since I left.'

'And how do you find it when you do come back? It's taken a pasting, hasn't it?'

She dipped her head in acknowledgement. 'It certainly has. When I picture it, when I'm away, it's the same as it was when I lived here. Then when I get here, it's like a shock all over again. The ruined shops — like Blacklers, where I used to go so often. The cathedral. St Luke's. All those landmarks.'

'I know what you mean.' His voice was warm and, like it or not, she could feel the old familiar response deep inside her. Damn it, she didn't want to make this easy for him.

'And you're based on the south coast, aren't you — at the same base as Dermot.' She tried to keep her tone clipped and neutral.

He nodded. 'Yes, you're right. He said he'd seen you, of course. Working in the East End. You must have been at the heart of the bombings a few years ago.'

Alice shuddered at the memory. 'Yes, we saw a fair amount of damage,' she said carefully, not wanting to give him any cause to express sympathy. Besides, words could not describe what had happened to Dalston and its surrounds during the Blitz. 'As you must have too.'

He gave a slight smile. 'Well, yes. You could say that.'

She knew that was a huge understatement, just as hers had been. 'But you're all right — you've emerged unscathed.'

'Just about.' He looked at her, his gaze unwavering. The noise from the concourse seemed further away as he spoke again. 'And so have you, Alice. You know, you haven't changed a bit.'

She pushed a stray lock of hair behind her ear. 'Don't be silly,' she said swiftly, 'I'm six years older and look what's happened in that time. I don't fool myself that I haven't changed.'

'Not to me, Alice.' He seemed to be about to say something more and then stopped. 'That's to say . . . if things had been different . . . no, that's not right, but you're as wonderful as you always were . . . '

She stared at him.

'Sorry, that's coming out all wrong. I didn't mean to put you on the spot like that.' He drew a breath. 'There's so much to say, Alice, and we've never had the chance before.'

'You could have written,' she said mildly. 'Dermot's had my address all this time.'

'I know, I know. But it didn't feel right. Not with what I wanted to say. Anyway, you might have refused to read my letters — you might have ripped them up and thrown them on the fire. I wouldn't have blamed you.'

She narrowed her eyes, knowing that she might have done just that.

'Are you sure you won't come for just one cup of tea, Alice?'

Now she really was tempted, even though every sensible bone in her body cried out against the idea.

He could sense her wavering, as he bent to pick up her grip, which still lay by her feet in their well-polished but well-worn black winter boots.

The moment was broken by the station guard she had spoken to earlier, who called out to her as he hastened past, puffing slightly: 'You're for London, aren't you?'

She nodded as he told her, 'One's just about to leave, change of platform. Hurry, that's it over there. You'll make it if you run.'

'I'd better go,' Alice said at once.

'I'll help.' Before she could stop him, Mark had grasped her bag in the same hand as his own and slipped his other arm through hers, rushing her expertly through the other passengers and speeding her to the opposite platform, where the new train was filling up, everyone buzzing as they were caught out by the suddenness of the change of plans.

She couldn't help it, the warmth of him at close quarters, the sensation of his breath on her face as he drew her into his side, the words he'd just said — and even more what he hadn't said — made her head spin. This couldn't be happening.

'All aboard,' called the guard, a couple of carriages away.

Mark pulled open the heavy door to the nearest carriage, but put his hand on her arm as she went to step in. 'Write to me,' he said, his voice full of intensity, as far from that casual conversation as it could possibly be. 'If you write I won't destroy your letters,

161

I promise. It's the same address as for Dermot.'

'I . . .'

Before she could demur, he had grasped her hand in its leather glove, the heat passing through the supple fabric. She could not bring herself to take her hand away. 'I never forgot you, you know. I've thought about you ever since I left. I know I made a mistake. Forgive me, Alice.'

'All aboard!' The guard was at her carriage now. 'Up you go, miss. Stand back, sir, train's about to depart.'

Mark had no choice but to obey as Alice swung her bag up and in, the guard slamming the door behind her. 'I don't know,' she said through the open window. 'It's been so long, Mark, and I don't know if I can . . .'

The whistle drowned out the rest of her words. Mark was looking up at her, in an agony of hope and despair. All his worldly air of calm possession had vanished, and he was the man she remembered all too achingly well: passionate, determined, with all his attention fixed solely upon her. She held on to the window frame, rooted to the spot by the power of his attention, the force of his plea.

As they pulled away from the platform, she could hear him calling to her: 'Write to me.' Then the noise of the train increased and rose over all other sounds, obliterating the words. They rounded the corner out of Lime Street and the station receded, leaving only the views over the devastated city they had both called home for those precious, passionate years. In her head she could still hear him: 'Write to me.'

★ ★ ★

Lily hugged herself in delight. Before her on her bedside table lay another of those notes on impressively heavy paper, written in that confident, commanding hand. Donald wanted to meet her again and this time he promised their evening would not be cut short. He apologised a thousand times for the abrupt finish to their cocktails. He hinted that this coming assignation could go on a very long time, should Lily wish it to.

She knew what that meant. She wasn't born yesterday. No, she was sophisticated. He wanted more from her than conversation; those last moments before they'd had to part had made that very clear. Did she want the same? She wasn't sure.

What she did want was to mix in the circles of those people she had seen in the Magpie Club. The women who wore the height of fashion without a care in the world, the men whose suits had been cut with little regard to clothes rationing. Sometimes she hated the very word 'Utility'. It was so restricting. She wanted clothes like theirs, and their jewellery, and their outlook on life. It was within her reach, she could just feel it. She touched the bouncing edge of her bright blonde hair, knowing how it made her stand out. She could hold her own with those people, given a chance to practise.

A noise along the corridor outside brought her back to earth. It was late; she'd finished her evening meal over an hour ago. Most of the nurses were getting ready for bed, preparing for the next morning's rounds. She had thought everyone on this floor had already retired. Lily got to her feet, and tucked the precious sheet of paper under her pillow. Then she went to the door and opened it, unsure of what she might see.

163

Ruby was struggling to move a big box along the wooden floor, the rag runner having been moved aside.

'Hello,' she said softly. 'Did I disturb you? I'm trying to be as quiet as possible but this one is too heavy to lift and so I'm having to kick it along.'

'Kick it along? Why, what are you doing?' Lily had rarely seen Ruby up on this floor, let alone kicking a box down the corridor.

'Didn't you hear?' Ruby asked. 'Edith's moved out to live with the Banhams until her baby is born. That means I can move into her room.' She pointed to the box. 'I didn't realise I had so many things. I had hardly anything when I first arrived, but I must have picked up more than I thought. All those trips to the market, I suppose.'

'Oh, I see.' Of course Lily remembered that this had been the plan all the time, that Ruby was only in the makeshift downstairs room until a proper space became available. It had meant over two months of cramped accommodation for her. Had things worked out otherwise, it might have been Lily herself who'd had to endure it. She shuddered. Guilt prompted her to be helpful.

'What can I do?' she offered. 'Shall I fetch anything else?'

Ruby grinned at her words. 'That's really nice of you. I'm almost finished, though. Do you want to come in and see what the room's like? I've moved things around a bit.'

Lily's curiosity made her accept immediately. She loved seeing how the other nurses ordered their near-identical rooms. She was always on the alert to learn something, pick up any tips on how she could

164

improve her quarters, even though she doubted if Ruby had much to suggest in that department.

'Go on, then.' She went over and bent to pick up one side of the big box. Together they manoeuvred it into the room formerly occupied by Edith.

Ruby had had no time to unpack properly and clothes were piled on the bed, a much smaller heap than Lily's would have made. Lily glanced around. No photos. She didn't have any either — she didn't want her past getting in the way of her journey to a successful future. She wondered if Ruby felt the same or if the other nurse simply didn't have any photographs. After all, they were never cheap.

'Don't you have any pictures of your family?' she asked.

Ruby pulled a face. 'I've got one of us all somewhere. It'll be in my bag, I expect. I didn't unpack it before as I knew I'd be moving again after a while, and I'd already wrapped it up in newspaper so it wouldn't break.' She fished around in a big cotton shopping bag. 'This is it.' She cautiously undid layers of old paper, keeping them to one side for future use — nobody wasted newspaper any more.

'That's us,' she said, passing the dark wooden frame to Lily. 'Luckily the glass didn't break.'

Lily stared in fascination at the black-and-white photograph in her hand. There was Ruby, hair very neat, in Sunday best, smiling shyly for the camera. In front of her sat a thin, older woman with a care.worn face, also trying her best to smile, the similarity in their sharp features suggesting it was Ruby's mother. To her side was another woman with a smugly self-important expression, clasping the arm of a nondescript man in army uniform whose expression showed

165

he'd rather be anywhere else. At the back stood a tall young man, his hands resting on the older woman's shoulders. He stared confidently into the camera, almost in challenge. He too wore a uniform.

Ruby pointed at him. 'That's my brother Colin. We had this done just before he joined up. People used to say we look alike.'

Lily nodded dutifully, although she couldn't really see it. She thought he looked like trouble personified, nothing like his shy sister. 'Who are the other people?'

Ruby came around to her side. 'That's my sister Beryl and her husband Terry, when he was home on leave. Beryl and Colin are twins.'

Lily regarded them. 'They aren't very alike,' she observed.

Ruby shrugged. 'They are sometimes. They both get this same look on their face when they want to tell me off. That's our mother in the front. Me dad died ages ago.'

'Oh, I'm sorry,' Lily said automatically. She peered at the picture closely. 'Your brother and sister must be quite a bit older than you — is that right?'

Ruby took the frame and put it on top of the cupboard by the window, with its blackout blind firmly down. 'Yes, there's a ten-year gap between us. Mum used to say she was so worn out with the twins that she couldn't stand the thought of any more kids for ages after that.'

Lily nodded — Ruby recited this as a piece of unquestioned lore. It made her wonder though. Of course there were all sorts of reasons why there might be such a long gap between children. Perhaps her husband worked away from home much of the time. Maybe she was sick. Or she just didn't fall pregnant.

Or, and this was something nobody ever talked about, she might have taken steps to ensure she didn't have another baby until she was ready.

As a nurse, Lily had sometimes been asked about this by women who were desperate to avoid another pregnancy, and she had always found it difficult to respond. In her training hospital such things were deeply disapproved of; some of her matrons had been very religious and forbade the merest mention of the topic. All the same, she knew as well as the next nurse that there were times of the month when you were more likely to conceive, and if you were lucky enough to be regular then it was a matter of counting. Not that she ever intended to rely on such methods.

She also knew that some men would routinely carry something they'd wear to prevent them being caught out by unexpected and unwanted fatherhood. When she'd been in the habit of going to the dance halls, would-be suitors would whisper that they had something with them so she needn't worry — as if she would find that so enticing she would give in to them at once. Not on your nelly. But it was a question that had lodged in her mind for when the time came, all the same.

'. . . your family much?' Ruby was asking. Lily shook herself.

'Sorry, I didn't catch that,' she said lamely. Ruby didn't seem to mind.

'I asked if you missed your family much?'

Lily gave a little laugh. 'Oh no, not really. There's so much to do here, isn't there? We're busy every minute of the day. I don't have time to miss them much.' In truth, she rarely gave them a second thought.

Ruby began to hang up her clothes, carefully

shaking out the creases before threading them onto hangers. 'I've had this frock since before the war began,' she said cheerfully, and Lily bit back her first thought which was that yes, it showed. 'Not that I get much chance to wear frocks these days, not really. You always have lovely clothes, Lily. Do you go out much, from here I mean?' She turned to take more hangers from the rail.

Lily was so excited at the idea of seeing Donald again that she decided she could be friendly and confide in the other nurse. There was no need to keep the whole thing a secret — and that might make it seem sordid. There was nothing underhand about it. 'Well, I've been out with a very lovely man a couple of times,' she said, hoping it sounded casual, as if she was asked to do this regularly and she just happened to have selected him as the lucky candidate.

'Oooh, you dark horse!' Ruby was instantly intrigued. 'How did you meet him? What's he like?'

Lily was pleased with this reaction, and so she told Ruby the full story, or at least the best bits. She left out that strange little man in the rather cheap coat who'd put paid to their enjoyment the last time at the cocktail club. She concentrated instead on how handsome Donald was, what excellent taste he had.

Ruby was impressed with the description of what he looked like, demanding more details, but less so about his worldly behaviour. 'He sounds a bit stuck up to me,' she said frankly. 'Colin had a friend a bit like that, thought he was better than everybody. Drove us all mad, he did. Nothing was good enough for him. We stopped asking him round in the end.'

Lily was affronted. 'Oh no, you've got it all wrong. Donald's not a bit like that. He takes people as they

168

are.' Although it struck her as she said this that she didn't really know if it was true.

Ruby sensed that she had put her foot in it. 'That's all right then.' She gave Lily a quizzical glance. 'Even so, don't you want someone a bit more like you?'

Lily frowned. 'What do you mean? Are you saying I'm not worthy of someone like that? I'll have you know I could have my pick of men. I'm not short of offers. Donald and me are exactly suited, that's what he said to me last time we went out.' Which wasn't so far from the truth, she assured herself.

Ruby took a step back in the face of her friend's touchiness. 'Good, I'm glad,' she said shortly.

Lily inwardly berated herself. She shouldn't be cross with Ruby. The shy nurse probably had no experience with men. She wouldn't know how these things worked. Just because a girl came from a different background, it didn't mean she couldn't aim high and improve herself, if she tried hard enough. This wouldn't have occurred to Ruby. The likes of Donald would never ask her out. 'Donald likes me for who I am,' she reassured her. 'He's not trying to make a fool of me, or take advantage, or anything like that. I can spot that sort of thing a mile off.'

Ruby nodded dubiously. 'If you say so.' She lifted the last of her clothes from the bed, tucking them into a drawer as the little wardrobe had run out of hangers. 'There, that's all done. I'll be able to find everything in the morning now. Thanks for helping, Lily.' She gave a small yawn and tried to cover it.

Lily recognised that it was time to go. 'It's getting late. I'd better be off — get some beauty sleep.' She flashed her eyes and Ruby had to laugh.

'Thanks again,' she said, opening the door to the

corridor and then shutting it behind Lily as she departed.

Well, thought Ruby as she sat on the bed, tired from her exertions. She'd just been talked down to, if she wasn't much mistaken. Trust Lily to put on all these airs about her fancy man. Personally, she didn't like the sound of him much. In fact, she would go as far as to say she wouldn't trust him one bit. Perhaps she had got it all wrong and Lily was simply getting carried away with the thrill of being courted, the early throes of romance. Ruby wrinkled her nose. Somehow she didn't think so. When you grew up around a brother like Colin, with his gang of friends, you learnt how to spot them. She'd bet a week's wages on this Donald being anything but what Lily took him for.

170

17

Many hours later than she'd intended, Alice got off the bus in Dalston and turned onto the side street that would take her back to Victory Walk. The train had already been late departing from Liverpool's Lime Street, and the journey had grown steadily worse. They'd all had to change at Crewe, onto a train crowded with soldiers coming south from Scotland. Then that had pulled abruptly into a siding, where it stayed for many hours, before eventually resuming its slow progress southwards in the dark of the night.

Alice had stood for much of the way, managing to sit on her bag in a corner of the corridor in an attempt to grab some rest. She had scarcely cared. Her brain had been far too agitated to allow proper sleep, or even to fully register the discomfort of the trip. The shock of seeing Mark would have been bad enough, coming as it did on top of the worry about her mother. Then for him to come out with that extraordinary farewell — she did not know what to make of it.

Alice had spent the past few weeks putting Lily's offhand conversation to the back of her mind. Now it seemed as though that was the tip of the iceberg. He'd said he'd made a mistake. He wanted to start again, that was what he must have meant. Her head ached, trying to comprehend the idea.

For so long this had been all she'd wanted. Then she had taken her future into her own hands, left Liverpool and her position in the big hospital, and moved to London to train as a district nurse. She'd made a success of it too, with no help from Mark whatsoever. She'd come to believe that his betrayal was actually the best thing that could have happened to her.

But that had been before she'd known he'd changed his mind. Her head swirled around and around. Did he mean it? Well, he would have had too much pride to say something like that unless he was deadly serious. The expression on his face as he'd stood on the platform was genuine, no doubt about it. He couldn't have changed that much in six years.

What might it mean for her if she allowed him back into her life? Alice knew that she had changed too in the intervening years. She was no longer the young nurse just starting adulthood that she'd been when they had first met. True, she'd never been one for wild escapades; she'd been steady and responsible, way before beginning her training. Yet she'd thrown herself into the joy of being with him. She had loved every moment of their growing closeness, the unbridled happiness of knowing she loved him and he loved her in return. She was the envy of many of her fellow nurses, and life had seemed to open up, its prospects boundless.

When Mark had told her it was over, not to wait for him as he didn't know if he would be returning from Spain, at first she had been too stunned even to cry. It had felt like a very bad dream. How could someone so constant, so passionate about her, so loving, have switched course and turned away? The shock of it was worse than losing a limb. Then the pain had begun and she had thought she would never recover. Her heart had been ripped out, the agony unbearable.

Yet, she had recovered. She'd done more than recover. She had built a new life for herself. Moreover, it wasn't boastful to acknowledge she was good at what she did. More than good — she was one of the best, and it gave her deep satisfaction. She had always told herself that a condition of this was to do it alone, not to risk being derailed a second time. Nursing was simply more important.

Was that true, though? Other nurses had boy-friends, fiancés, even husbands. They managed to balance commitment to their work and to a personal life. She didn't know if she could do so too. So much of her energy and emotion went into her work; it was all-consuming. But maybe it did not have to be like that.

She had to talk to Edie. Edie was the only person who would understand. She'd been her closest friend and only true confidante, the one person who'd seen the depths of her agony. Edie had managed to find that balance between her devotion to her work and her deep love for Harry. She hadn't felt she was divid-ing herself into two to do it.

Despite her exhaustion, Alice almost ran the final few steps to the nurses' home, up to the shiny navy door. It was early; she might be in time for breakfast. The door was already unlocked, no doubt by Gla-dys. Alice turned the polished handle. She'd find Edie right away.

'Good morning!' Fiona was in the hallway, a stack of files in her arms. 'Welcome back, Alice. We assumed your train was delayed. My dear, you look tired. Have some breakfast and then catch up on your sleep. I presumed you wouldn't have much of that on an over-night journey, and so you don't have to work until the evening rounds.'

Alice could hardly take in what she was saying, but

remembered her manners. This was a very kind offer. 'Thank you, yes,' she said, 'it was a bit of a marathon.' She set down her grip. 'I'll be all right after a rest. Is Edie up yet, do you know? Is she in the canteen?'

'Ah.' A concerned expression flickered across Fiona's face. 'Of course, that was the morning you left . . .'

'What's happened?' Alice was instantly alarmed. 'She's all right, isn't she?'

'Yes, yes, all's well,' Fiona said quickly. 'It's just that you've been away a little longer than you first thought, and that's all fine, you needed to see your mother. The big news here is, Edith's decided it was time to stop work now she's six months into her pregnancy, and so she's gone to live with the Banhams, as planned.'

Alice stood perfectly still. 'With the Banhams,' she repeated like an automaton.

'Well, yes. As she always intended to do. Are you quite sure you are all right, my dear? You've gone white as a sheet. She's perfectly well; she just found riding that bike too hard.'

Alice nodded dumbly. Edie wasn't here. She would have to wait to speak to her. She was too tired to think straight but she'd been absolutely counting on having this conversation now, before she exploded with the effort of holding in all the conflicting emotions. It wouldn't be possible. Edie was over at Jeeves Street.

'I have to see her,' Alice burst out. 'I need to speak to her right away.'

Fiona looked surprised but did not pry. 'Why don't you have some breakfast and take some time to freshen up,' she suggested, 'and then you can pop over to see her. Give her time to get up, in case she's enjoying her first few days without morning rounds.'

She smiled broadly. 'Whatever it is, it's bound to feel better after a cup of tea and some porridge, now isn't it? You're tired, my dear, don't feel you have to dash off. It won't do you any good in the long run.'

Alice swayed a little, knowing the supervisor was right, as usual. 'Yes, I'll do that,' she said faintly.

'Oh, and before I forget. Post came for you.' Fiona turned and picked up an envelope bearing Alice's name from the shelf behind her. 'Now I must be about my business. These forms wait for no man.' She smiled kindly as she hurried up the stairs towards her office, leaving Alice staring at the handwriting.

Joe.

She sank onto the lowest step of the stairs, her hand trembling. Suddenly she was filled with longing, for his steadiness, his calmness, his sheer understanding. He had never deceived her, let her believe one thing while planning to leave. He was utterly reliable, a rock, even though he was far away. How she wished he was here now.

Slowly she rose, gripping hard on the newel post. She could not be seen here close to collapse. She'd have to say it was because of the difficult journey if anybody asked. She couldn't tell anyone here the real nature of her trouble.

Picking up her travel bag, she forced herself to mount the stairs, up to the first floor and then to the attic level. Pure homing instinct propelled her through her bedroom door, and she sank down once again, this time on her own bed.

Now she could no longer pretend she was thinking straight. Mark, back after all this time, wanting them to resume where they'd left off — but how could she trust him after what he'd done? Joe, writing to her

175

from who-knew-where: a total contrast, but only ever her friend. Yet she knew the connection ran deeper than that. Mark; Joe. The two faces swam before her eyes, bringing tears to them. You're tired, she told herself severely. Stop this. It will get you nowhere.

Aching all over now, she struggled out of her coat and pulled off the fine dark green gloves, then took off the black winter boots. That used up the last of her energy and she curled up on the bed, still holding the unopened letter. Mark; Joe. Her last thought before dropping into an exhausted sleep was that she had to see Edie. She felt as if her very life depended on it.

★ ★ ★

Several hours and a long nap later, Alice was feeling more like her old self. She washed her hands and face, brushed her hair and left it loose for once, and then put on a change of clothes. That in itself felt like a big improvement.

Then, the letter from Joe in her pocket, she set off on the short walk to Jeeves Street. Even if she hadn't needed to see Edith so badly, she would have gone to see the Banhams to check that they too had had a similar letter with its news: Joe hoped to have a short spell of leave soon. Normally Alice would have looked forward to that with no hesitation, but now it had suddenly all become more complicated. She frowned, and decided not to think about that until later, when she could get Edie on her own.

A letter had clearly arrived at the house on Jeeves Street as well, as everyone was agog with the news when she arrived. Flo's happiness showed in the way she moved around the welcoming warm kitchen, as

176

sprightly as she had been before the war. 'Did you fill the kettle, Mattie? Never mind, I'll do it.' She hastened to make tea before anything else.

Edith smiled and then immediately apologised. 'I meant to wait for you to come back, but then events took their own course,' she confessed. 'I couldn't ride that blasted bike for one more day, and Fiona knew it. So here I am. A lady of leisure.' She was sitting in the comfy old chair, her feet resting on the fireguard.

'Don't listen to her,' said Mattie, moving a pile of laundry dried and ready for ironing. 'Sit yourself down, Alice. Edie's been running round like a mad thing ever since she got here.'

Edith shrugged. 'Well, I like to help out when I can. Especially while I can still reach around the bump.'

Flo set the filled teapot on the table. 'So, now, Alice, you'll know about Joe, won't you.' She poured out four cups. 'The thing I can't work out is where he is now. Have you any idea?'

'You know he can't say, Ma,' Mattie pointed out. 'He'll be in trouble with the censors if he does.'

Flo tutted. 'I know that as well as you. Hasn't he put in one of his book clues like he normally does?' Her raised face was full of hope.

Alice shook her head. 'No, for once there's nothing like that and I don't know any more than you.'

'That's odd.' Flo's face clouded a little. 'Do you think we should be worried? Is that a bad sign?'

Alice wished she knew the answer to that one, but kept her voice optimistic. 'I shouldn't think so.' She began to think out loud. 'It is unusual, though. Perhaps it means he's between bases, or ships, or something like that. We wondered if he was heading to Italy but we never knew that for certain. Though from what

177

we can piece together, things are going our way over there at the moment. Maybe he's on his way back before going somewhere else.'

'Well, if you can't work it out then I don't know who can,' Flo sighed. 'With any luck we'll hear it from the horse's mouth soon enough. I'll have to start baking his favourite things to eat. I'm sure they don't feed them properly in the navy.'

'He won't have had anything like your cakes and biscuits, that's for sure,' Edith said loyally.

'I'm so sorry we don't have anything to offer you right now,' Flo said. 'We ate the last of the flapjacks yesterday and I haven't got the ingredients for any more yet.'

Edith looked up. 'That reminds me, I must sort out my ration book. I should register at the shops near here, now I don't have to give most of my allowance to the cook at Victory Walk. I'll do that today.'

Alice spied her opportunity. 'I'll come with you if you like. It'd do me good to stretch my legs after that train journey.'

Flo looked at her and seemed to catch her under-lying urgency. 'You can make sure she doesn't overdo it,' she suggested. 'But finish your tea first.'

'Spit it out, then,' Edith said, the second the heavy front door had closed. 'I can see something's up. What happened in Liverpool?'

Alice tucked her hand through her friend's arm and started to tell her. Once she had begun she found she couldn't stop, and it all came pouring out in a rush. 'So you see, I don't know what to think,' she said, coming to a halt on the corner near the main road.

Edith looked up at her taller friend, the spring sun-shine making her dark blonde hair almost silver.

178

'Blimey,' she said forcefully. 'Didn't see that one coming, did we?'

'Not at all,' said Alice, immediately comforted by the 'we'. She wasn't in this alone. Edith would help her. 'Even with what Lily said, I didn't imagine this. What should I do, Edie?'

Edith began to walk slowly along the pavement, staring down at its cracked flagstones. 'I can't tell you that,' she said seriously. 'Only you know what's in the depths of your own heart.'

Alice nodded. 'I think I'm still in shock. I can't see clearly. I'm all of a muddle.'

'No wonder,' Edith said grimly. 'For him to come out with something like that, after all this time!'

'He can't expect me to change everything just because he's had second thoughts.'

'I should think not!' Edith said hotly.

'I can't and I won't. He's got no right to think it,' Alice declared. 'But then, to be fair, that isn't what he said. I'm making assumptions. He only asked me to write to him, not alter my life to suit him.'

They were approaching the grocer's shop, its window zigzagged with sturdy tape to protect the goods from bomb-blast damage. 'Let's walk on past and then turn back,' Edith suggested. Then she looked her straight in the eye. 'The other thing, Alice, is what about Joe?'

'Well, like I said, I don't know where he is any more than Flo does — '

'That's not what I meant,' Edith interrupted. 'Obviously I'm concerned as I couldn't ask for a better brother-in-law, but it's more a matter of you two when you're together. I know you always tell me you're only friends, and it's no good saying if only circumstances were different and "what if" and all that sort of thing. It's just, it's plain to see how close you are. He's going to be home soon with any luck. Are you going to say anything to him?'

Alice shook her head, feeling a blush on her neck and face. 'I don't think so. Or maybe yes, perhaps. Edie, I just don't know.'

Edith glanced up at her friend. 'It's too much to decide yet, isn't it? Come on, I'd better go into one of these shops — I should register at this butcher's and then we'll go back to the grocer's. You've got to give yourself time to work out how you feel, that's what I reckon anyway.'

'You're right.' Alice shoved her hands into her coat pockets. 'It's too big a decision to rush into. I'll have to sit tight until things settle into place. But Edie, the thing that nags at me over and over is that I don't know if I can ever trust him again. Mark, I mean. He let me down so badly and I don't know if he has any idea of quite how awful it was. He was off having adventures in Spain while I was left high and dry. It's all very well for him to say he's made a mistake. I don't think he knows the half of it.' Alice nodded sadly and said once more, almost to herself: 'I don't know if I can trust him.'

18

'What are you doing, Gladys?' Ruby asked, poking her head around the door of the district room. It was Friday evening and she was surprised that the other young woman was still here. 'Why haven't you gone home yet?'

'Tidying this place up a bit,' Gladys replied. 'And then I'm going out directly from here. My mother can sort out the rest of them for once. I made a nice lamb stew for them all earlier; all she has to do is heat it up and dish it out.'

Ruby looked more closely at what Gladys was up to. 'Is that a broom handle?' she asked.

Gladys nodded. 'That's right. It's how you keep these pieces of mackintosh from sticking together — you got to roll them around something and a broom handle is easiest. Can't have them ripping in two when you nurses want to use them when you're treating a patient, can we?'

Ruby instantly remembered the little boy having his tonsils taken out. She'd had to use the mackintosh sheeting then. He'd made a good recovery, so after next week she wouldn't have to see him any more. He was back to chasing around the house with his little sister, wearing his mother's nerves thinner with each passing day.

'Where are you going this evening?' she asked, starting to replace the items she'd used from today's cases as she spoke: castor oil, Vaseline, surgical spirit.

'I'm going to the pictures with Ron,' Gladys said

with a big grin. 'Gert and Daisy are on up at Clapton. Want to come?'

'Oh, no.' Ruby tucked her new supplies tidily into her Gladstone bag. 'I don't want to be a gooseberry.'

'You won't be,' Gladys assured her, stowing the rolled mackintosh back in its cupboard. 'Me sister is going to be there and Belinda said she might come along too. And remember I told you about Ron's friend Kenny? He'll be there as well if he ends his shift in time.'

Ruby looked dubious. She wasn't at all sure if she wanted to be set up like this. At least it sounded as if it was a big group of friends, not just a couple with add-ons. Moreover, she did like Gert and Daisy — the comic characters always made her laugh. After such a busy week she could do with that; not all the patients were recovering as fast as little Roy.

'Well, all right,' she said, suddenly filled with the urge to do something different for once. 'Yes, why not?'

Gladys automatically straightened the boxes of Dettol as she passed them. 'Really? You'll come? You won't regret it,' she predicted. 'We might even go for a half of shandy and a bit of a sing-song after. I mean, you don't have to, but just to warn you. Ron always says it does you good to let your hair down a bit at the end of the week. I tell you straight, I'm looking for-ward to it. I done three nights in a row at the first-aid station and a change of scene is just the ticket.'

Ruby nodded. Even Gladys, who she knew to be dedicated to her duty, felt like this sometimes. Per-haps it would be a good evening. She had to try, or she might as well have stayed at home with Beryl and her mother.

'I'll go and get changed,' she said, refastening her bag. 'How long have I got?'

Gladys pulled a face as she tried to recall the details. 'It starts at seven o'clock, that's the newsreels,' she said. 'See you down here in the hall at six thirty? Then we can walk up there together and meet the others in the foyer. It's not too cold out, the walk will do us good. Bit of fresh air and all that.'

Ruby smiled. 'I'll go and get my glad rags on. Well, what pass for glad rags.'

'It don't matter what you wear, you'll still have a good time,' Gladys said cheerfully. 'I don't have no fancy clothes, but Ron says he likes me the way I am. Good job, cos that's what he's getting.'

Ruby laughed as she left Gladys to finish her work. She ran up the stairs, smiling: an unexpected night out! All at once she felt the weight of responsibility lift from her shoulders. She'd done what she could for her patients — and now she deserved to enjoy herself. Things were falling into place. She liked Gladys and also Belinda, from what she knew of her. Despite her mother's doubts, people did like her. She was making friends.

★ ★ ★

Lily hugged herself in anticipation. Finally, Donald had made good on his promise and was taking her out properly — no interruptions allowed. She'd taken even more care with her appearance, brushing her gorgeous hair till it shone like pale metal, blotting her special dark red lipstick and slightly rouging her cheeks to emphasise their natural rosiness. She'd debated long and hard what to wear, but really didn't

183

have anything as smart as the little black dress. She'd have to hope that the different accessories would make it seem new and stylish. Donald seemed the sort of man who would notice.

She'd bumped into Ruby on her way out, and the other nurse had seemed excited. She too was going out — but only to the pictures in Clapton with Gladys and her friends. Really, the two evenings could not be compared. Lily had tried to be enthusiastic and wished her colleague a good time, but hoped her condescension hadn't been too obvious. From Ruby's face, she might have got that wrong. Never mind, that was the least of her concerns.

Donald was to meet her in Piccadilly. Lily had had to check where this was, but it turned out not to be too far from where they'd gone before. She liked the centre of town — it had an infectious energy to it, war or no war. People were dressed up. Some men wore dinner jackets, and women had elegant coats with fur collars and plenty of jewellery. Lily hoped her best necklace would not look too tawdry. It had seemed the height of fashion when she'd put it on earlier, but now she thought perhaps it was a little too obvious — big and shiny, clearly not genuine stones but glass substitutes. She would have to save up for something truly classy if she was going to make a success of herself in Donald's world.

She could see him now, waiting on the corner opposite the Royal Academy. For a moment she hung back, to savour the sight of him. He was in a different overcoat, this one darker, but cut to the same fine shape, emphasising his height and broad shoulders. She shivered a little at the thought of those strong arms around her. His hair had been slicked back just a

184

touch, not thick and glossy with Brylcreem like some of the younger men who'd tried to capture her interest in the past. His shoes were buffed and far from the clomping boots that many of her patients wore. She let out a small sigh. She could look at him all day.

Donald turned in her direction and caught sight of her, bringing a wide smile to his face. She stepped quickly towards him, clutching her good leather handbag to her side, the one she'd triumphantly snagged in a John Lewis sale years ago, before their building in Liverpool was bombed. It would do for any occasion, the assistant had assured her, and Lily hoped this was right.

'You look ravishing,' Donald breathed, placing both hands on her shoulders and gazing appreciatively at her figure belted tightly into the maroon coat. 'Shall we?' He offered her his arm and once again he drew her tight in against him and she clung happily to the luxurious fabric of his sleeve. People cast envious glances at them as she was led along the wide pavements, recognising how good-looking they were and what a well-matched couple they made. She gave some of them a swift smile, not too much or it would look immodest.

Donald turned down a well-proportioned street a short way, to the pillared porch and wide steps of a hotel. 'I thought we could have another try at drinking cocktails here, and then their restaurant is pretty good,' he said. 'Would that suit you?'

Lily nodded eagerly. 'It looks perfect.' She felt a warm glow spreading through her. This was even more upmarket than the club. She would bet that the strange man in the nasty coat wouldn't get through the doors here. Given the reception the doorman gave her, she herself was entirely respectable, though. She was on her way, she could sense it.

Donald led her into a small but beautifully appointed bar, and Lily almost gasped. There was no sign of the slightly shabby, make-do appearance of even the nicest places she'd seen so far. It was as if the war was happening somewhere completely different and had not touched these blessed walls. Pictures of classic scenes in gilt frames were everywhere: landscapes, solid-looking buildings, groups that reminded her of the paintings she'd had to pretend to admire when dragged around the municipal gallery when she'd been at school. She should have listened more closely.

Never mind, Donald wasn't here to talk about the pictures. He made sure her coat was safely taken, that she was comfortable in a well-padded chair of deep blue velvet, and that a martini was ordered. 'They'll have olives this time,' he assured her, and Lily tried to look enthusiastic at the shiny little berry in her drink when it came. As before, he had whisky, in an even more impressive cut-glass tumbler.

He was most attentive, and conversation flowed as easily as the martini slipping down her throat. Now she knew what to expect it was much better. She decided she enjoyed the taste. Half the delight was that she sipped it while his deep voice asked her questions, gave his opinions on world affairs, speculated what the other people in the bar might be doing. 'That chap over there is a diplomat, I'd put good money on it,' he said, pointing to a grey-faced elderly man in one corner. 'Did you see which newspapers he was glancing at? Not only *The Times* but a French and American one too.'

Lily raised her eyebrows and pretended she knew what he was talking about. She'd never seen a foreign newspaper, let alone read one. Until she moved to Victory Walk she'd never met anybody who read *The Times* either.

'How about that couple over there?' she wondered.

'You tell me.' He brought his face close to hers, his eyes alight with mischief.

Lily gave this some thought. 'They've come up for the weekend from somewhere in the country, but not far away — they don't look as if they've been standing up on a train all day.'

'Very good.' He gave a wicked grin.

She squinted a little to check the details of the woman's jewellery. 'They're married; she's wearing a thick gold ring.'

He laughed. 'Doesn't prove anything. It might be a family heirloom. Or,' and he brought his mouth tantalisingly close to her ear, 'she might well be married but not necessarily to him. Wouldn't you say?'

'Donald!' Lily was a little shocked, but exaggerated her reaction, as she sensed that was what he wanted. 'I thought this was a respectable hotel.'

'Oh, it is.' He set down his tumbler and turned it so that the amber liquid picked up the subtle lighting and sparkled warmly. 'Even so, I wouldn't blame them, would you? We've all got to find ways to console ourselves in wartime.' He smiled again and Lily relaxed. For a moment she thought he'd sounded cynical, but he was being generous.

She knew plenty of people would judge such behaviour harshly, but she didn't want to come across as too prim. 'I'm sure they deserve to have a good time,' she said, as neutrally as she could.

'Live and let live, that's what I say,' Donald declared, raising the whisky to his lips. 'Not that I'm against

187

marriage. Far from it — where would we be without it? It's just that in uncertain times such as these, it's hard to plan for the future.'

Lily nodded. She could understand that sentiment.

Nobody knew what would happen to them from one day to the next. She'd assumed she'd get married one day, but she was in no rush.

'If I married I would most likely have to give up nursing,' she said, ignoring the fact that she knew of several exceptions to that rule. 'I couldn't do that. I care too much about my job.' Which, on some days, was not far from the truth.

'Of course you do.' Donald was instantly earnest. 'That's one of the things I admire about you, Lily. Your dedication to what must be a difficult job. I never get tired of you telling me all about it. You mustn't sacrifice your personal happiness though.' He paused and reached for her hand, giving it the lightest squeeze before releasing it. 'Even nurses are allowed a little fun, I hope — am I right?'

Lily blushed. Donald admired her! He was treating her as a woman of the world, who worked in an important profession and who had a sophisticated outlook on personal matters. 'Oh yes, you're right,' she breathed, looking into the mesmerising depths of his eyes. She felt his hand squeezing hers again as she held his warm and inviting gaze.

★ ★ ★

The daylight had all but faded as Ruby and Gladys set off for the cinema. Belinda had decided not to come as her brother was unexpectedly in town, and she would go to their parents' for the weekend.

188

Gladys was describing the last film she'd seen, something with Tommy Trinder, but Ruby was finding it hard to concentrate. She was a bit annoyed with Lily. That parting comment about having a good evening, while clearly implying she herself wouldn't be seen dead going to the pictures in Clapton — who did she think she was? When it came down to it, she was just a nurse, the same as the rest of them. She had no right to her high and mighty attitude.

'. . . and it made me think, what's my favourite film. What's yours?'

Ruby gave herself a shake and brought her attention back to her companion. 'My favourite film? What, of all time, do you mean?'

Gladys nodded as she strode along the road that ran down the north side of Hackney Downs. The shapes of the trees loomed beyond her. 'Yes, pick any one, whichever you liked best. I reckon mine's *Casablanca*. I didn't see it when it came out cos I was too busy with the little ones but Ron took me just after Christmas. It was lovely. Mind you, I enjoyed it more than he did.'

Ruby giggled. 'I liked that one as well. That Ingrid Bergman, wasn't she lovely? And it was so sad with her and Humphrey Bogart.'

'I liked the music best,' Gladys admitted. Ruby started to hum 'As Time Goes By', and Gladys joined in with the words, singing the whole first verse. Ruby stopped in her tracks.

'Gladys! You can sing! I never knew!'

Gladys shuffled her feet a little. 'I sing a bit now and again,' she said shyly. 'Of course, you weren't here for the carol concert. I did a solo this year. I don't get much chance otherwise, but I enjoy it now and again.'

'No wonder you want to go for a sing-song after the film,' Ruby said, picking up speed again. 'You could go on stage with a voice like that.'

Gladys laughed. 'Not on your life. My sister, the one what's a Land Girl now, gave it a try and all that brought was trouble in spades. I'll stick to me carols, thank you very much.' They rounded the corner onto the Lower Clapton Road and turned towards the cinema near the big junction. 'There they are!' Gladys cried, pointing towards a tall young man with a face almost hidden in a vast woollen scarf, a shorter man wearing glasses, and a young woman who bore a resemblance to Gladys. The man in the scarf waved and then thrust his hand back in his pocket as if embarrassed. 'That's Ron, well, Ronald,' she said happily.

'He seems very nice,' said Ruby, though it was hard to tell. As they got closer she could see he had a kind face and that his eyes really did light up at the sight of Gladys. He looked as if he might kiss her hello, but it seemed he was too nervous in front of everyone. Still, he didn't object when she took his arm.

'This is Ruby,' Gladys said, as she snuggled against Ron's big coat. 'Ruby, here's my sister, Shirley, and this is Kenny.'

Ruby nodded as the introductions were made, and took in Kenny. He seemed pleasant enough — nothing outstanding but nothing terrible either. She laughed to herself. He was a far cry from Humphrey Bogart and she was no Ingrid Bergman, but it didn't matter. She wondered if Gladys had told Ron to ask him along specially, but there was no indication of that. Shirley was chattering away at nineteen to the dozen, and everyone else was listening.

Ron had already bought the tickets and they piled

into the foyer of the Ritz, with its Art Deco twirls of decoration. They made their way up to the circle, and Ruby found herself between Kenny and Gladys. She was quite glad it wasn't a romantic film that they were to see but a comedy. Soon they were joining in the raucous laughter all around and she quite forgot to be shy or worried that she and Kenny had been deliberately set up. It was fun to let go with a crowd of other people, and Kenny didn't try anything on. She was glad; she didn't think that Gladys would bring along someone like that, but you never knew. Her brother Colin's friends always used to boast what they got up to with girls in cinemas, and she wasn't keen to try anything along those lines.

As the house lights came up, she felt altogether friendlier towards her new acquaintances — sharing the laughter had broken the barriers — and she chatted happily to them as they all headed back down the stairs. 'They look like upside-down lighthouses, don't they,' said Kenny, noticing her staring up at the impressive tube-shaped lights above.

Ruby giggled. She thought that sounded funny and clever. 'They do,' she agreed. 'I wouldn't want to have to clean them. They're enormous, and how would you get a ladder up there?'

'Maybe they don't bother. Maybe they wait for Jerry to fly over, then when the bombs drop they blast all the dust off them,' suggested Kenny.

'Ooh, don't say such a thing.' Ruby exaggerated her fear, and he laughed along, teasing her.

'So, are you coming down the Duke's Arms now for a bit of a singalong?' he asked casually.

'Gladys is going to sing, isn't she,' said Ruby, her voice full of admiration for her friend's talent.

'She will, all right. And she lives near the nurses' home so we'll all walk back together,' Kenny said. 'Then you needn't worry.'

Ruby nodded, noticing that he hadn't put her on the spot by offering to walk her back, but he'd made sure she knew she would be safe. That was a very considerate way of putting her at her ease. 'In that case, do you know, I just might,' she said cheerfully. She hadn't had such a good night out for ages.

* * *

Lily suspected she shouldn't have had that second martini, but she was really getting quite fond of them. Now Donald had poured her some wine with her meal, apologising for the restricted menu. 'You should have seen this place before the war,' he sighed.

'It's lovely,' she said sincerely. They'd had a sort of casserole, which was immeasurably better than the stews that Cook and Gladys conjured up at the nurses' home, and then a delicate little sweet dish that she couldn't pronounce but was like custard with meringue in it.

He took her hand once more across the starched white linen tablecloth. 'Not as lovely as you, Lily.'

She giggled, enjoying the flattery. Everything was just a little bit blurred.

'No, I mean it,' he said, gazing at her intently. 'Shall I tell you something?'

'Go on, then.' She wondered what it would be.

'I don't have to work tomorrow.'

'Oh?' It was not surprising; it would be Saturday after all. Then again, he did seem to have to work at odd hours.

192

'No, it will be a day of leisure. How about you?'

Lily shook her head. 'No, I'm not on Saturday rounds this week.' Alice and the two Irish nurses were covering them.

Donald nodded slowly. 'And so you won't be in a rush to get back?' he asked. 'Might you be tempted to stay?'

Lily blinked. 'Stay here? In this hotel?'

He held her hand a little tighter. 'In this hotel. Yes. I took the liberty of reserving a room. It's a very nice room,' he continued persuasively. His thumb stroked her palm.

Lily did her best not to look shocked. That felt sudden. And yet . . . and yet she had known what he might ask. What should she do? What did she want to do?

'Don't let me rush you,' he said, letting go of her hand and moving his seat back a little way from the table. 'You don't have to decide right away. But I should like it very much if you were to stay.' He smiled that special smile again, those laughter lines deepening at the corners of his wonderful warm eyes.

Lily tried to think straight but the cocktails and the wine were muddling her brain. She knew all too well that you weren't meant to do this sort of thing — respectable girls did not stay with handsome men in hotel rooms unless they were married to them. Yet that was an old-fashioned view. They were at war now and people behaved differently. What was it he had said — something about 'if circumstances had been otherwise'. Who knows what he might have asked her then, whether he would have been thinking they could have a future together. He had said she was lovely. Wasn't that almost the same thing?

Lily asked herself what a sophisticated woman from

his circle would do. She'd bet they wouldn't worry about what anyone else would say. A worldly woman would make up her own mind.

She smiled a dreamy smile at him. 'That sounds wonderful,' she said.

★ ★ ★

Ruby hadn't been to many pubs before, but she immediately liked the Duke's Arms. Her mother had always said that no respectable woman would be seen in such a place, but there were plenty of other young women in there and none of them looked shady. Of course her mother had never said as much, but she'd implied that any woman going into a pub must be a prostitute — or as good as one.

However, the women Gladys and Ron waved at looked perfectly normal. 'That's Clarrie and Peggy, they were at school with Billy the ARP warden and the Banhams,' Gladys explained as she took off her serviceable winter jacket. 'They work at the gas-mask factory and like to come here once the week's over — though I bet they'll be doing shifts over the weekend anyway.' 'What would you like to drink?' Ron asked, pulling his wallet from his inner pocket. Ruby looked dubious. 'I don't rightly know. What do you usually have, Gladys?'

Gladys shrugged. 'I like a shandy,' she said, 'but don't worry if you don't like it. They got lemonade, even if it's a bit watered down these days. Peggy used to always have port and lemon, I remember.'

Ruby pulled a face. 'Oh, I don't think I'd like that,' she said. Her mother would sometimes get a bottle of port in for Christmas, and she'd hated the rich smell

194

of it. 'I'll have a shandy then. If I don't like it, you can have it.'

'You'll make me go all tiddly,' Gladys grinned. 'One half is about all I can manage. I still got to come in tomorrow morning and sort out your breakfasts, you know.'

Ron pushed his way through the maze of customers to reach the bar, which was gleaming with polished wood and brass. Gladys led Ruby to a small table in the corner and set about finding enough bar stools. 'Don't you want to sit with your friends from the factory?' asked Ruby, worried that her presence was stopping Gladys from enjoying this second half of the evening.

'No, they're with a big group and I hardly know the others. Besides, we won't hear a word over there closer to the bar, it's so noisy,' Gladys pointed out. 'We'll have some of our shandies and then we'll start up a sing-song. I wish Mary was here, she can play the piano all proper. We'll have to get the barman to do it — he's not bad but he ain't a patch on Mary.'

'Blimey,' said Ruby. 'I didn't know she could do that.'

'Oh yes, she always plays for the concerts,' Gladys said. 'Thank you, Ron, that's lovely.' Ron had returned with a tray of glasses, which he carefully lowered to the little wooden table.

'Where are the rest?' he asked.

'Shirley's gone to powder her nose. I hope you got her lemonade, she ain't strictly old enough for nothing stronger,' Gladys replied. 'Kenny went to say hello to Peggy and Clarrie but he's on his way back over here.'

'There you go, Ken,' Ron said as his friend returned. 'Pull up that stool beside Ruby, and here's your pint.'

Kenny beamed. 'Cheers,' he said, raising his glass and getting froth over his upper lip, as he sank down onto the stool.

Ruby looked across at him and laughed. He didn't seem at all bothered about his beer moustache. She liked that — he seemed an easy-going sort, not like Colin's pushy friends. She sipped her shandy and it wasn't too bad. Gazing around, at the bright lights and groups of friendly people, she felt again that certainty that she had done the right thing in leaving Hammersmith.

Gladys drank a little of her shandy and then stood, nodding to the barman, who caught her glance. He made his way to the piano as she went across to stand beside it. They conferred rapidly and then he played the unmistakable first line of 'As Time Goes By', and Gladys began to sing.

The pub fell quiet and after a few more lines some people began to sing along.

'Want to join in?' Kenny asked.

Ruby shook her head. 'I'm no singer,' she admitted. 'Gladys has a lovely voice, doesn't she?'

Kenny agreed. 'We'll just sit and listen, then,' he said, raising his pint again, and Ruby smiled. She could hardly think of a better way to spend the evening.

★ ★ ★

Lily lay awake, watching the faint play of anti-aircraft lights scraping the sky, muted by the thick fabric of the curtains. She had never been in a hotel room like it — she'd hardly been to any hotels at all, but the very few had been nowhere close to the luxury of this place. Donald must be very well off to be able to afford it. He still hadn't said what he actually did, but it was obviously something important and urgent. It must pay well.

She could see the silhouette of him now, his chest rising and falling as he breathed deeply beside her in the wide bed. Memories of what had just happened gave her a warm glow. He had treated her so well, not rushed her, reassured her, and she had happily fallen into his arms. In truth the memories were a little confused as the effect of all the alcohol was only just beginning to wear off. All the same, she felt loved and cared for and convinced that she had done the right thing.

Even better, Donald accepted her as a woman of the world. He'd brought her here to this gorgeous hotel, this sumptuous room, and treated her like a princess. No expense spared. He was special and she basked in the glory of having him beside her.

He had said she was lovely . . . that was almost the same as love, wasn't it? Lily gave a small sigh. She wasn't sure if she was in love with Donald, or not yet. What she did know was that she loved what being with him brought — the meals, the cocktails, the glamorous people and surroundings. She, Lily Chandler, from a small terraced house near the docks on the Mersey, was here in a luxury hotel. Look how far she had come, and it was all down to her determination. She wondered how far she could go from here. As her eyelids began to close, Lily held on to that feeling of excitement, of the world opening up before her. Best of all, Donald thought she was lovely.

197

19

Alice nodded absent-mindedly to Ruby as she passed her on the top landing. She still hadn't got used to Edith not being there in the room where she'd slept ever since they'd joined the home on Victory Walk. Several times a day she'd catch herself thinking that she'd knock on the door to see what Edie thought of this or that, before stopping herself just in time.

She could do with Edith's advice now, but it would have to wait. Alice couldn't abandon her morning round simply because she had received a letter. It was hardly a matter of life or death, even though it might once have felt like that.

She had turned the idea of writing to Mark round and round in her head but had done nothing about it. Now he had beaten her to it. She didn't have to open the envelope to know who it was from — she could never forget his handwriting, although she had destroyed all the old letters he'd sent her when they were still together. Typical doctor's handwriting, she thought grimly, almost unreadable. It was a scrawl, no doubt done at great speed.

There was one sheet of thin notepaper inside, covered in the same sprawling script. Mark said he would quite understand if she wanted to destroy the letter and wondered if she'd even opened it. If she had got as far as reading it, he just wanted to let her know that he meant what he'd said on the platform at Lime Street Station. It wasn't simply something blurted out in the shock of seeing her again; he had been going over what he would say to her for years, if he happened to bump into her. He had made a mistake. He had never forgiven himself for being so stupid. He hoped she would somehow find it within herself to forgive him and give him the chance to put things right. He had finished by repeating his plea for her to write to him.

That was all very well for him to say, but she was still too hurt by what he had done. His letter did nothing to change that. She resisted the immediate urge to rip it into tiny pieces, but she didn't want to keep it either. In the end she reread it twice, folded it and put it in the waste-paper bin. She did not need to hang on to it to remember what it said.

Now she was running late. She hurried to the bike rack and grabbed her old boneshaker, swinging her Gladstone bag into the basket in the front. First case was an old man who'd gone down with pneumonia, and his recovery was not being helped by his house suffering damage from a bomb blast. The house next door had been so badly affected that the residents had moved out, leaving their party wall exposed and freezing cold. Alice hoped that the man, who was a sweet-natured old fellow if somewhat forgetful, could be persuaded to move in with his daughter. That would be the best treatment he could have, but it was beyond her powers to enforce.

Before she reached her destination she was brought to a halt by a young girl waving. 'Miss! Nurse!'

Alice pulled hard on the brakes and finally they responded. 'Pauline!' She looked at the girl, taller now than when they had first met, but still with the inquisitive expression and lively air. 'How are you? Haven't seen you for ages, not since we did that knitting. You aren't missing school again, are you?'

Pauline shrugged. 'Not really. I'll go later, promise. I got to fetch something for Ma first. She ain't well, not at all.'

Alice frowned. 'What's wrong with her?'

Pauline shrugged again and sighed. 'I don't rightly know, miss. She ain't herself. She's taken to her bed and says she feels hot, so I been tryin' to cool her down but it's no good. She says she ain't hungry but she's gotta have something, so I'm goin' down the market to see if I can find something to tempt her.'

'Perhaps it's a late case of flu,' Alice suggested. 'If she's got a fever she'll need to keep up her fluid intake. That means making sure she drinks enough.'

Pauline nodded. 'I know, miss.'

Alice bit her lip. It was easy to forget that Pauline had grown up a lot since that first encounter. She'd been caring for her little brother for as long as Alice had known her, and the mother had played very little part in the upbringing of either of the children, as far as Alice could tell. 'Have you thought about calling in the doctor?' she asked carefully.

'Oh, miss.' Pauline's voice said it all. 'You know Gran don't hold with doctors if she can possibly avoid them, even after you came and sorted out her legs and all that. Ma's the same. She says they're a waste of time and money.'

'You know we can manage the money side of things,' Alice said hastily. 'Don't you go worrying about that.'

'That's as may be, miss.' Pauline looked down. 'It ain't up to me.'

Alice glanced at her watch. 'Pauline, I have to go, there's a very sick old man waiting for me. But listen, you make sure that you ask the doctor to come and look at your mother if she gets any worse. Never mind what your gran says. Otherwise you'll end up missing school again and you're doing so well. I know because Miss Phipps tells me.'

'Does she, miss?' For a moment Pauline was that eager young girl again, trouble written all over her but intelligence sparking from her face.

'Yes, so promise me you'll do it.' Alice knew she had to get going, and climbed back onto her bike, ready to pedal off.

Pauline sighed, the cares of the world descending on her young shoulders once more. 'I'll do me best, miss. I can't say no more.'

★ ★ ★

Lily had floated on cloud nine through the days since the night she had spent with Donald. She'd barely paid any attention to her colleagues and, although she'd smiled and appeared to be listening to her patients, she would have struggled to describe in detail what any of them had said. Her mind was solely on what a wonderful time she had had and when she might see him again. As usual she had to rely on him contacting her to say when he would be able to take time off from the demands of his work.

It was frustrating not to have the chance to know in advance and plan properly, but it couldn't be helped. Whatever it was that he did, it was obviously hush-hush. Lily had persuaded herself that it was maybe top-secret work for the government. He was exactly the sort of person who would be chosen for such a position.

She'd even thought about refusing when Alice asked

her a favour, as she would sooner have spent the time daydreaming about Donald. Then good sense had asserted itself and she'd realised she had better agree, as it would have looked very bad if she'd flatly said no. Pressure of urgent cases had meant that the senior nurse had not been able to pop in to see someone who wasn't strictly under the care of a doctor but who was cause for worry all the same.

'I'm needed for a patient with suspected peritonitis, but I've got a feeling this woman could do with a visit,' Alice had explained late one afternoon, just when Lily had thought she would be able to call it a day. 'Will you go in my place? It's not far from here. You don't have to stay long but it would put my mind at rest.' Lily had reluctantly picked up her bag once more and headed out into a fine drizzle that soon soaked her outer clothing.

The house had been one of the worst she'd ever seen, and the smell was beyond awful. It brought to mind her old neighbour's dog, only a hundred times worse. The only person there with the slightest ounce of good sense was the daughter, Pauline, a scruffy but sharp girl of about eleven, who was concerned for her mother. 'She's ever so hot,' she fretted. 'She don't like to stay indoors but she ain't moved for ages.'

Lily had rushed through the usual TPR checks, as required of her — 'Never fail to look at temperature, pulse and respiration', as her ferocious first matron had insisted every day of her training — but decided everything was close enough to normal. Well, the temperature was up, and the pulse a little erratic, but she didn't know the patient and it might be a temporary fluctuation. Lily certainly didn't want to get caught up with this household. She decided she'd mention it to Alice the next time she saw her but otherwise there was no urgent need for concern. She'd come out in horrible weather — she'd gone above and beyond, and enough was enough.

Now she swiftly made some weak cocoa — the smallest splash of milk, and no sugar — to tide her over until the evening meal, putting the tin of powder back in the cupboard in the service room. She almost collided with Ruby as she made to return to the common room.

'Hello, stranger,' Ruby grinned, stepping quickly to the side to avoid the sloshing hot drink.

Lily took a breath. Was Ruby making fun of her? 'Hello,' she said cautiously.

'Haven't seen you around much this week,' Ruby went on, pulling open another cupboard door and reaching for a jar. 'You wouldn't think we had rooms on the same floor, would you?' Lily was about to reply when Ruby carried on, not expecting an answer. 'Have you tried this? They said it's made from chicory. Brendan was selling it on his stall, so I thought I'd try it — smells a bit odd but we'll see.'

They were both obviously having a quick pick-me-up after the afternoon rounds, and Lily couldn't very well back away now that Ruby had her cornered. So she waited while her colleague added hot water to the brown powder and stirred it, creating a sharp aroma.

The pair of them carried their drinks into the common room and Lily knew it would be rude not to sit with the other nurse, so she settled in a chair opposite Ruby near the side windows. 'What's it like?' she asked, nodding at the cup.

'Hmmmm.' Ruby tried it and pursed her lips. 'It's

all right, I suppose. It makes a change. It would be much nicer with sugar in it, but there's not much point in getting a taste for that. Do you want to have a go?' She offered Lily the cup.

Lily shook her head. 'No, thanks all the same. I'll stick to what I know.'

Ruby did not take offence. 'Fair enough.' She sipped some more and pushed the cup away. 'How are you, Lily? I don't think I've seen you since Friday evening.'

At the very mention of those magic words, Lily's face lit up. 'Perhaps you're right. Did you have a good time, in the end?'

Ruby also smiled at the memory. 'I did, thank you. Very good. We saw Gert and Daisy in *It's in the Bag*, and it was ever so funny. Then all Gladys's friends were going to the pub, one near here, and so I went with them. Guess what — Gladys can sing. She got everyone joining in. She did "It Had To Be You" and all sorts from the films. She's good, she honestly is.'

'Gladys?' echoed Lily in disbelief. It was hard to imagine the mousy kitchen help standing up in front of everybody, let alone having a decent voice. That was a waste of talent and no mistake. She suppressed a shudder.

'Yes, I know, you wouldn't think it, would you? We had a lovely time,' Ruby went on happily. She toyed with the cup handle. 'What about you?'

Lily had wondered what to say if she was asked. She didn't think it would be a good idea to tell the full story, sure that plenty of the nurses would disapprove of what she had done. They probably all held conventional views and would not understand that she was sophisticated now, and could behave differently. Nevertheless, she was keen to share some of the elements of the evening.

'Donald took me to a beautiful small hotel near Piccadilly,' she said, watching to see if Ruby was impressed by this. 'It was terribly smart. Everyone was all dressed up, you can't imagine. I suppose I was the youngest person there, but nobody stared.' Except Donald, she thought, remembering the intensity of his warm gaze. 'We had the loveliest food, and there was a sort of custard with sugary islands in it — you'd have liked it.'

'I'm sure I would,' agreed Ruby. The lack of sugar was one of the constant frustrations of the wartime diet — they were all suffering from its absence. 'Did you go anywhere else? Dancing or anything like that?' She sat forward eagerly.

'No,' Lily said. She wondered whether Ruby would understand if she explained what they'd done after the meal. Perhaps it was better not to, as Ruby was not sophisticated enough to approve of Lily's decision. 'Just the hotel. It really was perfect, there was no need to go anywhere different,' she added.

Ruby nodded. 'Well, if you get taken to somewhere like that then it's nice to make the most of it.' She stood up. 'It's no good, I can't finish this stuff. I'm going to tip it away and get changed. I might even have five minutes' shut-eye — I've had an afternoon of surgical dressings and I'm beat.'

Lily nodded in sympathy, as she knew how exhausting changing dressing after dressing could be, with the need to maintain strict hygiene at every turn. When you felt that you never had enough equipment with you, even after refilling your bag twice a day. 'See you later, then,' she said.

In fact she was quite relieved that Ruby hadn't

wanted to stay and chat for much longer. She wanted to cherish the memory of that wonderful evening, and was far from sure the other nurse would have appreciated the finer points: the chilled glass for the cocktail, the expensive jewellery on the other women, the soft lighting. Not everybody would enjoy such things, but she herself knew how important they were now. To think that a few weeks ago she didn't even know what a martini was. She was learning fast and loving every minute.

★ ★ ★

Ruby trudged up the stairs and went to the little bathroom at the end of the attic floor, to wash her face and hands. She really was very tired after all those visits. Splashing water over her face made her feel a little better. She looked at her reflection in the mirror, taking in the still-neat dark hair, the pale face, a little thinner after the weeks of relentlessly cycling around the district. Perhaps she didn't look so bad. There was something about her posture now that showed she wasn't quite so cowed by everything. Being accepted by a new group of people buoyed you up.

She couldn't think of much worse than being stuck in some boring little hotel on a Friday night. Even with custard and sugar islands, it simply did not sound like much fun. Perhaps Lily genuinely liked it or, Ruby suspected, she thought it was the sort of thing she ought to like and was trying to persuade herself that she did. How complicated, and what a waste of time.

Ruby would prefer a night out at the Duke's Arms any day. As for Donald, he sounded like a proper stuffed shirt. Lily was welcome to him. Ruby wondered if she might hear from Kenny soon. He'd been the perfect gent as they'd all walked back to Victory Walk. She might be wrong but she thought she'd read something hopeful in his farewell glance, had the sense that he'd enjoyed the night as much as she had. She'd made a new friend — that would do for now. It was certainly a thousand times better than being cooped up in a polite little dining room with someone who didn't want to go dancing. What a terrible way to spend a Friday.

20

'Honestly, that new nurse.' Mary scowled as Alice sat down at the same table to eat her breakfast.

'Which one?' asked Alice, well used to her friend's bad temper in the mornings. She took a first bite of toast.

'Lily,' Mary growled. 'I don't mind that she came to join me, even though I hate having to have conversations with anyone this early — present company excepted,' she added hastily. 'But she wanted to talk about cocktails — at this time of day! Asked me if I liked martinis and what else would I recommend! Really, she has no idea.'

'Hmmmm, not what I like to think about first thing in the morning,' Alice agreed.

'It's enough to turn your stomach,' Mary declared, still finishing off her porridge and scraping the bowl. 'Do you want that second slice?' she asked hopefully.

'I'm not sure yet.' Alice flashed a smile at her friend. 'How's Charles? Haven't heard you mention him for a while.'

Mary's expression changed. 'That's because I hardly see him, even more so than usual. He's terribly busy and can't say with what. Now and again he talks about planning and then clams up. You know how it is.'

'I do,' said Alice, beginning to add a smear of precious marmalade to her other piece of toast. Her mind whirred into action. Charles was involved with the planning of something; Joe couldn't say where he was. There was a connection, she was sure of it. A major event was brewing.

'He'll have more time for me soon, he says,' Mary went on. 'I know I used to think it was all a cover for him having someone else, but now I'm reassured it's simply pressure of work.'

'Of course it is,' Alice said immediately. 'Charles isn't like that, he's completely trustworthy, and he adores you.'

'He does,' said Mary. 'Besides, he wouldn't have time to see anyone else. He's tired enough as it is, poor lamb.'

Alice took a quick sip of tea to hide her reaction to this comment and to curse herself for thinking of untrustworthy men. She was still unsure what to do, but before Mary could quiz her, Gwen came across to their table.

'Alice, good, I'm glad I found you,' she said without preamble. 'I'm afraid you are needed right away.'

Alice immediately set down her cup. 'What is it?' she asked, brushing crumbs from her skirt in preparation for swinging into action.

'You saw the Morley boy two days ago, didn't you?' the deputy superintendent asked.

'Yes, little Albert. He has whooping cough, poor thing.'

Gwen looked sympathetic. 'Yes, that's the one. We've just had a call to say he's taken a turn for the worse and has had a convulsion. His mother is in a terrible state. You're the only one she trusts — will you go at once? Sorry to have interrupted your breakfast,' she added politely, but all three of them knew that was the least important thing.

'Of course.' Alice rose, pushing the slice of toast towards Mary. 'Here, you can have it after all. I'll eat later.'

She followed Gwen from the canteen and Mary made the most of her extra slice. It would be a shame to waste it.

As she rose to leave, Ruby came across with her own tray of breakfast.

'Do sit here, I'll be off in a minute,' she said hastily, indicating the chair that Alice had just vacated, but establishing that she wasn't in the mood for a protracted discussion.

Ruby nodded, her face troubled. She was in no mood to chat either. The confidence she had enjoyed earlier in the week had crumbled in the face of a letter from her mother and her sister. In the blink of an eye she was back to where she began, unsure of herself and convinced everyone would soon find that she was a fraud and no good as a nurse. She knew it was stupid to feel this way after a few familiar but cruel comments from Beryl, but there it was.

'Everything all right?' Mary asked, picking up on the younger nurse's anxiety.

'Yes, thank you,' Ruby said quietly, in no mind to elaborate. She would sound silly if she did. She didn't want Mary to think badly of her. While she didn't admire Mary quite in the way that Lily did, she respected her experience and reputation. Everyone knew that Mary was one of the most reliable members of the Victory Walk team, and she had no desire to come across as stupid.

Mary looked up sharply as Gwen reappeared, a concerned expression on her face. 'What a morning!' she exclaimed. 'It never rains but it pours. Two rather alarming cases in the space of a few minutes. Never mind, you're exactly the sort of person I want for this, Ruby.'

Ruby blinked in surprise. 'Me?' she said blankly.

'Yes, you, Ruby.' Gwen was sounding businesslike now, back to her usual efficient self. 'It can't be helped, but Alice has already been called away to another case, one at the other end of the district, and she'll have to take great care not to transfer the infection to which she will be exposed. I cannot let her go straight to this new case. It would normally be hers as she's well acquainted with several members of the family but there's no time to waste if it's what I suspect.'

'Goodness,' said Ruby faintly. She felt bombarded by this news. It sounded serious and as if it required a nurse who could be fast and decisive. The way she was this morning, she had no idea if she could cope. What she really wanted to do was to crawl back into bed and pretend none of it had happened.

'What is it?' Mary asked.

'The doctor has been called in, most unusually, by a child in the family rather than an adult,' Gwen explained. 'Apparently the mother has been ill for some days and has taken to her bed, totally out of character. She wouldn't allow the doctor to be called but she's apparently deteriorated further and her young daughter took matters into her own hands. The report is of fever and incoherence. Ruby, you'll have to keep your wits about you.'

Ruby felt as if her wits had deserted her, just when they were most needed.

'Are you sure it's me you need?' she managed to stutter out.

Gwen nodded vigorously. 'Absolutely certain of it. Look how well you performed under pressure at that tonsillectomy. You managed a difficult surgical matter and you won the trust of a potentially problematic

211

family. You are discreet and that is important. I don't want to bias your opinion when you actually attend the patient, but please bear in mind that discretion might well be necessary.'

Mary looked askance. 'This sounds like a riddle,' she remarked.

'No, no, it might be a simple case of fever. It's not for me to say. I merely caution you, Ruby, to be on your mettle and observe every detail. Of course you would anyway. I have faith in you, complete faith.' She smiled meaningfully and Ruby felt herself respond to the senior nurse's words.

'Really?' she gasped.

Gwen maintained her smile, not revealing her surprise at the young nurse's diffidence.

'Totally. We have all observed how you have adapted to and coped with the many surprises working on the district can bring. You don't fall apart when there is a crisis. You have kept a calm head when plenty would not have managed to do so — including some with far more experience than yourself. That is precisely what might be needed in this new case. Do finish your breakfast, but then come to my office and I'll let you have the address.'

Mary nodded as well. 'You'll be just what this woman needs, Ruby,' she assured her.

Ruby took a deep breath. Damn her sister and her thoughtless remarks. Now that a little time had passed she could see how she'd fallen straight back into her old pattern, believing what Beryl said rather than trusting in her own abilities. Now here was the deputy and one of the most experienced nurses telling her that they had faith in her. More than that — she was the only one here who could do the job. Her skills were needed. There was no real choice.

'Of course,' she said.

★ ★ ★

The young girl was waiting outside the squalid-looking small terraced house, kicking her feet against the whitened kerbstones. As Ruby got closer she could see her face was pinched with anxiety. The medical notes had listed Pauline as being eleven years of age, but she appeared both younger and then much older at the same time. Younger, as she was not tall for her age and did not have a spare inch of flesh on her, but older too, as her eyes gave away that she had witnessed far more than most eleven year olds, her shoulders drooping with the weight of responsibility.

She looked up at the sound of the bike's brakes. 'Where's Nurse Lake?' she demanded. 'We always have Nurse Lake.'

Ruby took a deep breath. That was a fine welcome. 'Nurse Lake was called out first thing this morning,' she explained. 'I'm Nurse Butler. We work together, so I'll be able to help you just as well.'

Pauline's suspicions were not allayed. 'We had another one of you lot come and she weren't no good,' she said bluntly. 'She weren't in here five minutes. I don't want nobody what don't know what they're about. Besides, I ain't seen you before,' she went on. 'I came to your home and everything. Several times, with Nurse Lake. You wasn't there.'

Ruby propped up her bike alongside the front door and lifted her Gladstone bag from the front basket. 'Well, I'm there now,' she said, determined not to waste time. 'I wouldn't have known to come here

213

otherwise, now would I?'

Pauline nodded reluctantly, unable to argue with that. 'You better come in, then. Ma's downstairs.' She pushed open the front door.

Ruby had been warned about the likely state of the house, which was just as well, as it was on a par with the worst that she had seen. It was cluttered, filthy, and the smell was overwhelming. When Pauline pulled the door shut it was gloomy, as the window had not been cleaned for a very long time and the rag that served as a curtain might never have been washed at all.

But Ruby's experience of the past few months kicked in and she was no longer rooted to the spot with horrified shock. Instead she glanced around, waiting for her eyes to adjust to the dimness. When they did she realised that one pile of rags at the back of the room was actually a human being, covered in a crocheted blanket. 'There's me ma,' explained Pauline. 'She's ever so hot. She ain't moved for days, not really, and usually she never stays in.' Suddenly her voice cracked. 'Can you help her, nurse?'

'Let's see.' Ruby moved carefully across the floor, which was covered with domestic bits and pieces — used cups, odd items of clothing, a couple of toys. Pauline swooped down to grab those. 'I told me brother to get them out the way,' she muttered.

Ruby asked Pauline to show her where she could wash her hands, although there was only cold water. Then she came back in from the shared yard and crouched down to her patient, careful not to let her own clothes touch the floor, and proceeded to carry out the same checks that she undertook for every case: temperature, pulse, respiration. She carefully noted the figures for each, and nodded thoughtfully.

214

'You're right, she is very hot,' she said, trying not to let any alarm creep into her voice. She'd never come across such a high fever, not on the district nor in the hospital. 'How long has she been like this?' she asked.

'Too long, miss,' Pauline said succinctly.

'And you've been giving her cold drinks?'

'Ever since she got took poorly, miss. And I wipe her face with a cold flannel, even though she don't like it.'

The woman moaned but Ruby couldn't work out if she was trying to say something or not.

Gradually she worked her way through the notes that the doctor had left, annotating the chart where necessary, noting that the fever had risen since he had visited, more and more convinced that here was another case of septicaemia. She knew she must not worry the child any more than she could help, and cast around for a subject to distract her. 'Nurse Lake was teaching you to knit, wasn't she?' she began. 'She told me about it. In fact, I was there when Nurse Banham bought the wool.'

This brought the first hint of a smile. 'Was you, miss?'

'Yes, she was sure you'd like the colour. That pretty red.'

'I did, miss. I tried ever so hard.'

'I'm sure you did. Weren't you making a scarf?'

Pauline shrugged. 'I wanted to. But I haven't been able to finish it.'

Ruby rose from the patient and looked around for the bright wool. 'Why was that, then? Didn't you like it after a while?'

'Wasn't that, miss.' Pauline's face twisted. 'I lost one of me needles.'

215

Ruby frowned. 'That's a shame. Perhaps Nurse Lake can bring you another if she's got one in the same size. They're big things to lose though, aren't they?'

Pauline didn't answer.

Ruby paused for a moment. An idea was beginning to form and she hoped against hope it was the wrong one. She mustn't jump to far-fetched conclusions, but she framed her next question very carefully.

'And you mother, has she um, needed to spend a penny much recently?'

'Spend a penny? Oh, you mean go to the lav.' Pauline thought hard. 'We ain't got one ourselves, but you must have seen the privy what we share out in the yard when you washed your hands before.'

Ruby agreed, as the smell had been hard to miss. 'It's a long way to go if you're sick,' she sympathised.

'Oh, we don't bother. We got the po.' The young girl pointed to a china chamber pot in the far corner of the room. 'Usually me gran has it but I made her put it where Ma could reach it for once.' She paused again. 'Only, she ain't had call to use it, come to think of it.'

'What, not at all?'

'No, miss. I'd notice. It's me what has to empty it, after all.'

Ruby felt a cold shiver run down her spine. All the alarm bells now began to ring in her head. A lasting fever, extremely high. The patient drinking but not passing water. Incoherence. Now she knew why Gwen had chosen her to come here above any of the other available nurses. It was that same set of circumstances she'd witnessed back when she'd just started, only an even worse case.

216

Then there was the missing knitting needle.

Ruby had heard of such methods, though not from medical textbooks. It was the stuff of whispers, of muttered conversations. Some of the girls she had been at school with had heard of it from their big sisters, more confiding than hard-faced Beryl. If you were unlucky enough to fall pregnant and you didn't want the baby, you drank gin and sat in a hot bath. Even back then, Ruby had thought that pretty unlikely to be effective. Or, you could use a knitting needle.

Ruby struggled to imagine how desperate anyone would have to be to endure such pain. Now possibly here was the result — a raging infection. If the woman had done the procedure in this house, she might as well have swallowed poison.

'Miss?' Pauline brought her attention sharply back to the present.

'One more question. Is that your mother's coat over there?' Ruby had spotted an off-white garment hanging on the back door. Maybe it had been properly white once.

'What about it, miss? She ain't going nowhere right now.' Pauline was dismissive. 'Oh, you mean she might have to bring it to the hospital if she goes in? So she'll have something warm for when she leaves?'

'Maybe.' Ruby was evasive. This could be the final piece of the jigsaw. Gwen had told her that Alice had hardly ever seen the mother, despite knowing the family for many years — she was always out, and Pauline would sometimes say she was working but never at what. There were a few professions that needed a white coat, but Ruby doubted if the woman was anything medical or worked in a laboratory. However, since the blackout had been in place, prostitutes were known to favour white or pale coats so that they could still be seen.

There was no proof but it all made a terrible sense. This was why Gwen had emphasised discretion. Why she had smiled with such meaning. There were some things that were never written on the charts or forms or messages for the doctor, certainly not when a patient or relatives could see them — some not at all.

Ruby's heart sank. If this was what was behind the woman's fever, then she might well never need the coat for coming out of hospital. She might not be leaving it at all.

'Where's your little brother?' she asked.

'Me gran took him down the shops,' Pauline explained. 'She don't like doctors and nurses much. She only let me ask for help when she thought it would be Nurse Lake.'

'Well, never mind.' Ruby knew it was time to act. 'I'm going to call for an ambulance to take your mother to hospital and it will probably be here before they get back. So she'll be none the wiser which nurse arranged it. But that will mean you will be here on your own. I don't like to leave you.'

Pauline shook her head. 'That don't matter, miss. I'm used to it.'

Ruby realised that was most likely true, but decided she would ask Alice to call around later anyway. If what she suspected was correct, Pauline's troubles were only just beginning.

21

'I can't believe it, Brendan. I can't thank you enough.'
Fiona stood in the centre of the common room, staring in wonder at the miracle the ARP warden had brought about. Against all the odds he had somehow managed to have the big windows mended. Not only had he found the boards to block them up temporarily, so that the home was secure, if very dark. Plenty of people were making do with waxed linen instead of proper panes, which at least let in more light, as well as the cold. Better than that though — now he had found real glass.

'How ever did you do it?' asked Gwen.

Brendan smiled cheerfully. 'Don't you go worrying that it was dodgy or nothing like that,' he said. 'I know what people say about us traders down the market, that we're all up to something. No, this is totally kosher and above board. I got mates in the salvage teams, and they know about the availability of this sort of thing.'

'But there's a waiting list,' Gwen said severely, not because she lacked gratitude but because she could not bear the thought that this wonderful gift might be tainted in any way.

'There is, but there's priorities,' Brendan said patiently, knowing what Gwen was like. 'You ladies are priorities. We can't do without you, none of us can. You look after all the sick people day to day and all the extra injuries from the bombings. Can't argue with that.'

Gwen nodded, still not quite able to take in the transformation of the room to its old, bright self.

Fiona was delighted. 'It's strange, we'd got used to it, and while the evenings were still dark it was almost cosy,' she said, 'but now the daylight is lasting for longer, I admit I did feel the difference. While the nurses all have their individual bright rooms, here is where we all congregate, here's the beating heart of the home. Natural light lifts the spirits, it's a fact. We need as much of it as we can get.'

'Exactly.' Brendan could not be happier. 'Even better, you got all your frames repaired and strengthened and proper locks put on.'

'Good,' said Gwen at once, thinking that there would be no easy way to get around the curfew now.

'It's important,' Brendan went on. 'I don't have to tell you that there are all sorts of unscrupulous types out there who'd love nothing better than to get into these premises. You're sitting on a gold mine with your medical stores.'

Fiona frowned. 'I'm well aware of that. It's a matter for discussion at most of my committees. We've had a few instances of equipment going missing, mainly being stolen in transit.'

Brendan's face clouded over. 'It fair makes me spit. We see it down the market all the time. There's those what have got no morals at all. They see all this as a way of getting rich quick. They steal people's coupons, or they forge them and sell them on. You got to be watching out for it all the time — it's exhausting is what it is.'

Gwen pursed her lips. 'It's exploitation, pure and simple.'

Fiona nodded. 'That's the word all right. Still,' she

220

clapped her hands together and turned to Brendan once more, 'thanks to you, we're safer than we were before. It's nothing short of marvellous and we can't begin to tell you how much we appreciate it.'

The ARP warden smiled once more.'You don't have to. Just knowing you ladies are protected again is thanks enough. We can't have no harm coming to you. Now I best be off. Young Maurice is getting the hang of setting up the stall, but I don't like to leave him to it too often. Ta-ta for now.'

★ ★ ★

By the next evening, Fiona's mood had grown more solemn. Everyone was delighted with the new and improved common room, but she had the sad duty of summoning three of the nurses to break to them the news they had dreaded.

'Alice, Ruby, Lily, sit down,' the superintendent said as the younger women came through her office door. She coughed a little. No matter how many times she did this, it was never easy. The only way was to plough straight in.

'I'll come directly to the point,' she said as soon as they had settled on the hard wood chairs on the other side of her desk. 'I'm afraid to say that your septicaemia patient has died, Ruby. Alice, of course you are very familiar with the family and so you need to know this too. And Lily, I understand you dropped in to see her unofficially before we knew how bad things were, and you must now hear the news we feared.'

Ruby groaned. 'Oh no.' She shut her eyes tightly, but the image of the feverish woman under the crocheted blanket was vivid in her mind.

Fiona gave them a moment to take in what she had said, knowing that even if they had thought it might happen, that was a very different matter to having the truth confirmed. Then she spoke again. 'You couldn't have done anything more for her, Ruby. None of you could. You called the ambulance as soon as you were sure how bad her condition was. There was nothing, absolutely nothing, you could have done at that stage to save her. She was simply too sick.'

Ruby gulped audibly. 'Thank you. I know that really, but I feel . . . I feel . . . I should have saved her somehow.'

Fiona nodded, her face etched with sympathy. 'We can't save them all, Ruby. That is the sad reality. We would if we could, but we can't.'

Ruby stared fixedly at her shoes until she was reasonably certain the risk of tears had gone away.

'Do we know if . . . if . . . what I suspected was really the cause?'

Fiona twisted her hands. This was always going to be awkward. 'Officially, no. The cause of death will be listed as septicaemia but no further cause will be recorded.' She sighed and met the young nurse's gaze. 'Unofficially, I've been told that sadly you were exactly right. The woman had tried to perform an abortion — we don't know if she asked anyone else to help or not, and will most likely never know. However, as in so many cases, it went tragically wrong.' Again she gave the nurses a moment to absorb this. 'Gwen assured me that you knew the value of discretion in this case and her trust in you was well placed, Ruby. If any of this were to be written down then there might be legal consequences, and I cannot see how that would help anybody.'

Alice buried her face in her hands. 'It was my needle, wasn't it. One of the ones I gave to Pauline so she could learn to knit. I'd never have done it had I realised . . .'

'Stop that right now, Alice,' Fiona said forcefully. 'You are in no way to blame here. You were doing that young girl a kindness and teaching her a useful skill. The last thing you would have imagined is something like this. It just goes to show how desperate that poor woman was, to steal her own daughter's knitting needle.'

'I know, but like Ruby, I feel responsible somehow. If only I hadn't — '

'If you hadn't then the odds are that she would have used something else,' Fiona said. 'I'm sorry but it's true. People react with drastic measures when they are backed into a corner. It might sound brutal but that's simply the case.'

Lily sat thunderstruck, unable to say a word. She had seen this patient early on. She had assumed nothing too terrible was amiss — but she knew deep down that her judgement had been affected by her urge to leave the horrible house as soon as possible. Might she have queried the slightly raised temperature otherwise? She would never know now — and she would have to live with that.

Alice nodded silently, battling with her guilt, which threatened to overwhelm her reason. 'Poor Pauline,' she said bleakly after a while. 'She might think it's her fault, when it wasn't at all.'

Fiona gave a half-smile. 'And that's where you can come in,' she said. 'She will need reassuring and also practical advice. She's now a motherless girl effectively bringing up her younger brother. She trusts you

223

though. You should look upon her as a patient and pay her regular visits for the time being. We will want to know that she can cope.'

'It probably won't make much difference in practical terms,' Alice replied. 'That's been the position for ages, years even. Gran helps a bit but the mother was hardly ever there.'

'Doesn't mean that Pauline won't miss her though,' Ruby added, understanding of the complicated situation dawning on her face. 'It's still her mother, even if she wasn't much of one.'

Fiona nodded and thought once again how their trust in Ruby had been repaid. She might be inexperienced but she saw straight through to the heart of the situation. It didn't matter what profession the mother had followed and how little time she'd spent with her children, they were still bereaved. It wasn't a question of what sort of parent the dead woman had been. For good or ill, she had been their mother, and now she was gone.

'Ruby, Lily, you can back Alice up in this,' she said. 'If for any reason she is unable to attend, you now know the facts and can help out when necessary. I don't have to tell you that this conversation must remain completely confidential.' She glanced down at the formal note she had made about the cause of death. 'You may say it was as a result of septicaemia, which is absolutely true, but make no comment about the cause of the infection. The woman deserves some dignity in death, and the children will suffer if people start gossiping. We don't want that.'

'No we don't,' Alice agreed emphatically. For a moment she wished Edith were here so that she could unburden herself, but then recognised it was perhaps just as well; Edie knew her too well and could always tell if she was holding something back. Besides, Edith had enough on her mind as the birth of her baby drew closer. She didn't need to be party to this sad news.

'I won't say anything,' Ruby promised, deeply sad for the children and unwilling to make a terrible situation even worse.

'Of course I wouldn't either.' Lily just about got the words out. She fought to keep her voice from trembling.

Fiona rose. 'No, I'm sure you won't. That of course is one of the reasons you were asked to attend the patient in the first place. We were sure we could rely upon your discretion.' She flashed them a warm smile. 'Off you go now, and tomorrow we can begin to plan what little deeds of kindness we can do to help Pauline and her brother.'

Ruby made her way up the stairs, following Alice and Lily, none of them in much of a mood to talk. Ruby's heart was heavy with sorrow and, now that she'd heard the facts, she realised that this was what she had been more or less expecting since being asked to visit the little house. Suddenly she was overwhelmed with exhaustion, and rushed through her evening wash as fast as she could. She could not wait to crawl into the safety of her own bed.

Yet the way that Fiona had spoken to her lingered in Ruby's tired mind. That sense of total trust and confidence. There was not much good to be taken from the whole sorry episode, but at least there was this. It was not much of a silver lining, but under the circumstances it was something to value, nonetheless.

★ ★ ★

225

Lily gazed out of one of her bedroom windows, from where she could see that some of the remaining trees lining the streets towards the Downs were covered in blossom. Her mind was not really on the signs of spring though. Something wonderful had happened and it was a welcome balm after the shock and distress of the recent patient death. Her hands went to her throat and the silk scarf tied there.

It really was beautiful. Donald had selected it specially, telling her it was the closest he could find to the one she had admired in the Magpie Club. He'd explained it was a Liberty print, with all its swirls and repeated patterns, in a shade of green contrasting with a deep red, which went with one of her lipsticks. Lily could not help but be impressed. She had never met a man who took such care to notice what she liked and what suited her.

She'd tried it on as soon as he gave it to her in the hotel restaurant, admiring herself in one of the old gilt-edged mirrors. Then she'd allowed him to take it off when he led her upstairs later. She'd shivered with delight as his hands had touched the skin of her neck. He was unlike anyone she'd ever met and she could not get enough of him. She trusted him completely — he'd reassured her that he'd 'brought something' and it was typically thoughtful of him to take care of such matters.

As they lay in bed afterwards he had listened to her talk about her work, asking lots of detailed questions. He genuinely was interested, and not just in the incidents of high drama. Lily had told him about the sad death of the woman from septicaemia, which had affected her more deeply than she would have imagined just a few months ago. Also she could tell

226

what a toll it had taken on her two colleagues. She didn't like to see Alice and Ruby so down. She hadn't asked Ruby too much about what the scene had been like that day, but she'd made her tea every time she came back from her shift and kept an eye on her.

No, Donald was even interested in the mundane aspects of her day — what sort of things she carried around with her, how often she had to refill her supplies, what equipment was kept in the district room in case any of them needed it. He often asked about such things when they were together. 'Oh, you don't want to know about our old sheets of mackintosh,' she had joked, and he had assured her that if it was important to her, then it was important to him too.

She had spent the night in the luxurious room, the third time that she had done so. But the next morning, Donald had apologised and said he had to go to work, even though it was a Saturday. Lily could not really complain after the night they had spent together, but she would have loved to walk around the streets with him, arm in arm, like any normal couple in love. However, she respected that his work must come first. 'And anyway, it's my turn to cover the weekend evening rounds,' she had said to him as they parted outside the hotel's discreet but elegant porch. 'I must be ready for that.'

'Of course you must.' He bent forward and brushed his lips on her forehead, and she felt again that delicious tingle of pleasure. 'I'll see you soon, Lily.'

'I hope so.' She forgot to make a little play of reluctance or coquettishness, and waved as he turned the corner on the street of high terraced houses, so much more generously proportioned than most around Dalston.

There had been nothing for it but to return to Victory Walk, trying not to be too obvious about the fact she'd been out all night. Slipping upstairs to her room, she saw nobody and was fairly confident that nobody had seen her. She had a story all ready and prepared about bumping into an old friend, but it wasn't needed. Now she turned her back on the view of the blossom, and carefully folded away the precious scarf. Lily my girl, she silently congratulated herself, you really have come a long way since arriving from Liverpool.

22

'Are you going home for Easter at all, Ruby?' Gladys asked, shrugging into her canvas jacket before leaving for the day. 'You won't have to work for the whole of the long weekend, will you?'

The weather was warmer now and she was going to put in an hour at the victory garden before going home. They'd already started to plant this year's crop of vegetables, but that meant the weeds were springing up as well. You had to keep on top of them or they'd take every ounce of goodness from the soil, given half a chance.

Ruby paused at the bottom of the stairs. In the past she had enjoyed Easter with her family. When they'd been able to save enough ingredients, her mother would bake a special cake, and decorate it with some little eggs of imitation marzipan made with semolina paste. They'd go to the local church on Easter Sunday, and even Ruby had joined in the singing of 'Christ the Lord Is Risen Today'. The Sunday school children would make Easter gardens from whatever plants and bits and pieces they could scavenge, small lumps of rubble representing the stone that rolled away from the tomb. Ruby had done that herself as a child but had never won the competition for the best one.

'I don't think so,' she said. She would send a card, but dreaded the idea of trailing all the way to Hammersmith only to be berated for a list of her faults. She had gone back not long after Pauline's mother died, propelled by some deep urge to make sure that her own mother was safe and well, only to be met by Beryl's complaints as soon as she stepped through the front door. Ruby had spent the entire visit biting her lip, longing to say, 'If only you'd seen what I've seen.' She'd cut the visit short, claiming it would take her a long time to get back as all the buses had been diverted again — which was true.

'We're all going to the pictures on Easter Saturday,' Gladys said. 'Me and Ron and Shirley and Kenny. Maybe some others. We don't know what's on yet but that's half the fun.'

Ruby perked up. They had gone out, as a group, several more times since that first outing; sometimes with Belinda too, and once with the two factory girls, Clarrie and Peggy, from the pub as well, and each time she had sat beside Kenny and they had talked afterwards. He hadn't gone so far as to ask her out on her own, and she would have died of embarrassment sooner than ask him, but she sensed he liked her more and more. 'I don't think I'm working then,' she said. 'I'll come along, if that's all right.'

'Course it's all right. I wouldn't have said anything about it otherwise, now would I?' Sometimes Gladys had to make a big effort to remember how shy she herself had been until recently. She couldn't quite fathom why Ruby, who was winning a reputation for her excellent work and was well liked in the nurses' home, was so unsure of herself for so much of the time. It was as if she had to apologise for being there at all. Gladys's lips met in a determined line. If her new friend wasn't going to pursue a possible romance on her own behalf, then she would just have to engineer it for her.

'Well, then, I'll join you.' Ruby smiled in anticipation.

'You could always help me out in the victory garden if you have a spare half-hour,' Gladys suggested. 'I'm going to give beetroot a go this year. You can use them in all sorts of ways, you know. Like a vegetable, like we always used to do, or pickle them, or put them in cakes as they're so sweet. And you can use the juice like lipstick if you've mind to.'

Ruby looked doubtful. 'I don't think I'd want to do that,' she said hesitantly. Then she thought about how good it would be to be out in the fresh air, doing something useful with her spare time. 'But I'll help you grow them, Gladys. You'll have to show me what to do.'

'I can do that all right,' said Gladys cheerfully.

★　★　★

Alice was arriving back later and later after her shifts, as she made sure to drop in to see Pauline and little brother Larry as often as possible. To begin with Pauline had been subdued, almost afraid to talk about what had happened. Then, once she started, the floodgates opened. It was as Alice had feared; the young girl felt guilty about how her mother had died. She knew it was something to do with the missing knitting needle, even if not quite how it had been used. Alice was grateful for that and made no effort to explain. Part of her had hoped that the grandmother would step in and reassure the children, but that had been too much to ask. Gran took refuge in her normal comfort — gin.

That left Pauline in charge as usual, and gradually she had rallied. Larry, never the strongest of children when he was small, was in reasonable health now thanks to the rationed diet, which was better than the one he'd got by on before the war. He could be relied upon to do some of the basic shopping, though Pauline would carefully supervise which coupons he took where.

Janet Phipps, the teacher, was given the gist of what had happened and made sure both children had adequate dinners on school days. She also kept an eye on their hygiene. It was only an extension of what she had been doing for years. If she had any concerns she contacted Alice straight away.

The sky was still light as Alice hopped off her bike and pushed it over to the rack. If she hadn't been so exhausted, she would have gone to help in the victory garden, which she had enjoyed doing over the past few years, but her limbs would go no further today. Though she'd been doing her best not to think about it, she was still turning over and over the dilemma about Mark. She'd received another letter, in which he'd said the same again only more strongly. He was so deeply sorry for making such a big mistake. Could she ever forgive him?

Alice had not yet written back. While she didn't doubt his sincerity, her own positon had grown no clearer over the weeks since she'd seen him. She could not deny that he still affected her strongly — and yet she could also not deny that her trust had been permanently shaken. Could she go back to him, knowing that to be the case? Did she want to?

The bike refused to stand upright and clattered to the ground. Alice could have screamed. Nothing was going right. For a moment she gave in to the wash of emotions and felt very sorry for herself. She was tired, she was cross, and Edith wasn't around to jolly her along and bring her out of her low mood. It simply wasn't fair.

Then she caught the sound of a blackbird singing on a nearby branch and looked up, noticing that even more of the trees were blossoming, and that the rays of the fading sun were casting a bright gold-copper glow against the clouds. She gave herself a shake. What had she to complain about? She bent and picked up the frame of the bike and set it to rest properly this time. She was healthy, she had a job she loved and was good at. Her best friend was soon to have a much-wanted baby; there were less than two months to go. Set against all this, her own personal dilemma truly was not so huge.

Alice ran up the stairs to wash and change before the evening meal, willing her spirits to rally. Mary caught her on the landing. 'Alice! Just who I wanted to see. Do you fancy coming to a concert with Charles and me? He can get tickets on Easter Saturday. They're as rare as hen's teeth but he's managed it somehow. Actually, we don't even know who it will be, but maybe Moura Lympany. Do say you'll come!'

It was hard to resist Mary in full flow, even if you weren't tired. Alice recognised this was a very kind offer and that it would be churlish to refuse. Besides, Charles could often whisk them into the centre of town in his staff car, which was almost as much of a treat as a piano concert. 'That would be lovely,' she said gratefully.

'I'll tell him at once. See you downstairs!' Mary ran off, her abundant chestnut curls bouncing around her shoulders.

Alice smiled. It helped to have something to look forward to. She could not remember when she had last been to a proper concert — probably not since Charles had organised the last trip to one, many months ago. While it wasn't quite the same as going out with Edith, Mary and Charles were good company and never made her feel that she was in the way.

Putting on her boat-neck jumper after carefully hanging up her uniform, she felt better. This war could get you down; everyone was brought low by it from time to time. She shouldn't feel too bad about it. She was not superhuman — none of them were. Now and again it was all right to rail against fate.

She gave her hair a quick brush so that she would at least seem presentable. Now she was calmer. She'd go down to the common room and enjoy the evening meal in Mary's company. And there was no point in thinking about that other matter over which she had no control.

Joe was coming home on leave soon. There was still no clue when that would be or where he'd been. It didn't matter. She would see him soon. She had every faith that he would make it, or he wouldn't have said anything. He would not let her down.

★ ★ ★

Lily had waited and waited to hear if Donald would be able to take her out over Easter, but there was no word by the time Good Friday came. She knew she risked wrinkles on her forehead but it was hard to keep from frowning. It was most frustrating. He must know how eagerly she longed for his messages, but she could do very little about it.

Some of the others were going to church. 'Do you want to come with Bridget and me?' Ellen asked.

'Only we're Catholic, and you probably aren't.'

'I won't, but thanks for asking.' Lily made sure to be polite. She didn't want to go to any church; she was too on edge to sit still through a service. Maybe if Alice had asked her to go to the local one she would have accepted, just to have a chance for more conversation with her, but she hadn't. It turned out she had gone over to the Banhams' house, so that some of them could go to the church in which Edith had been married, and that had meant an early start.

Of course, if Mary had asked her to go with her she would have jumped at the chance, but the nurse she admired most of all had been rostered to do the first visits of the morning, so she was already off tending to a case of measles with complications.

Lily had her own patients to see to in the afternoon, and then she would be left kicking her heels in the evening, as there was still no word from Donald. Really, he worked too hard. What office could keep him so busy all through Easter? It was different for the nurses; some of them had always to be available, for their regular patients and for new cases. People didn't suddenly stop being sick or having accidents. But Donald didn't look like someone who ever got his hands dirty. It was deeply disappointing that she couldn't share some of her time off with him.

If she had expected an improvement on Saturday, her hopes were soon dashed. Mary and Alice were off somewhere together, and it must be to do something smart as they'd dressed up. Mary had her mother's understated jewellery on again, and Alice had put on her best skirt and jacket and let down her hair. Lily's jealousy knew no bounds when an army captain in uniform whisked them away in a sleek dark car. That must be the famous Charles. How she would have loved to be introduced to him, but it had not happened.

'What are you up to later?' Ruby had come up behind her and Lily hadn't noticed, as she stood at the corridor window on the attic floor, gazing down to the spot from where the staff car had departed.

Lily jumped, hastily fighting to recover her composure.

'Oh, nothing much,' she said.

'Because we're going to the pictures,' Ruby went on. 'You could come if you like.'

Lily sighed inwardly. This was the third time Ruby had asked her along, but she doubted she would enjoy the evening. Why would she want to spend time with Gladys and the dock workers when there was a chance that Donald would still get in touch?

'I might be busy,' she hedged.

Ruby glanced down to see what the other nurse might be looking at, and guessed that she had been watching the car. She could imagine what was going through her mind.

'We can't all have officer boyfriends taking us out,' she said lightly.

Lily breathed out loudly. 'No, I don't suppose so.'

Ruby wondered what else was going on behind her colleague's troubled expression. 'No word from your gentleman friend?'

Lily shook her hair and patted it back into place. 'No, not yet, but he's always so busy. He has to work when most people have time off. He's very dedicated.'

Ruby pursed her lips. 'What is it he does again?'

'You know I can't answer that,' Lily flared, more strongly than she'd meant to, but because it was true in two senses: nobody was meant to enquire too closely in case information got to the wrong ears, and so this made her sound patriotic and put Ruby in the wrong; on the other hand, she didn't know herself, although she would sooner die than admit it.

Ruby nodded, understanding more than Lily had intended her to. 'I suppose you're right.' She shifted her weight to her other foot. 'Well, do you want to help out over at the victory garden while you wait to see if he contacts you? Gladys showed me what to do and I'm going down there now. It's not far.'

Lily registered that Ruby's clothes were even plainer than usual and her blouse had a big patch on one arm. It was all very well for her: she had no nails to ruin. Lily had spent quite some time last night giving herself a careful manicure, and had no desire to get earth engrained in her soft hands.

'I really don't think I'd be much use at that,' she protested.

Ruby grinned widely. 'That's what I thought too. We've only got a little yard at home and never had no call to grow anything, but Gladys told me how to plant and weed. It's not even a proper garden — it was a bomb site a few streets away and they took it over so the land didn't go to waste. They got all sorts of things growing. You'd be surprised. Lots of the vegetables we've been eating have come from there.'

Lily knew this was something to be grateful for but she still didn't want to get her hands dirty.

'You go on,' she said. 'You'll be much better at it than me.'

Ruby could see through that one. 'Don't worry about ruining your nice clothes, I could lend you something that's on its last legs,' she offered cheerfully.

237

Lily gulped. She hated wearing other people's clothes. She'd had to wear her cousin's hand-me-downs as a child and resented it deeply. 'It's not that . . . '

'Besides, it's good exercise,' Ruby went on mischievously. 'Lots of bending and lifting — it helps you keep your figure.'

'Oh.' For the first time, Lily was tempted. Sometimes she secretly did exercises in her bedroom to maintain her shape.

'Yes, it strengthens and tones the muscles that normal nursing duties can't.'

Lily stared. Was Ruby making fun of her? Surely not.

'Of course if you'd rather not . . . ' Ruby made as if to leave.

Suddenly Lily saw it as a challenge. She couldn't be seen to dodge such a thing. 'Yes, all right,' she abruptly agreed. 'I'll find an old jumper or something. I'll meet you downstairs in ten minutes.'

Ruby watched her colleague disappear back into her room and almost laughed out loud. There, that wasn't so hard. They could certainly do with an extra pair of hands on the vegetable plot — even ones as beautifully manicured as Lily's.

★ ★ ★

'I don't believe you,' said Gladys, when Ruby told her who'd helped out earlier that afternoon. They were mixing mugs of weak cocoa in the service room, before heading out to meet the others. Ruby had changed out of her patched shirt and into one of her few good frocks, and she had added a bright brooch

238

borrowed from Ellen. It wasn't that being around Lily had brought out an urge to be smarter, but she had felt the need to up her game a little. It was good for everyone's morale if you looked good in public — but she drew the line at using beetroot juice on her lips, all the same.

'It's true,' she replied, leaning against the narrow counter. 'I teased her a bit and it did the trick. I know she didn't want to wreck her nails, but I lent her some spare gardening gloves. I got her tying wooden wigwams for when the peas and beans are ready to go out. Then she helped carry some of the tools into the storage box, where they'll be safer.'

Gladys beamed. 'Imagine that. I'm really pleased. We always need those jobs doing.'

Ruby cocked her head. 'Footsteps — I recognise them. Here she is now. Don't say anything about her nails, mind.'

'As if I would.' Gladys turned to face the doorway as Lily appeared. 'Lily! I heard you been down the victory garden with Ruby.'

Lily smoothed the sleeves of her cream blouse. 'Yes, we were there for a couple of hours I should think.' She didn't want to say too much. She was still battling disappointment at the lack of communication from Donald. Yet she was reluctant to admit that she had enjoyed herself today. At first she had winced at the thought of wearing someone else's gloves, and appearing in public in such old worn-out clothes. Anyone might walk by and see. Then she realised that nobody cared, and if she'd appeared at the garden in her usual finery, she'd have stood out like a sore thumb.

Moreover, she had liked the feeling of being out in

the open, moving about. The exertion had brought a becoming pink blush to her cheeks, she'd noticed on their return. That saved on rouge, for a start. Perhaps it wasn't a fib that exercise made the skin glow. Her arms ached a little from hauling the heavy tools from one end of the plot to the other, but it was a good sort of ache. She was almost looking forward to repeating the experience. Who would have thought it?

'So, will you join us tonight?' Gladys asked. 'We're going down Hackney Road, to see Arthur Askey's new film. It's bound to make you laugh.'

Lily hesitated. Sitting in a crowded cinema, feeling that you had to chuckle at something you didn't find funny, was not her idea of a night out. The last time she had seen Arthur Askey had been back in Liverpool, and she'd been uncomfortable, not knowing if her companions expected her to laugh or not and whether they would look down on her if she did.

'You don't have to,' Ruby chipped in, sensing her colleague's unease. 'It's up to you. Don't feel obliged or anything. We just thought you might like it, seeing as we had a good time this afternoon, didn't we?' Why does Lily make everything so complicated, she wondered. It's not as if we're asking her to audition for something. It's like she has all these hidden debates going on inside her head when all she has to do is say yes. Perhaps she doesn't want to enjoy herself and would rather sit around moping that her fancy man hasn't turned up.

Gladys drained the last of her cocoa. 'Right, I'm going to fetch my jacket. Don't worry if you haven't eaten yet, Lily, cos we often go for chips. There might even be pickled eggs.'

Lily winced. She could not abide pickled eggs. On

the other hand, she loved chips. It would be a far cry from the delicate sliced potatoes in creamy sauce that Donald had ordered the last time they were at the hotel. Still — Donald wasn't here to see.

It was true, she and Ruby had had a good time that afternoon. She might as well admit it.

'Thanks, Ruby.' She made a special effort not to sound condescending. It was clear they didn't think she would be doing them a favour by coming along. It was a simple offer from her colleagues to go out on an equal footing. Perhaps she could set aside her usual way of approaching social situations and accept it for what it was. 'Yes, why not? I'll go and find my handbag, shall I?'

Ruby beamed. Blimey, who'd have thought it? Twice in one day, the high-and-mighty Lily was risking enjoying herself like any normal person.

'See you at the front door in five minutes then,' she said cheerfully.

23

'You're absolutely sure this was deliberate?' Fiona's forehead creased in concern as the policeman turned to face her.

He was middle-aged and walked with a slight limp, one of the older members of the force who had most likely seen service in the Great War. His face spoke of years of experience and she trusted his judgement. That was just as well, as her own faith in humanity had just taken a blow.

'I should say so, yes.' He made a comment in his notebook and returned it to his pocket. 'Those sharp marks next to your window locks indicate that somebody has tried to force them with an implement, probably a knife of some kind. It's hard to see how else they could be there. A bird pecking for insects wouldn't make a mark like that. And you say the windows and frames are all new, so it can't be wear and tear or from the weather.'

Fiona nodded sadly. 'Yes, we sustained quite bad damage in this area during the last round of bombing and we sat in the semi-dark until we were given these wonderful new windows. They've not long gone in.'

The policeman looked at them carefully once again. 'Just as well they were in such good condition,' he said, running a finger along the inside edge of the wood. 'If they had been old and flaky, the burglar could easily have gained access. He was probably counting on getting his knife into a gap near the lock and forcing it. Only now there aren't no gaps. You foiled him.'

'Well, I suppose there's that to be thankful for.' Fiona folded her arms. 'We can't change anything, so what's done is done. Still, I'm very grateful that you informed us. We can be more on our guard in future. What a piece of luck that whoever it was chanced to be disturbed by your colleague on patrol.'

She tried hard not to show how shaken she was. It would not help matters. She had to breathe deeply and recover her nerve. It didn't do to imagine what might have happened if a burglar had managed to break in. The conversation with Brendan resurfaced: 'You're sitting on a gold mine.' The black-market value of all their medical stores would be considerable, and they'd had a new delivery just last week. Could anyone outside the inhabitants of Victory Walk have known?

'Try not to worry,' said the policeman affably. 'I doubt it will happen again. It's much more likely that word will get round that it's not as easy as they thought to break in here. That should make you safer, if anything.'

Fiona looked at him sharply. 'Does that mean that neighbouring nurses' homes and doctors' surgeries will be at an increased risk, then?' When he did not reply at once, she hastily drew her own conclusion. 'Very well, I shall contact them straight away and warn them. We can't have any link in the chain short of resources. They'll have to step up their security.'

'It wouldn't hurt for them to do that, at any rate, although I wouldn't want them to become unduly alarmed,' the policeman said solidly, somewhat taken aback by the tiny superintendent's sudden burst of energy. He hadn't met her before.

'No indeed. However, it is my duty to let them

243

know that such people are operating in this area. Of course one hears about it, but it's quite another thing to encounter it for oneself.' She smiled at him. 'I shan't start a panic but they do need to be informed. None of us has the capacity to spare.'

The policeman made as if to leave. 'I'd best be off, but rest assured I'll tell you if we hear anything more. In the meantime, by all means tell your fellow super. intendents to be on their guard.'

'Thank you, Constable.' Fiona saw him to the door. She had managed to put him off until most of the nurses had gone out on their morning rounds, so that she could come up with a way of telling them without causing a major scare. Only the cook and Gladys were aware that the policeman had visited. Gladys was coming down the hallway now, a dubious expression on her face.

'Is something wrong?' she asked. 'Has anybody had an accident?' It was always the first thing they all thought of when a policeman turned up unexpectedly.

'Not exactly,' Fiona replied. 'In fact, you might say we've had a lucky escape.' She paused to think. 'I'll announce what's happened over our midday meal, but come with me, Gladys, and I'll show you now, and explain what we think is behind it.' She drew the young woman along with her down the hall.

★ ★ ★

'Who would do such a thing?' Mary asked indignantly once they had all been apprised of the situation at lunchtime. 'It's those spivs, I'll be bound. It's disgusting, people trying to profiteer by stealing our supplies.

244

We need them to save lives and all they think about is money.'

'Well, we don't actually know that,' Alice pointed out. 'All we know for certain is that a policeman doing a late-night patrol walked by and heard a noise, and when he shouted out he heard footsteps running away. Then this morning they found those marks on the new window frames. Are we sure we're not putting two and two together and making five?'

Mary tossed her hair and glared at her friend. 'How else would you explain it then?'

Alice shrugged. 'Don't blame me, Mary, I'm just saying. Do we rule out coincidence?'

Belinda drummed her fingers on the table. 'You know what, Alice, in this case I reckon we do. If it was a one-off then I'd be more inclined to agree with you, but it isn't.'

'Really?' Lily was part horrified, part secretly thrilled to be sitting at the same table as the senior nurses and therefore close to Alice and Mary. She hardly dared to join in as they seemed so much better informed.

Belinda turned to her. 'You won't know my friend Miriam, Lily, as she's not a nurse. She's actually a good friend of my parents, and by chance also of Gwen. We're both Jewish and we help other Jews who are fleeing persecution, mostly from Austria as that's where our families were originally from.'

'Oh,' said Lily, unsure what else to add. She'd heard of all this going on but didn't realise anyone in her immediate circle was affected.

'She can do this because her husband's a very successful businessman here in the East End. Well, he's noticed a big increase in items going missing; either raw materials on their way to his factories, or finished goods vanishing before they reach their destinations. We wondered if he was being targeted because of being Jewish, but then other business contacts told him the same was happening to them. It sounds pretty organised. So why wouldn't they go after medical supplies too? It's not as if they're available down the market. They're specialised. If you stole them you could make a killing on the black market. Sorry, bad choice of words.'

'No, you're exactly right,' Alice conceded. 'On both counts. It does sound as if it was deliberate — and if that's what's behind it, then lives are at risk. What if they got hold of stocks of insulin, for example? That's basically holding people's health to ransom.'

'Good job Brendan sorted out our windows,' Mary said vehemently. 'When all this is over, we'll have to think of a way of rewarding him. I'm sure Charles can come up with something. I'll ask him as soon as he has finished whatever it is he's so tied up with . . .' Alice looked at her meaningfully and she changed the direction of the conversation. 'At least it'll stop you getting in after curfew, Belinda. That'll make Gwen happy.'

'Don't look at me,' Belinda protested, grinning, 'we've all done it. All right, Alice, maybe not you. And I don't know about you, Lily.'

Lily blushed, in full knowledge that she hadn't even bothered to sneak back in after the ten o'clock deadline had passed, but had simply ignored it and stayed out all night. The others spared her embarrassment and did not pursue the question. It also made her hot with anger that anyone should stoop so low as to try to rob their vital stores.

'Anyway I shan't need to get in late for a while,'

Belinda went on. 'Last time David was in town — that's my brother, Lily, he's a pilot — he said it would be his last leave for some while. He's going to be tied up with some operation for the foreseeable future, although I've no idea what. So I shall be spending my evenings doing good works. Belinda Adams, spinster of this parish.'

'Good, you can help me with the WVS talks,' said Mary at once.

Lily grinned, liking how Mary had seized upon that chance so swiftly. All the same, she could not put aside her horror that anybody could be so callous as to try to steal their precious supplies. As Belinda said, it wasn't as if you could go to the market and simply buy them. Everything had to be ordered in advance and carefully monitored, as running out of any one item could prove fatal, and yet they couldn't hang on to medicines indefinitely. They went out of date for a start. Or other areas might need them more, depending on a number of factors — local rates of infection, which places had been bombed most heavily, lots of things. It was a complicated balance and she didn't envy Fiona and Gwen for having to manage it.

She'd never really thought about it when she began working on the district, but trying to explain it to Donald had crystallised it in her mind. He'd been so understanding, happy to talk about the most boring aspects of her work, not minding at all when she meandered on, telling him how they'd almost run out of dressings once and how long she'd had to wait to replace her special nailbrush when she'd lost it while on a visit. She was sure one of the children of the household had pilfered it but had no proof.

'Probably thought it was a toy,' he'd said, and she

had thought how sweet and understanding he was, always ready to think the best of people he didn't even know. She considered the little boy in question to be a proper handful and a potential criminal in the making, but hadn't said so. That would have made her sound mean and churlish.

Lily had never troubled him about the details of the curfew. She had made light of the fact that she was meant to be back at the nurses' home before ten o'clock, without fail, or else run the risk of big trouble. She'd laughed about other nurses climbing through the big back window, but didn't want him to think she'd consider such drastic actions. She was too sophisticated for that. Many of the other nurses laughed about it too, as Mary was doing now, and Lily had heard that she'd been known to come in that way in her early days at the home, back before she'd met Captain Charles and such measures became unnecessary. Then again, Alice didn't look as if she approved, and Lily couldn't imagine the serious nurse getting a leg-up from a friend to wriggle under the raised sash. It was known that Belinda was tall enough to manage without help, but few of the others could have done so. Lily briefly wondered how Edith would ever have got anywhere close to the window ledge, being almost as short as Fiona. Still, that wouldn't matter now.

'Prison's too good for them,' Mary was saying now, and Lily nodded vigorously, furious that anybody would consider stealing from Victory Walk and also privately delighted to be part of this conversation and able to show her hearty agreement with her more experienced colleagues.

24

'Are you sure you're all right to be walking this far?'
Alice asked. She didn't want to alarm her friend, but
Edith was getting bigger almost before her eyes. For
ages she'd carried her bump neatly, but in the past
few weeks it had grown far more noticeable. This was
the home stretch for her pregnancy, and Alice didn't
want to tire her out unnecessarily.

'Of course I am. If I'm not then I'll tell you,' Edith
replied, more snappy than usual. She drew her cardigan around her — in fact, Flo's cardigan, Alice
realised, a baggy one in pale blue that had seen many
years of service. No doubt it was now the only one
that would fit.

They were walking up the main road towards Stamford Hill, passing the Victorian cemetery to their left.
Neither suggested wandering around inside, but carried on up the long incline. It was an excuse to get
out into the warm sunshine as much as anything else,
now that late spring was beginning to turn into early
summer. Alice knew it might be one of the last walks
she took with her friend with it being just the two of
them.

'So, Joe's leave is postponed again,' she said.

'Looks like it,' said Edith, less sharply now. 'We got
a short note just like you did. No idea why, and still
no clue where he is or what he's doing.'

'And I'm none the wiser,' said Alice. That was one
more thing she was trying not to worry about, as she
had no control over it. He would have his reasons, but

she heartily wished he had not raised their hopes by mentioning it in the first place.

Edith strode along, determined not to show any weakness. 'It won't be his fault,' she said, her cheeks rosy with the effort. Alice noticed how, now the sick. ness that had plagued her for so much of the pregnancy had retreated, Edith was truly blooming in these last weeks. Her dark hair shone, and she'd allowed her once-short curls to grow a little now she didn't have to pin them back for work. She'd moved into a different stage of life, Alice recognised.

'I know.' Alice was sure this was true and logically it could not be otherwise, but still, some part of her felt hurt at his continued absence. She'd counted on him coming home. Without realising it, she had been hoarding news she wanted to tell him, ideas she wanted to discuss, things she couldn't share easily with anyone else. It had become her habit. Now she would have to wait, the same as everyone else, and she couldn't help but feel obscurely cheated.

Edith glanced at her, as always aware of what she wasn't saying as well as what she'd actually put into words.

'It won't, don't even think it,' she insisted. She paused, pretending to catch her breath, and gave the taller nurse a quizzical look. 'So . . . have you heard any more from Mark?'

Alice looked away, back down the hill. A bus was drawing up at the nearest stop, a crowd of passengers alighting with shopping and small children, whose high voices drifted towards them.

'Once or twice,' she admitted.

'What did he say?' Edith demanded, her dark eyes bright.

Alice shuffled her feet. At last it was warm enough to dig out the shoes she'd put away last September: a pair of peep-toe pumps, in warm maroon. She didn't get many chances to wear them. 'Well . . . more of the same,' she said slowly. 'He hasn't changed his mind since we saw each other. He keeps asking me to forgive him.'

'And will you?'

'Forgiveness is one thing.' Alice spoke carefully, putting into words the thoughts that had been circling around in her head for so long. 'He can't expect me to forget, though. You don't forget something like that.'

'I should think not,' Edith said hotly. 'So you've told him to leave you alone, then?'

Alice shuffled some more. 'Not exactly.'

Edith frowned.

'I mean, not in so many words.' Alice grew more and more awkward. 'What I said was, I couldn't forget how he had betrayed my trust. That's the truth. He might see it differently but I can't help that. He let me down and there's no getting away from it.'

'I know. He left you and then you had to cope with it all on your own. Of course you can't trust him again. He can't expect you to.' Edith's expression showed her deep sympathy for everything Alice had been through. 'So he knows you can't trust him in the future, then?'

Alice gazed up at the clouds for inspiration, juggling the wild mix of emotions that the question stirred up. 'I didn't quite go that far, to be honest. But you're right, I don't feel that I can.'

Edith shook her head decisively. 'You've got to tell him that outright, Al, or he won't get the message.

Men are like that. Half of them hear only what they want to hear. If he sees a chink of hope, then he'll be on to it like a dog after a bone. Because that's what you want, isn't it? Isn't it?'

'Of course,' said Alice, but she knew she wasn't totally convincing.

'Oh, Al.' Edith raised her hands and then let them drop again with a sigh. 'You aren't secretly thinking you might take him seriously, are you? Not after everything? Tell me you aren't even considering it.'

Alice rubbed her hands together. 'No, not really. It's just . . . he's still Mark. Part of me really, really wishes I could trust him again, that we can make it right this time. But — '

'But the other half of you knows you can never trust him and so it will never work,' said Edith bluntly. 'You know it, Al. Of course it's tempting; it must be flattering to hear he never forgot you, that he knows he was wrong. But that's because he *was* wrong. Doesn't mean it would be all right second time around. If you can't trust somebody then there's no point. That's what you'd say yourself, you know it is.'

'I know.' Alice still could not meet her friend's eyes.

Edith squinted up at her. 'This hasn't got anything to do with Joe not coming back when we thought he would, has it?'

'Of course not,' said Alice at once, too quickly.

'Alice Lake, whatever is going on?' Edith asked. 'You aren't thinking right for once. Look, just because we're all missing Joe doesn't mean you have to go soft on Mark. It doesn't make sense. You know that as well as I do.' She gazed anxiously up at her tall friend. 'Don't *you* go making a mistake this time. See what happens when I'm not there every day to keep you

252

on the straight and narrow. You got to come and see me more often so I can check up on how you really are.' She grinned. 'Come on, let's go back. No, I'm all right, but Flo will be worried.'

'If you're sure that's all it is,' said Alice, her own cares forgotten in an instant in her concern for Edith. As they walked more slowly now back down the hill towards the turning for Jeeves Street, she reflected that her friend had put her finger on the dilemma yet again. It made no sense. But there it was, all the same.

★ ★ ★

'Something wrong, Lily?' Ruby caught Lily's expression as she hesitated at her bedroom door.

'Oh, not really,' said Lily over-brightly, shaking her gorgeous golden hair.

Ruby was not fooled. 'All the same, do you want to come in for a chat?' she offered. 'Seems like ages since we had a chinwag. Maybe not since we went to the pictures that time.'

Lily looked as if she might refuse but then relented. 'Yes, why not. I'm not quite ready to turn in for the evening, after all.'

In truth she was glad of the distraction. She didn't particularly want to be left with her own thoughts, which were making her uneasy. A break from them would do her good. She was sure she was exaggerating things but, even so, it would be a relief to get away from them.

The last couple of times she had seen Donald, he had not been his usual lovely and kind self. In fact, if she was to be totally honest, he had been short with her, rude even. They had met for a meal at the little

Italian restaurant where he had taken her for their first date, but the staff had not been so welcoming. If she hadn't known better she would have said they were cross with him for some reason, but that did not make sense and she must have got that wrong. There had definitely been an atmosphere though.

He had not made any pretence of offering to escort her home, or even as far as the bus stop. Although he had gone through the motions of being interested in her day's work, it had felt as if he couldn't get shot of her soon enough. He'd given her a perfunctory kiss, barely more than a peck, and set off into the twilight in the complete opposite direction to her, or indeed to his office.

Then, at the weekend, when she had thought a visit to the discreet hotel would make everything better, it had — if anything — been worse. They had of course ended up in bed in one of the gorgeous rooms with the opulent fabrics and gold-tasselled lamps, but Donald's mind had been elsewhere. He kept asking her the same questions and not paying attention to her answers. Then, when she had laughingly pointed this out, he had come close to losing his temper with her.

Lily flinched at the memory. He'd had no call to behave like that. He should appreciate her company and treat her accordingly — she had assumed that was part of their unspoken arrangement. If she'd wanted to spend time with grumpy older men then she could have visited umpteen of her patients, many of them tetchy and grouchy. At least they had proper excuses — they were ill, or recovering from illness, and plenty of them felt guilty at not being able to fight, or carry on with their work on the home front.

However, she was sure Donald had his reasons. Perhaps his work was even more pressurised than usual and he couldn't put it to one side. He'd never properly spoken of it and she didn't like to ask. It was easy to share the day-to-day activities of her nursing rounds, but obviously his profession required more secrecy. She admired his discretion and so she couldn't really complain. Times were hard for everyone.

Gratefully she followed Ruby into the room that she was making more and more her own. It was a relief not to have to pretend. Ruby had seen her letting her hair down and hadn't thought any the worse of her; Lily realised that she had not had many friends like that. She could perhaps dare to relax her guard, or at least a little. That went against her nature, but it was so tiring keeping it up all the time, trying to gauge every situation, work out what behaviour would be to her best advantage and play that role.

'How's Kenny?' she asked, out of politeness and, now she came to think of it, out of genuine interest as well. He wasn't her type but he wasn't a bad person. Part of her shuddered at the thought of socialising with dock workers; she needn't have come to London for that as there were more than enough in Liverpool. Yet she could not deny that Kenny and Ron were good company.

'Oh, too busy to come out much these days,' Ruby sighed. 'Gladys says Ron's the same. Sometimes when there's so much cargo to sort out they can't get away, and they scarcely get a chance to sleep before getting up and unloading the next lot. We'll just have to wait until things are quieter.' She spoke with some pride, knowing that the young men were involved in vital war work, and often at great risk to their lives. She

255

brought out a tin and offered it across the neat little bed. 'Fancy a biscuit? My mother sent them.'

Lily raised her eyebrows. 'Yes, please. If you can spare one.'

'Please, try one. She kept some preserved ginger and now and again she makes a few of these and sends them over.' Ruby wondered how they would compare to the fancy fare that Lily spoke of eating in her posh restaurants, but honestly couldn't see how her mother's biscuits could be bettered. Judging from Lily's reaction, she was right.

'And how's your gentleman friend?' Ruby asked lightly.

Lily's for once unguarded face immediately clouded over. Ah, so there was trouble in paradise. Ruby supposed if Lily wanted to tell her then she would, but she said nothing, simply shrugged.

'Go on, have another.' Ruby recognised the signs of disappointment, however well concealed. She couldn't exactly offer her advice if it wasn't asked for, even assuming she'd know what to say. However, she could ply her friend with ginger biscuits. They made everything seem better, at least.

★ ★ ★

Gladys was pleased that Ron had finally managed a couple of hours off, and had arranged to take her to the Duke's Arms. 'Auntie Ida can see to Ma for once,' he told her as they settled on a bench in the beer garden, the first time this year that it had been warm enough. 'Otherwise I don't know when I'd have the chance to see you. We're working all hours flat out.'

Gladys sipped her half of shandy and shaded her

eyes with her other hand, as the angle of the setting sun was directly in her face. Still, it was beautiful — the coppery light lit the small area, the big pots of geraniums — just coming into flower — set out in an effort to make the place cheerful, the much-mended back fence. She breathed out in contentment.

'You're doing your bit,' she said proudly. 'We can't do without the likes of you. You must be tired.'

'Not too tired to see you,' Ron grinned. He shifted a little closer to her so that their arms were touching. He didn't go in much for public displays of affection, but Gladys was happy to have him here at her side, knowing it was important for him to see her. She felt the same. He was brave and reliable and she couldn't have asked for more.

'No Billy or Kenny tonight?' she asked.

'Nah, Billy's on ARP duty later and he wanted to see the kiddies first,' Ron said. 'Kenny started the early shift and then worked straight through so he was fit to drop. It's not like him to miss a trip to the pub, but even he has his limits.'

Gladys nodded. 'It stands to reason. He can't keep going without some sleep. A shame though, cos I wanted to ask him about his intentions towards Ruby. He likes her, don't he?'

Ron snorted. 'It's no use asking me, Gladys. Me and him don't talk about such things. He was narked when I didn't like his last girlfriend, and then it turned out I was right cos she led him a merry dance then dumped him.'

'That weren't right. She was married and everything.'

Gladys had not approved either. 'Ruby's not like that. She's a nice girl.'

Ron laughed. 'You're playing Cupid, aren't you.'

He took a swig of his pint. 'He might do all right without your help, you know. He's a grown lad, is Kenny. Old enough and ugly enough to manage himself.'

Gladys tapped him playfully on the chest. 'I'm only giving them a bit of encouragement. Kenny deserves better than someone trying to mess him around. And Ruby's not had it easy — she don't say much, but you can just tell. She could do with bringing out of her shell.'

Ron's eyes sparkled, appreciating that Gladys was trying to be kind to their friends. Then he looked up as two young women approached. 'Hello there, Clarrie, Peggy. You just finished at the factory?'

'We have.' Clarrie plonked down on the bench opposite them. 'Mind if we join you?' Peggy came and sat beside her, happy that the answer would be no.

'We just got off, both of us done a double shift today,' she said, setting down her lemonade. 'Boy, I'm glad to get the weight off my feet. Bet you are as well.'

Ron and Gladys nodded.

Clarrie drank some of her lemonade and made a face. 'Oooh, it's even more watered down than usual. Never mind, it's cold and that's what matters.' She pulled back her serviceable headscarf to reveal her deep red hair, backlit by the setting sun. 'Did I hear you saying Kenny's been messed around, Ron? Wait till I tell you what just happened to me.'

Ron shook his head. 'That was before, Clarrie. Gladys has introduced him to her new nurse friend and she won't do anything like that.'

'Of course she won't.' Gladys smiled, keen to get Clarrie and Peggy on her side. 'I'm not interfering, just trying to smooth the way for them a bit, cos they like each other but Ruby's shy and Kenny's all cautious since that last girlfriend. So I'm giving them a

258

helping hand, that's all. Like what any friend would do.' She gave Ron a straight look. 'But what do you mean, Clarrie? Don't tell me you've been treated bad by someone.'

'Well, now.' Clarrie sat forward and took another draught of the watered-down lemonade before launching into her tale. 'Me and Peggy tried to buy some make-up ages ago, it was still winter, wasn't it, Peggy? We queued up for what felt like hours, only it had all gone by the time we got served. So we went out of this shop down near Dalston Lane, and then this man comes up and offers to get me some lippy on the QT. I said, "You must be joking", and thought that was that.'

'Go on.' Gladys was all ears.

'Well, damned if he don't turn up again a while later. He's dressed all smart, acting like what he's the bee's knees, but I can tell there's something wrong, so I don't give him much time. He's seen us coming out of the factory and so knows where we work, and back he comes again a few weeks later. Makes out he's all sympathetic we have to do such long shifts. Asks these little questions about what exactly we do, what stuff we use to make the masks and whatnot.'

'Goodness, that's a bit cheeky. I hope you didn't tell him,' Gladys breathed.

'Course not. What do you take me for?' Clarrie laughed to take the sting out of her question. 'Anyway, he has another go, and he tries it on with me — just like that! Blatant as could be! Do I want to come out with him for an evening, he'll take me up West, he knows this special little hotel?'

'No!' Gladys was horrified but fascinated. Clarrie clearly hadn't come to any harm and was relishing telling her story.

'He did. I says to him, I bet you do. You look like the sort what goes to special little hotels. But I reckon that's too high a price for a lipstick!'

'You never!' Gladys clapped her hand over her mouth in delight.

'Bloody nerve,' muttered Ron, who hated to hear of anyone taking advantage. 'Good job you told him where to go.'

Clarrie shrugged. 'Never did get our lipstick, did we, Peggy? But if that's what you have to do to get it, I'd rather go without.'

Peggy nodded. 'It would have come in handy, cos James gets leave this next weekend and he's coming all the way down from East Anglia to see me. But he don't care if I wear it, or not really. We just want to see each other.'

'Course you do.' Gladys knew Peggy's boyfriend was a GI who was stationed too far away to visit very often. 'It won't matter to him one way or the other.'

'I can't wait.' Peggy's face had lit up at the thought of him, and Gladys was pleased for her friend. Peggy had married her childhood sweetheart but he had been killed at Dunkirk. She'd had a terrible time until she'd met James. Gladys fell silent as Clarrie and Ron began comparing the length of the shifts they'd been asked to work recently and her thoughts drifted. What a horrible man, to ask Clarrie such a thing. And why would he want to know so much about the factory? What business was it of his what it made these days? Everyone still called it the gas-mask factory, and if people guessed it produced anything more, it wasn't done to talk about it. You never knew who might be listening.

Such as thieves who would turn such information to their own benefit for a start. Despite the warmth of the evening, Gladys felt a shiver go down her spine. Thieves like the ones who had tried to break into Victory Walk. War or no war, there were some despicable characters about. It sounded as if Clarrie had had a lucky escape.

25

Lily could see that something had changed. The warmth of the evening had meant that Donald had suggested walking along the streets around the Embankment before finally offering to take her for a drink, but it wasn't that. He was going through the motions, she could just tell.

Perched on a high stool in a quiet pub with a view of the slow-moving river, she waited for him to bring her a glass of lemonade. She didn't fancy anything stronger. She was beginning to wonder if she'd ever liked what he'd bought her before — had she just tried to enjoy those glasses of wine because that was what was expected of her? She certainly didn't want one now.

She had made an effort with her appearance, as usual — tonight she'd gone for her navy blouse and the more subtle lipstick. After all, it was the middle of the week. She'd dug out her lightest jacket, and carefully hung the maroon coat next to lavender sachets at the back of her wardrobe so that it would keep for next winter. She was as confident as she could be that it wasn't the way she looked that had brought about the change.

Donald sat opposite her now, handsome as ever but barely masking his bad mood. She wondered if she should joke prettily and try to tease him out of it. Suddenly she felt it was all too much like hard work. She twirled her glass with her thumb and fore-finger, watching the bubbles rise in the clear liquid.

'Did your sister use up all her lipstick yet?' she asked casually. 'You never said if she liked it.'

For a second he looked confused, but then his features settled with practised ease. 'My sister? Oh, well, she doesn't go out very much. She doesn't get much call to use it.'

Lily sighed. 'What's she like, then? You must be very different to one another, if she doesn't go out.'

He shrugged. 'There's not much to say. She's a little older than me, doesn't have the energy any more.'

Lily sipped her drink, wondering if lack of energy ran in the family. Certainly Donald seemed to have lost most of his. She allowed her gaze to roam around the pub, observing how the angle of evening sunlight reduced the few other customers to silhouettes against the wooden panels. Donald was staring into the distance in the opposite direction, evidently as bored by the sleepy place as she was. Then he drew himself more upright.

'Ah.' He straightened his tie. 'Looks as if there's someone over there who needs to talk to me. Excuse me, this shouldn't take long.' Leaving his briefcase on the stool next to her, he pushed away from the table. 'Keep an eye on that, there's a good girl.'

Good girl! Who did he think he was? She twisted around in annoyance, watching Donald's back as he strode towards the exit. Scurrying after him went a smaller man, presumably the one whose business wouldn't take long.

Something about him jogged her memory, even though she hadn't been able to see him properly in the glare of sunlight. She shook her head. It would be a silly coincidence — and yet it made a kind of sense. The man bore a strong resemblance to the one from months ago in the Magpie Club, the one with cheap clothes, who'd made Donald so angry, only she hadn't been able to recognise that at the time. Even though she'd seen him only the once, the man had made an impression on her, as she had thought he was such an unlikely person for Donald to know.

Now she began to think differently. Perhaps that was exactly the sort of person Donald did business with. What evidence did she have that he worked for the government in a hush-hush position? None at all. She'd taken his bland hints and made them into something that had no basis in fact. It had all been her fantasy.

If he wanted her to keep an eye on her briefcase then she would do exactly that. Carefully she reached for it and tried its clasps. They sprang open at the first attempt; he'd not bothered to lock it. Either he had nothing to hide or he thought she was too stupid to look inside, or she wouldn't understand its contents if she did. Lily drew a sharp breath. She might have been silly when it came to Donald — but she was far from stupid.

The first thing she saw was a small flattened cardboard box. Cautiously she picked it up. Empty. She squinted at its slightly smudged label and had to bite her lip not to exclaim aloud. It was a long name that would make little sense to most people but one that she was very familiar with. A painkiller — a strong one, and hard to get hold of. Gwen was always worrying that stocks were running low.

Beneath it was a sheaf of papers. She scanned them quickly, again aware that they would be incomprehensible to the lay reader. Not to her. They were lists of drugs, with amounts and dates scrawled beside them.

Almost like a shopping list, Lily thought, the pieces falling into place. What if Donald was nothing to do with the government at all, but a petty criminal instead? One of those spivs that her colleagues hated so much — that she herself had been so furious with. He must be a pretty high-up one — she couldn't see him getting his hands dirty, and those clothes showed he had a more than decent income. She gave a stifled groan as she recalled their conversations over the past few months.

What she had taken for loving interest in the details of her day could also be him pumping her for information. Every time she'd complained about having to take her turn tidying the district room, he'd patiently asked exactly what she'd had to do: how many boxes of which drugs or pieces of equipment she'd had to move, what was easily available and what was scarce. She'd described case after case and what she'd used each time, and even what her colleagues had dispensed too. There had been a week when they'd nearly run out of insulin; she'd told him everything.

She put the paperwork back in the case, shaking with anger. It could easily have been him who'd tipped off the would-be thief. Donald himself would be above all that; he would be an information man. Perhaps his interests were widespread — she recalled those sharp looks in the Italian restaurant. He might have a finger in every black-market pie. Business was business, and he'd all but told her some of those places found it hard to keep going in the current conditions. Who better to receive a friendly welcome than the man who could get hold of everything — and how might that sour, if the supplies dried up?

She gulped down the rest of her lemonade and

barely looked up as Donald returned, this time without his badly dressed sinister shadow. 'Fancy another?' he asked, his voice calm as if he'd been out discussing the coming week's weather.

She looked at him with new eyes. 'Perhaps not,' she said. 'After all, I don't want to keep you from your important business. That's obviously where your mind is this evening.'

'Now, Lily, you know that's not fair,' he said, a little edge creeping into his voice. He cleared his throat as if to recover his casual tone. He passed one hand through his elegantly styled hair. 'It's not that I wouldn't love to take you somewhere tonight, but that's just not possible.'

'Of course.' She smoothed her skirt. 'Are you going to have another drink?' she added, although he had not finished his beer.

'Ah.' He pushed back his light tweed jacket sleeve and checked his big, shiny watch. 'Maybe not. In fact, I should be getting back soon. Sorry, I didn't make it clear I couldn't spend very long with you this evening.'

'Oh?' Lily cocked her head and gave herself a moment to gather her thoughts. Then she threw aside her caution. 'Do you have to get back to your office?' she asked, quietly at first but then letting her voice rise. She got to her feet, setting the wooden stool aside. 'Is it that hush-hush work you have to get back to so urgently?' She rounded the little table and stood at his side, her eyes now on a level with his.

He smiled uncertainly, then put on his best reassuring tone. 'Now, Lily, I know you're disappointed — '

Lily threw back her head and laughed, at which the few people in the dull room finally looked up and took notice. 'Disappointed? Oh yes, I'm disappointed all right. But not for the reason you think.'

'What?' Now he was flustered. 'I can assure you that I've got something unavoidable and urgent . . .'

'Oh, don't bother to lie any longer, Donald.' Lily was sick of the whole charade. 'This business of yours isn't for the top-secret war effort, is it? You're nothing but a common or garden crook. Every time you have to run off, it's for another black-market deal. Lipstick, perfume, medicine, it doesn't matter what, does it? As long as you can steal it and then sell it at a profit.'

Now everyone was interested. Silence fell. The bartender put down the pint glass he had been polishing so that he could be prepared for trouble.

Donald looked stunned and then hurt. 'No, what-ever do you mean? I've told you — '

Before he could stand, Lily whipped back her arm and slapped him hard around the face. 'All you were interested in was what I knew about the movement of drugs around the East End. Oh, and you got your bit of fun on the side. As it happens, your henchman didn't manage to get into our stores and you're not going to get anything more from me.' She picked up her cherished handbag. 'Well, you can wave bye-bye to all of that. Any more attempts to burgle us, we'll know who to blame. Don't you dare forget it.' With that she turned on her high heel and dashed out, leaving Donald with his hand over a burgeoning red mark on his handsome face, too stunned to go after her.

The barman picked up his glass and began to polish it again.

★ ★ ★

Lily had no idea that she could move so fast in her high heels, but desperation gave her wings. She wove in and out of the pedestrians on the pavements of the Strand, thinking only of putting enough space between her and the horrid pub before Donald decided to come after her. If he decided to come after her. Instinct reminded her that if she got as far as Aldwych she could pick up a bus heading towards Liverpool Street.

Finally she halted outside the Waldorf Hotel, gasping for breath. At least this was one place Donald hadn't taken her. She didn't think she could bear to see any of those bars or restaurants again. Let alone the Magpie Club. As she waited for the bus, she thought what a good name that was for it — full of shiny and tempting things. How she had been taken in by its superficial glamour.

Her feet were killing her but she forced herself to stand straight, wincing as her new blisters rubbed the shoe backs but not giving in to the pain. It was what she deserved. Now the full impact of the evening was beginning to hit her, and inside she was crumbling. As she climbed aboard the bus and took her seat on the top deck, well away from any other passengers, she closed her eyes but would not permit herself to cry. The bus trundled along and she held tight to her resolution not to give way to her emotions.

'Last stop. We're terminating here. Everyone off, there's a burst water main,' shouted the conductor, and Lily wearily hauled herself onto her agonisingly painful feet, ready to stand in the now-cold street until a replacement bus came to ferry them all on a different route.

As the wind rose and funnelled around the corners

268

of the tall buildings, the grand façades of banks and offices, pockmarked from years of shelling, Lily realised that anger was her strongest feeling by far. That was followed by shame at getting everything so wrong. There was little sense of lost love. So perhaps she hadn't been fooled so heavily; her heart might yet be intact. It had been such a gorgeous image, she and Donald looking like such a well-matched couple, going to glamorous places, but maybe deep down she had known that it was unreal. He'd been having a bit of fun, with the added possibility of taking advantage of her professional information, and she had played her part to a T.

Finally the replacement bus turned up, and she collapsed onto a seat on the lower deck this time. What an evening. She took out her hanky and carefully wiped her face. No reason to look like a victim, she reminded herself. It was Donald who was in the wrong. At least she would make it back before curfew.

★ ★ ★

Ruby lay on her bed, still dressed in her old shirt and skirt. She was too awake to get ready for sleep; her mind was going over the cases of the day, even as her body was tired from an hour at the victory garden. It was strange to think that she'd never bothered with such things before. Now she felt a major sense of achievement at picking a bunch of early radishes.

So she was alert enough to hear footsteps coming up the stairs and the telltale creak of the floorboard just along from the end of the top landing. Automatically she rose and went to her door, edging it open. Lily was tiptoeing down the corridor.

269

'Lily? You all right?' She could see the other nurse was trying to be quiet and hadn't expected anyone to be about.

'Oh, Ruby. Fancy you still being up.' Lily was attempting to sound normal but something was wrong.

'Ah — yes, yes, I'm all right, just went to meet a friend. I'd have been back sooner but the bus had to terminate early — you know how it is.'

'Yes, of course.' Ruby looked more closely at her colleague. 'You made it just in time then — it's just turned ten.' She paused. 'You sure everything's fine? Do you want to come in for a minute?'

Lily sagged a little against the wall but shook her head. 'Really. Thanks but not tonight. I'm tired, that's all it is.'

Ruby nodded dubiously. 'Well, if you're sure.' She waited but Lily said nothing further. 'Right, well, I'd best be getting changed and ready for bed.'

'Me too.'

'Good night, then.' Ruby gave the other nurse one more chance to say something further, and then shut her door again, puzzled and not convinced.

★ ★ ★

Lily just managed to get her door open and then shut it firmly behind her before the tears came. She threw herself onto her bed and buried her face in her pillow, desperate to muffle the sound, knowing Ruby was awake just a few yards away. Even now she was concerned not to make the wrong impression.

Damn Donald and his good looks and persuasive ways. She had so wanted him to be what she'd

270

imagined, to live up to her ideal of the worldly man who would sweep her off her feet and transport her to a more glamorous world. Since she was young she'd seen pictures of that kind of life in the newspapers and magazines or on the screen at the cinema. It had seemed beyond her grasp, growing up in a small but respectable terraced house near the Liverpool docks. Her parents had loved her and spoilt her as much as their slender means allowed, but she'd always hankered for something more.

Knowing that her natural good looks set her apart from the others, first at school and then in nurses' training, she'd almost felt it her due to be able to reach that magic world. She channelled all her energy into finding the right way to break into the hallowed inner circle. It had become second nature to angle every word and action towards that end.

Now all that effort had come to nothing, as she'd come a cropper and had little to show for it except two half-used tubes of lipstick. Perhaps she'd throw them away in the morning. She couldn't imagine ever wearing them again.

Gradually her sobs subsided and exhaustion overwhelmed her. She forced herself to hang up the navy blouse and pull out its creases, and carefully place her high heels under the wardrobe. She put on her most worn-out cotton nightie, which brought comforting memories of home, a place where she didn't have to pretend to be anyone else. Then she sat on her bed and waited for any remaining sounds of life in the big house to die away, before she moved to go down the corridor to the bathroom. The last thing she wanted was for anyone to see her with a tear-stained face. Lily Chandler did not cry.

271

Safely behind the locked door of the chilly bathroom, she washed her face and patted it carefully with her flannel. It had her initials embroidered in the corner; her mother had done this the week before she left. Lily gulped, guiltily remembering how she'd not even unpacked the photograph of her parents.

The best she could do now was to get as good a night's sleep as she was able, and then she would think about what to do next come the morning. As she made her way back to her room, she was so tired she thought she could have nodded off on her feet.

Finally switching off her light, she felt sleep overcome her. Donald was not worth crying over any longer. Whatever he had done, she knew that her patients would be waiting for her in the morning. So would her colleagues — the ones who didn't give a jot if she had new clothes or perfect make-up, just as long as she worked hard and played her part in the team of district nurses. The team in which she was gradually finding her place, in which she was judged for her expertise, not her looks.

26

Alice approached the grand main entrance to Victoria Station, her heart in her mouth. It was time to make up her mind once and for all, and she dreaded it. Nevertheless she knew it had to be done.

The station had been the target of many enemy bombs during the Blitz, and some of the damage was still clear to see. The Grosvenor Hotel next door had taken a proper pasting. She wouldn't fancy staying there any time soon. Still, the trains had kept running and now there had been no attacks there for nearly three years; she was as safe here as anywhere.

Alice had chosen the station as it was neutral ground. She felt a strange reluctance to have this conversation closer to home. Neither did she want to travel any further; there was always the risk of disruption and she had to be back on shift this evening, covering the late rounds. Whatever happened in the next few hours, she had to be calm and collected by then.

Mark had offered to come to the East End, to meet in or near the nurses' home, but she didn't want that. It felt like her own territory, one that hadn't been touched by his betrayal. Of course Dermot had given him instructions just how to get there, but she had suggested somewhere mid-way instead. His train up from his south-coast base would arrive at Victoria, and that would suit her very well. It was big enough for anonymity.

She knew that she was dragging her feet, putting off the moment of stepping onto the concourse.

Self-consciously she patted her hair to make sure it was how she wanted it. She wanted to look smart, in control, when in fact she felt anything but.

Alice slowly made her way to the agreed meeting place, the end of the furthest platform. She didn't want to be late but hated the idea of standing there waiting — just as she had waited all those years ago, for a word from him to say that he had changed his mind. Well, she was done with waiting for him any longer. She clenched her jaw. She had to say the words she had rehearsed over and over in her head — but there he was, already at the arranged spot, and the speech she had memorised vanished completely.

It being early summer, he was in a light jacket this time, a dark tie loosely knotted at his throat, casual cotton trousers with turn-ups. He looked up and smiled as he caught sight of her and against her wishes her heart thudded in response. Alice tried to focus on any changes to the Mark she had known. The hair beginning to recede, the crow's feet, the skin which hinted that he spent too much time indoors. It was no use. Her heart betrayed her, reacting to that once-beloved face.

'You came.' His smile grew wider. 'I didn't know if you would.'

'Of course I came. I said I would.' Alice didn't add that she always kept her promises — it was not in her nature to let anyone down.

Mark nodded as if he had taken the unspoken point, the implied rebuke. 'You look . . . wonderful,' he added.

Alice winced with embarrassment. She had dressed carefully for this meeting, wanting to look smart but not inviting in any way. He was not making this easy.

274

'How was your journey?' she asked, knowing that she sounded stilted.

He raised his eyebrows a little. 'It was all right. No delays — as you can see for yourself.'

She nodded hesitantly.

A crowd of young women in the dark green sweaters of the Land Army disembarked from the newly-arrived train at the platform and flowed around them, giving Alice a few moments to steady herself.

'Well,' Mark began again once the sea of Land Girls had gone, 'you got my letters. You know what I want to say to you, Alice. How sorry I am for what happened, what a stupid decision I took back then. I was young, I was an idiot. I know that now.' His face started to show the strain, his voice was low and with the hint of a shake.

'You followed your principles,' she said slowly. 'But I would have waited. You only had to ask.'

'I didn't think it was fair to do that.' He looked away.

'You didn't give me the choice,' she said, trying not to sound bitter.

'No. Like I said, I was an idiot.' He cleared his throat and met her gaze once more. 'But Alice, I'm asking now. Will you give me a second chance? I can't make up for the hurt I caused you and all those years we've wasted being apart. That's not possible. We can start again though. I'll never hurt you like that again.'

For a second she was tempted. It would have been the easiest thing in the world to fall into the old pattern, to melt into his arms, rest her head on his shoulder where it fitted so well. And yet, what did he mean, wasted years? She had not wasted her time since they had last met. She had gone on to qualify as a nurse, and then a district nurse, and spent valuable years helping patients, even saving lives. She would not call that a waste of time. He no longer knew her. That one comment proved it.

Alice took a small step back. 'No,' she said.

His eyes shut in pain. 'Give me a chance, Alice,' he said, the shaking in his voice more noticeable now. 'You're the only woman I've ever loved. Let me show you that I mean it.'

She shook her head, her face more certain. 'It's no good, Mark. I can't put aside how you let me down. Yes, it was terrible and I never want to feel anything like it ever again, but it's in the past. I'm not the person I was back in Liverpool. Our lives have changed. I can't say yes.'

He reached his hand forward. 'You don't mean that, Alice, you can't.'

She gasped. He didn't believe her even when she told him how she felt, directly to his face. 'I do mean it, Mark,' she said, conviction filling her now that the crux had come.

'No. That can't be true. Alice, say you'll try again. Forgive me.'

She could see that his pain was real, but now she was sure that she had taken the right course. 'I might forgive you, Mark, but I can't forget what you did,' she said frankly. 'It means I could never fully trust you — we could never be happy together now. We had our chance but it's all over.'

'Alice, stay. You're upset and I don't blame you . . .'

'Mark,' she said with patience, though she was keen to end the conversation, 'I'm not upset. I'm sure. I'm sorry if it's not what you want but I'll keep to my decision.' Her voice softened a little. 'Goodbye, Mark.'

She turned, and her last sight of him was of his face, almost dazed, as if he was unable to believe that he had failed to persuade her.

Alice stepped out of the concourse and onto the pavement outside, hardly able to believe it herself. She had finally told him what she had wanted to say for so long. Wherever her future lay, it would not be with Mark.

★ ★ ★

'It's going to be a busy day for me!' Ellen was packing her leather bag at top speed. 'Two of my ladies have gone into labour. One's a couple of days late and the other's two weeks early. I thought I'd have lots of time in between the pair of them, but now it looks as if I won't.'

Ruby stepped back from the door of the district room to give her colleague more space. 'Good heavens. How will you manage? You can't be in two places at once.'

Ellen laughed. 'Just watch me. I nearly can. They live only a couple of streets apart, for a start.'

'All the same.' Ruby's head was spinning at the idea of everything that would need to be done.

'One's already had two children and her pregnancy has been very straightforward. We're not anticipating any problems, touch wood.' Ellen turned and knocked her knuckles against the door of the old oak lending cupboard. 'Also, she's got a lovely big kitchen — she's at the end of the terrace and they have more room. Loads of hot water, everything clean as a new pin, it'll be grand. So I can be doubly sure I won't infect the other lady.' She added a fresh pair of rubber gloves to her items. 'As for her, we'll just have to see. She's

277

much younger, and it's her first child. She's quite thin, but the doctor expects she'll be able to deliver her baby without complications all the same.'

Ruby gave a small smile. 'I've never delivered a baby. I've been present at births when I was training, but I haven't had much to do with pregnant women on the district.' Except for those ones who lost their babies, she reminded herself. That was the opposite end of the spectrum.

Ellen added a couple of cotton face masks to her collection. 'Oh, it's the best part of the job, let me tell you. There's nothing quite like it. Those first few minutes of a baby's life — it's a rare privilege to be there.' She fastened her bag. 'There, I'm done. But say now, Ruby, did you never think of taking the extra midwifery training? There used to be a bursary for it — Fiona would know all about that. You'd fit the bill, I'd say.'

Ruby was nonplussed. 'Do you think so?'

'Sure. Why not?'

Ruby shuffled her feet a little. 'I don't know. I'm not that long out of my district training, I suppose.'

Ellen nodded. 'Ah well. You've most likely had training up to here for the time being. All the same, think about it for the future. People will always need midwives. You could work wherever you want. Travel a bit, if that's what appeals to you.'

Ruby frowned. 'Oh, I'm not sure about that. I haven't ever thought about leaving London. It felt like a big step just moving from west to east.' Then she worried that she might sound rude, given who she was talking to.

Ellen laughed. 'Oh, don't worry, it's not for everybody. I thought long and hard before leaving home.'

'Don't you miss it?' Ruby couldn't resist asking.

Ellen nodded. 'Of course. Sometimes I wake up and think I'm back in Dublin, and wonder why everything sounds different. Or I'll smell something cooking when I go past a house, and it takes me straight back to my mother's kitchen.' She shrugged. 'It helps having Bridget here — we trained together, you know. She's met my parents when they came to help me move out of my first nurses' home, and my younger brother once when he came up to Dublin.' She sighed. 'I don't know when I'll see them all again, to be honest, but we knew what we were signing up for. We're needed more over here than at home, that's the long and the short of it.'

Ruby felt a lump in her throat. For all that she dreaded seeing her sister, at least she knew she could get back home if there was an emergency, or simply if she missed her family too much, though that was yet to happen. For Ellen and Bridget that would be well-nigh impossible. 'You must be very brave,' she stuttered.

'Not a bit of it,' Ellen said briskly. 'No more than any other nurse. We all have to get on with the job in hand, don't we? No matter what the circumstances are. No point in wishing for a nice tidy hospital ward when the patient's in a house that's been bomb-damaged. You do what you can.'

Ruby blinked, acknowledging that was the truth.

'What's the most difficult birth you've had?' she asked, feeling daring for asking the more experienced nurse such a question.

Ellen pulled a wry face. 'Now you've got me.' She paused. 'Since you ask, it was with a mother who was quite small. Her baby was overdue and it was a devil

279

of a job to get it out and make sure they were both all right. Touch and go for a few moments there, and no mistake.'

Ruby's face grew concerned. Before she could stop herself, she blurted out what had just come into her mind. 'What about Edith? Do you think she'll be all right, then? She's not very big, is she?'

Ellen paused, and her face showed that she too had had this thought. 'Well, as it happens, I might well be at her birth. She spoke to me about it ages ago, long before she stopped work. She knows all the risks, of course.'

'Of course.' Ruby was hanging onto her colleague's words, hoping she could allay her own worries.

Ellen took a deep breath, as if recognising how anxious her younger colleague was. 'There's really no need for concern at this stage. Edith's healthy as can be, aside from a nasty run of morning sickness that went on a bit longer than usual. She's fit — you know as well as I do that you can't do the job unless you are. She knows what she should be eating and how much rest to take. Yes, she's not what you'd call large, but she's not exactly delicate either. As long as she doesn't go a long way overdue then she should be perfectly all right.'

'Really?' Ruby suddenly couldn't bear the thought of any harm coming to the senior nurse who had been so kind to her from the moment she'd arrived at Victory Walk.

'Really.' Ellen was all firmness now. 'Don't you dwell on that, Ruby. She'll be grand, just you see. Now I had best be getting along. Her baby is still a few weeks off, but I'd better attend to these two who look as if they are intending to arrive today.'

280

Ruby nodded, somewhat reassured. Edith would be in the best of hands, she knew, and all her training would help when it came to the moment. There was no point in worrying. There was plenty to keep her occupied with her own patients — and then there was the matter of what was going on with Lily. She didn't like to think of her colleague being upset and not being able to confide in anybody. True, Lily had been offhand and stuck up at times, but no one deserved to have to bottle up their pain. One way or another, she would get to the bottom of it.

★ ★ ★

Alice took a deep breath and looked at herself in the mirror. She couldn't quite believe this day had finally arrived, weeks after she thought it would happen. Joe was coming home on leave at last, and she wanted to be at her best.

She'd imagined that she would wear the boat-necked jumper her mother had made, as he wouldn't have seen it before. However, now it was late in May and the weather was warm, too warm for wool. She'd had to go through her wardrobe, shaking out all the light blouses and dresses she'd put away the year before when the cold snap began. She couldn't remember which he'd seen her wearing and which he hadn't. It really didn't matter, but it was something to concentrate on, to avoid any more troubling thoughts.

She held her blouse with the pattern of red berries at arm's length, trying to recall when she had last put it on. Then she decided it wasn't right and hung it up again. What was wrong with her, she wondered. She never usually bothered about such things. In the end she settled on her plain sky-blue blouse with the mother-of-pearl buttons. If she teamed that with her navy skirt, she could wear her maroon peep-toe pumps, which would look smart but not showy. That would do. After all, she didn't have Edith near at hand to advise her any more.

She would walk over to Jeeves Street, where Flo was preparing a special meal. She had been hoarding ingredients to make her eldest son's favourite dishes ever since he'd first written to say he would be back on leave. Alice could imagine her now, the kitchen window steaming up with the heat from the range where a chicken would be roasting. Mattie would be peeling carrots and potatoes. Edith would be insisting on helping and the others would be insisting that she didn't.

Alice had checked with Gladys if there was anything she could take along from the victory garden, but it was still too early in the season for much to be ready. Instead she had picked some flowers to make the table cheerful. A few had taken to growing along the borders of the garden, seeds blown in from when people still tended their plants in window boxes, and she had even tried a few in odd pots in the Victory Walk back yard by the bike racks. They brightened the little space, and Gladys assured Alice they could spare some sweet peas.

Alice's gaze fell on her wastepaper basket. An unopened letter lay in it, with Mark's writing on the envelope. There was no point in reading it — she knew what it would say, but it would not change her mind. On her way back from Victoria a few days ago, she had waited for a rush of remorse and regret, but none had come. All she'd felt was a huge sense of

282

relief. Having dreaded the confrontation, wondering if she would have the strength to keep to her resolve, instead a weight was lifted from her shoulders.

The important thing now was that Joe was coming home and she would finally see him again, not just make do with his letters. They had become less and less frequent, and yet she counted on them to brighten her day, buoy her up when everything felt too hard. But if it was bad for her, how much worse would it have been for him, on his ship, heading for who knew where? The danger would be unremitting.

She had so much to talk to him about. She hoped there would be time for them to spend on their own; she had no idea how long he would have before his leave was up and he would have to return to his base, wherever that was nowadays.

Alice had thought long and hard about whether she should get him a gift to mark his making it home at last. After all, she owed him a Christmas present and at least two birthday presents. She felt it was a special occasion and wanted to find a way of showing him she knew how important it was. It couldn't be too big; there would be very little room on board his ship.

She had ventured into the centre of town on one of her precious afternoons off and wandered the bookshops on the Charing Cross Road, wondering what would be the perfect gift. It had to be something fun, not too serious. She rejected choice after choice, for being too weighty, or depressing, or silly, or books she knew he'd read already. Several times she was tempted to buy something for herself but had resisted. This trip was about finding the ideal book for Joe, not a treat for her.

Then she came across it, on a low wooden shelf

near a bright sunlit window. A couple of years ago, they'd gone together to see Humphrey Bogart and Mary Astor in *The Maltese Falcon*. They had both enjoyed it hugely and had quoted lines at one another for a long time afterwards. Now here was the book on which it had been based — and not only that novel, but the author's complete set, all in one volume. It would be perfect. Five stories for the price of one, and not taking up much room either.

The shop assistant had asked if she wanted it wrapped, and Alice had said yes. That way she wouldn't be lured into reading it herself and wanting to keep it. Perhaps Joe would let her borrow it at some point in the future. She had sat on the bus home with *The Complete Novels* of Dashiell Hammett safely stowed in her handbag, happy in the knowledge that Joe would enjoy it — and would think of her while reading it.

Now she took the present, still in its wrapping, and put it once again in her bag. For some reason she didn't want anyone to see it on her way out. She knew one or two of the others would tease her, say Joe would have other things on his mind, that she was wasting her money. Or perhaps it was more that she wanted to keep it just between the pair of them, something that only they would fully understand. It would make him remember their trip to the cinema; there had been a raid the previous night and they had expected the sirens to go off again at any moment, and so making it through the full film without interruption had been a triumph.

Carefully she edged on her maroon shoes. She had saved her last pair of nylons for this visit, but as luck would have it, it was warm enough to go without. Mary had managed to get hold of them; they had

284

been a present from Charles and she had been kind enough to share them. Mary wouldn't have told her she had been silly to buy the detective stories for Joe, although she would have had no interest in the book or the film. She would understand that this was one of Alice and Joe's shared enthusiasms. Mary herself didn't like films about crimes — 'There are enough of those about already,' she would say, if asked along to the cinema when one was showing. 'Give me something cheerful instead.'

So the nylons were still in their packet, in the drawer, awaiting another special occasion. Alice grinned. Some of the nurses had resorted to trying to stain their legs with tea and then drawing a thin line down the backs of their calves to represent the seam, but she had never attempted it. Tea was rationed anyway; she would far rather drink it, given the choice.

She lifted her cotton jacket from its hook and folded it over her arm. Even if it was too warm to put it on now, she might need it later. She'd spent so much time thinking about what to wear that now she was in danger of running late. Not that any of the Banhams would mind, but she didn't want to miss a moment of the event.

Gladys had kindly put the slender bunch of sweet-pea flowers into a jar of water to keep them fresh. Alice retrieved them from the kitchen and then wrapped their stems in a piece of wet newspaper so they would not dry out on the short walk to Jeeves Street and the Banham household. Flo wouldn't appreciate dead flowers, even if she'd be too polite to say so. The petals were a wonderful deep red, mixed with some so pale as to be almost white. They made a lovely contrast and Alice was pleased with them. She gave them a little shake so that the excess water wouldn't drip on her dark skirt, and then she was ready.

Stepping over the threshold at the nurses' home's big front door, she drew a deep breath. The day had finally come; she would see Joe again. He was really home at last.

27

Ruby had never tried to mend a bike before and wasn't quite sure where to start. She'd returned from her rounds in the afternoon and twice the front wheel had resisted where she wanted it to go on the way back. Gritting her teeth she had wrenched the handlebars around and manoeuvred the clunky frame into the yard at Victory Walk. She'd had enough. She dashed inside to hang up her uniform and change into clothes that didn't matter, and then returned to the bike rack, pitching up her sleeves.

Belinda saw her and wandered over. 'Trouble?' she asked.

Ruby explained the problem. 'I don't want to make a fuss but I'm not sure what to do,' she confessed.

Belinda hefted the bike from the rack and wheeled it to and fro, then tried to turn the handlebars. There was an ominous sound of creaking. 'I see what you mean,' she said. 'I reckon it needs oil. Wait here and I'll fetch some.' She was as good as her word and a few minutes later she had shown Ruby what to do, and there was no more creaking when they tried to wheel the bike around the yard.

Ruby sat back on her haunches. 'How did you know that?' she asked, impressed. 'Did your brother tell you? Mine never let me near a tin of oil.'

Belinda squatted down beside her. 'Sort of, but we were just kids and I've forgotten most of what he taught me,' she admitted. 'No, my friend Geraldine who drives the ambulances reminded me. They have to sort things out if anything goes wrong — there's no time to wait for a mechanic to come and mend it for them. So fixing a bike is easy in comparison.'

Ruby was even more impressed. 'I can't imagine. Well, thanks for helping. I was dreading getting back on it.'

Belinda got up, brushing dust from her skirt. 'Think nothing of it. Now you know what to do.' She went back inside the home through the side door.

Ruby lifted her face up to the sun, enjoying its warmth. It was good to be outside, to make the most of the bright daylight, enjoy the birds singing. It didn't seem possible that only a few months ago they had all had to huddle in the refuge room, in the dark, hoping the enemy aircraft would not bomb the house. If she didn't look around too closely, didn't turn to glimpse the houses over the back wall which had caught the force of the hit in the last raids, didn't notice the fresh mortar around the replacement windows, she could pretend none of it had happened.

She couldn't stay here much longer though. The others would be returning, needing to put their own bikes in the racks, and she was in the way. Ruby hauled herself upright, her gaze wandering over the small collection of odd containers being used as pots, and the sweet peas that grew from them. Bigger pots behind them showed the young shoots of beans, Gladys's latest idea.

There was a movement at the big windows, a figure coming to look out from the common room. Ruby waved. It was Lily, who had now noticed her too. Lily, who had seemed to be avoiding her ever since that evening when she'd sneaked in just before curfew.

Ruby decided now was the ideal time to seize her

chance. Who could resist a walk on a fine afternoon like this? She would ask her colleague to come along, and then she'd get to the bottom of whatever it was that was so troubling her.

★ ★ ★

Lily crossed her arms defensively across her chest, tugging her neat cardigan more tightly around herself. Ruby's suggestion had caught her on the hop and she hadn't been able to come up with an excuse to say no. Not that she minded being outside on a day like this, but she would far rather have gone for a wander by herself. That way she wouldn't have had to face any tricky questions.

She'd done her best to throw herself into work after that awful final evening with Donald. He wasn't worth wasting time over, she told herself repeatedly, only to remember how she had loved the sensation of being held in his strong arms, the smell of his aftershave, the way the light would catch on his dark hair. Then she would remind herself that he had been a criminal all along. Yet even though she knew that to be the truth, it didn't stop her longing for what she had thought he was offering.

She had been far too ashamed to admit any of this to anyone, keeping her sadness buried deep within. Nobody needed to know. It wasn't as if spilling her secret would change anything. No one could help; it was all down to her. She had to hold her head high and shut all of them out.

That had worked until Ruby had come beaming into the common room, refusing to take no for an answer. 'Look at that sun, it'll do you a world of good to go for a walk in it,' she had said, and Fiona, passing through, had nodded in approval.

'Exactly right, Ruby, exactly right. If I didn't have all these forms to fill out, I swear I'd join you.'

After that, Lily could not escape.

Ruby had led her towards the Downs, where the trees were now fully in leaf. People were working on their strips of allotments, weeding, sowing and digging. Lily wondered if she should volunteer for more hours at the victory garden and show willing to contribute to its valued crop of vegetables. It wasn't as if she had to keep her nails beautifully manicured any more.

'So, Lily, I don't seem to have seen you around much lately,' Ruby began.

Lily shrugged. 'I've been working, same as everyone else. And you've seen me at mealtimes.'

Ruby gave her a dry look. 'You know what I mean.'

She waited to see if any answer would be forthcoming, and when there was none she carried on. 'That evening when you came in at curfew — something was wrong, I know it was. You didn't say what. You don't have to, I can't force you . . .'

'I should hope not,' said Lily quickly.

Ruby sighed. 'I thought you might want to talk about it, now that we've got a bit of space on our own,' she suggested. 'A trouble shared is a trouble halved, isn't that what they say? I wouldn't go blab. bing to anybody. I can keep my mouth shut, if that's what has been bothering you.'

Lily let her gaze turn from the busy allotment to her friend. 'It's not that,' she said. 'It's just that you can't do anything to change what happened. No one can. So it's best to leave it alone.'

'All right.' Ruby appeared to give in, and they walked a little further along the wide path that ran along one side of the big open space. She looked up at the branches, spotting a blackbird finding a new perch.

Lily stared straight ahead, a wave of sadness washing over her. Ruby was only trying to help. She wasn't prying — it was a genuine offer of friendship. Maybe she shouldn't bat it away too hastily.

'The thing is,' she began, edging her way in cautiously, 'well, you know I told you I had a . . . a gentleman friend, a while ago now.'

Ruby nodded. 'Yes, of course. You went to a hotel together, you said.'

'That's right.' Lily let out a long exhalation. 'We did. Quite a few times, actually. It was lovely at first — he said all sorts of lovely things and treated me so well, I thought it must mean something . . . but I was wrong.' She spoke quietly, keeping the tremor out of her voice.

'Go on.' Ruby was all ears.

'It all started to feel different. Like he wasn't really listening, or only to certain things I said. I began to wonder what it was, but for a while I didn't put together all the obvious signs. I suppose I didn't want to, that was the truth. It was all too lovely, being taken out to places like that. I didn't want it to end.' She stopped abruptly, afraid that she would sob aloud. She bunched her hands into tight fists, willing herself to maintain control.

'Must have been horrible,' Ruby sympathised. 'I mean, when you know something is wrong but can't put your finger on what it is.'

'Sort of,' Lily managed to reply. She gave another long sigh. 'Turns out he wasn't what he let me think

291

he was. All that money he had to spend — it came from the black market.'

She hated admitting it. It made her appear gauche and gullible, and anything but sophisticated. Then again, this was Ruby — who had never seemed to set much store by appearances.

Ruby nodded, not shocked or horrified, for which Lily was grateful. 'The thieving so-and-so,' she said. 'He led you on, then. He let you think he was all respectable and above board.'

'Oh, it was all very grand,' said Lily bitterly. 'He didn't promise me anything, not really; he was just happy to string me along. He'd say things like, the way things were at the moment meant it was too uncertain to plan for marriage, or that everyone deserved some pleasure in their lives . . . I thought it meant we'd have some kind of a future, but not yet, not while the war was still going on. He was happy for me to believe that.'

They were heading towards a busy section of the allotments, with gardeners calling and shouting at one another across the beds.

'Let's go down here,' Ruby proposed, taking Lily's unresisting arm and steering her towards one of the quieter exits on the Downs.

Lily agreed, relieved to avoid any curious faces. She hadn't cried after all, but she wasn't sure if the danger was entirely past. She didn't want to break down in front of strangers.

'I should have known better,' she said bleakly. 'I mean, why hadn't he been conscripted? I just assumed he had an important hush-hush job that paid well.'

'I don't know about that.' Ruby lightly patted her arm before releasing it. 'You're hardly to blame, Lily.

Not if he took advantage of you. No one will think the worse of you for that.'

'Oh, they will, believe me, they will,' Lily said immediately. 'People love to point a finger, tell you that you've done wrong.'

'Some people, maybe,' Ruby said, 'but not ones who matter. Anyway, why should you care what they think? It's none of their damn business when it comes down to it.'

Lily almost took a step back. This was such a refreshing way of looking at the matter, and perhaps not one she'd expected to hear from Ruby, whom she'd always considered too shy and anxious to have such opinions.

'Do you really think so?' she asked cautiously.

'Yes I do,' Ruby said staunchly. 'You can't be blamed for wanting to have a bit of fun, Lily. We all deserve to have that. God knows we work hard enough. Some of the sights we see would have your finger-pointers running for cover. We've got to be tougher than that. Let them say what they like. I know you aren't a bad person. You work hard, and you've even started to do your share in the victory garden. If you want to have a proper meal in a posh hotel, then who am I to say you can't?'

'Really?' Lily could hardly believe that Ruby was so strong-minded in her support. A few months ago she would have dismissed the other nurse, thinking that anyone so reserved and nervous wouldn't have any ideas worth listening to. She would have thought her too unworldly, too drab and dull. How wrong she had been. 'I suppose I was taken up by the showiness of it all,' she admitted. 'I loved going to places I never could have afforded otherwise. It was exciting. I never stopped to think of where some of his friends got their money. Not one of them ever asked me what I did for a living, they wouldn't care how hard the likes of you and me work. All they saw was a pretty face.'

Ruby laughed a little. 'Well, I wouldn't know. I've never been anywhere like that. And people don't stop and stare at my face — no, don't say anything, I know I'm no great shakes in the looks department. It don't matter, though. I used to think it did but it's not nearly as important now.'

Lily shook her head. 'Don't be so hard on yourself,' she said. 'I could show you a few ideas if you like: how to do your hair a bit different, what other clothes you could wear, which colours would suit you best — things like that.'

Ruby looked as if she was going to protest but then she smiled. 'Maybe. It would be a bit of fun, wouldn't it? Perhaps, like one Friday or the weekend, before we go to the cinema.'

Lily managed to smile back.

'That's better,' said Ruby encouragingly. 'We'll plan something to cheer ourselves up, that's what we need.' She glanced sideways at her friend. 'Is there something else, Lily? Have you not told me everything?'

Lily tried to cover her mistake at once. 'What, isn't it bad enough that I've been walking out with a man, and went to stay with him in a hotel?' she said, not quite keeping the bitter edge from her comment. 'Most people would say that's more than enough.' She tossed her head.

Ruby narrowed her eyes in concern. 'You're not . . . you're not in the family way or anything?'

Lily blinked slowly. 'Thank God I'm not.' She was surprised Ruby had the nerve to raise such a question, but then again she was a nurse — she would have

294

known what went on in the hotel and what the consequences could have been. 'No, before you ask, we made sure that didn't happen. You know. He brought something with him.'

Ruby nodded dubiously. 'Sorry to intrude like that but I wondered if that was why you were still worried. Because you are, aren't you?'

Lily took a few more steps along the path to the exit, which led into a narrow street of small terraced houses. The voices of the allotment holders were fading into the background. She pushed back the sleeves of her cardigan and then pulled them down again, unable to decide whether to say anything further. However, Ruby didn't look as if she was in the mood to give up easily. Perhaps airing her suspicions would help.

'All right,' she said. 'There is something else. It might be nothing. I've got no real proof.'

Ruby waited for Lily to catch up with her. 'Go on, then,' she said. 'Maybe it will help to tell me. I'm not the one who's been betrayed. I might be able to see if you're worrying about nothing or not.'

Lily shut her eyes briefly as if trying to work out how to begin, and then she started to explain.

'He wanted to know so much about my job — not the patients, but the equipment, how we restocked the bags, when items ran low . . . I thought he was being kind and taking an interest, but after the attempted break-in . . . Then right at the end, I looked in his briefcase when he left me alone with it.' She described what she had seen. 'I can't be certain that he was behind what happened to our home, but he might have been. If not, then it was someone in the same line of business.'

Ruby's expression turned grim. 'I can't think of many people who'd want to know about us restocking our bags. So you haven't reported it to anybody?'

Lily shook her head. 'I told him straight out, if anything like that happened to us again I'd know who to blame. Then I thought I might go to the police, I was so angry. I wanted revenge more than anything. Now that a bit of time has passed, I've calmed down a little. Revenge isn't good, is it? It only makes more trouble, in the end.'

They passed through the gate and into the little street. Ruby clasped her hands in front of her, gathering her thoughts.

'That's true,' she said seriously, 'or at least I think it is. I can't say I've ever taken revenge myself, but I can't see how it would help, not in the long run. As long as you're sure he won't be back for a second go.'

'I don't want to be a snitch,' Lily said glumly.

'It's hardly the same as telling tales at school,' Ruby pointed out. 'But I can see it might get complicated and, like you say, you don't know for sure. Sounds as if you caught him out and he'll think twice about coming near us in future.'

Lily brightened. 'Thank you, Ruby. That makes sense. I couldn't see past how angry I'd been, I wasn't thinking straight.'

'Well, no wonder,' Ruby replied at once. 'That's only natural, when someone treats you bad like that. You can't be expected to carry on as normal. It stands to reason.'

Lily smiled in gratitude. Who would have thought it, Ruby offering sage advice, and putting the whole sorry affair into perspective? 'You were right. It did help to talk about it. I didn't think it would, but it did.'

Ruby smiled back, looking Lily straight in the face. 'I'm glad,' she said. Then her expression changed.

'What ... what is it?' Lily thought she might have misread everything, even now.

Ruby pointed behind Lily, to her right. 'Look over there,' she said. 'Lily, is that smoke? It looks like smoke. And unless I'm mistaken I can smell something burning. I'm not imagining it, am I?'

Lily wrinkled her nose. 'No, you're right. I can smell it too. Oh no, that smoke is getting worse. Come on. We'd better see what's happening. We might be able to help.'

28

Alice knocked on the front door but didn't wait for an answer before walking in. She knew they would all be busy. For a moment she stood still, listening to the sounds of the Banham household preparing for one of its famous celebration meals. To the untrained ear it would have seemed like pandemonium, but she knew — beneath the noise — it was all highly organised.

The door to the kitchen abruptly opened and little Gillian shot out, dressed in a new smocked pinafore. 'Alice is here!' she shouted and then disappeared again.

There went the chance of a quiet entrance, Alice thought, gripping her bunch of flowers. She had better get them in water before they wilted. Even as she tried to concentrate on the immediate task, she was wondering where he was — the cause for celebration, the returning naval hero. She wanted to be prepared for the moment she saw him but suddenly felt jittery and unsure of herself. It had been so long.

Mattie appeared through the open kitchen door.

'There you are! I thought I heard Gillian shouting that you were here. Come in, come in. Are those for us? What lovely flowers.'

'I'll fetch a vase,' Alice said, thinking that Mattie was becoming more and more like her mother Flo with every passing day.

'They're in the back kitchen, on the little shelf beside the sink — do you know where I mean?'

'Yes, I know exactly.' Alice shrugged out of her jacket, hung it on the one remaining spare hook and went through to the small back kitchen with its big sink and taps worn shiny with use.

Flo waved at her from where she was basting the roast at the far side of the big main kitchen. 'What lovely flowers!' she echoed.

Alice smiled back and cast her eyes around. There was Edith, rising to come across to her, and little Alan toddling towards his grandmother. No sign of Joe. She picked up a glass vase with a narrow neck and filled it, then carefully unwrapped the wet newspaper from the stems.

Edith grinned up at her. 'Are they from the back yard?' she asked. 'I heard Gladys had taken up growing sweet peas as well.'

'They are.' Alice finished arranging them and took a good look at her best friend. 'How are you then, Edith? Seems like ages since I saw you.'

'Hardly,' said Edith lightly, wincing and then trying to cover it.

Immediately Alice set down the vase. 'What is it? Are you all right?'

Edith hastily glanced over her shoulder to check that Flo and Mattie had not seen or overheard. 'It's nothing. Honestly. Don't say anything.'

'About what?' Alice was worried now.

Edith bit her lip. 'I've just had the odd twinge. It's really nothing. Not a contraction or anything like that, so don't take on. Please, Al, don't say another word about it. This meal is for Joe and I don't want to spoil it. My time will come soon enough.'

'Are you sure? It's a bit early but these things happen.' Alice thought that in the brief time since she had last seen Edith that her bump had grown even larger. Officially she was not due until a couple of weeks into June, but it was now the end of May; the baby could decide to arrive any day now.

'No, really, it's just uncomfortable now and again. No more than that.' Edith spoke quietly but with determination. Then she deliberately changed the subject. 'Don't you want to know where he is?'

Alice eyed her friend carefully. 'All right, if you're certain. And yes, of course I do. I thought he might be in here.'

'He's upstairs, he'll be down any minute,' Edith assured her. 'He was giving Stan a hand with fixing the shelter door — the hinges had gone wonky after the last raids. Then Stan said he could finish up on his own and Joe had better make himself look respectable.'

'I should think so.' Flo came across to wash her hands at the sink. 'Alice, what a nice blouse. It matches the blue of your eyes. And the sweet peas, that's very kind of you. How about a cup of tea, now you're here?'

Alice noticed, not for the first time, that Flo's hair was turning grey at the temples and the lines on her forehead and around her eyes were more pronounced. 'No, don't trouble yourself, I'm not thirsty.'

'It's no trouble,' said Flo at once.

Alice could have kicked herself. 'Honestly, it's warm outside and I'd rather have a cup with the rest of you later.'

Flo looked at her askance but gave her the benefit of the doubt.

'What can I do to help?' Alice continued.

'Don't be silly, you're our guest,' Flo replied, but Edith, knowing how Alice would be feeling, brought her over to the big table, which had been covered with the best cloth, embroidered around the edges. 'Can you sort out the cutlery?' she asked. 'My bump's too big to sit straight now, and if I twist for too long then my back starts to ache.'

Alice agreed at once, and began to go through the best cutlery, brought out only for special occasions. She was concentrating so hard that she missed the moment Joe came downstairs, and stood watching the scene before him as he leant against the door frame.

Then she realised the room had grown quieter and that Flo and Mattie were looking towards the hall, although Edith was looking at her. With a strange prickling sensation at the back of her neck, she slowly turned around in her seat. There he was.

For a moment she could hardly take him in. During the long months of absence, she'd imagined him so often that she'd been afraid she'd forgotten what he looked like in the flesh. Then her gaze steadied and that rush of recognition pulsed through her. His thick, dark hair, his intelligent eyes now focused on her, his toned physique — no new injuries and no obvious sign of complications from his old ones, when his ship had been attacked. That face, the expression which told her he understood her like nobody else did. For a moment it was like coming home.

Almost at a loss for words, she rose. 'Joe.' She smiled broadly as he broke into a grin. 'I see they've got you working already,' he said, and made to step across to her, but his way was barred by Alan, rushing across the rug for attention. Joe hefted him up and lifted the little boy towards the ceiling, resulting in screams of delight.

'Don't you mess him up, I've only now put him in

301

that clean shirt,' Mattie warned, setting down a big bowl of marrowfat peas. 'If he gets overexcited, it'll be your fault.'

Joe set his nephew back on the ground. 'Now you listen to your mother,' he said, mock-sternly, but Alan was not fooled for a moment and hooted with laughter.

'I despair,' said Mattie. 'He's just like his sister, pays me no heed.' Her voice showed she didn't mean it.

Joe settled on the seat beside Alice and she could feel the heat radiating from his body, he was so close. 'Alice,' he said. 'How are you? How has it been round here lately?' His tone was casual but she could sense the layers of deep concern in it, the genuine wish for her to be well and happy.

Before she could give him a proper answer, Stan came in from the back, calling his greetings, Flo began to take out the roast and Mattie flew around bringing plates and the gravy jug and more vegetables than Alice would have thought possible. Billy and Kath arrived just in time, shooing their children into the corner to play with Mattie's, and the welcoming pattern of a big Banham meal started to unfold. Alice sighed to herself. She loved this place and had had some of the best meals of her life here. Yet she yearned for a few moments alone with Joe. It was almost like a physical need, like being thirsty for water after a long draught. However, she knew she would have to wait.

* * *

It was one of those streets where many of the houses had been bombed and so stood empty. Ruby could well imagine that before the war it would have been chock-full of people who all knew one another. If a fire had started then, someone would have run for help long before it could have taken hold.

Now, though, only a handful of anxious residents clustered along the whitewashed kerb. Many of them were elderly, and Ruby automatically wondered if they ought not to go back indoors and sit down before they came to harm. Several leant on sticks and one was visibly shaking.

Now was not the time to be shy, although Ruby had to swallow hard before gathering the courage to approach a small group of strangers. Lily, however, had no such moment of doubt.

'We're nurses,' she announced, loudly so that the oldest of them could hear her. 'Do you need help? Are there any casualties?'

'You don't look like nurses,' complained one of the grey-haired men at the back. 'You're just girls. You're far too young to be nurses.'

Ruby had to smile. She hadn't heard that comment for a long while, although when she first started she had had to put up with it all the time. Lily tutted impatiently. 'We're off duty and so we aren't in our uniforms. Is anybody hurt? Was there anyone inside that house?' Behind her, the smoke had turned into flames, beginning to lick at the window frames on the upper floor of the two-up, two-down.

A woman at the front stepped forward. She was younger than many of her neighbours, with an air of competence. She pushed a dogtooth-patterned head-scarf back from her brow. 'There's usually just Mr Hawkins,' she said, her voice a little husky. 'I went as close as I could around the back and called out to him, but the smoke drove me away. I couldn't see nothing, but I got Cassie here to get on her bike and fetch the ARP warden.' She indicated a girl of perhaps eleven years old, who had been hiding shyly behind her. 'She's ever so fast on that thing, you got him in no time, didn't you, Cass?'

The girl nodded solemnly and her dark plaits bobbed around her shoulders.

'Oh good, so the ARP warden's here,' said Lily, relief evident in her voice.

Ruby had a thought. 'What did he look like?'

The woman didn't hesitate. 'He was quite big, a bit red in the face, wide shoulders. He seemed to know what he was about.'

Ruby nodded. 'Sounds like Brendan,' she said. 'I wondered, as I know that Mr Banham will be at their big family do today — Alice was going over there earlier. And Billy will be there as well. So that really just leaves Brendan on this patch unless they'd got in reserves.'

'Well, that's good,' said Lily, 'everyone always says he's one of the best. All the same, we should maybe make ourselves known, see if he needs back-up or anything before the fire brigade get here.'

Ruby agreed, but then a memory surfaced. As she and Lily approached the house, she dropped her voice. 'We should make sure he's all right,' she said. 'He doesn't broadcast it but he's got bad lungs. Smoke's the worst thing for him. He had TB when he was younger, that's why he couldn't join up.'

'Oh no.' Lily's tone changed from confident to much more concerned. Like Ruby, she had come across plenty of patients who had or had suffered from TB in the past, and she knew what that might mean for them. Brendan was liable to have lasting weakness.

'He'll have been trained about smoke inhalation, he'll know the dangers,' Ruby said, as much to convince herself as Lily. 'God, it's hot, isn't it? I don't see how we can go much further.'

The closer they got to the front door of the narrow house, the more impossible it seemed. There was no point in putting themselves at risk. On the other hand, she knew they could not just walk away and leave Brendan to get on with it. There was no way of knowing how long the firefighters would take to arrive.

'That woman said something about going round the back,' Lily pointed out. 'We could try that. It's better than nothing and we won't get any nearer out here.'

'Good idea.' Ruby didn't hesitate. 'There's bound to be an alley in between some of the houses — look, a few doors down, let's go through there.'

Lily needed no second bidding and they hurried through the dark opening, emerging onto a small path running between the back yards and those of the next street. It was plain to see which house they had to go to as now flames were visible around the chimney.

'Do you think it started as a fire in the grate that got out of control?' Lily asked, shielding her eyes as she looked up at the bright light.

'I don't know. We'd better hurry.' Ruby wrestled with the back gate, which was so rotten as to be almost falling apart. 'Brendan!' she called as they entered the narrow yard, empty apart from a few old boxes and a frayed washing line. 'Brendan! Are you in there? Can you hear me?' Without thinking, she reached forward and touched the back door knob, pulling her hand away as if stung. 'That's red hot!' she gasped.

'Is your hand all right?'

'I'll think about that later,' Ruby replied at once, not wanting to admit she had burnt herself. She took off her cardigan, bundled it up and wrapped it around the handle before trying again. This time she got the door open, and foul-smelling smoke poured out into the yard.

'Brendan!' she shouted, her eyes now streaming and red.

There was a noise of violent coughing and then an old man staggered out towards them, gasping in desperation. He wore a sagging woollen jumper and baggy trousers, barely distinguishable in the gloom of the smoke-filled room, which Ruby assumed was the kitchen. 'Are you Mr Hawkins?' she croaked, now using her rolled-up cardigan to shield her mouth and nose.

He coughed again and almost fell. Swiftly Ruby and Lily caught him by his elbows. 'Over there,' suggested Lily, indicating the far corner of the yard with a tilt of her head. 'Let's sit him on that old box.' Cautiously they helped him to relative safety and lowered him to where he could sit and catch his breath.

'Mr Hawkins, did you see the warden?' asked Ruby anxiously. 'A big man in ARP uniform? Your neighbour said he'd gone in to find you.' Even as she asked the question, her heart sank, thinking of what it must be like inside the house. The heat was rising all the while and they were some way away from the building; heaven knew what it was like in the kitchen and beyond.

The old man wheezed and his eyes were watering, but if it was from the smoke, tears or both, Ruby could not tell.

306

'He came and woke me up and told me to get out,' he croaked, slowly and with huge effort.

'Where is he now?' demanded Lily.

The old man raised an unsteady hand and pointed to his back door. 'In there. He's still in there.'

29

Alice could not remember the last time she had eaten so much. Flo had pulled out all the stops to welcome Joe home, and had managed not one but two types of fruit crumble to finish with. 'You've got to try the other one,' she had insisted when Alice had attempted to say she'd had enough.

At least now she could help out by gathering the bowls and serving dishes, and the big jugs that Flo had filled with creamy custard. 'It's not made with real eggs but I got this special powder,' she had admitted. 'Tastes all right though, doesn't it?'

'I don't know how you do it,' Edith had confessed. 'Mine always goes lumpy.'

Flo had beamed with pleasure. 'Years of practice,' she'd explained.

Alice took the crockery into the back kitchen and began to stack it on the draining board, filling the serving dishes with water so that the burnt bits at the edges could soak.

'Now you leave that to us, Alice,' Mattie called.

'Yes, we'll go into the parlour and have some nice biscuits with a cup of tea,' Flo added. 'Stan's got some whisky, haven't you, Stan?'

Alice raised her eyebrows. 'Thanks, but not for me,' she said. She caught Flo's disappointed look and added, 'I mean, not yet for the tea and biscuits. I'll say no to the whisky if you don't mind.'

'I'll have your share,' grinned Billy, from where he sat with an arm protectively around his wife

308

Kath's shoulders.

The adults began to move from the table into the next room, Edith walking slowly, Mattie and Kath carrying small plates and the biscuit tins. Alice began to rinse the cutlery, taking special care as it was Flo's best set, when Joe came through with more bowls and set them alongside the serving dishes. 'Leave that for a while,' he suggested. 'It won't hurt for a minute.'

'Yes, but I don't want the juice to stain the silver . . .'

'Leave it, Alice,' he said, more forcefully. Then he smiled, so that she knew he wasn't cross. 'Just for a bit. The world won't come to an end if you don't do the washing-up immediately. How about a walk? It's still warm outside,' he added persuasively.

Alice put down the cutlery and wiped her hands on a tea towel. For a moment she fought with her instinct to act like a grateful guest and tidy up. Then she looked at his face and decided he was right — it could wait. 'It might be nice to walk off that big meal,' she said, 'although it was delicious, of course.'

'Of course. Just enormous.' His eyes sparkled with amusement.

'It was pretty enormous.' She hung up the little towel and he followed her out into the hallway.

'Just getting some fresh air,' he called through the parlour door, as Alice took her jacket from its hook. He held open the front door for her as she stepped out onto the street, still warm in its early evening sunshine.

'Which way would you like to go?' she asked as he shut the door behind them. 'You're the visitor, you choose.'

He laughed. 'Not quite a visitor. It is my house, after all.'

'You know what I mean.'

'All right, then. Let's head towards Butterfield Green.' They turned down Jeeves Street and began to saunter along.

Alice thought it would be the most natural thing in the world to take his arm, but she didn't move to do so and he didn't offer. Instead they walked side by side, almost touching but not quite. She could hear the sparrows chirping from the big privet bush on the other side of the street, and somewhere a robin was singing loudly, defending its patch against a rival.

'You've been away a long time, Joe,' she remarked. 'We were wondering what you've been up to.'

He inclined his head. 'Well, I did write to you and to Ma. You knew I was still in the land of the living.'

'You did. I always look forward to your letters.'

'Do you?'

'You know I do.' She hardly needed to tell him. 'But we couldn't work out where you were. That's unusual.'

He gave a short laugh. 'That was the idea.'

'Why? I mean, you always managed to let us know before, even if it was pretty general.'

He turned his gaze up to the pale blue sky, with the clouds beginning to pick up the edges of the dipping sun. 'Now, Alice, you know I can't say.'

'We thought you were headed towards Italy at one point.'

'I might have been,' he replied evasively.

Alice fought the urge to demand to know what had been happening and lost the battle. 'So you didn't go to Italy? Or did you go and come back?'

He sighed. 'Oh, Alice. You know I'd explain if I could. It's better if I don't, or at least, not now.'

She looked up at him. 'Not now but maybe later

you will? After what, then?'

He shook his head. 'You know I can't say. Really, I'd love to tell you, but it's best if you don't know.'

Alice glanced around, at the terraced houses that had been scarred from years of raids and yet which still looked respectable; the residents prided themselves on keeping this road as neat and tidy as could be, under the circumstances, because it helped morale. With the gentle heat of the late May evening, some people had left their windows open. She gave a wry smile. As a nurse she should approve of fresh air at all times; but now she realised that their conversation could drift in to all these parlours and bedrooms, and Joe could not risk anyone overhearing.

'I understand. But I'll keep you to your word — when all this is over, you're going to tell me everything.'

He laughed and looked down at her. 'It would be my pleasure. Everything I possibly can, anyway.'

She raised her eyebrows but he would not expand on that cryptic comment.

Butterfield Green was quiet, with no sign of the mothers who brought their young children there to let off steam during the daytime. Alice knew that Mattie and Kath often took their families here, as it was close enough for small legs to manage and made a change from the cramped back yards. Now it was enclosed and more private than wandering along the streets, cooler because of the greenery. She could just make out the sounds of a wireless from a house on the corner. The news was ending.

'So, how have you been, Alice?' Joe asked now, and she looked at him, detecting a change in his voice. He stood facing her and she had to raise her chin to meet his eyes; he was taller than his father, taller even than his brother. 'Don't say you tell me in your letters. I know you do, but it's not the same.'

She laughed a little but could see he was serious. 'I . . . well, it's been strange,' she began. 'My mother wasn't well, and that meant I was worried, really worried, and not like we've all been because of the raids. I felt I should be able to do more for her but I just couldn't.'

He nodded. 'Of course. But she'll know that. You're a good daughter to her, Alice.'

'Am I? Sometimes I'm not so sure.' She glanced down quickly at her feet and then gulped, remembering what had happened as she left Liverpool. 'It's made me think I'm the responsible one now — she's not there to look after me any more, it's the other way around.'

'I know what you mean.' His eyes crinkled in sympathy. 'I can see how Ma is gradually moving more slowly, not that she'd admit it.'

'You can't say anything. She'll be upset,' Alice interjected quickly.

'I realise that. It's looking after everyone that keeps her going, that keeps them both going.'

Alice nodded, thinking that some time soon they'd have another small life to look after, to give them an extra reason to carry on.

'It makes me value what's waiting for me back home, on these rare times that I can return.' He stopped and she wondered what he had been about to say.

'How long is your leave?' she asked.

'Probably another couple of days. That's when I'm booked to go back to . . .'

'. . . whatever you can't tell me.'

'Exactly.' He smiled ruefully.

312

Alice let her gaze sweep around them and then smiled back. 'But perhaps it's something that's been in the air for a while.' She recalled all the little comments Mary had casually dropped about Charles being unable to go out because he was planning an important matter for the army. Mary, being Mary, never had the slightest interest in asking what it might be. Then there were those occasions on which Fiona had returned from one of her committees, and speculated about a detail to Gwen, before realising that Alice was close by, and hastily changing the subject.

'Oh, Alice, you're doing it again.' Joe's voice was part frustration, part admiration. 'You know I can't confirm . . .'

'But just say for a moment that it's big enough to involve you in the navy, and the army, and the air force . . .' Belinda's brother having that unexpected weekend home ' . . . and it's what logically must have been in the government's mind for ages . . . and it has to wait for the right weather . . .'

'Alice, don't even think . . .'

Nobody could hear her if she spoke quietly. 'It's the invasion, isn't it,' she said. 'At last. We're invading France. Liberate France and then liberate Europe. It makes sense.'

He shut his eyes and then looked at her and raised his hands to grip her shoulders. 'Hush, Alice, don't say it, not even here. Forget you ever mentioned it.'

She knew she'd hit the nail on the head. But more immediate now was the sensation of his hands, warm through the thin fabric of her jacket and blouse. 'I . . .'

'Don't say anything more.' Then, from nowhere, he leant forward and kissed her, not the brief touches of his lips when saying goodbye, but a proper kiss, on the

313

mouth, warm and then hot with long-hidden passion. For a second she didn't know what to do — and then, all thought abandoned, she reacted and returned it, not caring that anyone might come along and find them, not caring about anything else at all.

She could not have said how long it lasted, but found herself out of breath when they finally broke apart.

'I . . .'

'Don't say it.' He held her tightly to him, her face pressed against his warm chest in its warm cotton shirt, her breath coming unsteadily. She let him hold her, knowing that this was what she had desired for so long, realising how right it felt, how well they fitted together. How had it taken her until now to admit it? She had been so cautious, so keen to do the right thing, not to risk letting herself be hurt again, to put all of those feelings aside.

Who had she been fooling? Only herself. Not Joe. And, a little voice said, probably not Edie either.

'What I wanted to ask just now,' he said, his voice loaded with emotion, in a way she had never heard it before, 'was, will you wait for me, Alice? You know what's going to happen next, in a very short while. I don't know how close I'll be to the action, but the odds are I won't be far from it. I don't know when I'll be home again, how things will go. But I do know that if I know you're waiting for me . . .' He could not continue, and she recognised he was shaking. She held him as tightly as she could, not wanting to let him go.

He murmured something against her head, his face in her warm hair.

She looked up at him.

'Perhaps I shouldn't have said that. Perhaps it's too much.' He was backing down before she was even fully certain of what he'd said.

'But what . . . ' She still wasn't sure.

'I can't help it. Maybe I should have told you ages ago, maybe I shouldn't have said it at all. I can't help it, I have to tell you. I love you, Alice. That's all. Plain and simple.'

She gasped and could scarcely draw a breath.

'I know, it's too much, I'm sorry. But I had to say. I don't know if I'll be coming back at all, we never know. I couldn't go ahead with what's coming without telling you.'

'Joe,' she said softly, burying her head once more against his chest. 'Joe.'

'You don't have to say anything, I know this is a shock,' Joe said, stroking her back, touching the warm skin of her neck with his broad hand. 'You'll have been thinking of nothing but your work and worrying about your mother, you won't have been wondering about me.'

'No, that's not true,' she admitted. 'I do think of you, all the time.'

'But not like this. You couldn't have known I'd come back and say this.'

'Maybe not . . . but ...'

'Don't give me an answer now,' he said, his breath hot against her forehead. 'Have some time to think about it. I'd rather you did. I don't want to make you feel you have to say yes just to put me off.'

'As if I would,' Alice protested.

Still he held her against him. 'Promise me you'll sleep on it and give me a proper answer tomorrow,' he said. 'This is no passing fancy, Alice. I hope you know that. I've wanted to tell you for so long, but I didn't know if you felt the same.'

She finally looked up at him again. 'You must know . . . can't you tell . . . ?'

He bent and kissed her once more, long and hard and exactly how she had always wanted to be kissed by him, even if she'd never dared to admit it.

At last they stopped to catch their breath, and he looked at her solemnly. 'We'd better go back — Ma will worry,' he said. 'No, don't answer me now. Tell me tomorrow. I want you to think this through, Alice. Tell me tomorrow. Promise.'

She nodded, recognising that this went far, far deeper than anything she had ever been asked before. 'Tomorrow, Joe,' she said. 'I promise.'

30

'Is this right? Do you think this is where he meant?' Ruby choked out the words as she pressed forward down what she thought must be a hallway. She could not see properly as the thick smoke obscured everything. She reached behind to check that Lily was still there.

Ruby had tended to old Mr Hawkins in his back yard as well as she could, while Lily ran around to the street in front once more, to fetch the helpful neighbour. The woman speedily agreed to help Mr Hawkins to a safer spot to await the firefighters, leaving Lily free to join Ruby in the search for Brendan.

Lily coughed. 'It must be along here somewhere. Mr Hawkins said he'd fallen asleep in his chair. It can't be far. It looked like a small house from the outside.'

Ruby stumbled onwards, keeping one arm outstretched in front of her. Her eyes were streaming constantly and with her other hand she held her cardigan over her nose and mouth. Her rational mind told her that it would do her no good to keep breathing in this foul smoke, but they had to find Brendan. There was nobody else to do it.

'Are you there, Lily?' she asked shakily.

'I'm here.' Lily's voice was several tones lower than usual but she was not far behind.

'Here's a door.' Ruby used her cardigan to test the handle but it was wooden and not too hot to touch. 'I can get it open . . . it doesn't feel right though.' There was a clatter as something fell to the floor. She moved her hand forward again and came into contact with a vertical surface. 'I don't think this is the room, Lily. It's more like a cupboard.'

Lily coughed again. 'Sounded like a broom falling over or something like that.'

'We must be under the stairs then.' Ruby gritted her teeth. She'd thought they had found the right place but her hopes had been raised too soon. They would have to carry on searching.

She backed out of the broom cupboard and felt her way along the wall of the hall, catching her finger on what must have been a picture frame, scrabbling for the next door. She knew time was precious but she didn't want to fall. It was good to know that Lily was right behind her, that she wasn't alone. She didn't want to think about how afraid she would have been without her colleague. Her thumb knocked into a piece of wood — maybe this was the next door frame. She touched her fingertips to it — yes, a door frame. 'Why have you stopped?' croaked Lily.

'This might be it, this time. Yes, that's more like it.' Ruby explored the door and space immediately beyond. 'It's another room, it must be the one at the front. Brendan!' She tried to raise her voice but it came out cracked and strange. The noise of the flames upstairs was growing louder. 'Brendan! Are you in here?'

'Here's got to be in here,' Lily said. 'I'm going to crouch down and try to search the floor, in case he's fallen or collapsed or something like that.'

'All right.' Ruby reached forward again, the heat from the ceiling above her making her scalp sear with pain. Then she too bent lower — didn't they say that it was safer to be close to the ground in a fire? It felt slightly easier. She shuffled along, banging into a piece of furniture with a sharp edge — maybe a small table.

There was a dull thud to her left. She peered through the smoke to see the indistinct shape of Lily coming to a halt. 'Brendan! Is that you?' Lily spoke fiercely now, the urgency of their search filling her voice. 'Ruby, I think this is him — he's on the floor, he's not answering.'

'Is he all right? Is he breathing?'

'I can't tell.'

'We'll have to get him out,' Ruby said decisively.

'How? He's so much bigger than we are.'

Ruby thought fast. 'We'll drag him. I'm right beside you now — I can feel his boots. I'll take his legs. You take his arms, and we'll manage as best we can.'

Lily grunted. 'I've got to fasten something over my mouth to help me breathe, then — I've been using my hand. One moment, I've found a hanky in my pocket. I'll just tie it across my face.' There was a brief pause. 'Right, off we go.'

'Right you are.' Ruby heaved and raised the heavy legs of the ARP warden and staggered back the way she had come, banging into the table again, keeping her head as low as she could. Her back ached ferociously but she told herself she could worry about that later.

'Go on, go on, you're doing well,' Lily encouraged her, taking her share of the weight.

Ruby misjudged where the doorway was and hit her leg on the frame, but she ignored the pain, edging through the opening and out into the hall. Now it was easier as she knew she simply had to keep going in one straight line, without tripping over the cracked lino. She edged backwards, past where the broom cupboard must be, into the kitchen. The smoke was not quite as thick in here, and she could make out the shape of Brendan in his dark uniform and Lily with her pale hair a few feet away.

'Almost there,' she gasped.

'My arms . . . I don't think I can hold him for much longer.'

'Don't stop now, Lily, you can do it, you really can,' Ruby croaked. 'I can feel the fresh air from outside. Just a few more steps, come on, we'll make it.'

Her throat rasped and she longed for a cold drink of water, of anything. She'd never felt pain like it. With her last ounce of strength, she dragged her feet over the back doorstep and out into the little yard.

Lily stumbled after her, narrowly managing to avoid dropping Brendan's body. They rushed the final few feet to the end of the yard and fell in one heap, too exhausted to go further.

Ruby took a moment to gather herself, trying to think straight. Her overwhelming urge was to lie down, to rest, but she knew she could not. 'We've got to check his airways,' she whispered.

'Let's try to sit him up, see if he can cough to clear them,' Lily said, pulling herself into a kneeling position. 'Brendan, listen, we're going to move you again. Can you hear me?'

She leant forward and caught him firmly around the arms by his thick uniform, tugging until he was almost sitting, with Ruby pushing from behind. 'Brendan!' she called hoarsely. 'Can you hear us?' Still the flames roared.

Ruby thought for a moment that it had all been for nothing, that he could not respond, that it was too late and he had died there on the little living-room floor. She rubbed his back, willing him to make a noise, a groan; anything at all to show that he was all right, that he was still alive.

'Do you think we didn't get him out in time?' she asked quietly, afraid to say it any louder in case it was true. She had seen death before, of course — but nothing as personal as this. This was Brendan, who had been kind to her from the first moment of meeting, who had looked after Kath when she had no money, and who had come to the rescue of all of the nurses when their common room had been ruined by the bombing raid. Nobody deserved to die — but it was so much more unbearable when it was someone who was fundamentally so good.

'He's going to make it, he is, aren't you, Brendan?' Lily wasn't going to give up without a fight.

Ruby tried to join in the encouragement but her voice failed her. Diligently she kept rubbing his back, thinking that surely he must cough, must gasp for clean air.

'That's it, that'll help,' Lily went on. She seemed to have found her second wind and had enough enthusiasm for both of them. 'Keep at it, Ruby, you're doing a grand job.'

Ruby felt she was wilting but would not stop, moving her aching arms, trying through sheer force of willpower to make Brendan show a sign of life.

She was at the point of asking Lily to take over when there came a faint splutter and then at last a definite cough. Brendan was breathing. He was alive.

'Do it again, Brendan!' Lily cried. 'Give us a nice cough, now. That's right. You're going to be fine. It's me, Lily, and that's Ruby behind you. Cough for us, show us how you can do it.'

Ruby sagged in relief but now dared not stop, urging the warden's lungs to work, to cough out all the noxious substances he had inhaled in the burning house.

'Don't try to speak, just cough,' Lily instructed. 'We can talk later, can't we? Just cough, Brendan, that's right.'

Brendan spluttered and tried to disobey, attempting to say something, but it was beyond him. Ruby felt that it didn't matter, the fact he was breathing was enough. And then she could hear the noise of approaching feet and, like a miracle, the first two firefighters burst through the rotten gate from the alley, swiftly followed by Geraldine from the ambulance station.

If she was surprised at the state of the two nurses, she didn't show it.

'Don't worry, we've got him now!' she exclaimed, beckoning for a colleague with a stretcher to come through. 'Let's pick him up straight away and out of the way of the firemen. That's right. We'll take him around the front where we're parked up and then on to hospital.'

'He's only just started breathing,' Lily said, remembering to pass on as much useful information as possible. 'He was passed out on the floor inside the house — we don't know how long for. He's got lung damage from childhood TB.'

'Thanks. I'll make sure they know.' Then Geraldine was taking one end of the stretcher bearing Brendan and was off, at a practised half-walk, half-run.

'We'd better get to safety ourselves.' Lily said, shakily rising to her feet. Then she started to laugh. 'Oh,

322

Ruby, you should see what you look like. You're in such a state. Your face is all black, and your hair looks as if you've stuck your finger in a plug socket.' She giggled uncontrollably.

Ruby didn't know whether to be offended or not, whether to laugh or cry. In the end she did a bit of both. 'Well, you're no better. You're all filthy. Look at the state of you — you've got a funny line across your face and it's black above it and smudgy grey underneath. Must be from where you tied your hanky. Is that it there?' She pointed at a scrap of material lying beside Lily's feet.

Lily bent to pick it up and began to laugh even harder. 'That's it. Only it isn't a hanky.' She gulped and held her sides. 'Come on, get up, Ruby, you'll trip up the firemen if you stay there. Ugh, this thing is ruined. Never mind, it did its job.'

Ruby cautiously stood up, feeling as if she'd have to learn to walk all over again. Her sense of balance seemed to have deserted her. It was a very strange and disorienting sensation. 'Why, what is it?'

Lily snorted and held up the wispy square. It bore the traces of a swirly pattern but its former colours had been destroyed and, if it had once been beautiful, it was now just a rag.

'Come on,' she said, linking her arm through Ruby's and helping her unsteady colleague retrace their steps back down the narrow lane and little side alley through the gap in the terrace — the path they had taken just a few minutes ago, but what felt like hours since. 'This bit of old rag was a scarf,' she went on. 'I thought it was beautiful. Donald gave it to me. It used to be really silky, and he told me it was from Liberty but I bet it was a knock-off. Anyway it served

323

its purpose. Best thing he ever gave me, in fact.' She laughed again.

Catching her eye, Ruby joined in. 'Good job he did, wasn't it? It came in handy — you'd have been in a right pickle back there without it. Who'd have thought it?'

Lily hooted with laughter, as if it was the funniest thing she'd ever heard. Ruby knew she was letting off steam, they both were, as a reaction to the extreme danger of the recent events began to sink in. So it was that they rounded the corner of the alley, arm in arm and laughing, to be greeted by the group of neighbours, now far more of them, all clapping and cheering.

'Let's hear it for the nurses!' called one of the men, and the young girl with the plaits waved in excitement. 'Hip, hip,' and everyone joined in, shouting 'hooray!'

Ruby stopped in her tracks, embarrassed to be the centre of attention, and aware of what she must look like, but Lily waved back and beamed at them all. 'It was nothing, we were just doing our job,' she wheezed. 'It's the firefighters who are the brave ones.' Even now, a team of firemen was tacking the blaze at the front of the house, as the flames had spread to the ground floor and the living-room window.

Ruby noticed what they were doing and gasped, the urge to laugh leaving her as rapidly as it had come. They had been on the other side of that window just minutes ago. Any later and they would indeed have been too late. Brendan would have been burnt alive. And so too might she and Lily, she realised. They had had the closest of escapes.

Yet here they were, alive and being feted by the residents of the narrow road. The sensible woman who

324

had been such a help now brought them glasses of water and bade them come and sit on her low brick wall. 'Give them a bit of room, can't you see they need to catch their breaths,' she scolded the neighbours, who wanted to press around and congratulate them.

Ruby eased herself onto the wall, sipping gratefully from the heavy glass beaker, and let the evening sun wash over her. She could not even begin to think about what she and Lily had just done. That would come later. For now, it was enough to take joy in the fact of being alive.

31

There was a time not so very long ago that Gladys would have balked at going anywhere near a pub, let alone entering one on her own. She had grown bolder since those days, though, and anyway, it was almost as if the Duke's Arms didn't count. They knew her in there and she could count on finding friends inside. Besides, Ron had so little spare time at the moment that it was unfair to expect him to come the extra short distance to collect her from Victory Walk or her family's house. It was quicker by far to go along by herself, and that meant she would have more precious minutes with him. Her face grew warmer as she approached the welcoming building, and not only because she had walked there so fast.

She'd taken the time to change into a fresh blouse and skirt after finishing at the victory garden, and to brush her hair until it shone. It would never bounce like Mary's or curl prettily like Lily's but it was the best she could do. At any rate, judging from the look on Ron's face when he glanced up and saw her as she came through the big door, he liked what he saw. He rose as she went over to the wooden table in the corner. Kenny was there too, and he half got up, constrained by the angle of the table. He looked tactfully away as Ron and Gladys greeted each other; nothing too obvious, but to give them a couple of seconds of privacy. Then she sat down.

Ron waved at the barman, who nodded. He knew what they wanted by now.

'How was your day, then, Gladys?' Ron asked, his eyes bright with happiness now that she had joined them.

'Oh, it was ever so busy. I been cooking and cleaning since the break of dawn, and then down the garden hoeing the weeds. That ain't the big news though.' She broke off as the barman came over with a half of shandy for her along with pints of beer for Ron and Kenny.

'Go on, then,' Ron said, lifting his glass and taking an appreciative sip. 'Oh, this hits the spot, this does. Me and Kenny been hard at work since first thing as well.'

'We have,' Kenny confirmed. 'So . . . your friend didn't fancy coming along tonight, then?' His expression grew hopeful, as if one of the others was about to push open the heavy door to the outside world.

'My friend? You mean Ruby?' Gladys checked, although she was pretty sure.

The tips of Kenny's ears went a little redder. 'Well, yes, of course. Ain't she coming tonight?'

Gladys shook her head. 'I need a drop of this and then I'll tell you. That's the big news.'

Kenny's face froze. 'What, is she all right?'

Ron made a face. 'Keep your hair on, Ken.'

Gladys nodded, drank her first mouthful of shandy and set down the glass. 'She is, Kenny, but she's in hospital with Lily just to make sure.'

Kenny nearly leapt out of his seat. 'In hospital? What, why, what's happened? Gladys, you got to tell me.'

'Sit down, Ken, can't you see she's trying to.' Ron put his hand on his friend's forearm. 'Go on, Glad.'

Gladys grinned quickly and shyly at him, because

nobody else had ever shortened her name, and she knew it meant she was special to him. Then she explained the events of the late afternoon and early evening, culminating in the two nurses returning home, but then Geraldine and the ambulance crew turning up and informing them they had better come into hospital to be checked. 'They were breathing all this horrible smoke, they might have hurt their lungs,' Gladys finished. 'They couldn't really talk proper or nothing. They was wheezing a lot. So it's best they go and get looked at by the doctors. Fiona said as what they don't have to work until they're better.'

'That's only right,' said Ron admiringly. 'Fancy Ruby doing all that. That's real bravery, that is.'

Kenny swallowed hard. 'I'll say.'

'I'd have been terrified,' Gladys confessed. 'They said it was red hot in there. Ruby had singed bits on her hair, they're going to have to cut it shorter.'

Kenny's face fell. 'Oh no, her lovely hair.' Then he shut up abruptly, obviously annoyed with himself for blurting out such a personal comment.

'I always told her that she had lovely hair,' said Gladys. 'It'll grow back, she ain't got a burnt scalp or nothing. You could tell her that though, when she's better, Ken. She never thinks she looks nice.'

He took a slow draught of beer. 'Maybe I will,' he said quietly.

Ron raised his eyebrows at Gladys as he too raised his pint, and she looked back happily, not having to say 'I told you so'.

Before she could rub it in, there was a rush of air and the big door opened again, the brass handles flashing in the last of the daylight. Gladys noticed idly that the frosted glass panels with their engraved pattern of

328

intertwined ribbons had survived the raids, and felt glad that something so fine had lasted.

'Evening! Thought you'd be in here.' It was Clarrie and Peggy, once again straight from their factory shifts. 'We won't stop long, as I'm back on fire-watching duty at ten, but we could do with a half, couldn't we, Peggy?'

'I'll get them,' Ron offered kindly. 'You two sit down here with us and take the weight off your feet. Gladys can tell you the news from the nurses' home while I do.'

He stepped nimbly over one of the low bar stools and the young women shuffled into the space he had vacated, sighing with relief.

'I haven't sat down for seven hours,' Peggy groaned. She raised her feet and flexed them to and fro, in their sensible flat shoes. 'No wonder my ankles are all swollen. To think I used to wear those high sandals. I bet they won't fit no more.'

'Don't talk nonsense, you're just tired,' Clarrie admonished her. 'So, what's the big story then. Gladys?'

Gladys told them, and Kenny's face revealed all she needed to know about his feelings for Ruby. 'So you see, we got two heroines at Victory Walk,' she finished.

'Blimey,' said Clarrie. 'I wouldn't want to do that. I mean, I know I watch for fires three evenings a week and we're taught what to do if one breaks out, but I don't know if I'd go into a burning building. Especially without proper protection and everything.'

Peggy's eyes were wide. 'Me neither. Makes me go all shaky just to think about it.'

'You'll be better when you've had a drop of shandy,' Clarrie predicted.

'Day like we've had today, it was almost enough to get me back on the port and lemon,' Peggy stated, rubbing her tired eyes. 'Honestly, Gladys, as if that double shift wasn't enough, I got a letter from Jimmy earlier.' She felt in her pocket and drew out the envelope with its distinctive looped writing on the front.

Gladys was concerned. 'He's not ill or anything, is he?' She knew how much the American soldier meant to her friend.

'He ain't given you the elbow?' asked Kenny.

'Course not,' said Clarrie crossly, protective of her friend.

Peggy grinned sadly. 'No, nothing like that,' she said. 'But it's almost like an embarkation letter. He says not to worry if I don't hear from him for a while. He'll be thinking of me but there might not be many letter boxes.'

'Better keep your voice down,' said Clarrie. 'Even if that got through the censors, we don't know who might like to know such a thing — even in here.'

Peggy put the cherished letter back in her pocket. 'I'm worried, that's all — it's only natural. I know damn well what he's signed up for and what that might mean, it's not exactly a surprise, but I hate it when I'm reminded of it. I'll make extra sure to keep this safe.' She tapped her pocket lovingly with her hand.

Kenny nodded slowly. 'Yes,' he said, as if making up his mind about something. 'Of course.' He stood up. ''Scuse me, Gladys.'

She looked up at him. 'Where you going, Ken? Ron's got the drinks, look, here he comes now.'

'Had an idea,' Kenny said, and added no more as he made his way over to the bar, crossing paths with the returning Ron on his way.

330

As they sipped their drinks and reassured Peggy that her soldier would be all right, Gladys could see that Kenny was busy at the bar. He seemed to have begged a pen and piece of paper from the barman and was writing something, his tongue poking out of the corner of his mouth as he concentrated. He was clearly putting a lot of thought into it, whatever it was.

Eventually Clarrie drained her glass. 'That's enough, it's twenty to ten,' she said. 'I'd better get going. It's nearly time to stand up there on the roof watching the stars.'

'A nice way to spend the rest of your evening.' Ron smiled.

'Got to be done,' said Clarrie matter-of-factly. 'Here, Ron, mind your great feet, let me out.'

'All right, all right.' Ron made a show of fussing, standing to enable Clarrie and Peggy to slide out from behind the table. 'Leave your glasses, I'll take them back.'

'Thanks, Ron.' Clarrie looked across the bar. 'Bye, Kenny. What're you doing that's taking so long?'

Kenny's ears went red again as he folded the piece of paper and hastily tucked it into his shirt. 'Nothing, nothing. You off, then?'

He came back over as the two young women said their farewells.

After they'd gone, Kenny waited until Ron had gone over to the bar with the empties before speaking to Gladys.

'Here, will you do something for me?' he asked, his tone serious.

'Well, yes. What do you mean?' She couldn't help but be worried — she'd rarely heard Kenny sound like this.

331

He brought out the piece of paper. In the absence of an envelope, he had folded it tight and tucked the ends in, and now he pressed it into her hand.

'Will you give this to Ruby?' he asked, his eyes searching hers for any signs of mockery or doubt. 'It's important. Don't tell nobody, not even Ron.' He sat back hastily.

Gladys was surprised by his intensity, but recovered quickly. She wanted to smile, guessing what the letter might say, but realised that Kenny would not appreciate it. 'Yes, of course,' she said. 'Mum's the word.'

He nodded gratefully, but said nothing as Ron came back with another round of drinks. 'I know it's midweek but we deserve it,' he said cheerfully. 'Have I interrupted something?'

'No, not a bit,' said Gladys at once.

32

Alice awoke early, with a jolt of energy shooting through her. For a moment she could not remember why today was so important. Then the events of yesterday came back in a rush — the conversation with Joe, how he had held her and kissed her and that she had kissed him back. He had asked her to wait for him, but not to answer at once, to give him her reply today. He didn't want to rush her into saying anything; it was far too important.

She threw open the attic window and breathed in the fresh air of first light. The dawn chorus was still in full swing. She knew with a flood of certainty what she would say.

Being in Joe's arms was completely different to anything she had known before. It made her even more certain that her decision to turn Mark down had been the right one. She had responded to Joe as a woman who knew her own mind. He had awoken something that had been simmering beneath the surface for a very long while, perhaps even from the first time they had met. They had fallen out immediately, but would that have happened if there had not been a deep and fundamental attraction between them? Alice smiled, recalling the summer's day, the picnic, how horrible she thought he had been. Funny to think of that now.

She wondered what to wear. On the one hand, she knew he would not mind in the slightest. On the other, she felt it was one of the most important days of her life and she wanted to mark that. She had time to

spare; the Banhams would want to have their breakfasts in peace, to get the children up and dressed,
Gillian ready for school. Despite the butterflies in her
tummy, she would have to wait a while. Slowly she
went through her wardrobe, such as it was, dismissing
anything too frayed or patched, or too drab. There
was a frock she had not worn since the warm days of
the previous summer, pale green with cream polka
dots, cap sleeves and little pintucks on the bodice. It
felt fresh and bright. It would be perfect.

Taking her time, she wandered along to the bathroom, washed, changed into the cotton frock and
brushed her hair, leaving it down, and chose a small
gold chain to put around her neck. It had been a birthday present from her parents, and she felt it would
bring her luck. For some reason she wanted a small
part of them to be with her today; she wanted their
approval of what she was about to say. She knew they
would be happy at her choice, as they had only ever
wanted the best for her. She was sure they would love
Joe, when they finally met him. Sighing, she wished
she knew when that would be.

She opened her bedroom door and sounds rose up
the stairs from the floors below. Her colleagues were
up and preparing for the day ahead. Alice had been
excused from morning rounds, but she knew she
would have to work later as Ruby and Lily were off
sick, recovering from the effects of the fire. She was
in no hurry to join everyone in the canteen; better let
those who had to work first thing have first claim on
the porridge and toast. It would be better all round if
she herself was one of the last to eat.

Ellen waved to her as she reached the ground floor.
'I've another lady due today!' she called. 'Down on

334

Evering Road. I think you might know her — Mrs Parfitt.'

Alice frowned and then nodded. 'I do know her. I treated her for a broken wrist last year. So she's having another baby? She's got two children already, hasn't she?'

'She has.' Ellen fastened her bag. 'That husband of hers has a job with the post office and so she's had him under her feet all this time.' She gave a wide smile. 'Wish me luck, those other kids are proper handfuls. I hope they've gone to their granny's. See you later.'

Alice smiled back as her colleague made off for her working day. Mrs Parfitt would be in good hands, no matter if her older children were there to help or hinder.

She helped herself to toast but was almost too excited to eat. She shied away from sharing a table, her thoughts racing, in no mood for conversation. Alice flicked idly though a copy of the previous day's *Times*, but of course there was no hint that the invasion was imminent. She could not concentrate enough to follow the articles. Folding the pages, she pushed it away and then hurriedly finished her toast, before someone noticed and teased her for not completing the crossword. It could wait until later.

It was now a respectable hour to go visiting, but still she made herself walk slowly along the pavements between Victory Walk and Jeeves Street, to ensure she didn't arrive at an awkward time. Mattie would have left for her shift at the gas-mask factory; Stan would have gone to work by now as well. Flo would have taken Gillian to school, and would be back by now to mind Alan, while Edith put her feet up. Or perhaps she had taken Alan over to Kathleen's, to play with little Barbara.

Maybe Joe would be checking the repairs to the Anderson shelter while he waited for her. He'd want to know that the family would be safe in his absence. At the start of the war, he and his brother Harry had not hesitated to sign up, but their one consideration had been for the welfare of the ones they'd be leaving behind. It had not stopped them from leaving, but she knew that worry was never far from Joe's mind.

Alice paused at the corner of Jeeves Street, nervous now that the moment was upon her. She straightened her collar and touched her finger to the slender gold chain, reassuring herself that her mother and father would be with her in spirit, would be pleased and excited for her. Then she walked the final few paces towards the house that was almost as dear to her as her own back in Liverpool.

Flo must have seen her coming as she didn't even have to knock.

'Alice! We were just thinking about you. I'm so glad you're here.'

Alice was slightly surprised by the greeting but smiled and followed Flo inside. She had no way of knowing what Joe had said to his mother about their brief absence yesterday. Perhaps her arrival had been expected by everybody. 'Where's Joe?' she asked as she came through into the kitchen.

Flo looked puzzled for a moment and then she gasped a little. 'Oh, of course, you won't have heard. He's gone.'

For a moment Alice felt dizzy and the sound of Flo's voice was distorted, as if it was coming from underwater. She must have misheard.

'Gone?' She put out her hand to a chair back to steady herself.

'Yes, it all happened ever so fast.' Flo clasped her hands together. 'It was only just light this morning and a telegram came. He had to go that very minute. There was barely time for him to pack his bag. I didn't even have any baking ready for him to take, after all my plans.' Her voice shook but she ploughed on. 'He wouldn't say what it was, he proper clammed up. I had some leftover biscuits from yesterday and I just about had time to put them in a paper bag and he was gone.'

'Gone.' The realisation hit Alice with a sickening thud. She had missed him. It was too late. He had left without hearing her answer and now he might never know. Worse, if she had come over as soon as she'd woken up, then she might have caught him. She had delayed out of politeness and now he had gone.

'But you've come to see Edie, haven't you?' Flo's tone became urgent. 'That was like a miracle, you turning up so early this morning. She's upstairs, Alice, she's been asking for you.'

Alice stared at her, unable to form any words.

'Yes, even with all that palaver going on first thing with Joe, she's been wanting to see you.'

Alice gathered herself. 'Is she all right?'

Flo turned towards the door. 'You'd better come to see for yourself. I told her to stay in bed and that I'd get word to you.'

Alice followed her, trying to prepare for what was about to happen. 'Is it . . .'

'Yes,' said Flo, only one thing on her mind now. 'It's the baby. It's coming early.'

★ ★ ★

337

One look at her best friend told Alice that things were not going well at all. Edie's forehead was covered in a shiny sheen of sweat and she was very pale. 'Al,' she managed to gasp, but then that seemed to cost her too much and she fell silent except for a series of groans. Alice took her hand.

'Edie, have you been having those pains since yesterday?' she asked urgently.

Edie gave the smallest of nods.

'Right.' Alice knew that there was no time to lose. Flo would not have brought her upstairs so fast if everything had been going to plan. Flo had had three children and been present at her first grandchild's birth; she had realised something was amiss. 'I'm going to fetch Ellen. She's your preferred midwife, isn't she? I know exactly where to find her.' At least she did if she was still at Mrs Parfitt's, Alice thought, sending up a prayer that her colleague had not moved on to another case. 'I'll be back as soon as I can.'

Edie had no energy left to agree or protest. Alice tore herself away, unable to look back at her friend's face, not daring to think about what might happen after she had left. It might still be early in her labour; the pains of the previous day might not have been full contractions. Then again, Edie might not have wanted to say anything so as not to spoil Joe's special meal. She had to hurry.

'I'm going to get Ellen right now,' Alice told Flo as she passed her in the hall. 'She should be with another mother-to-be, only a short way away, and that woman's had two children already. Edie will be the priority.'

'Hurry,' was all that Flo said, holding open the door, her face creased with worry.

Alice set off at a run, knowing that finding Ellen would be only half of the story. She had made up her mind to go from there to see Dr Patcham and ask him to call in as well. She considered whether she was overreacting because Edith was her best friend, but decided she wasn't; even though she was not a trained midwife, Alice had seen plenty of women in labour. She had to trust her gut instinct that this was not right.

Thank goodness that when she was choosing nice clothes this morning, she had still opted for flat shoes. Her breath was ragged but she kept up her unaccustomed pace, pausing only when she saw two young women on the opposite side of the main road. They were looking at her too, and waving. Alice ran over to them, neatly avoiding one of the buses heading for Stamford Hill.

'Alice! Whatever's the matter?' Ruby asked.

'Can we help?' added Lily, her voice lower and huskier than normal but now without the dreadful wheeze.

Alice had to bend forwards and place her hands on her knees to catch her breath. Part of her wanted to demand why these two were out at all, when it would have been better for them to rest. The other half shouted that this was a golden opportunity and she should make the most of it. 'Are you feeling better?' she asked between deep gasps. 'If you are, then I have a favour to ask you.'

Ruby nodded at once. 'We thought a walk would do us good. It's such a fresh morning — and we haven't come far.'

'Then maybe you can take a diversion.' Alice made a swift decision. 'Lily, can you go to Mrs Parfitt's at

Evering Road and see if Ellen is still there. If she is, tell her she is needed urgently at Jeeves Street. Edith is in labour and she needs attention immediately.'

Lily's hand flew to her mouth. 'Of course. Anything to help Edith,' she said. 'I'll go right away.'

'Thank you.' Alice nodded gratefully as Lily set off, as fast as she was able.

'Ruby, this might seem like a drastic step but I need you to fetch Dr Patcham,' she went on. 'Tell him Edith's in her second day of labour and is struggling. I didn't have time to assess her but I can tell it's not going well, and I'm not sure even Ellen can make it right. I'd be terribly grateful if he could come over to Jeeves Street and put our minds at rest.'

Ruby stared for a moment, her eyes darkening with anxiety. 'Is it that bad?'

Alice willed herself not to break down. 'It might be. If I've overreacted then I'll apologise later — but better to act now and fast than to wait and see, only to find the doctor's too busy,' she replied, trying to sound professional and feeling anything but.

'I see.' Ruby took a deep breath. 'Then I'll go right now. Don't worry, I'll find him and persuade him. He knows you wouldn't make a fuss for nothing.' She turned and headed back the way she had come, leaving Alice alone on the pavement, hoping that the young nurse was right.

★ ★ ★

What felt like half a lifetime later, but was in fact only a couple of hours, Alice sat in the back yard at Jeeves Street, a cup of tea going cold in her hand. Opposite sat Flo, also holding a cup, and a teapot sat on a tray between them. Neither had really wanted the tea, but it was something to do, to pass the agonising time. Behind them, the roof of the Anderson shelter was bright with the green of home-grown vegetable plants. Mattie had transformed it into a useful patch of garden.

Ellen had rushed over as soon as Lily had found her and immediately set about making Edith more comfortable, but she was evidently concerned. She had given Alice and Flo the task of heating water and fetching towels, although Flo had done most of this anyway. Everyone had been mightily relieved when Dr Patcham arrived, as unruffled as ever.

'Your fine colleague Ruby impressed upon me that time was of the essence,' he said, as Alice showed him where he could wash his hands. 'I know she's not one to flap or exaggerate, so I came as soon as I could. We absolutely cannot have Nurse Banham in trouble. Now I know that you and Mrs Banham senior will naturally want to be at the bedside, but I must ask you to stay where you are. Between Nurse Devlin and myself, we'll fill the space. We'll call you if you can be of assistance.'

Alice had had no choice but to agree, and she knew it made sense. However, every atom within her cried out to be upstairs in the bedroom, where Edith was fighting to deliver her baby. Alice put down her untouched tea and dug her fingers into her palms, willing her friend to succeed with all her might. How she wished Joe was here. He would tell her not to worry, that Edith was a survivor, that she hadn't come through the past few years to be beaten by childbirth.

Flo looked into her face and Alice wondered again if Joe had said anything yesterday. Whether he had or not, now was not the moment to broach why she had happened to be on the doorstep this morning. Let Flo think it was divine providence, or whatever she wanted to believe; there was nothing to be done now. It made Alice long for Joe all the more sharply.

She'd hoped to spend the morning reliving those delicious moments when Joe had kissed her and held her. Instead she was fervently hoping that her best friend would make it through her ordeal and that, somehow, mother and child would be well.

Flo reached across and took her hand. 'Edie's very strong, Alice,' she said. 'We mustn't forget that. She might be small but she's no pushover.'

'I know.' Alice wanted at that moment to cry, to sob for her poor friend who so desperately wanted this baby, Harry's baby. She couldn't even begin to think what might happen if it went dreadfully wrong. What would become of Harry — surely fate would not be so cruel as to pluck him from the brink of death at Dunkirk, only to have his wife and child die in their own home? No, she must not let her thoughts go down that route.

'It seems to be going on for so long,' she sighed. 'I know it isn't, not really, and that first babies can take ages, but surely we'll know something soon.'

Or, said a little voice in her head, no news is good news. While we're out here in the sunshine, then there's still hope.

Flo simply squeezed her hand again and made no reply.

The seconds stretched into minutes, the minutes into another hour. Flo made more tea, and neither of them drank that either. 'A shame to waste the tea leaves,' Alice said guiltily.

'I'll tip them on the roses,' Flo said.

★ ★ ★

Alice could not have said how much more time had passed, but the sun had passed overhead before there was a sudden flurry of activity. Footsteps sounded from the kitchen and then the back kitchen door was flung open and Ellen came through. At the same time a faint cry could be heard, and then a louder one, and then the unmistakable wail of a baby.

Alice and Flo jumped to their feet.

'How are they both?' Flo asked, getting the words out before Alice could.

Ellen wiped her dark hair back from her reddened face. 'It was touch and go for a while there,' she confessed. 'Gave us all a bit of a fright, you might say. There, you can hear that the baby's arrived and is doing all right.'

'A boy or a girl?' Flo demanded, the energy flooding back into her now that she knew she had a new grandchild.

Ellen smiled for the first time since leaving the home that morning. 'A girl. A little girl. She's small but there's nothing wrong with her lungs, as you can tell.'

Flo beamed. 'They'll be able to hear her down the market at Ridley Road,' she exclaimed.

'And Edie?' Alice asked, whereupon the smile faded from Ellen's face.

'Truth be told, she's very weak. The doctor had to do a bit of an operation there. We'll give her a little while to come round and then we can see how she goes from there.'

'What sort of operation?' Alice asked, but Ellen shook her head.

'I'll explain later. You'd better come up and meet the baby. Am I right in thinking you're to be her god-mother, Alice?'

'That's right.' Alice had been deeply touched when Edith had asked her. However, she had imagined it would mean buying nice presents at Christmas and birthdays, taking the child on little trips when old enough, giving her gentle guidance on how to tell right from wrong. The full meaning of what she had promised struck home. If anything were to happen to Edith . . .

'Come on, then,' Flo said, back to her determined self. 'We'll do no good sitting around down here.'

She raced up the stairs like a woman half her age and Alice followed, dread slowing her steps. Don't let Edie die, she silently chanted over and over. Not Edie.

The wailing continued and then Dr Patcham appeared at the bedroom door, his white hair bright in the shady hallway. In his arms was a small bundle wrapped in towels. Flo stepped forward and gasped as he handed over her granddaughter, who gurgled and ceased her crying immediately, almost as if she knew that these strong arms would take care of her and defend her no matter what. Alice peered into the nest of towelling and caught sight of a tiny red face, eyes screwed tightly shut, crowned with a thick head of deep brown hair.

'Harry's hair,' she breathed.

'Yes, and won't he be pleased.' Flo was smiling even as a tear tracked down her cheek. 'Your daddy was so proud of it, he used to say it was his crowning glory. But now he's got you to be proud of, hasn't he? Oh, my little darling. We won't let any harm come to you, not ever in your life.' She leant in and kissed the tiny forehead and the baby snuffled contentedly.

Alice gulped and then put her head around the doorway to see how the mother was faring. Dr Patcham was arranging the bedcovers over her. 'She's still breathing; it's a little on the shallow side but she's still with us,' he assured her. 'Give her time, that's what she needs. She's been through a bit of an ordeal.'

Ellen glanced at him with concern. 'Now, Alice, as you're the godmother, I've got to ask you, does the child have a name? Did Edie say what she had decided?'

Alice shook her head. 'She didn't say. We thought she still had a few weeks to go.'

'Ah, the best-laid plans,' said Dr Patcham benevolently.

'Edie's Catholic, isn't she?' Ellen said.

'Yes, although she's not strict. She and Harry got married in the local church, it's C of E. And she stood godmother to Mattie's little boy in the same church.'

Ellen nodded, not in disapproval but with an air of practicality. 'In that case — '

'Nurse Devlin, Nurse Lake, let me say something,' the doctor interrupted. 'I do realise that as members of your profession you are in fact permitted to perform the last rites in emergencies, but that won't be necessary here. No, I firmly believe that Nurse Banham will pull through. I confess that if you'd asked me when I first got here whether her life was in danger, I would have had to admit that it was, but now — with the baby safely delivered, and barring any unexpected developments — I feel confident that Edith will recover. Let's not hurry her. Rest will be the best thing for her now.'

'Then let's all go back down to the kitchen where

it's nice and warm,' suggested Flo, carrying her precious bundle with great gentleness as she descended the stairs once again.

'I'd feel happier if the child had a name,' Ellen said quietly. 'Not as a nurse, you understand but — but for myself.'

Flo looked at her enquiringly but made no comment. Instead, she held out the baby to Alice. 'Here, you take her. I'm going to put the kettle on once more and, I don't know about you, but this time I'm going to drink that tea. I'm parched. I hadn't even realised it until this minute. You must feel the same.'

Alice took the child and raised her so that she could see her face. Then she looked up at Flo and Ellen, smiling with certainty.

'It's true that Edie never spoke to me about what she wanted to call her baby,' she said. 'Also, if it had been a boy then I wouldn't have known. But as it's a girl — well, there's only ever one name that she would have wanted to give her. There's no doubt about it.'

'Really?' Ellen was impressed. 'You know her that well?'

Alice nodded. 'I know why she became a nurse in the first place. She had a sister who died when they were young. Edie never got over the feeling of being unable to help her then. That's why she fought so hard to get her training. She'll want this little girl to have her sister's name. So, this is Teresa.'

'Teresa Banham,' Flo breathed, setting down the full kettle. 'What a lovely name. Welcome to the world, Teresa Banham.'

346

33

'You most certainly will not.' Fiona folded her arms and regarded the two nurses seated in front of her in her office. 'You are to rest, let me repeat, rest. That is not compatible with working an afternoon shift. You will stay inside and allow your lungs to recuperate.'

'But you'll be left short as Alice isn't here . . . '

'That's very noble of you.' Fiona fixed Ruby with a stern look and then relented a little. 'I understand your reasons and I admire your dedication, but if you go running around now then you might set back your recoveries. Therefore you will not work today. We shall manage perfectly well. Gwen herself has volunteered to cover some of Alice's round.'

Ruby slumped a little in defeat but Lily was not cowed. 'We feel ever so much better,' she protested.

'Will you listen to yourself?' Fiona looked heavenwards for a moment. 'Nurse Chandler, you're practically croaking. Don't even pretend to me that you haven't got a sore throat. I've been nursing people since before you learned to tie your shoelaces, so don't think you can fool me. I'm glad you're feeling better, but there is no way on God's earth that either of you will go on the afternoon or evening rounds. Do I make myself clear?' She smiled slightly to soften her pronouncement.

'Yes,' muttered Ruby. Lily nodded sadly.

'Very well. I cannot have you two putting yourselves at further risk. You acted swiftly this morning, and for a second day in a row that might have helped save a

347

life. Don't think we don't appreciate it. But it must not be at the price of your own health. I can't afford to lose you now that you are experienced working on the district.' She stood to indicate the meeting was over.

Ruby followed Lily out of the first-floor office, absorbing Fiona's closing comment. They were counted as part of the experienced team now. She could feel proud of that. If she was honest, she did not feel well enough to work a full shift; the effects of the fire had not vanished overnight, much as she would have liked them to.

'Let's go and have a cold drink downstairs,' Lily suggested, her voice breaking on the last word, as if to demonstrate that Fiona had been right all along. 'It's too warm for tea. We'll see what we can find.'

Ruby followed her friend, pressing her hands gingerly against her ribcage. She had all but run this morning over to Dr Patcham's surgery, and it had taken its toll. Normally she would have done so without a second thought, but this was not a normal day. Still, the main thing was that Edith had had her baby. Alice had got the message through via the ARP network and they knew that it was a girl and both mother and baby were safe. The rest of the details could wait.

Ruby had not forgotten Edith's kindness back in January, in those first nervous weeks of learning the ropes. The more seasoned nurse had had no reason to go out of her way to be friendly, particularly as she had been coping with a difficult pregnancy, and yet she'd done so all the same. The discomfort of a bit of pain in the ribs was nothing set beside the chance to help ensure her baby arrived safely into the world.

The common room was bright with afternoon

sunshine and Gladys was opening the big windows to the back. 'Come and get some fresh air,' she called. 'Isn't it wonderful news about Edith's baby? I wonder when she'll be well enough to bring her over for a visit.'

'Not for a while yet, I shouldn't think,' Ruby said, finishing her sentence with a cough, which made her clasp her ribs again.

Gladys was instantly concerned. 'Hark at me, blathering on. Let me bring you something for that cough. How about some of my fruit cordial? I keep some hidden away for special occasions.'

'We could wet the baby's head,' croaked Lily.

'Sounds as if you could do with a dollop of honey in yours,' Gladys observed. 'Cook's got some at the back of a cupboard. I'll fetch it right now.'

Lily smiled gratefully and wandered over to the windows, pulling out a chair to sit beneath the open sash. The scent of sweet peas drifted through from the back yard. Ruby nodded towards the flowers, in their varied shades from pale pink to deep crimson. 'We could pick a few and put them in jars, liven the place up,' she suggested.

Lily nodded. 'We could. Let's see if Gladys has any spare.' She sank down onto the chair and coughed. 'That's better. Maybe Fiona was right — it's too soon for us to go back to work. I feel as if I've been run over by a bus.'

Ruby chuckled. 'I know. I was cross at first but now I'm glad. I don't think I'd have been much use today, to be honest. I couldn't have lifted anyone for a start.'

'We did enough of that yesterday.' Lily's arms still ached from when she had half-carried, half-dragged Brendan out of the smoke-filled house. 'I wonder how

Brendan's getting on. They'll have kept him in.'

'Bound to have.' Ruby stretched out her legs and winced as the movement sent a jolt through her rib-cage. 'He won't be back at the market for a while, I'd say. Or patrolling as a warden.'

Lily pulled a face. 'Then they'll be a warden short. They were at full stretch as it was.'

'Perhaps somebody else will step up and join them,' Ruby said. 'Oh, thank you, Gladys. That's just what we needed.'

Gladys set down a tray of glass tumblers. 'Lime cordial, my favourite. Here, this one with a spoon is yours, Lily. Thought I might as well come and join you, take my afternoon break while the going's good.' She pulled up another chair, with a faded padded cushion tied to its seat.

The three of them sat facing the flowers, enjoying a rare moment of peace in the nurses' home. 'Imagine, Edith's a mother now,' Ruby mused. 'I can't quite believe it, even though I know it's true. Do you think you'll ever have children?'

Gladys shrugged. 'I spent most of my life so far bringing up my brothers and sisters. I expect I will one day but there's no rush. I got enough on me hands as it is.'

Lily looked thoughtful. 'I don't know,' she said slowly. 'I'm in no rush either. I prefer grown-ups to babies, to be frank. Does that sound awful?'

Gladys laughed out loud. 'Some people would say so. But I know what you mean.'

Ruby had gone quiet. 'I never really thought about it before,' she said after a while, 'but do you know, I think I would like children one day. Even after all the things we see round here, how wrong it can go — but

350

yes, one day. When the war is over, of course.'

'Of course,' Gladys and Lily echoed together.

Lily sat upright. 'Have you got any spare jam jars, Gladys? Or something we can use for vases? We thought we could pick a few sweet peas and put them around in here, make the tables look nice. And they'll smell lovely too.'

Gladys nodded. 'Bound to have. We kept some jars in the kitchen — they'll be in the cupboard behind the knife rack, under where all the saucepans are. Give me a mo to finish me drink and I'll fetch a few.'

Lily stood up. 'Don't worry, I'll go. I feel loads better after that honey.' She proved it by not coughing as she made off.

'That was kind,' Gladys said. 'That's a bit of a surprise, when you think of how Lily was before. I never knew what to make of her to begin with but now I can see she's got a softer side after all. And she's not as well as she pretends, is she? And neither are you,' she added, narrowing her eyes a little.

Ruby tried to laugh it off. 'We're better than we were yesterday, honest we are. They wouldn't have sent us home from hospital if they hadn't thought we'd improve on our own. That's the trouble with living in a house full of nurses, you can't get away with anything.'

'Well, that's a good thing,' Gladys replied. She felt in her skirt pocket, trying to extract whatever was stuck there. 'Here, while Lily's busy, I've got something for you.'

Ruby was taken aback. 'What do you mean?'

'Don't worry, it's nothing to worry about.' Gladys worked it free and brought out the now-creased piece of folded paper. 'I went down the Duke's with Ron

351

last night and Kenny was there. He said to give you this.'

'Kenny did?' Ruby's eyes were like saucers.

'Yes, that's right. Even Ron don't know about it, so stick it away somewhere safe before anyone sees,' Gladys suggested.

'What does it say?' Ruby wanted to know, even as she tucked it into her own skirt pocket.

'I don't know,' Gladys said, beaming with smugness, 'though I think I can guess. Read it later when you're alone,' she grinned.

★ ★ ★

It was twelve hours since she had stood at this window, Alice thought, and what a twelve hours they had been. She had woken with such hope, been plunged into despair, then had come a period of fear bordering on panic, before relief and then joy had followed in quick succession. She was utterly wrung out by the whirling emotions of the day.

She had left Jeeves Street only once Edith had begun to come round, sore and disoriented but most definitely alive. Alice had almost cried when Flo had placed the baby in its mother's arms. Edith had looked up at Alice and the expression on her face made everything that had gone before worthwhile. 'Here's Teresa,' she breathed.

'Alice guessed that already,' Flo had said, standing back to give the two friends a minute alone. 'You chose the right godmother, Edie.'

'I know,' Edie had replied happily. 'She can have your name as a middle name, Al.'

Now Alice watched the treetops shifting in the early

evening breeze, fully in leaf and blocking the sight of ruined roofs and roads. She had lost count of how many gaps had appeared in the terraces since she had moved into this room. Too many, that was for certain. Maybe by the time little Teresa was old enough to notice, it would all be over and rebuilding could begin.

So much of that would depend on the success of this week to come. Alice shivered at the idea. There would have been months of planning leading up to this point, secret rehearsals, troops being moved under cover of darkness, false trails being laid. Now Joe had been spirited away to join his crew, before she'd been able to give him her response.

She drew out her writing case and unscrewed the cap from her fountain pen. If she couldn't tell Joe in person, then the next best thing would be to go back to what they'd done for years. She thought for a moment and then set pen to paper.

He'd want to know about his new niece, and so she gave him the heavily edited highlights. She added how she had managed to narrowly miss him, and how deeply sorry she was not to have seen him. Her heart was pounding as she wrote, willing him to understand just how strongly she felt. She had to have faith that he knew her well, and would pick up exactly what she meant, how much he meant to her.

Alice bit her lip. She had to finish this and take it to the post so that it would catch the earliest possible collection. 'Please stay safe and come home to me,' she wrote at the bottom of the page. 'I'll be waiting, just as you asked. Of course I will. All my love, Alice.' She was shaking as she wrote the last line. She had never ended a letter this way before. He would know that.

Carefully she addressed the envelope and sealed it, letting her lips linger on the lightweight paper. She could only hope that this reached him before he set off for whatever was to come. She could do nothing to speed it on its way. Only time would tell. Her message of love was in the lap of the gods.

34

'More milk, Ma?' Ruby picked up the little jug with its slightly cracked handle. 'You know you don't like your tea too dark.'

Her mother looked a little anxious at the indulgence and then nodded gratefully. 'I will, now you come to mention it.'

Ruby grinned, pleased to be able to do something for the careworn woman in front of her. 'There you are.'

They were in a small tea shop on the western edge of Kensington, a single bus journey for Mrs Butler. She had protested that she didn't like to go back to the West End and the Lyons' Corner House that Ruby had taken her to before, as it was too far. Bus trips made her nervous; she might get lost and there might be problems going home again. Ruby had resisted, replying that anything else would mean she herself had to travel twice as far. It didn't really matter. She didn't mind any more.

A week after the fire and the frenzied activity of the morning after, Ruby was finally more like her old self, with a pain-free ribcage and all her energy back. Lily was almost fully recovered as well, and even Brendan had been discharged from hospital yesterday — although they'd heard he wouldn't be back at the market for a while and his nephew would have to step up and take charge of the stall. To be fit and well again was a wonderful feeling, and Ruby was happy to spend her last free day travelling across the city to see her mother. Even better, Beryl had been unable to come along at the last minute. Ruby struggled to recall the last time she had seen her mother on her own.

Had she ever noticed before just how tired the older woman looked? She was thinner than ever, her hair streaked with grey, the skin on the back of her hands showing wrinkles and her fingers red and chafed from years of hard work. She wore a carefully pressed but faded print frock under a light coat, much mended at the cuffs.

Ruby felt smart, even glamorous, by comparison, in one of the outfits she had made from material bought at Ridley Road. She had taken up Lily's offer of advice on what colours to wear more often, and had chosen a pale rose cotton, teamed with a shiny navy belt. Her hair had had to be trimmed after the fire had damaged it, and Lily again had taken charge, snipping away at the sides and nape of the neck in order to create a proper style. She had then lent Ruby a navy and white scarf to tie at her neck.

Arriving at the tea shop, Mrs Butler had stared at her younger daughter in amazement. 'You seem . . . different, Ruby,' she had stuttered, as if unable to match the young woman in front of her with the diffident girl of six months ago.

'Not really,' Ruby had said. 'I had a bit of a haircut, that's all.'

Now she stirred her tea and smiled, trying to put her mother at ease. The place was almost empty at this time of the morning, later than elevenses but too early for the lunchtime rush. It was not as smart as the Corner House and Ruby had thought that might mean her mother would feel more at home there, but

356

perhaps it was being away from home at all that was her problem.

'Have you heard from Colin?' she asked.

Mrs Butler shook her head. 'No, no, we haven't. We think he might be caught up with all that business last week.'

The one topic on everyone's lips was the Normandy landings, after the news had come through. The scale of it all was hard to imagine. There was an air of barely suppressed excitement, that this really might mark the beginning of the end, mixed with a caution not to hope for too much too soon.

'It's hard not knowing, isn't it?' Ruby agreed, thinking of all the young men fighting their way onto the beaches in their quest to liberate France, and then all of Western Europe. If Colin was there, then probably so were many of his old friends — they'd joined up together. Then there were all the ones she'd met or heard of through the nurses: Edith's brothers and her brother-in-law, Joe, Peggy's fiancé, Belinda's brother. And so many others, leaving their loved ones waiting for news.

'How've you been, then?' asked her mother, obviously wanting to change the subject. 'What you been up to? You write us them lovely letters but I know you can't tell us everything.'

Ruby always kept the gory details out of her letters, and stuck to general comments, which meant that her family really had very little idea of what her life in Dalston was like.

'Well, what would you like to know?' she asked. 'You won't want to hear about my patients. It's not always very nice.'

Her mother had sat up straighter. 'As it happens,

357

Ruby, I would like to know. I'm made of stronger stuff than you think. It's that Beryl who has a delicate stomach. She might pretend otherwise, but she's the one who doesn't like to hear about blood and all that. I'd like to hear what you do. If you don't mind, that is.'

So, Ruby began to tell her. About how she had arrived at Victory Walk, not knowing anybody, afraid of what was to come but not liking to say. How Edith had been kind. The first few cases, feeling out of her depth and getting lost. Then the most difficult times: the visit when she thought the patient's husband might hit her. The overwhelming responsibility of attending the little boy having his tonsils out. The horror of last week's fire. And then, the incident she still regarded as the worst one of all, Pauline's mother and the manner of her death. She hadn't intended to tell the full story, but sitting in that quiet little café, for once having her mother's full attention without Beryl's interference, she wanted to let it all out. It was one thing to share it with other nurses; now she had to let her mother know just what she'd gone through, for better and for worse.

Her mother's face went from shock to sadness to something else again, and towards the end she reached for her handkerchief. Ruby noticed the unimportant details — it had a lace edge and some embroidery in one corner and had once no doubt been for Sunday best. Her mother had dressed up for this meeting, in her own way.

'Oh, my little girl,' she said. 'You been through all that, and we never knew. Oh, what a thing to happen.' She was shaking as she put her hand over Ruby's and squeezed it hard.

'It's all part of the job, Ma.' Ruby didn't want to make light of it, but felt she had to reassure her somehow.

'You must be so brave, Ruby. I don't think we realised that. To see such things.' Her mother blinked hard and to Ruby's dismay began to cry. Silently the slow tears fell down her worn and care-lined cheeks.

'Ma, it's all right. It was weeks ago, it's over and done with. The little girl's looking after her brother and we all keep an eye on them,' she hastened to say.

Mrs Butler shook her head slightly. 'I know you'll see them right,' she said. 'It's not that.'

'What then, Ma?' Ruby waited, alarmed now, as the silence stretched out.

Finally her mother shifted a little in her seat and an expression of resolution crossed her face. 'I might as well tell you, Ruby,' she said, so softly that her daughter could hardly hear her. It was no more than a whisper. 'I'm only saying it cos Beryl ain't here. She must never know, you got to promise me.'

Ruby had no idea of what might be coming. 'I promise,' she said, all concern for her mother's distress.

'The thing is . . . ' She appeared to lose her nerve but then ploughed on, her hand shredding the little hanky. 'Well, after I had the twins, me and your father was living in just the one room. Horrible, it was. He was out working all hours and I didn't go out much, not even to see your gran, cos we was on the top floor and I couldn't manage with two babies going in and out. Then I found out, well, you know, I was in the family way again.' She paused to take a deep breath. 'I didn't think I could cope with any more. There was no space and no more money coming in, nor likely to be. I — I did a dreadful thing.'

'Go on,' said Ruby, with a sickening certainty about

what her mother was going to say.

'I did away with it,' said her mother in one hurried rush. 'I done it. I put something in myself and did away with it. I didn't even tell your father, not at the time, only he come home that night and found me. I was in a dreadful state.' Her eyes were glassy now. 'He said he didn't think I was going to live. He got a doctor, it cost all our savings. He saved my life but I was never the same since.' Her trembling hand reached for her tea cup but then she pushed it away.

'I was lucky they never called the police. But I had my punishment all right. My insides was never the same. Well, you'd know, being a nurse. You know what happens.'

Ruby nodded, able to imagine only too well.

Her mother's face softened. 'We thought that was it, no more children. After a bit, your father got a better job and we moved to a bigger place. We kept trying but I thought I was being punished when nothing happened. When you came, you was our little miracle, Ruby. I can't tell you how happy your father was. Ten years we'd been trying and we thought it wasn't possible, but you showed we was wrong.' She gave a sniff and then smiled. 'You don't know what it meant, Ruby.' Her hand grasped her daughter's once more and she fell silent, totally drained now that she had made her confession.

Ruby's mind reeled. She could hardly think about what it had been like — her own mother having to commit that act of desperation. Then to feel guilty for so long — and, she recognised, that guilt had never gone away. Even her own arrival had not absolved it. It explained so much: why her mother was so protective, so fearful.

360

'Oh, Ma,' she breathed. 'I'm glad you told me.'

Her mother nodded, relieved now. 'I could never speak about it to a living soul, not after your father died, and he never wanted to hear about it much anyway. I can never tell Beryl. She wouldn't approve, she wouldn't understand.'

'No, she wouldn't,' said Ruby, with rock-hard certainty. Her judgemental sister would not have a clue what drove women to do such things.

'When you said you wanted to be a nurse, I was so proud. I know I never said but I was.'

Ruby nodded but frowned. 'But you were a bit afraid, weren't you? It made you remember that time and you were scared somehow.'

Her mother nodded. 'I know it don't make sense. See, you've grown up, Ruby, you understand these things. You're a good daughter, you are. Not many would sit here and not blame me. You don't, do you?'

'Never,' said Ruby at once. 'You were stuck between the devil and the deep blue sea. I can't blame you. Nobody can unless they've been in your shoes. Maybe not even then. Don't go feeling bad, Ma. These things happen. More than you'd probably guess.'

Her mother tightened the grip on her hand. 'You're my reward for all that, Ruby. Now look at you, out in the world, saving lives. I can hardly believe it, my little girl. And so smart as well.' Her eyes shone with pride and Ruby almost cried at the sight. When had her mother last smiled, really smiled?

'Now tell me all about your new friends.' The time for confession was over. Her mother pulled in her chair, and Ruby seized the moment to order more tea.

'You'd like the nurses, Ma,' she said. 'They've taught me lots, about nursing and everything else too.'

361

'Have you made any special friends, then?'

Ruby laughed. 'It's funny, cos my best friend now is someone I didn't even like much at first. She joined on the same day as me. She was ever so stuck up, made out she was better than the rest of us.' She poured two fresh cups from the pot and added milk. 'She's ever so pretty, though, so lots of people don't mind and she gets away with it.' She chuckled. 'Only she had a bit of a bad time with her gentleman friend and then she changed. Turns out she was nice underneath it all — it just took a while to find out. She did my hair,' she added, patting it at the back, still getting used to its new shape. 'She was the one in the fire with me, getting the warden out. She's really brave, only you wouldn't have known it to begin with.'

'She must be, to have done that,' her mother agreed.

'And she's a good nurse too. I've seen her with her patients, being all kind and sensible, though she'd never have admitted it.' Ruby laughed again. 'We got all sorts over at Victory Walk, Ma, but I couldn't have wished for a better place to live and work. You should come and visit one day.'

'Maybe.' Her mother's voice was full of caution. Then she looked roguish. 'And what about a gentle-man friend for you, Ruby? You never showed much interest before.'

'Hmmmph,' Ruby replied. 'You know what Colin's friends got up to, Ma. That's enough to put you right off.'

'I'm glad to hear it,' said Mrs Butler. 'I worried that one of them might turn your head, carrying on with their nonsense like they used to. I'm glad it had the opposite effect.'

Ruby grinned and said no more on the topic,

allowing her mother to tell her about their old neighbours and who'd moved in across the road. When the time came for them to part, she hugged the older woman with new-found respect. 'We should do this again, Ma,' she suggested.

'Maybe,' Mrs Butler said. 'Beryl might not like it though. You got to make allowances for her little ways, Ruby. She ain't tough like you are, not underneath. It's all mouth with her, though I says so myself. She would never do your job in a million years.'

With those words echoing in her ears, Ruby made her way to the bus stop for the first of three journeys back across town. That was a bombshell all right. So her mother didn't agree with everything Beryl said after all. It was making allowances, not condoning her thoughtless criticisms. Her mother thought she was brave, and smart. Ruby thought she might burst with happiness.

Besides, she'd be taking another bus this evening. Kenny had asked her to go to the pictures with him, and not with all the others on this occasion. They had decided to meet down near Liverpool Street, so that they wouldn't run into anyone they knew. She didn't even know what they were going to see, but she didn't care. She was going to spend a proper evening with Kenny, and she found she couldn't wait. Her heart skipped a beat at the very idea. He was a good, kind man and not bad looking either. And he was interested in her — not the flashy, made-up girls who they sometimes saw in the cinemas. Her, Ruby Butler.

War or not, suddenly her world looked very bright indeed.

Acknowledgements

Many thanks to Teresa Chris, Kate Bradley and Pen Isaac for all their help and enthusiasm for the nurses of Victory Walk. Special thanks to the staff of the Queen's Nursing Institute for generously allowing me access to their fascinating archive.